LESLIE PIETRZYK

The Unnamed Press
Los Angeles, CA

The Unnamed Press
P.O. Box 411272
Los Angeles, CA 90041

Published in North America by The Unnamed Press.

1 3 5 7 9 10 8 6 4 2

Copyright © 2018 by Leslie Pietrzyk

ISBN: 978-1-944700-51-5

Library of Congress Control Number: 2017963879

This book is distributed by Publishers Group West

Cover design & typeset by Jaya Nicely
Cover Artwork by Jennis Li Cheng Tien

This book is for
my sister, Susan,
and for Lisa

CONTENTS

PART III: THE END

PART IV: WHERE EVERY STORY TRULY BEGINS

Early versions of these chapters were previously published in the following magazines and journals: "Shadow Daughter," *Hudson Review*; "Give the Lady What She Wants," *Gettysburg Review*; "How We Leave Home," *Cincinnati Review*; "Bad Girl," *River Styx*; "Headache," *WIPs* (*Works [of Fiction] in Progress*); "The Devil's Daughter," *Midwestern Gothic*.

Silver Girl

THE DEVIL'S DAUGHTER

1980
(fall, freshman year)

My roommate arrived first, staking her claim. Probably someone told her to do it that way, her cum laude mother or Ivy League dad or an older sibling or cousin in college. I had no one telling me anything. So I didn't know to take the overnight bus to Chicago from Iowa instead of the one arriving late in the afternoon, meaning when I unlocked the dorm room door I saw a fluffy comforter with bright poppies already arranged on the bed along the wall with the window, cracked open to grab the only breeze. Several dozen white plastic hangers holding blazers and skirts and blouses filled the closet with the door where F U wasn't gouged into the wood.

I rubbed my fingers along the grooves of those letters, imagining a deeply angry freshman girl digging a nail file from the clutter of her purse and carving those letters into the wood, while, at the library, her roommate wrote a smart paper about Jane Austen, or blew her boyfriend in a car parked by the lake, or spray-painted acorns lustrous gold for table centerpieces at a sorority mother-daughter tea. I hoped my roommate wouldn't be that angry girl.

Also, I hoped I wouldn't be.

I admired the precise lettering—straight, even; a challenge creating perfect lines in the cheap veneer—and then slid open this closet door to find a handful of flimsy, misshapen wire hangers. I trailed my fingers along them once, twice, noting their musical jingle, and then hung up my skirts, blouses, and blazer (singular). These items filled about a foot of space, even including my parka for winter. I bunched the rest of my clothes—T-shirts, underwear, jeans, socks—into two of my four dresser drawers, organizing furtively, as if I didn't want to be caught taking them from my duffel and trunk. Then I stared into my roommate's open closet, counting, adding, trying to do the math to determine the algebraic equation that would tell me how many combinations of outfits were possible with ten blouses and nine blazers and sixteen skirts and three dresses and a handful of scarves and—

The doorknob jiggled and I had only enough time to slide shut her closet and grab my plastic-wrapped Kmart Bluelight Special markdown sheet set before the door popped open and a girl with bright turquoise eyes wedged her head through the doorway and said, "Got any masking tape I could borrow?" Her eyes were the color of things I'd seen in *National Geographic*: lakes, oceans, seas, vast skies stretching above plains and pampas, velds and savannas and deserts. Later, I learned she wore colored contacts, which, for a long time, made me believe she saw the world through a blue haze. "I'm Jess, next door, from Oak Lawn, comm studies major." She pushed the door wider, angling herself into the center of the frame.

I didn't want her to leave, so about her request for tape I said, "Hang on, maybe," and I rooted in the chaos of crap at the bottom of my trunk, pretending I might logically expect to find a roll of masking tape, when no one had told me to bring such a thing to college—though apparently no one had told her either.

"Did you meet your roommate yet?" she asked me.

I shook my head. "Just her stuff, all of it," and I swept one arm in a wide semicircle encompassing the glossy stereo system on the cinder-block-and-plank bookcase and plastic milk crates filled with records and her half of the school-issued bulletin board tacked with photos of perky girls with waves of dark feathered hair, so many girls and so much hair that I couldn't tell if each was a different girl or if I was seeing the same one in a fun house of mirrors, over and over, this same girl, my new roommate. Dangling off a plastic thumbtack was a strand of pearls like the pearls I owned, but I was guessing hers were real, unlike mine, which weren't.

"She's from Fort Lauderdale," Jess said. "Voice major. Already planning to pledge Theta, she told me, because she heard from someone it's the best house on campus. But so sorry to say there's no way they'll take her because she's Jewish."

I leaned back on my heels, abandoning the fake search for the imaginary roll of masking tape. It was a whirl of information, in a language foreign to me—not the words, but how they were put together, and also the whole. A sorority wouldn't want a Jewish girl? A girl with nine blazers and sixteen skirts? With three rows of wool sweaters stacked six or seven each? A girl so cavalier with pearls that she draped them over a thumbtack? I wouldn't be that casual with my fakes, which my mother and I picked out for my birthday at the jewelry counter at Younkers department store. They were 30 percent off, but the saleslady acted like they were full price, nestling them into a white box between two pillowy squares of cotton. I kept them in that same box. There were maybe four or five Jewish kids in my whole high school, and no one treated them any differently. Though it suddenly occurred to me that if I wasn't one of them, how could I know?

"Not that I told her that," Jess continued. "But some guy at the comm studies welcome this morning gave me the rundown. Probably I heard wrong." She slipped the rest of the way through the door and bounced onto my roommate's bed, puckering the red poppies. I recognized the stitching along the leg seams of her jeans: Calvin Kleins, crisp like how Brooke Shields wore them, and on top, a man's white dress shirt with the cuffs rolled higher than anyone would roll sleeves, up to the middle of her top arm muscle. The sleeves looked strange that way, but also purposeful, and I felt I was the one in the wrong for not understanding that purpose, which was a different wrong than the tightness I felt seeing my roommate's stacks of sweaters. Those sweaters spiked my gut with jabs of anxiety: I would never have enough, even if I could buy up a whole store, an entire mall. The sleeves, though, maybe I could learn—if I paid attention. If I paid attention, my sleeves could be interesting and purposeful.

Jess was gazing straight at me with those inhumanly blue eyes, maybe following the exact path of my thoughts. I was hunched in front of my trunk, also from Kmart. It wasn't exactly made of cardboard, but it wasn't real suitcase material, leather or even plastic. A little like cardboard, but definitely reinforced, with two pull-tab metal latches and a lock that had bent both of the dinky keys that came scotch-taped to the trunk's inside. It was a heavy and ridiculous piece of luggage, but I had read Agatha Christie mysteries where characters traveled with steamer trunks on a train, and this wasn't that, but it felt close. If it wasn't this Kmart trunk, it would have been musty vinyl suitcases from a neighbor's garage sale. My mother said the trunk was practical because I could double it as a coffee table, putting things on it, "a TV or record player," she had suggested, without suggesting how those things might appear.

But the trunk wasn't practical to haul around. After my father left me at the bus station, a long-haired man with a lisp helped heave it into the luggage hold in the belly of the bus. In Chicago, a man wearing a snowy-white navy uniform took one side handle while I grabbed the other, and we walked lopsided down the street to the el train, and together we lugged the trunk up the stairs and he pointed me to the correct side of the platform. But when I got off in Evanston, people streamed around me, unwilling to be drawn into my problem, so I dragged the trunk by one handle, pretending not to hear the screeching and clanging beating the metal stairs. I dragged it eight blocks on the sidewalk, to registration, including getting lost and trudging two blocks I didn't have to. When I found the registration line, some of the dads helping their daughters jumped in, and my arms ached enough that I let them, despite their daughters' eyes needling me, petulant, pouting for me to find my own father instead of hogging up theirs. Now, the trunk was a scraped-up, shredded, banged-apart, embarrassing mess, barely a functional trunk, let alone a "table" where my roommate might stack her silvery-sleek stereo components. Much of the fake brass trim lining the edges of the trunk was bent and mangled, including a six-inch prong forking up off the bottom seam. I'd already gouged my calf against it, enough to bleed.

Jess shifted her weight, and the bed ground out a wrenching groan, like a strangled elephant, a sure sign that my roommate hadn't sat on this bed before claiming it. Jess bounced again and again, making the bed screech, a tiny smile jiggling her face as if she knew exactly what I was thinking. I was wary of smiling back. I had no idea why she rolled up her sleeves the way she did or how her eyes were that dramatic blue; there were many things I didn't know, so many I couldn't even say for sure what they all were. I should not have come to this school, lugging a cardboard trunk behind me—yes, time to admit it was cardboard, time to admit I was a Beverly Hillbilly, not even a Joad.

I fingered the dangling metal strip, then tenderly stroked my thumb along its razor edge, wincing at each jag. As she watched, I tugged, peeling the metal inch by inch off the trunk, the slow ratchet making me think of a dentist drilling deep, drilling to somewhere painful that would end up hurting real bad.

Jess laughed, like the tinkly keys of a piano. "That's the most pathetic piece of luggage I've ever seen. It looks like it went through hell. Where'd you come from, anyways?"

"Hell," I said. "You got it. I'm the Devil's daughter, and he sent me to college here."

With one last tug and a hard twist, I worked the piece of metal the rest of the way off and so there it was, overflowing the palm of my hand. I looked at the horrible, twisted, meaningless scrap. What was I supposed to do with it? The garbage can was—yes—in my roommate's half, by her desk. I drew in a breath, a deep, calculated breath. I was here, wasn't I? And hadn't I gotten myself here, no thanks to anyone else? The Devil's daughter would know when to take a chance.

So. "I want to pledge Theta, too," I ventured. Trying out the unfamiliar word was like sliding chocolate on my tongue, that same lingering melt, that craving. "Since I'm not Jewish, I figure I've got a shot, right?"

Jess laughed again. "They'll love you, Devil's daughter," she said. "Because I love you already."

We were joking—both of us laughing, not meaning anything mean—but we shouldn't have been, because anti-Semitism was wrong, wrong, wrong, a sin, sin, sin, and those discriminatory Theta girls were evil—we knew that—and since neither of us was Jewish it was especially wrong to laugh even this tiny bit, even at evil Theta girls. And a week later, when my roommate actually was cut by Theta after a single round of sorority rush—suspiciously the only sorority of seventeen to do so during three weeks of rush, to cut her and her real pearls and her sixteen skirts—and she flopped sobbing across her screechy bed, with Jess and me tag-teaming on how Theta was stupid, that she was too good for those stuck-up bitches—reciting every platitude she wanted and needed to hear, because we all three of us knew that those platitudes kept us from the truth none of us could bear to speak—that's when I felt most terrible for those jokes with Jess. It didn't matter that my roommate and I already deeply despised each other, that I'd decided up front to stay with her the whole year anyway, partly because it was easy enough to avoid the room, easier than paperwork and chancing someone else's unwanted roommate, but mostly, really, truly, I was afraid that calling attention to myself to someone in authority meant they would snatch away the financial aid. And Jess lived next door, after all.

But that was later. What was right now: my guilty laughter with Jess and that awful hunk of metal heavy in my hand, the mangled trunk and my cheap Kmart sheets still shrink-wrapped in the package, those words: *Because I love you already.* She had spoken them easily and simply, like tossing a beanbag to a child, so she couldn't have recognized what I did: That they were the words I longed most to hear. That it really wasn't so terribly hard to say them. It wasn't. That this was news to me was the real news to me.

That night I lay in bed listening to the scrape of my roommate's breath, her off-kilter rhythm unaligned with my own. It was four in the morning and I'd counted at least a thousand imaginary sheep. I was not-sleeping in this ten-by-fifteen room, 250 miles away from the house in Iowa where I'd grown up. It was like that house didn't exist anymore. It was gone. Everything was gone. Everything except now. I wasn't rational. I knew I wouldn't sleep even one minute this first night. I didn't.

"You're not afraid of much, are you," Jess had also said—a statement, not a question—so she didn't expect an answer. She could believe what she wanted, and I didn't have to lie.

Part 1:
The Middle

HEADACHE

1982
(fall, junior year)

The phone on the kitchen wall rang. Jess and I stared at it in surprise. Though we had been sharing this off-campus apartment for a week already, we still didn't feel as though we belonged here, and the ringing phone seemed to emphasize exactly how out of place we were.

"You answer," she whispered.

It was eleven A.M., hardly a time for whispering, but I whispered back, "No, you," and then we laughed.

Freshman year we were crammed into the hormonal all-girls dorm that had been built with money donated to the university in the early 1960s by some uptight woman who feared the coming sexual revolution. The school packed all the freshman girls there. The halls smelled like hair spray and popcorn, and someone was always crying in a bathroom stall about what a boy did or didn't do. The joke was that entire floors of girls synced their periods. It was a place to escape from. The next year, we escaped to north campus, the land of frat parties and Frisbees slicing through the quad and stereo speakers propped against window screens on sunny days.

Now, we were juniors, living together off-campus on the first floor of a small stacked duplex half a block from the el tracks. I had arrived the week before she had and was already immune to the screech and rattle of the trains.

The phone kept ringing. This was before answering machines, before voice mail, email, texts, and Skype. Letters and phone calls were all we had. This was a time when not answering a ringing phone was an act of subversion. We wanted to be subversive—or I did, secretly. That was something we had in common, secret desires. Secrets.

Jess picked up. "Hello?" Her voice croaked, and she spoke more forcefully. "I mean, hello."

I laughed. We laughed a lot. We laughed at everything back then. Everything was funny.

She listened for a moment, her face knotting into annoyance. "I'm not coming back home, Mom. No." Then she twirled, letting the extra-long cord wrap around herself once, twice, her back to me now. "No," she repeated, the word swelling. "I said no."

A pause. I watched her shoulder blades jutting and sharp through her ex-fiancé's White Sox T-shirt.

"Stop," she said. "I told you not to call until Thursday at the earliest." She emphasized the last three words. I imagined a black line underscoring them.

I ran to the front door, yanked it open, and pressed the doorbell, which ding-donged loudly. Back in the living room, I leaned over the wall cutout to the kitchen. Her mother had placed a vase on this ledge that I guessed eventually would get knocked over and broken. Hopefully, it wasn't expensive. It looked like crystal, but I couldn't tell crystal from glass. There had been white roses in it, but Jess shoved them in the trash two seconds after her parents left from their weekend visit.

"I've got to go," she said into the phone, giving me a thumbs-up for being clever. "Someone's at the door." She untwisted herself and replaced the receiver with a gentle *click*.

Jess's sister had died over the summer in a gruesome car accident with two other seventeen-year-old girls, who also died. They'd been at a Rush concert at Rosemont Horizon, and Linda was driving. There were headlines in the local papers, above a row of yearbook photos of the girls, who were all pretty, all smiling with straightened teeth and shiny dark hair and neat turtleneck sweaters. Mary-Louise Donohue, from down the hall freshman year, clipped and mailed me the articles, because she lived in the same suburb as Jess and read about what happened, and good thing she did, because Jess never called to tell me herself. It was a whole folder of clippings, as if Mary-Louise had thought I wouldn't believe just one article.

Of course I called up Jess right away, of course, though that meant long-distance charges I'd catch it over with my parents. Our conversation was awkward and bizarre, like being trapped in an elevator with someone's grandpa. I waited for Jess to bawl and for me to say, "There, there," or "Everything will be okay," but she didn't cry, which meant I didn't know what to say. "It must be awful," I said, or "You must be so sad," or dumb things like that. "Yeah," she said, or things like that. Finally: "Should I be at the funeral?" I had asked, and she said, "Why? It's too late. Over. Done," then told me she had to hang up, that someone needed the phone. It was that "why" that I didn't understand—or want to understand. She shouldn't be afraid of needing me, her best friend. Secretly I was worried something would happen with the apartment and our plan to move in together, that she'd back out—hers was the name on the lease—but she called a week after the awkward conversation, excited because an aunt was moving, meaning she was giving Jess a bookcase, a dresser set, and a bunch of kitchen stuff, including a blender that was almost brand new and a toaster oven. I knew exactly what to say to that: "Great!"

I barely knew Linda, just that Jess called her a snotty brat and hated how she was the favorite. Jess's parents had visited campus and taken us out to dinner sometimes on weekends, but only once Linda had been there. Or the times when Linda was with them, I wasn't invited or had to study or was working one of my jobs. When I was with Jess and her parents, we talked about the weather and Jess's classes and maybe my classes and Jess's boyfriends, especially after she got engaged, and Chicago trivia and sights, since I wasn't from the area and they all were, and sometimes Chicago politics if her dad was in the right mood. Basically, he thought everyone from the mayor on down was a crook. The only good politician was Ronnie Reagan, and Washington would wreck him if he didn't watch out. There was a lot of talking; the meals were almost all talking it seemed, always someone asking something or telling a story prefaced with "Here's one that will really make you laugh, lovey," or, if it was a sad story, "Here's one that will about make you cry, lovey." They called each other "lovey" in closed-off, private voices and gave tons of cues so everyone at the table knew how to react, exactly how to feel about this particular issue, whether it was all the rain we were getting or the new exhibit at the Art Institute or whatever donkey thing the mayor was up to. It was all a cinch. Jess acted like a talk show host, rolling through topics as if she'd jotted them down ahead of time on index cards; her parents were like guests, waiting for her direction. Like if she weren't there, there'd be only empty silence between the two of them. I mostly sat there, answering questions that bounced my way, mentally reminding myself to eat slowly and not look piggish.

My own sister was much younger than me—ten years younger— and after I got the folder with the newspaper clippings, I stared at her often, tucked up in the battered fake-leather recliner in the unfinished basement, an afghan heaped on top because even in summer it was frigid down there. She was working her way through my old Nancy Drew books a second time, trying to stay in exact order, lining up each completed yellow-spined book on her bookshelf like a trophy. She was so quiet sometimes I had to remind myself of her name: Grace. I brought to school several framed snapshots of her, which I right away set up on Jess's aunt's hand-me-down dresser in my bedroom. But they made me feel guilty, so I shoved them into a drawer and filled the empty space with bottles of nail polish. I hadn't said good-bye to her when I left for school this time. Grace just woke up and I was gone. Maybe my mother concocted some baloney story about why, or not. Probably not. I had to believe this would be okay. I had to. When I stopped feeling so awful I'd pull Grace's pictures out of the drawer and arrange them nicely. I'd send her a surprise gift or something. I'd do something. Jess didn't know. I couldn't talk about my sister when hers was dead, when hers was a snotty brat. I barely mentioned Grace anyway. Jess probably couldn't remember her name.

Now.

Now. Back at the kitchen table with its mismatched set of chairs (the "semifurnished" part of the rental, along with two saggy twin beds, a couch with an ugly mustard slipcover, a tweedy brown La-Z-Boy, a coffee table stained with water rings, and three wobbly floor lamps), Jess said, "My mom says to come home because she heard all these news reports about people dying from poisoned Tylenol."

"Why are people eating Tylenol if it's poisoned?" I asked.

She laughed. "You sweet dope, they don't know it's poisoned. They have a headache, and next thing you know, they're dead." She laughed again, a bark this time. She had bunches of different laughs, which also reminded me of a talk show host. Like there were different kinds of funny, so you always had to match up the right laugh to the right joke.

"Who's poisoning the Tylenol?" I asked.

"They don't know," she said.

She rested her hands palms down on the kitchen table. There was a faint white line across her ring finger, from the engagement ring, which had a diamond so big it looked fake, a diamond big enough to cast a shadow. She still had the ring, though the fiancé's lawyer-dad sent a certified letter on fancy stationery demanding it be returned. We weren't supposed to say the fiancé's name out loud anymore.

"My mom says we should throw away our Tylenol if they're capsules," she said. "If they're extra strength."

"What if we get a headache?"

"Suffer through it, I guess. Endure the pain." She shook her hands as if she'd known I was staring at them, then stood and walked into the bathroom we shared. I heard her wrestle with the sticky sliding mirrored door of the medicine cabinet. "Aha!" she exclaimed, and she returned to the kitchen, cupping two plastic bottles in her hand. On paper and back-to-back, we were the exact same height, except that she felt taller. Her eyes were blue and mine were muddy and brown. She had sunlit wavy hair, lush like a doll's hair. My hair was too soft, too limp—like mouse fur—not quite blond, not quite brown. A color you'd forget immediately, even if you were staring straight at it. Most times I felt like a shadow standing next to Jess, but other times I felt like she was my real sister, my only true family.

She plunked the pill bottles on the kitchen table. One of them rattled slightly. The other, I knew, was brand new, with cotton stuffed inside. I had bought it yesterday at the drugstore, because I didn't come from the kind of family where you could grab things from home to take to college.

"They look incredibly dangerous," I said.

She nodded. "Totally."

"We're lucky we're still alive." Immediately I wished I had kept my mouth shut. It seemed like a bad thing to say, knowing what had happened to her sister this summer. But Jess laughed. She unscrewed the top of the open bottle and dumped out about ten capsules. With one finger she rolled them into two rows of five, then into three rows of three and flicked the extra so it spun for a fast moment. The capsules looked set up as if they were pieces in a game with complicated rules and scoring.

"The other bottle is full," I said. "I bought it yesterday at Osco."

"My mom said it's only bottles bought in Illinois so far," Jess said. "Around Chicago."

"Mine is from Osco," I said. "Right here in Evanston."

Jess unscrewed the cap and tugged out the lump of cotton wadding. Then she dumped out those capsules at once, fast, so they tumbled and rolled along the table, caught by Jess's fingers, guided back to the center of the table with the others. She lazily circled one finger through them, swirling and combining the contents of the two bottles. I panicked to see that many pills on the table. What if Jess's mom was right? What if they were poisoned? What if I had taken one yesterday or this morning? A psychosomatic headache immediately pressed into my temples.

Jess lifted one capsule, barely as long as her pinkie nail, pinching it between her finger and thumb, peering at the seam between the red half and the white half. "Seems easy to pop it open and then dump in the poison," she said.

"People don't do that," I said. "Who does that?"

"One Halloween my sister found a razor blade in a Snickers after trick-or-treating."

She'd never told me this. It seemed like a story that might have come up. "I didn't think that really happened," I said. "I thought adults say this to scare kids so they can't have fun."

"My sister slashed up the roof of her mouth and tongue," she said. "They drove her to the emergency room and it was on the news."

"One of your neighbors did that?" I said. "Did they catch the guy?"

She shook her head, still staring at the Tylenol as if mesmerized, either by the capsules or this memory. "Tons of people hand out Snickers.

Plus, my sister said she swapped with her friends for more Snickers bars. She's so stupid and picky about food, and that's about the only candy she likes. She was out for hours, all over town, and got a pillow-case-full of stuff."

"But the police—"

"Never found the guy," she said. "Did nothing."

There was a silence. Jess's sister seemed incredibly unlucky to me. The phone rang again.

"Don't answer," Jess said.

I counted ten rings as I imagined Jess's mother in their house in Oak Lawn, sitting at a kitchen table much nicer than this one, where the chairs all matched, worrying that her remaining daughter was going to die after swallowing an extra-strength Tylenol capsule laced with poison. I imagined her sneaking a cigarette, a sweaty glass of white wine nearby. Maybe there was an untouched turkey sandwich on a plate in front of her, the bread hardening slightly, the smear of mayo stiff and congealed. I imagined the tinny burr of an unanswered phone echoing in her ear. I imagined a daughter who wasn't able to talk about her sister's car accident, a mother who laughed on cue. *Here's a story,* I imagined her saying, *this one will scare the crap out of you.*

I jumped up and grabbed the phone, but no one was there. The dial tone felt lonely.

Jess said, "For a while they suspected my dad, because nothing happened to any other kids in the neighborhood. Everyone else's candy was fine. They x-rayed everything. Only my sister. That one candy bar. So maybe it wasn't random."

"My god," I said. It wasn't that I couldn't imagine a family where a thing like that would happen, because I could, because I knew for absolute fact that families did plenty of bad things. Just not Jess's family. I thought about a muttering old man at his workbench, grubby fingers sliding a razor blade deep into a Snickers bar and nestling it into a plastic pumpkin with the rest, offering his candy to witches and clowns. A man who might be any man.

"They questioned my mom," she said. "Privately, away from him, and you know what she said? She said, 'It wouldn't surprise me if he did.' I was on the stairs, listening, and she flat-out said that. To cops."

"Wow."

"What I always wanted to know then is, so why'd she stay with him? I mean, if she thought he would do something like that?" Her voice turned dreamily singsong, as if she were a child reciting a familiar story.

"Yes, why?" I singsonged back. I stood and moved to the window. The leaves on the maple tree in the yard next to ours were tinged yellowy red. It was amazing the tree knew to change color every year, year after year, until it died or got chopped down. It felt so impossible, though it was an obvious fact of nature. We read a poem last year in one of my literature classes, about a girl named Margaret who was bummed out about a tree turning colors, and it ended up that what she was really bummed out about was the fact that she would die eventually. The professor told us she wrote her dissertation on that poet, so she dumped her lecture notes and started talking all fiery and almost cried when she read one of the lines. We were embarrassed, but I also liked seeing that someone could care deeply about a poem.

"You should call her," I said, still looking at the tree. "Just tell her you're throwing out the pills." I had a way of staring that made things blur and fuzz, get sort of prettied up around the edges, and I was doing that. It could last for ten minutes sometimes, my ability to stare. People didn't know when I was doing it, even if they were speaking straight at me, even if they were yelling. No matter what was happening in the now, I had this trick of staring and being blank.

"She wants me to go back home and I'm not," Jess said. "She didn't want me to come back to school this fall. Because of my sister. She's crazy, turning crazier by the day. I'm the only sane one there. It's like without me, nothing there is normal. It's a nuthouse."

"She's worried," I said. "She cares about you." That comforting blur, condensing everything into nothing, into static. I kept up the same singsong voice Jess did, as if we agreed the things we were saying—*why? why stay?*—didn't much matter.

"What she cares about is..." but Jess didn't finish the sentence, and I didn't ask her to.

We hadn't spoken this way for ages, probably not since those freshman-year nights in the dorm, at four in the morning, after all the pizza was eaten, even the nibbled-down crusts rattling in the box, sitting side by side on my twin bed, looking across at the Monet posters taped to the cinder block walls, my pretentious roommate somewhere with her boyfriend-with-a-car, the flexible desk lamp bent into a glowing U, and I felt cradled by deep darkness and the sense that the world was asleep, that maybe I was far enough away to let up, if only for these few moments. Jess would pose questions, and we'd wrestle out answers and laugh and then drop into dead-serious whispers, then laugh again, because everything felt hilarious or dead serious. My breath scraped my throat when I thought about the two of us talking across entire nights like it was something so normal, until finally I had to ask, desperate to sound casual, "Why do you even talk to me?" but the sentence burbled out on a wave of neediness and stupidity, and I crushed a pillow over my face. She laughed like I was hilarious, not dead serious, and declared, "There are people who listen to the words and then people who listen." I couldn't admit not knowing which group I was supposed to want to be in, but I relished the warm relief of being sorted into the right one.

It would never be me breaking the spell; it was always her saying, "Guess I should get some sleep or something," and she'd wander back to her own room, pulling open the door to a slash of bright hallway light that stabbed my eyes. Last year, she had her boyfriend, so the late nights were with him. This year would be like a reunion, I figured, I hoped.

Now, I knew I should listen to her talk about her dead sister and find out if she really was a snotty brat, if her parents really liked her best. I should want to find out what was going on in a family that actually wasn't perfectly normal like I'd thought, where the mom believed the dad might slide razor blades into kids' candy bars, or where that's what the mom might tell the cops, or where she or Jess or possibly even the sister might lie about the whole entire thing. Jess had lied plenty when we first met, about things that didn't matter, like her shoe size and what the cute guy in sociology said to her after class, but I hadn't minded. It made her more interesting. Because lots of people lie. Lots of people lie all the time. Recently she had caught her fiancé—Tommy; she wasn't saying his name anymore—in a big fat lie, about the thing you'd expect—being with another girl, his ex-girlfriend, actually—and that's when it was finally over and the whole ring fight started. No one really needed that ring; sure, it was a lot of money, but both Jess and the fiancé had tons of money, and I mean tons of money. For me, throwing out an entire bottle of Tylenol that I'd paid full price for, not on sale, was kind of a big deal, but those two bled money. If the ring disappeared entirely, neither of them would starve. I thought a ring was a dumb thing to spend so much money on, but weren't people always spending money on dumb things? Recently, I'd started getting a lot of headaches, and extra-strength Tylenol worked the best. Or so I thought. I'd learned about the placebo effect in a psych class. The ring was in an envelope under her mattress, she'd told me. Like the princess and the pea, I said, but the effect was ruined when I had to explain the story.

Possibly Jess was lying about the razor blade in the Snickers bar or her mother was lying about the Tylenol. It was possible the fiancé wasn't in love with his ex-girlfriend. The tree looked like lace in my eyes. Or like a fast pencil sketch. My sister, Grace, liked to draw. That's the other way she spent her time, drawing. She was either reading or drawing. Two silent activities, done alone. She wasn't all that great at drawing, but she sure liked it. Lots of pictures of animals, of horses. Before Nancy Drew, she read my horse books. That was something about my family, that no one complained about space for books. She'd probably find my Agatha Christie mysteries next. Boxes of those library-sale paperbacks with ripped covers were stacked in the basement. Also, she still liked stories I imagined just for her, about the Silver Girl. I told a thousand stories last summer, a big fat blur of the Silver Girl. We sat together in the kitchen at night, only the two of us, and I'd spin out sentences, and she wasn't like a kid who ever acted bouncy happy, but she sure liked these stories and not being alone. What I could do was type up a Silver Girl story and send it to her, once a week or now and then. I imagined her folding up the pages in half, in half again, hiding them inside a Nancy Drew. I'd be careful about big words, because she was too embarrassed to look things up when she didn't know; she just skipped ahead. When I told her that was kind of a bad habit, she asked if I was mad at her.

Now, I was supposed to be paying attention to Jess, listening to her talk about her dead sister for the first time. That's what a friend does, a friend who got the furniture the aunt who was moving gave to Jess. Jess bought a new dresser from a furniture store in Oak Lawn and had it delivered. I didn't have to confess straight out, how no way could I buy even one stick of furniture. So now I asked, "How's your mom getting crazier?"

Jess said, "She slapped a lock on my sister's bedroom door and she's the only one with the key, so no one else can go inside."

That was another name Jess didn't say: Linda. I remembered from high school Spanish that the word *linda* meant "pretty." Linda looked pretty in the newspaper photograph, but no prettier than the average pretty girl. I didn't like staring at her picture, knowing she was dead. Like spying. But I kept the clippings and brought them to school with me. I don't know why.

"That's crazy," I agreed.

"She sleeps in the guest room," Jess said. "Locked door there, too."

"Also crazy," I said.

"No way am I going back to that house," Jess said. "No way. This is my grand escape."

Without the fiancé, she would have to pay closer attention to getting a job. She wanted to work in public relations or something with the media. One of those jobs where they want people with a lot of energy. I imagined a calmer sort of job for myself. A lot of students from our school ended up in entry-level assistant jobs at one of the big Chicago ad agencies, because the founder of the agency graduated from here. A building was named after him. I wanted to end up there, though people complained it was a terrible time for getting jobs. I could type fifty words a minute. I could make coffee. I didn't have a great need to do more. I just wanted a place to show up every day and a paycheck. I wanted files with typed labels in alphabetical order. I wanted an office supply cabinet filled with Wite-Out and boxes of Bic pens in blue and black ink. An enormous Xerox machine spitting out copy after copy, that fluttery whisper of paper moving across mornings and afternoons. I wanted, really, never to go back to Iowa. That was what I wanted. Like Jess: *No way am I ever going back to that house.*

Different but the same, longing always for more than what I had. I liked that we suddenly had this in common.

"What's your mom do in that bedroom?" I said. Abruptly my eyes snapped into focus—a tree again, a tree—and I spun around. Jess had popped open several of the capsules and was pouring white powder into a tiny, loose pyramid. She set her fingertip at the pointy part and pressed lightly, smushing down, then started re-mounding the powder.

"You'd think you'd be able to see the poison," she said.

"Maybe you can," I said. "Maybe these are fine. Maybe we won't die if we take them for our headaches."

Jess said, "It was my sister."

"Linda," I said, because it was weird not to say people's names. That's what names were for, to use them when people were real, right? To say "Linda" and to think of that pretty girl in the newspaper clipping. Also, maybe I wanted to shake Jess up, knock her concentration. Also, I don't know why, but Jess made me nervous sometimes.

"The razor blade in the Snickers bar," Jess said. "She did it herself. She told me so this summer, like a week before driving to that concert. Why would—"

I sat down immediately. The chair squeaked. It was going to be the chair that drove me crazy the whole year, squeaking and squealing, rickety besides, but it would be disruptive to pop out of this chair and jump into another. "No," I said. "That can't be."

Jess dribbled more powder into her growing pile. It looked like cocaine, which I had done a couple of times without liking it. It was supposed to be glamorous, probably because it cost so much money. Jess said, "Easy to sneak a razor blade out of some old paint scraper in the garage. If you pulled the wrapper carefully enough, you could re-stick the edges together."

"Anyone can buy razor blades from the drugstore," I said. "That's just a normal thing."

"Like Tylenol." Jess raised the red half of an empty capsule. "Looks like plastic. I can't believe it dissolves in your stomach." She smiled. "Remember, my sister was the one driving," she said. "Which is also normal, right?"

"No," I said again, such a stupid word, so defenseless.

Jess stuck out her tongue and touched the open edge of the capsule to it. "Less see if it melz," she garbled.

I imagined taking Jess's hand, guiding it down to the kitchen table, setting it flat, and tracing the white line of her missing diamond ring with my own finger. I imagined saying some word that was smarter and stronger than "no," some word that might be meaningful. I imagined that English professor sitting at night in a library somewhere with a thousand scribbled index cards, reading about that poet, reciting lines to herself until she cried. I imagined a day when I might be perched on an office chair at a cool, clean desk with an in-basket and a telephone with blinking lights and buttons that I knew how to operate, when I might simply pick up the phone and say something easy like "Mr. Smith's office," pen poised to jot down a number. I imagined how many asses had sat in this squeaky chair, how many conversations had happened around this kitchen table, how many secrets there were in the world, in this room, in my head.

That pile of powder on the table could be all poison, I thought, all contaminated.

I grabbed one of the open capsules and placed it on my own tongue. "Racth ya," I said. "Go." It felt impossibly light, tasted like nothing. My heart pounded loudly, suddenly fast.

Jess laughed, and I laughed, both of us keeping careful balance of the empty capsules on our tongues. A regular, ordinary laugh, as if I were any normal friend, as if we were simply girls who randomly met when we were eighteen. As if the world weren't changing, now or ever; as if I hadn't done those things with her fiancé, with Tommy, all those times; as if I wouldn't again tonight or any night if he showed up at the library looking for me, wanting me. As if something could stop me.

Strategies for Survival #8: Mental Health

(spring, freshman year)

Nothing would get me inside the student mental health center. But sometimes I walked by the brick Georgian—which had been a family's house before the university sprawled its way onto Orrington Avenue, snapping up buildings for quirky departments like geography and African studies—and its University Counseling and Social Services, which was called UCSS but that we rearranged to CUSS, or maybe only Jess and I did that, one more word for our private vocabulary. Sometimes when I walked by, I stopped across the street, maybe to tie my shoe, maybe to admire the prickly holly planted in front, maybe to stare at the people trudging up the brick walkway on the lifeless gray day, backpacks hanging limply off one shoulder. What was wrong with them, I always wondered, that they couldn't fix themselves? What was wrong with me? What had they done? Or was it what *hadn't* they done?

JEWELS

(fall, junior year)

"I can't do anything right." It was Jess's mother at the front door, around dinnertime the next day, when the Tylenol scare filled the paper and the TV. Jess wasn't home, and I was the one opening the door, telling her Jess would be back around ten, though that was an optimistic guess. I had been trying to write a paper that didn't want to be written. Most of my papers were like that until about midnight, when suddenly they would get done in a mad clatter of typewriter keys, but it wasn't a schedule that felt normal, so I resisted it, thinking each paper might be the one that I could write in a state of calm. I had typed my name at the top of the piece of paper. That's how far I had gotten; that's how well this paper was going. Ten years from now I wouldn't remember the paper or the book the paper was about.

Jess's mother stood on the porch, fingers twisting the single strand of pearls around her neck, as if it were a rosary, though Jess had said that her mother didn't trust Catholics even though Jess's father once was one, so I didn't mention the comparison. Her purse was unzipped, one strap dangling, flapping open so I could see into it; instead of a clutter of makeup and receipts and a billfold, there were several small rubber-banded white boxes, like the kind for jewelry. It seemed like a peculiar thing to cart around, and I wondered if this was what always was inside her purse or if this was something new. Jess claimed she was going crazy.

"You could come in and wait for her," I suggested, tacking on, "I mean, if you want," in a way that implied she shouldn't really want to.

Jess would flee if she spotted her mom's silver Cressida parked on the street outside.

She stepped through the door, her face making that little crinkle it did when she was working to pretend she wasn't uncomfortable. She liked me a lot, but she was suspicious of this apartment. On move-in day, there had been a lecture about extension cords and electrical outlets; a warning about candles burning in empty rooms; and much concern that the refrigerator wasn't cold enough, that the thermostat was off. Jess had ignored it all, but I pressed the back of my hand against damp milk cartons, as if gauging a fever. Now, I remembered the pile of white Tylenol powder that neither Jess nor I had wiped off the table. She would assume her daughter was a cokehead. Probably better than thinking we were messing around with Tylenol. Seven people were dead. No one knew how much poison was out there, who was doing such a thing. It seemed like it had to be someone trying to kill one person specifically and cover it up, maybe to get insurance money, like in a TV lawyer show, or maybe it was a disgruntled employee. There had to be an explanation. A reason. A plan. Someone would get caught in the next day or two, everyone said, because who would do this thing, kill random people with headaches? A twelve-year-old girl was dead. A little girl.

"Let's sit in the living room," I said, though when Jess's mother had been here before she sat at the table. She told us how growing up she was the youngest cousin, so she spent hours sitting in the kitchen while her mother and aunts played cards after the housework was done. Jess was bored with stories from before she was born, and these were boring stories, but I pretended to enjoy listening to them when her mom got on that track. I headed her off before she could reach the kitchen table, scooping a clutter of Jess's fashion magazines from the sofa, and she sat down, balancing on the edge. Her back stayed as straight as a pool cue.

I perched on the arm of the saggy recliner, working to get my back as straight as hers, but that hurt so I relaxed into a slump, into my usual approximation of a parenthesis. Her pearls made me wish I wasn't wearing sweatpants bunched up to my knees. I tugged them down but was reminded why I'd slid them up: splotches of grease from when they snagged in a bike chain while riding along the lake with some boy. I didn't like bikes but the boy did. She could probably see the Rorschach stain even after I crossed my legs.

"Oh!" I said. "Would you like some water? Or I think there's Tab."

She said, "Where is Jess?"

"At the library," I said, which distracted me into wondering about Tommy, Jess's ex-fiancé, so I pushed the lie more forcefully. "There are readings on reserve. You know how it is."

"Not really," she said. "I didn't get to go to college."

I guess I'd known that, but it seemed like an accusation now, like she wanted to fight me because I knew "readings on reserve" and she didn't. "It's when professors—"

"No one thought I should waste my time with school," she said. "Get married and have babies was all anyone expected from me. All I expected from myself." Her back was so straight. Watching its perfect straightness strained my eyes. I didn't want to hear her mention Linda. I sensed she was about to, just as I suddenly sensed those little boxes in her purse had to do with Linda. I thought of that locked-up room no one but her was allowed in, Linda's bedroom. Jess always complained to me that Linda was the favorite, that Linda got away with anything. I didn't know if this was true, but Jess was absolutely certain.

"I'll get some Tab," I said, jumping up, heading to the kitchen. I was afraid she might follow me, but luckily no. I opened the refrigerator, which contained a sweaty container of yogurt that I instinctively rested my hand against, half a loaf of bread, two curling pieces of leftover pizza on a plate, and no Tab. To save money I drank water, which I claimed to love, though Jess told me I should drink or eat anything she bought. The problem was she often forgot to go shopping. Plus she was the one with the car, and Tab was heavy.

"Water's fine," her mother said, as if reading my mind. "No ice," which was also lucky since there were only two cubes in the tray and I wanted them. I took as long as possible, but it wasn't hard putting together two glasses of water, even with refilling the ice tray.

I set the glasses on the coffee table, then remembered we owned coasters, so I found them and moved the glasses onto the cork coasters. She said, "I have those same coasters." She seemed amused.

"I bet maybe Jess took them from your house," I said.

"I never especially liked them, so good."

There was a silence. I tried to imagine owning enough things that you might forget what you owned. What a luxury. I drank my water and the ice clinked noisily, or so it seemed. She barely moved. Her lack of movement was making me itchy, itchy and crazy and wanting to scream. None of that made sense.

She said, "This thing with the Tylenol has me spooked."

"I know."

"You forget that anything can happen, anywhere, even to a nice family."

"I know."

"That's why"—and, yes, here came the swoop toward the purse, as she reached in and drew out two white boxes—"I want to leave these here, with you." She set the boxes on the table. Though they were each only as wide as a deck of cards, they sounded heavy, or heavier than jewelry anyway, with a slight rattle. She pulled out more until there were eight altogether, stacked up in two columns of four. The rubber bands pressing around the lids looked off bundles of asparagus or other produce. Funny that someone who owned so many things that she didn't miss a coaster set would squirrel away used rubber bands.

"You mean leave with me to give Jess," I corrected.

"With you," she said. "Not Jessica."

I half smiled, maybe at the official name. Like we knew different people.

Another silence. I honestly wanted to pick up the boxes—whatever they were—and carry them into my room and drop them into a drawer and never look at them again until she needed them back, but I knew that she expected me to ask what was inside. It was unavoidable. She was going to tell me.

Still, I didn't ask. We both stared at the little boxes, and when I glanced up, her eyes looked so glossy and sad that I finally said, "What are these?"

She pounced on my question: "Every day since Linda died, I walk to the park, to the pond she liked as a little girl. Every day I find a rock or two and bring them home. These are those rocks."

"Wow," I said.

"I can't have them with me or look at them anymore," she said. "There are too many."

"Well, could you—"

"Don't tell me to throw them away." Her voice was as sharp as her back was straight.

"I'm sorry," I said. I don't know what I had been about to say, but it wasn't to throw them away. "I'll take care of them for you." I imagined my life ahead, these boxes cluttering the bottom of a drawer or stuck in the back of the closet or packed into a moving van.

Maybe she wanted me to ask why she was giving them to me and not to Jess, but, actually, when I looked into her eyes—blue, like Jess's eyes, only a lesser, paler blue—I didn't care why. I just was happy suddenly, and I immediately had to look away because being even a little happy right now seemed wrong.

Then she said, "You have a sister."

I nodded.

"Jess and Linda weren't particularly close." She sighed so fast I almost missed it.

I nodded again.

"But there was deep love between them," she said.

Another nod. I could do this if all I had to do was bob my head. A layer of sweat thickened behind my knees.

"Your sister is also younger, right?" she asked. "You and Jess are both the older sister?"

"She's four years older," I lied. "She lives in Arizona, where she's working as a park ranger"—something I knew nothing about. Not a smart lie. A stupid lie. A stupid, pointless lie. I squeezed my fingernails hard and deep into the heels of my hands.

A line of concern dug into her forehead. "Oh, your mother must worry about her, out there with all the rattlesnakes and, well, a job like that."

I smiled. "My sister is tough as nails. I've never seen her cry once." I kept smiling. I could smile and smile. This part about not crying was true, I realized, and suddenly it was harder to smile.

Jess's mom blinked several times and then pointed to the boxes. "I might want them back someday," she said.

"I know. Just say so."

"Jess would throw them away," she said.

"Maybe not." Of course she would. She would make fun of her mother to me, scattering sentences with the word "crazy" and bringing up how Linda was the favorite. Then she'd spill the rocks into a metal garbage can outside, where they'd clunk and rattle, and over the course of the week, we'd drop in sloppy trash bags that smelled of banana peels. By garbage day, she would have forgotten the rocks entirely. Only I would imagine them being tipped into the truck, being driven away with the other junk.

"But you," she said, "I trust you." That same surge of joy, as she stood up and cupped my chin with one hand, tilting my head so I looked up at her and the tiny creases in her makeup, like cracks in an old oil painting. "You understand what sadness is. You know. We both do."

My eyes prickled with sudden tears. I couldn't help it. She held my face steady so I couldn't shake away those tears. Her eyes, too—but she kept herself still in that miraculous way she had, until one tear dropped free, gliding down the curve of her cheek, and she let go of me and sat down, straight as before. She dabbed her face with a tissue from her purse and announced it was supposed to rain tomorrow afternoon.

There was chitchat—with the boxes still stacked on the table—and then she told me she couldn't wait for Jess, though she needed to see her because of this whole Tylenol scare, that she needed to see both of us, that my parents must be so worried, that it was a scary, insane world where people do the things they do. "Just scary," she said, "and just insane that we're not safe in our own home." She repeated "our own home" a thousand more times. Maybe it only felt like it.

She scribbled a note to Jess, left. I wrote my paper. I don't remember what it was about. Maybe *Jane Eyre.* Maybe Thomas Hardy. It seemed I was always reading Thomas Hardy in my classes. Jess came home just as my paper-writing vision was kicking in; she was looped from meeting a guy from her Theories of Persuasion class for drinks at the Orrington Hotel bar because she wanted copies of old midterms from his frat's test file. "Bleah," she said, "he's got the fattest face in the world, like the rump of a blimp," with a huge sigh to remind us that her ex-fiancé's face was flawless. She said she'd deal with her mom's note in the morning, that her mom was crazy, that everyone was crazy, that she hated men. She didn't notice the rubber-banded boxes on the coffee table.

At about five A.M., with my paper wrapped up, I collected the boxes, carrying them into my bedroom, and set them on the hand-me-down dresser where the nail polish was, where my sister's pictures used to be. It seemed disrespectful that the nail polish was nearby, so I dumped the bottles into a drawer. I didn't like half the colors anyway, shades Jess had tired of. The boxes were tidy, a neat stack, even rows: a wall. I liked that they contained sadness. I liked that the sadness was not exactly mine, and that rubber bands safely held the boxes shut, and that really, if I did open one of the boxes, I would see only meaningless rocks. I liked that Jess's mom had given them to me and not to Jess.

I pulled my sister's pictures out of the drawer and propped them up behind the boxes, arranging them tallest to shortest.

As I collapsed into bed, my temples bulged with an abrupt headache, and all I could think of was that Tylenol powder still on the table. It could be poison, which was crazy, crazy. The darkness felt like a thing knotted around me, until finally I was asleep, and the next morning it was so simple to wipe away that white powder with a damp paper towel and take my typed paper off to class.

Strategies for Survival #4: Lists

(winter, freshman year)

Jess and I kept lists. I started her on that, which sometimes she would out of the blue thank me for, like it was a big thing. It was something. Not a big thing, but something. There was a book I obsessed over when I was younger, *The Book of Lists*. Everything was in there, like lists of favorite sexual positions and lists of kings with syphilis. The book had been banned from our school library, so I read it in the reference section of the public library, sitting off in the corner by the overgrown spider plants, feeling immoral and dirty, but relieved to have a specific reason to feel that way, flipping the pages for an hour (how long you were allowed to keep a reference book). I loved the library but hated its endless rules. So I made my own book of lists that I shoved under the mattress, one of those bound composition books with the mottled black-and-white covers that I filled with lists: Animals I Sort of Look Like; Middle Names That Are Better Than Mine; Favorite Foods to Eat When I'm Sick. My lists weren't ambitious, never offering plans or goals for the future. They merely reported the facts of the moment, which is what I thought lists did: report information. State what was, not what might be.

Jess and I started keeping lists around early December of our freshman year, when winter bit down. We were at Osco because Jess had spilled her eye makeup remover and needed more, and I had to escape my psychology textbook because I was self-diagnosing manic depression. As we roamed the overheated aisles, we landed in school supplies in front of a stack of those composition books, and I gasped the tiniest bit in surprise, because that time in my other life felt distant and far removed, so other—as if I were a snake spotting a dried, shed skin tangled in the branches of a brush, startled it used to be mine.

Jess was especially observant of tiny things: "What's the matter?" she asked. She unzipped her parka, finally, and pushed back the fur-edged hood; I had started sweating the moment we walked into the store and draped my coat awkwardly over one arm. I looked like a shoplifter, but so many old people shopped here they kept the thermostat at eighty.

"These notebooks," I said, letting my hand rest on the top of the stack. In Iowa, Drug Fair offered them two for a dollar on sale, which was when I stocked up. There was a white square on the front with lines for your name and the subject, which I left blank, not wanting to muck up the smooth sheen of the cover; my handwriting was pedestrian, readable but ugly, and I often studied handwriting, hoping to find something pretty to incorporate into my own: a crosshatch through a Z, a tilted dash instead of a dot over a lowercase *i*, almost like an accent mark.

Jess lifted the top notebook from the stack, slipping it out from under my hand. "I'm buying this," she said. "Want one?"

I shook my head no (she didn't need to know I had only a quarter in my pocket), but she grabbed another and dropped both into her basket. She was already buying me a black L'Oréal eyeliner pencil and a pair of Hanes ultra-sheer hose in nude. She said the hose I wore made my legs look fake, like plastic. I would always end up with something new whenever I went to Osco with her. But I had to be there or else she wouldn't bring anything back. As if anything not in her line of sight didn't exist.

It seemed daring to admit this to her: "I wrote up lists in these notebooks. When I was a kid."

Jess got it right away: "Records to Take to a Desert Island. Favorite Picture Books. Cities to Visit Before I Die. Best Mixers for Bourbon. Worst Hangovers. Most Idiotic Dates."

"Like that," I said.

"Like a diary, but quicker," she said. Her eyes locked on to me, into me, like I had breathed a secret out and she had breathed it right in.

"Yes," I said.

"I want to go back and start one," she said. That's how she was, deciding something that fast and doing it that fast, and so we were done trolling the aisles of Osco.

In her dorm room, we boiled water in a hotpot—tea for her, a mix of instant coffee and powdered hot chocolate for me that Jess called disgusting—and the room took on that steamy early-winter quality of dimming late-afternoon light that is only Chicago: a white-gray sky pressing low outside, leaning flat against the cold window pane; the small circle of yellow lamplight never all the way reaching wherever I sat; a crushing loneliness seeping inward, edging closer and closer, as rhythmic and persistent as breathing; old snow and crusted slush rimming the salt-stained pavement outside. The first Edward Hopper painting I saw I understood immediately because of these Chicago winter afternoons, and the first time I heard Beethoven's *Moonlight Sonata*. There should be coziness to these moments of winter, relief at being inside and warm as darkness settled in, but through all my years in Chicago, I never felt cozy or relieved during those wintery twilights, only anxious as I waited for fully night, or fully spring.

I sat at her desk, and she sat crosswise on her unmade bed, the puffy down comforter scrunched at one end like something discarded, a crumpled Kleenex. The books on her desk were also askew, and I longed to restack them: either largest to smallest in a pyramid, or with the bindings all matched straight and even, or with the bottoms aligned. But I stared at the blank page of my composition book, at the blue Flair pen in my hand, at the evenly spaced lines across the white paper.

"Let's do our ideal man," she said. "Our future husband." She wrote for a minute, and I listened to her pen scratch. Abruptly she said, "Should these be in order?"

"Do what you want," I said, but obviously priorities were crucial. The idea was to hone and make judgments. This is better than that: Anne with an *e* is a better middle name than Ann without. It's slightly better to look like a tiger than to look like a lion. Without order, what you wrote was no better than a random grocery list. "I number mine," I said.

She tapped her pen on the page. "So rigid with your rules. How can you be like that?" she asked.

"How can you not?" I joked back, not joking.

I watched the top of her pen bob across the paper. Without looking up, without pausing, she said, "I'm just writing everything down. Who cares about the order?"

Who did care about the order? Who cared that the most favorite food to eat when you're sick was chicken and stars soup and the second most favorite was orange Jell-O? Who cared about any of it, long lists in a composition book, a kid sitting at a wooden table in the dark corner of the library memorizing the list of most active volcanoes? Again, I dared to admit something: "Number it at the end, when you're done. That's what I do."

"You mean write everything down first?"

"Fill in the numbers last," I said. "That's the best part. Deciding what's first."

"I'll try," she said. "But it's notably insane. Clearly you have a disturbed mind. Clearly you're crazy."

"Clearly," I agreed.

My lists had always been extremely private. But Jess expected us to read these out loud and debate the order of the items. "I've got dark eyes before dark hair," she said. "Aren't eyes more important than hair?"

"You say that until he goes bald," I warned.

She laughed. "Sense of humor is first, always. God knows I need someone who makes me laugh."

I was maybe tired of hearing about her list. She'd been going over it for twenty minutes, the minutiae of this imaginary man, a man who never wore sandals, whose chest hair wasn't gross but whose chest wasn't baby-butt smooth either; how he could be smarter than her about some things but she had to be smarter than him about other things; how he had to know all the different wrenches and which to use when; who ate Ruffles not regular potato chips, though I'd barely seen Jess eat potato chips, and pepperoni on pizza or maybe sausage but never green peppers; who thought Abraham Lincoln was the most heroic of the presidents; who wouldn't complain about going to the theater the way her father did, and the same with art museums, though also I'd never seen Jess go to an art museum.

I had a list I could trot out for her, but the truth was I didn't want to be married. Nor did I want children. I couldn't even want a house with a white picket fence. These seemed like odd, shameful secrets, so I kept them to myself. But while I couldn't want what everyone else wanted, I was always aware of that treacherous ache of wanting, that dark hunger. To avoid reading my list, I kept asking about hers.

Finally the afternoon shifted into night, and it was only ordinary darkness outside the window, and what we saw when we looked over were our own startled reflections. The dorm cafeteria was open for dinner, and I would go, and this list would be over. I could have stood up and said I was going to dinner, let Jess claim she'd see me later, knowing she wouldn't, knowing she either skipped dinner or ran in last minute to grab carrot sticks off the salad bar, a spoonful of sunflower seeds wrapped up in a napkin.

Instead I said, "What about money? You didn't write down that he had to be rich."

She tucked her pen behind her ear, which was an affectation she took up for a short while, and pushed aside her composition book. "That's not on my list," she said.

I let a silence grow, imagining it the way a wave built, built, then crashed into a cascade of foam.

She said, "Is that on your list?"

I looked down at my paper, pretended to read what I had written. Then I said, "Second."

"That's the most important?" she shrieked.

"Second most important," I said. "Number two."

"What's first?" she asked.

"He needs to be very smart," I said. "Maybe the smartest person I've met."

"Hmm..." She studied her list, did not meet my eyes. I knew she wasn't reading her words on the page. "Money shouldn't matter." Her voice was prim, starched.

"But doesn't it?" I said.

She shook her head. "I could love a man who was poor. You too. You're not shallow."

"But this is the ideal husband," I said. "Wouldn't the ideal husband be stinking rich? The *ideal*?"

"I'm not writing it down." She sounded angry, at herself, not at me, or maybe at me. I was almost happy to provoke her. People across the country had been laid off. People couldn't find jobs. I didn't have enough money in my pocket to buy this notebook at Osco. Didn't she know any of that? She capped her pen, drummed it rapidly on top of the notebook. *This is how hard it is to tell the truth,* was my casual thought.

"No one has to know," I said. "Like a diary. What's the point if you're not totally honest?"

"You'll know," she said. "You know now."

"I'll forget," I said. "Anyway, I'm the one who said it first."

"You did." She opened her notebook, wrote something quickly, then said, "Okay, Miss Honest Abe, now it's second. After 'He makes me laugh.' A funny rich guy."

"And a smart rich guy," I said. "Maybe they'll be twin brothers. With dark hair and dark eyes."

She laughed and tossed the notebook across her bed, into the folds of the crumpled comforter. I wondered if she would write another word in it, or if this was only a diversion for this wintery afternoon when no one wanted to study. But it turned out that she liked lists. Sometimes she read them out loud. Otherwise I caught the composition book somewhere—on a desk, tucked in her backpack, alongside a sociology textbook in a bookshelf.

As for me, I wrote some lists to make her happy—silly things like Grossest Food in the Cafeteria, and Zittiest Boys in Astronomy Class, and Dead Poets Who Probably Were Good Kissers. I read my lists to Jess and she laughed at the right places, even when she hadn't seen the zitty boys herself or never heard of Rimbaud. Those were my lists in those days. There were other lists in my head, but I didn't share those with Jess or anyone, or ever dare write them down.

WHAT DO YOU WANT
FOR CHRISTMAS, LITTLE GIRL?

(winter, before college)

It's hard to think back.

I took Grace to the mall to see Santa. My mother wasn't wasting money on a stamp for Grace's letter. "He's at the mall," my mother said. "It will be fun for you to tell him yourself what you want." The cue was for Grace to agree, so she did. The letter was cute, with drawings of ice skates and some doll she'd seen on Saturday morning cartoons. A silver baton. Special artist crayons. Books. She was about eight then, and I was a high school senior. But when we got to the mall, she abruptly refused to approach Santa, to nestle in his lap. No reason, just, "I don't feel like it," and we lingered outside the white picket fence bordering the fake winter wonderland snow and mirrors playing iced-over ponds. Plastic reindeer. Snowmen. Fake Christmas trees. Boxes wrapped up like gifts with sparkly bows as big as cabbages. Santa slouched in an oversized red-and-green sleigh, and the idea was to sit with him while a guy dressed like an elf took a picture. It was all very jolly—I mean, to an eight-year-old.

This Santa didn't look substantially better or worse than others, but as we watched for twenty minutes or so, plenty of kids cried and clung to their mother's arms; plenty of kids, not just Grace, took one look at the billows of that fake beard, the shiny black boots, and that gelatinous mountain of red velvet and heard the robotic "ho-ho-ho," and their minds clicked like Grace's: *Nuh-uh, nope, not even for a free candy cane.* The moms wrestled or bribed their kids up there anyway, and most ended up smiling and hugging Santa as the elf snapped the picture. "You sure?" I asked Grace a couple of times, and she shook her head. Not even for a baton and ice skates, which she wouldn't get anyway—or maybe the baton, since that was only a buck. "I don't have to have those things," she said.

As kids paraded onto Santa's sleigh, cozying into his lap for their private chat, I wondered if Grace still believed in Santa. Kids at school had to be speculating. She'd made that list, but even I made lists after I knew better, hedging my bets. My mother thought she'd be the one bringing her today, but she got called into work last minute, so I volunteered. My mother would not have been one to lurk outside the wonderland, watching everyone else's kids chatter at Santa. I imagined her seizing Grace by the wrist, marching her up the candy-cane-striped carpeted pathway, and, with a sneaky push toward the steps to the sleigh, barking, "Tell him what you want." I imagined Grace letting Santa's arms compress her into a furry hug, Grace unable to remember a word of her list. Before she left, my mother said, "Take care of her," as if she were doing the favor, not me, when I already took Grace plenty of places and heated up her dinner and washed her hair lots of nights. Then my mother handed over a fistful of coins that she snuck from my father's penny jar. "Buy her that pretty candy at the fancy card store," she said. Like I'd dump pennies onto the glass countertop at Kirlin's, with its carpeted hush and elegant glass cases arranged with rows of wafery pastel creams and jelly fruit slices and bins of pink and black licorice bridge mix and colorful Jordan almonds. Nuh-uh, nope, not even for glittery crystals of rock candy on sticks, not for that or for anything would I accept a handful of my father's pennies. So I had bus fare (which exceeded the price of a stamp, I noted privately) and not more.

Grace was still wearing her mittens—a good thing, because she'd lose one or both once she removed them; these weren't even a true pair. One was bright blue stripes and the other was black with cat eyes and whiskers. My mother had given up and handed over any old left-hand mitten and right. By now, maybe Grace didn't get that mittens were supposed to match.

"Are you sure?" I asked Grace again. "I could go, too, sit by you and Santa."

A pause, maybe thinking that over. An explosion of *ho-ho-ho*, and Santa boomed, "What do you want for Christmas, little girl?" and Grace's shoulders twitched, then went rigid.

"Okay," and I grabbed her hand and tugged her away from the alleged wonderland. "Let's just have fun at the mall. We've got time before the bus."

"He knows my list," she said, and as I nodded, she dropped into a whisper, "He knows everything."

"'He sees you when you're sleeping,'" I sang.

I thought she'd join in, but she whispered, "I wrecked it."

"No, no, no," I said. But Santa did have a creepy obsession about ferreting out who was naughty and nice. Grace was smart to be suspicious. "We'll have fun anyway," I said. "The mall is fun."

It wasn't. I associated the mall with my terrible job at Karmelkorn, which, because it was food service, paid less than minimum wage. I'd been working there since I was fifteen, being bossed around by a rotation of snotty thirty-year-olds who couldn't get better jobs and burning my wrist on the popcorn kettle, that sticky, scorched-sugar stink of caramel corn—the proper spelling, thank you—lacing my dreams, penetrating my pores. I had applications everywhere, but there was that stupid recession. Places all wanted college kids anyway.

This was our town's first mall and it wasn't complicated—a straight line of maybe twenty stores on either side of a center walkway—and I led Grace the length of it, on the side opposite Karmelkorn, so no one would see me, because I was thinking I might have to call in sick tonight if I didn't get Grace home on the three thirty bus. At the end was Drug Fair, which was a good place for wandering without feeling hassled. I mean, it was the last Christmas shopping weekend and we were two kids spending no money, so why would a nice store want us hanging around?

I steered Grace to the cosmetics aisle, where we sprayed our wrists with perfumes. Then we looked at nail polish, arranging our fingers under each plastic fingernail-sized shape in the vast Cutex display of dozens of colors, names that made me hungry—Raspberry Sherbet, Blueberry Pink, Pink Almond, Beyond Peach. Her too. I caught her stomach grumbling, and I giggled first so she would, too. We spun the rack of Timex watches, debating which to fake-buy, stuck in the end between Mickey Mouse with his gloved hands pointing to hours and minutes or the candy-apple-red watch face with the stretchy silver band. That's when the ladies at the cosmetics cash register intensified their laser glares and hisses of "some people," with "some" like a thousand letters long. There was the toy aisle, but why let Grace come across that doll she wanted? I would tell my mother she had to buy it because Grace was too young to hate Christmas the way the rest of us did. She could get me nothing, but Grace needed that doll off her list.

"Time to go," I said, and I grabbed her right hand—now without a mitten, which I hoped was in her pocket—and we cut through the checkout lane jammed with people waiting to buy what we'd been looking at. I suppose I was used to it, but Grace was a little kid. She hardly knew there were this many things out in the world, and only so much money.

Grace said, "I get it. There's no Santa's workshop," and I said, "Um," and she said, "Everything comes from the mall," and I said, "Um," and she said, "It's okay. I knew it last year," which I didn't believe, and I said, "We probably have to think about getting to the bus stop," which was all the way down at Sears.

I veered us to the opposite line of stores, away from the tempting A&W—not that she would ask about root beer, because she was good at not asking, better than I was about not wanting. That draft root beer was icy-tangy cold, so sweet, and the heavy mugs were as frosty white as the signs promised; sometimes I stopped by after an early Karmelkorn shift, that tiny luxury I allowed myself maybe a truer reward for my hours than the stinking paycheck. As we passed Musicland, I thought I spotted my friend Janey's pothead brother flipping through 45s, and I paused to catch his face, but when he looked up it was another pothead.

Grace stood outside the next store over, Waldenbooks, and as I reached her, she said, "A library! We can check out some books anyway," and I kept walking, pondering why I was wishing it had been Janey's pothead brother, and called to Grace, "It's a bookstore. You have to buy them," and her voice pierced the Christmas Muzak, "Books cost money, too?"

I stopped, stared back at her—one mitten on her hand, the other who knows where, and her mouth open in a little round O of true shock—and looped back to where she stood. I wanted to slug someone, hard, if I only knew who, because my little sister didn't know that, yes, books cost money, too, and fuck Santa Claus, fuck that spying bastard and his ho-ho-hos, fuck that massive American lie of a man—because here I was, having to shake Grace to the core of her heart, rattle that deep, deep book love she had. She was dopey and dreamy, a girl who lost mittens and didn't like to talk, but she was a strong reader, a smart kid, devouring books, reading like words were the air she breathed. Right now she was moving from horse books to my old Nancy Drews. There were scads of books in our house, a collection I'd carefully accumulated from garage sales and library discards, enough that I suppose it made crazy sense that she never thought of books coming from a store, or even a place beyond our house or the library, where I or sometimes my mother took her every couple of weeks, where the librarians knew her name and set aside books they wanted her to read. She read them all. Here are books, and here are more books: and they're all free. It made absolute sense. I mean, unless you understood that you lived in a world that had a hundred shades of nail polish when, I don't know, five or six might be enough. My fury was a living thing rattling my chest. I'd been born understanding a price tag was tacked on everything. How could she not know? I think I was angriest at her, though I didn't want to be.

She wouldn't cry. She never cried. I could say the bus was coming and she'd believe me and off we'd go. I never cried either.

So I smiled. I smiled at her standing in front of the wide Waldenbooks entryway crammed with cardboard displays of gaudy paperbacks and tables stacked high with holiday cookbooks, and I said, "Books do cost money, but we can buy one. We can go in and buy you a book." And I smiled and smiled, and finally she mustered a twinge of a smile, no teeth showing, and said, "Any book?" and I was about to explain about the price difference in paperback versus hardcover but I stopped: "Sure. Any book."

I had no plan. There was no plan that was possible to have, unless the plan was to glance down and discover on the floor the Christmas miracle of a dropped ten-dollar bill. That was my plan. I'd lifted trinkets—eye shadow, Carmex, M&M'S, just little junk—but it felt wrong and, frankly, harder to steal a book. Maybe the plan could be to tell her Santa would bring the book later. Santa to the rescue. Good one.

She dashed into the store, then halted, possibly overwhelmed by the clusters of shelving, the books towering to the ceiling along all three walls of the store, the tables loaded with fat thrillers, the hair-tousled women lustily pouting off the covers of the historical romances, and I caught up to her again. I said, "We'll go to the back with the Nancy Drews and horse books." We edged through the skinny aisles bordered with cookbooks and travel books and joke books and sports books and books about animals and planets and movie stars. Anything you wanted. Once something was important, there was a book for it, a title and an author's name.

The children's section was a jumble: puzzle books, paper doll sets, picture books, book report books like *The Yearling*, cardboard books for babies to chew, and series books, including three whole long shelves of yellow-spined Nancy Drews. There were numbers we didn't have; our set was haphazard, so I guessed Grace would go for #18, *The Mystery at the Moss-Covered Mansion*, our first gap (and one I hadn't read). She was desperate to follow in order. Me too back then, until I realized nothing ever changed in River Heights, which we were supposed to like about Nancy. But that fact made me despise Nancy. "They're all brand new!" Grace called.

A Christmas tree filled the end of the aisle, decorated with large red and green construction paper stars, and I let Grace poke around as she did at the library, flinging open books and plopping on the floor to read with immediate intensity, while I looked at the tree. It was a bad fake with stick-straight branches and scratchy, squared-off needles the color and texture of the plastic basket grocery store strawberries came in. Twinkle lights draped the branches, but one strand was burned out. It was worse than the Charlie Brown tree, especially with the construction paper stars Magic Markered with employee names. Or that's what I thought until I read the names more closely: KIM, AGE 10. STEVE, AGE 7. BRENT, AGE 14. TRACY, DAWN, ERIC, TIM, KEVIN, JULIE... It was one of those Secret Santa trees where you picked a paper star and bought a book for some kid. LISA, JAN, MICHAEL, another MICHAEL. Someone writing names in black caps off a list they'd been given, checking it twice, like Santa.

My face flushed hot, embarrassed and ashamed, as if I'd been caught doing something wrong, as if I'd read my own name up there. We weren't poor-poor, not Secret Santa poor. My parents didn't believe in crying, and they didn't believe in charity. No one in my family did. We don't give to it, and we don't take from it—I'd heard my father holler that to my mother plenty of times. "We'll do without," she'd tell me later in a scorching tone to humiliate me for asking. That's why I rode the bus instead of getting to borrow the car, or getting my own car like some kids at school. That's why Grace's mittens didn't match, why we ate the bread heels instead of throwing them away like I'd seen Janey's mom do at their house, why we didn't have a dog or cat, why our sleds were flattened cardboard boxes, why times a thousand: because we could do without. For the whole rest of our lives, it seemed, we would do without, and it occurred to me, perhaps for the first time, that this had not been a choice for my parents. Only the acting proud was; that was what they had decided to *do*.

I stared at that tree for a million years, enough time for Grace to grow up and shrivel into an old lady. Enough time to be furious and then not.

I snatched a star off the tree. My hand trembled as I carried it up front to the cash register, where I got in line behind a man with a wall calendar with pictures of lighthouses. He asked for gift wrap. He refused the Santa paper, so someone had to come from the back with non-Christmas paper. His gift got wrapped. I was next. I sucked in lots of breath and arranged the paper star on the counter so the clerk could read the name. She said, "A Secret Santa—" and I interrupted: "This is my sister. She's here today, back in the kids' section, and I wonder if maybe we could just get the free book for her right now. It would mean so much to her. To Amy," I added, reading upside down off the paper star. It was red. Red was girls and green was boys.

The clerk looked like a college student, earnest, without makeup. Four inches of curly black hair haloed her face. She seemed startled, and her mouth twisted in confusion, a grimace that wasn't smiling or frowning, an expression that wasn't yes or no. She took off her glasses and polished each lens with the hem of her T-shirt. Stalling. She was going to call over the manager. Managers said no. My family also hated managers and bosses, cops and government do-gooders. People who had to be asked, people who granted permission. She lowered her voice into a whisper: "It doesn't work like that. I'm so sorry."

"Please," I said. I imagined my father listening to me beg. I imagined my mother pretending she didn't know Grace might want something simple like a brand-new book, unread by anyone else. I pushed their stupid faces to the back of my mind. "Reading is her favorite thing," I said.

She picked up the paper star. Maybe she was the one who had cut out the stars. Maybe that long list of poor kids hadn't seemed real to her as she Magic Markered each name. She put on her glasses and abruptly seemed a different person, her dark eyes larger, rounder, with purplish circles underneath, like she had a hard time sleeping. Like she might be the kind of person to be haunted by a poor kid wanting a book. Like she wouldn't want to remember me and my sad, begging face and this crooked red paper star when she was opening presents on Christmas morning. Like reading was also her favorite thing, like she was surprised that I might guess that, that I might understand her secret life, me, just a nameless stranger.

"She's a little kid," I said. "Eight years old."

A woman impatiently pressed behind me, a stack of hardcovers balanced in one arm.

"Please," I said, a little louder, so the customer could hear, could worry.

The clerk said, "One book."

There was a moment when I was supposed to thank her. That moment stretched. Finally I said what I could, which was "Merry Christmas."

"Merry Christmas," she echoed, though there was little joy in the words we exchanged, just a barter.

I rushed to tell Grace to hurry up, that we had to catch the bus, that she should pick out her book, that we had to get moving or be stuck at the mall forever, that this was the last bus, all kinds of alarming exaggerations so we'd be out of there before the clerk changed her mind or went on break or decided to bust me. I was sick to my stomach, not about lying—wasn't Santa Claus a big lie?—but for admitting want to a stranger, acknowledging I couldn't do without. I snatched up some books off a table, barely glancing at the titles, and said, "How about one of these? Look, rabbits on the cover!"

She said, "Are we both getting a book?"

I shook my head. "Just you. Only one. And we have to hurry." I shook my wrist wearing the watch. I was crazed. My throat was tight. Breathing felt unnatural.

She said, "Don't you want one?"

"No," I said.

"But they're new." She pressed her nose deep into the open book she held. "Smell how fresh it is."

I shook my head again, afraid I was going to yell at her, and then yelling at her: "You're the one getting the book, so pick it out right now before we miss the damn bus!"

She marched away, and I dropped the stupid rabbit books on the table and followed her to the next section over, mysteries. She pointed to the display of paperback Agatha Christies and said, "You like these," jabbing her finger against one: "This looks good."

It was *And Then There Were None*, showing a ropy hangman's noose on the front framing a sprawled-out dead body and a bunch of jagged rocks. No cuddly rabbits, nothing a kid would (or should) pick, definitely not a book to satisfy a Secret Santa looking to feel virtuous. "Do you have it already?" she asked, removing it from the display and handing it over. I flipped to the back cover, satisfying her by pretending I needed to read the description.

It was a classic, easily scooped up used; of course I had it. The school librarian had recommended it, hooking me on Agatha Christie. I still remembered the murderer, the trickiness of the story. I couldn't stand that this was the book Grace wanted, that she wanted for me. Her one book she would give to me. I couldn't stand that. I wanted her to be the kind of kid who cried and sulked because she wanted Nancy Drew #18 and #23, wanted #45, too; who thought it was "unfair" she got only one book; who "hated" me for being so "mean."

I wanted her to want them all, all the Nancy Drews, all the books. I wanted her to want everything, to *want*.

"Sure you don't have it?" she asked. "You have too many that look the same."

"Not this one," I said.

"Say thank you," she said, and giggled.

"Thank you," I said.

She hugged me, both mittens now missing. If she had a hat, it was also gone. "You deserve a new book," she said.

Up front, the clerk finished counting bills into someone's hand. When she saw us, she pinned Grace with a tremendous, embarrassing smile. "What'd you pick, sweetie?" she asked, and Grace lifted my forearm, showing off the lurid book in my hand. I stared at the fluorescent lights in the ceiling. Let her think we were scamming Waldenbooks for a $2.25 paperback. What explanation wouldn't be painful? Better to be silent.

The clerk said, "Get out," and I said, "We're going," and the clerk said, "The judge is the murderer," and I said, "We're going," and Grace called, "Merry Christmas! And happy New Year!"

As we left Waldenbooks on our way to the bus stop, I remember thinking, *Grace, age eight, how can I take care of you when you don't want me to?*

JINX

(fall, junior year)

Jess and I lingered at the water fountain in the library, across from the room with the best vending machines. It was her idea to hover, seemingly absorbed in conversation, rating the butts of guys bending over to drink. We flashed quick and—we thought—subtle signals with our eyebrows. We thought we were sly and hilarious, or Jess did. I thought we were embarrassing. But this was what Jess wanted for a study break, and I agreed since it was a step closer to forgetting her fiancé. Truth be told, none of the butts we saw was better than his, and Jess had to know it. *Tommy.* Not wrong to think his name.

An older guy, maybe a grad student, sidled around the corner and said, "You two are laughing a lot." Long blond hair hung straight down his back. His teeth held a pair of black plastic eyeglasses by the stem, so his words sounded tight and clenched. Instead of the preppy look everyone aspired to, he wore black jeans and a too-small black T-shirt printed, in all lowercase, with "anarchists unite—or not."

I looked into his eyes, trying to determine if he was talking to me or to Jess, and I felt Jess next to me, trying to determine the same thing. *Jinx,* I thought, the way kids did when they said the same word at the same time.

We were sideways from a floor-to-ceiling window, and when I checked my reflection, I stood straighter. Jess flicked her hair. I guessed she was thinking about the lipstick in her purse. Me too. So I flicked my hair because she had, and she promptly straightened up.

He folded the glasses and hooked one stem into a jeans pocket. "What's so funny?" he asked, saying it like he knew already. His back was to the wall, so I couldn't see his butt, but it had to be good. He wouldn't wear those jeans if it wasn't.

Jess said, "Just girl talk." Her voice overflowed with implication: that there was more, that maybe she'd tell him but maybe not, that time was endless and her flirty games could last into infinity, that a laugh now was as good as easing a tennis ball back at her with a single, graceful stroke. Three words equaled all that.

But he didn't laugh. That meant something. The silence grew awkward as he glanced my way, his unwavering gaze turning my face hot, though I tried not to show it. There were things I could have said, but I outwaited him. "Maybe you'll tell me," he said. "What's so funny?"

I said, "We're ranking guys' asses. And they don't even know."

Jess shrieked "Aaaugh" delicately and clutched at her chest with both hands, practically feeling herself up. "No, we're not," she said.

The guy locked on to my eyes. His were pale hazel. He didn't blink, and neither did I, and he said, "What about mine?" and he stepped to the water fountain and pushed the button, letting a stream of water arc as he twisted his head to watch us watching him, scooping back his blond hair with his free hand.

Jess tugged my sleeve like a child. "Let's go," she said, puffing out an impatient sigh.

I said, "A-minus." It was an A butt, which I'm sure he knew, but why give him the pleasure?

He twitched his butt in a goofy little wiggle. "Any extra credit?" he asked.

"Gross," Jess pronounced. Someone else would walk away. Not her. No way would she leave me alone with him now, convinced she was protecting me.

"Tough crowd," he said, twisting his head to drink from the fountain. Behind his back, Jess's raised eyebrows asked me: *Are you serious?* But he straightened and faced us before I could answer. Anyway, I didn't know the answer. What I liked about him was that he didn't like Jess best or maybe at all. I think I thought that was enough. I think I thought that was the point.

He slipped on his glasses, then pushed them way down to the tip of his nose and peered over the black rims. "This is a mother of a headache," he said. "Either of you got any drugs?"

"No," Jess said. Her mother's straitlaced voice.

He stretched wide both arms, hands posed like a Jesus statue, like we should place something precious into them. One palm had numbers written on it in red ink. "It's a headache," he said. "I meant aspirin or Tylenol."

I gasped. "You can't take Tylenol," I said. "It's been poisoned. Didn't you hear? It's on all the news."

"TV's for suckers," he said with a crushing but ridiculous sneer.

Jess unzipped her purse, which hung at her hip, and pulled out a white plastic bottle. "Here," she said, tossing it to him. The pills clattered lightly as he caught it.

"Don't take that if it's Tylenol," I said. "Really."

He examined the bottle through the lenses of his glasses. "It is," he said. "Extra strength." He knew, tacking that on on purpose.

Jess said, "It's been in my purse forever. It's fine."

He unscrewed the top and spilled two capsules into his palm, on top of the inky red numbers. Someone's phone number. A locker combination. A due date for a paper.

Why did I care? Trying to save the world. *Take the pills,* I thought, *you idiot.*

"Afraid?" Jess asked. I shook my head before realizing the question wasn't for me.

"You only live once," he said, and he cupped his hand to his mouth, then turned back to the fountain. Water arced. I wasn't looking at his ass. I was looking at Jess, but now she was looking at his ass. He could fall down dead in five minutes. It happened that fast. Why did no one else care? I almost hoped he would die to prove I was right. What showoffs. I remembered how Jess liked to say "Half of being brave is being stupid." "What's the other half?" I'd asked once. "Believing in luck," she'd said, smirking so I'd understand she thought of herself as lucky.

I unclenched my fists. I closed my eyes and quickly said, "I got to get back to my chapter." I walked fast, opening my eyes to watch my feet thud the floor, one after the other.

Behind me, Jess laughed and said to him, "You know what they say. Once is enough if you do it right." Her voice sounded like a pretty shower of confetti. He must have thought so, too, because he laughed right along with her. In the end, it was always Jess. I knew that.

Being quiet wasn't in Jess's DNA. But this was four A.M., when anyone else might tiptoe, or not slam shut the door, or not screech, "Shit," when something crashed, or might shush the guy who called, "Fuck, I'm standing in broken glass." The laugh was his, the guy from the library. Jess said, "Hang on." Crunching, footsteps turning to taps on the tile kitchen floor. "I have no idea where the broom is," she said, and laughed. He laughed. The rough ping-pong of drunk laughing jabbed my gut, making me think I might barf in the trash can, and I breathed quick, shallow breaths, then dragged the pillow over my head, cramming it down hard with my arm. Probably that vase her mother had put on the ledge between the dining and living areas, the one destined to break. Or a lamp. Or who cares. I wanted to shout, "Yes, I hear you! Now go to your room for God's sake, and I'll sweep it up tomorrow," but they'd spiral into laughter if I did or throw out some more curse words. I clamped the pillow tight against my mouth to shut myself up, the trick that worked, the pillow holding me a silent captive—through the toilet flushing, the sink running, footsteps; the fridge popping open, closed, open; and, finally, the soft click of Jess's door, and I knew they were quiet because they kept urging, "Quiet," and giggling and grunting and moaning. My sheets became a sweaty mess, not a cool spot anywhere. Each beat of my heart clawed at my chest. Jackrabbit breaths. I knew I wouldn't sleep, not as long as he was here, even as my mind spilled itself into emptiness.

At six or so, I snuck out to the other room and picked up shards of the glass vase with my fingers and carefully wrapped them in newspaper that I tucked into the trash. The apartment was quiet, draped in the morning gray of a day that hadn't decided which way it would go. Half this, half that. I didn't care about that guy. It wasn't that.

Anyway, Jess never saw him again after that night. She couldn't even remember his name. He called a few times, but I didn't give her the messages or bother writing the number. His name was Erik. He was very careful when he left those messages, saying, "Erik with a *k*."

It was kind of a powerful feeling to do that, to wipe him from existence.

THE THIRD RAIL

(spring, freshman year)

When Jess was bored, she liked to pull together a quick collection of new people. She'd weave herself a whole new domain populated by people she accumulated from random encounters: chatting in line to check out a library book or borrowing a pen in a lecture class or anywhere. She craved surprise, and it was no big deal, creating a sudden influx of new people just for fun. She wanted excitement, variety, new stuff to talk about. I didn't take any of this personally. She got bored with these new people quickly. The minute she did, it was like taking a broom to an old cobweb up in the corner and knocking it down. No thought that those dusty strands might be home to a spider. That these people might have believed they were real friends.

I was the real friend. We knew that.

I knew Jess so well that I could spot the onset of this particular boredom, the way you'd spot sniffling at the start of a cold. She'd pace the dorm hallway, lingering at each door's wipe-off memo board, reading scribbled messages as if hoping to find the answer to a question locked in her head. Or she'd gaze deeply at her face in her make-up mirror—not poking zits or practicing arching one eyebrow—but staring at her eyes, taking out her blue contact lenses and slipping on the glasses she refused to wear out, special-ordered Ray-Bans with clear lenses. She would sit still for ages, staring into super-magnification, dialing the mirror's glow to the greenish office filter, the harshest light. "It's all bullshit," she would pronounce, "right?" and I'd glance up from my book and agree, and there would be more, ranting about the exact vast thing that was the bullshit right this minute—politics, the world, men, capitalism, science, God—and I'd close my finger in my book to mark my page and listen. "Something's gotta change," she'd say eventually, "you know?" I'd agree, and the next day she'd be going on about some girl in her psych class with fascinating stories about volunteer coaching a high school softball team last summer on an Indian reservation in South Dakota; then that girl with the cool lace-up boots in the dorm elevator would become "Cammy, you know, on the fourth floor, the expert on the London punk scene"; then it would be "Oh, I forgot I said I'd go to a movie with some people tonight," meaning, *So I'm not going with you like I said I would.*

"Okay," I always said, whether it was Jess not joining me at the library, Osco, Saturday movie night at Tech, the frat party with the Eddy Clearwater Band. One fast word: "okay."

I couldn't tell if she wanted me to be jealous. I couldn't tell if I was.

In my head, I called them the test friends, like Jess was testing to see if they were better than me.

I could have created my own test friends. I knew how it worked. Everyone traveled in a pack in high school. Back there I was fringe, the quiet girl on the edge, no one's best friend but also not the one gossiped about. The closest I had to a best friend was Janey, whom they loved flinging the gossip on. No one claimed her, so Janey assigned herself to me. She was the friend I had so no one noticed I had no friends.

There were filler girls I knew here, props: Catholic girls on Sunday mornings hovering over free doughnuts after Mass at the student center, all of us forcing awkward chitchat with the priest; girls in lecture classes who swapped notes color coded with highlighter pens and set up study groups for the final; girls who didn't mind cheering through all four quarters on a sunny football Saturday, who understood rushing versus passing; girls along the dorm hall who made me laugh when we stood in our nightgowns, brushing our teeth at the bathroom sinks; girls who'd walk with me to Burger King for cheap Sunday lunch when the dorm cafeterias were closed. It was easy to feel surrounded by people. And I didn't mind the pleasant simplicity of surrounding others, which felt different from, and perhaps superior to, Jess's manic desire to rev herself up with a crazy kaleidoscope of new friends. I drifted and floated, whereas she crashed, usually about two weeks in, howling, "Well, tonight was a total suck," finding me to postmortem Cammy and her tacky boots and the pathetic (and gross) affectation of safety pins jabbed through earlobes.

So it was nothing when she told me she was going to brunch at the Third Rail with the latest batch, Teresa and Deedee. I gave the usual "okay." Then she said, "Come with. I want you to meet them."

I made her repeat the invitation because I didn't trust that I heard right. She laughed. "Are you afraid or something?" she asked, so right away I said I'd go. It was Sunday and no cafeteria and I had to eat and she knew it. I tried to imagine this would be fun, that I'd like these girls, that it was okay that Jess liked them.

The Third Rail—named for the electrical rail that powered the el trains—was famous for Sunday brunch. It seemed to be a spread of the usual stuff—waffles, bagels, the rest—but really, it was like all-you-can-eat dessert. So bowls of whipped cream for those waffles and tiny pitchers of hot fudge to take to your table. Chocolate chips in the cream cheese for the bagels. Chocolate chips in the pancakes. Chocolate chips to sprinkle in your oatmeal. Everything was turned into dessert or, if not, it was totally fattened up. Quiche was "quiche casserole" with a hash brown crust, three inches high, topped with a layer of sour cream. A man in a tall chef's hat carved roast beef, and if you didn't grab his arm to stop him, he globbed your meat with a coating of creamy horseradish sauce. Then there was the real dessert table, towers of densely frosted cupcakes and eight different types of cheesecake. Freshman girls kept the place in business, herding in, dragging visiting parents there, insisting guys spring for morning-af-ter dates.

Jess wasn't a brunch fan, calling it an excuse to eat like a pig and then sleep like a dog all day, but she went when her parents drove up with Linda, who for some reason loved the Third Rail—"Just to make me insane," Jess said. "All she actually eats is chocolate chip cream cheese. She licks it right off the knife blade. So embarrassing." I'd been a couple of times, with a cluster of penny-pinchers who lived down the dorm hall and had to be first in line when it opened at eight A.M., because anyone through the door before nine got two dollars off.

There was always a fight about whether to tip on the real per person price or the discount, which spiraled into "Why tip on brunch when all they're doing is carting off dirty plates?" Last time I shocked myself by advocating generosity, kicking in a couple dollars to jack up the tip, maybe because it mortified me hearing how my own thoughts sounded spoken. The penny-pinchers hadn't invited me since that betrayal.

I drove over with Jess on Sunday, at a more normal brunch time of 11:30, and because we were late, they'd found a booth. Sitting across from each other, you might think they were sisters because they both had red hair, almost as if Jess had decided, *Time for redhead friends.* They jumped up and tumbled into Jess's arms, all of them hugging gaudily, with relief. And because they were introduced to me so fast and because they both had a mass of curly red hair, but mostly because I expected them to be gone soon enough, I didn't keep track of which was which. They hadn't known each other until Jess came along. One was from Jess's psych class, and Jess found the other in line at the bursar's office, waiting to cash a check. A history major and a theater major. From Connecticut, from Phoenix. Chi O vs. Pi Phi, dogs vs. cats, vegetarian vs. meat, and so on—enough to make anyone think that these two girls with red hair wouldn't be friends without Jess as the link between them. They had been slumped in the booth, arms crossed, stuck in a slow-moving conversation that appeared composed of single-word answers, but the second they saw Jess, their faces bubbled into smiles. Compliments gushed to Jess on her oversized cardigan sweater, which I had complimented earlier, and there was talk about someone's new suede boots and someone else worried about rain on the way, all of this talk spilling at once, none of it special or beyond my own conversational skills, and then off to load up our plates. Jess returned with lettuce, raw spinach, alfalfa sprouts, and sliced mushrooms, no dressing—"rabbit food," one of the girls called it with a giggle, but Jess nudged aside the greenery to reveal the skinniest sliver of pumpkin-walnut cheesecake, and we all fake-gasped. With the penny-pinchers, the routine was five trips to the buffet, focusing on food they wouldn't feed us at the dorm, like expensive salmon, even if we preferred waffles slathered in whipped cream. I was too edgy to heap up with these redheads watching, so I had the least food—sauceless roast beef, three-cheese pasta salad, roll and butter balls, and two slices of cheesecake: almond amaretto and caramel turtle. Deedee and Teresa were fans of the quiche casserole, which came in three flavors (spinach-mushroom, bacon-Swiss, ched-dar-onion), and they had slabs of each, even the vegetarian. That and red hair were knitting them together. And Jess.

Jess poured coffee and passed around the cream. It seemed impos-sible to imagine conversation for two hours. I could fake a headache. But they'd talk about me if I left.

"So," one of the girls said. She looked at me, tilting her head as if I were a confusing piece of sculpture. "You know Jess how?"

"We met our first day," Jess said. "We're going to be roommates next year. After that we'll share a cute little apartment off-campus, then be maid of honor in each other's weddings, and finally live hap-pily ever after a block apart in Chicago till we're little old ladies."

"So then you're best friends?" the other girl asked. Coiled around her neck was a fuchsia-and-orange jacquard scarf that maybe would have looked good on a Frenchwoman or a Theta. If I had to guess, she was the theater major.

"Yes," I said, exactly as Jess said, "I don't believe in best friends."

There was an awkward silence. I smeared a glob of butter onto my roll, rubbed my knife across its slickness over and over, creating a per-fectly smooth surface. At home, we sprinkled salt on buttered bread, but I had forced myself out of the habit here.

"Oh, um," said the girl with the scarf.

"Me neither," the other girl said. "Ranking people is juvenile. And demeaning."

"That's not why," Jess said, and the girl turned deeply silent, as if slapped on the hand for grabbing candy. I had said "yes" because I thought I was supposed to, but now I concentrated on running my fork tines along the rim of my plate, unwilling to get caught with food cramming my mouth at the wrong time. No one asked, *What* do *you mean then, Jess?* though I felt we all wanted to. They were sliding me sideways glances. Jess told me they wanted to meet me, but I bet she had told them the exact same thing, that I wanted to meet them. I would have expected that I would be the one screwing up; I would be the one saying, "I don't believe in best friends." Maybe Jess wasn't screwing up. Maybe this is what she wanted me to know.

Jess said, "'Best friend' sounds so possessive, so reductive."

The red-haired girls looked at each other. Suddenly they looked like they had known each other for a hundred years, like they could tell what the other was thinking.

"I hate being boxed in," Jess said. "'Best friend,' one person holding all my secrets. Like I'm a possession. Thinking about a 'best friend' creates unhealthy competition. Like us right now." She kept talking and defending herself, but I stopped listening. What it was sounding like was that she didn't want these girls thinking I was already her best friend.

I cut a slice of roast beef into tiny, even squares, then those squares into tinier squares. The restaurant was noisy and too many people were walking around, squeezing past tables. There were a thousand different smells. Brunch was stupid. If I didn't get another plate, I'd be hungry later. The pizza restaurant I worked at was too slammed on Sundays to take extra time to make pizza for employees. Amazing how often I thought about food. All the time. There was so much silence at our table.

I felt these two girls and their stupid red hair feeling sorry for me.

I said, "My sister is my best friend."

The two girls sighed and smiled. "Oh, me too," they murmured. "Oh, yes, oh, I love my sister." They were so relieved, they started eating again. One of them picked up a chocolate-covered strawberry and bit into it. That Third Rail thing: a strawberry—but covered in chocolate. They started talking about their sisters: one was a real-life twin, which was secretly funny to me, though she wasn't an identical twin; her twin sister had brown hair, which was also secretly funny to me because the twin sister was at Brown University. I asked a lot of questions about their sisters, and in a few minutes I figured out that the twin was Deedee with the scarf and, yes, the theater major. Teresa's sister was two years older, in Paris on study abroad. She sent Teresa a Chanel perfume and powder set from Paris that smelled better than Chanel at Marshall Field's. We debated whether we liked No. 5 better or 19 or 22, and Jess wedged in to announce that her mother called Chanel too sophisticated for college girls but we said that was an old-lady thing to say. I could talk and listen and finally eat my slivers of cut-up roast beef, but what I was thinking was that I had won the conversation and beat Jess, and thinking that made me think, *No wonder she didn't call me a best friend, because what kind of friend did that?*

When they asked about my sister, I explained that she was several years younger but precocious for her age, and so smart and passionate. I was describing Phoebe, Holden Caulfield's beloved little sister from *The Catcher in the Rye*, but they didn't notice. "So adorable," they cooed, "next time bring pictures." I kept going, telling them about watching Grace ride the merry-go-round in Central Park while it rained like a bastard, buckets of rain, how crazy blue her coat was, though all that was Holden Caulfield, even the coat; though I'd never been to New York, which Jess knew. I wanted to talk on and on about my sister, tell these girls everything, because I missed her, I realized. I loved her. I could imagine this little girl as my best friend, until I remembered that I was spinning her from a fictional character, inventing her out of lies.

Jess never mentioned her sister, letting Teresa and Deedee assume she didn't have one, and I didn't tell them she did, not even when Teresa said, "I know a lot of only children who say that's best," and Jess agreed. We filled another plate with food, and another, and then we tried every flavor of cheesecake, even Jess, and they thought caramel turtle was the best, and Jess and I preferred chocolate chip. We poured hot fudge over everything. We filled a bowl with whipped cream that we ate with spoons. Deedee dropped a handful of sugar packets in her purse.

"Let's do this again," we agreed as we stood out on the sidewalk afterward. "It was so much fun," we assured one another, looping ourselves into hugs, waving good-bye as the two of them walked toward north campus. I knew they'd wait for Jess to call and she wouldn't, or to return a call and she wouldn't do that either. Maybe we'd run into each other at the library or at a party, and there'd be awkward chat, like about the weather. Maybe not even that. We were done with those test friends. I knew Jess wouldn't say it that way, but I knew that's what she was thinking. She didn't even offer them a ride.

She and I walked down Foster, toward her car. The sun felt surprising, like it should have been night, like somehow we'd been inside forever. There was a sense of time telescoped upon itself somehow, now expanding. I was waiting for her to speak first, which she finally did, as we jaywalked across the street, our strides matching, I noticed.

She was working to be all fake casual. I could tell. She said, "You know I was kidding, right? Of course you're my best friend."

The next moment felt long but wasn't, my mind flashing about what to say, how I might make her suffer, a little or a lot; the ways I could get back at her for her hurtful remark earlier. The knowledge that I had power, maybe more power than I'd imagined. "Revenge is sweet" was the cliché, but glowing brightest was this: relief is far, far sweeter, and so I said, "You're my best friend, too."

"Always," she said.

"Always," I echoed.

We would have to be. That was what being best friends meant, maybe: feeling so close, knowing so much, that you almost couldn't stand it. Almost.

THE GATES OF HEAVEN

(fall, junior year)

"I'm going to church tomorrow," I said to Jess. "The dead people are kind of haunting me." The little girl barely older than my sister, the Polish man and his family, the flight attendant, the others, including the ones maybe we didn't know about and anyone who might drop dead tomorrow because of a white plastic bottle on a shelf in their medicine cabinet, because they had bad luck or, some might say, because they were being punished. In such chaos, I wanted comfort: the familiar mumble of ancient words, that cadence, the utterly unchangeable rhythm of Catholic Mass. I wanted not false promises that all would be better or that this was God's will, but simply the *sound* of order. "Church is the sound of order," I told Jess. (And the place for guilt, I thought, though why feel guilty because my luck wasn't as rotten as theirs?) I don't know why I said any of it or bothered to explain why church, why now, when she would be asleep at 10:15 tomorrow morning, but I announced all this anyway in one long breath.

She said, "I'll go with you."

We were both so surprised that we laughed.

"You'll reek of the pope," I said. "One drop of our holy water will brand a crucifix onto your delicate sinner's skin. Your mother will disown you."

"Come on," she said, then jumped into a bad hillbilly parody: "I gotta see what this yeer 'hooooe-lee' communion's all about. I'm-a gonna get me some body a Christ." She was reading Flannery O'Connor in her Southern Women Writers class, picking up only the worst bits.

"No," I said sharply. "And stop with the voice. It's not funny."

We were in the kitchen, just home from the late show of a silly romance that made Jess teary, which meant she was thinking about her ex-fiancé, Tommy, though the point of going to a movie was to keep her from thinking about him. I was devouring forkfuls of cold Ragu spaghetti out of a Tupperware, though I'd eaten 90 percent of the popcorn she bought to share, though I wasn't hungry either now or when the popcorn bucket was in my lap. "Americans usually don't eat from hunger," Jess had informed me while paying at the concession stand, "it's boredom or anxiety. Trying to fill something that can't be filled."

Now she stared at me, an expectant look on her face demanding an apology for my snappishness. I gave an explanation instead: "It's a sin for non-Catholics to take communion."

"Well, whoop-de-do," she said. "Keep your dumb old salvation to yourself."

"Doesn't work like that," I said. "Catholics run a lifetime program. A commitment. What you want are the loons who dunk you in a river, then throw open the gates of heaven."

She rolled her eyes. "Why is me gobbling up a little white disk horrifically offensive?"

"I know it's dumb," I said. "Especially since I don't even take communion anymore."

"Then so what?"

I had been afraid the question would be *Why not?*

At the Catholic student center virtually the whole congregation went up for communion, even the hungover clot of us lurking in the back who showed up for the free, post-Mass doughnuts. Habit, peer pressure, took us up to the altar. Not me. I shuffled out of the way as they pressed up the aisles, the surge of them leaving me alone and out of place: a sinner. In Iowa, they taught us we weren't allowed communion if a mortal sin stained our soul, which made me worry about the several random people who remained seated at each Mass: Murderers? Or merely people who hadn't fasted the requisite hour before receiving communion? When my father whacked my shoulder, I dutifully stood and marched forward, his bulk looming half a step behind me. "Body of Christ," the priest intoned. "Amen," we agreed, mouths snapping wide, our outstretched tongues alert and ready.

One last dollop of spaghetti, then I burped shut the Tupperware, sliding it into the open fridge so I wouldn't have to wash the container. This conversation irritated me. Everything irritated me tonight, even the refrigerator light, overly bright and buzzy. There was barely any food, but I stared at what there was, mesmerized: cottage cheese, a bread bag with only heels, skim milk, two eggs, a stack of loose American cheese slices, rusty-looking lettuce, half a tomato in a baggie, mustard, mayo, packets of soy sauce, peanut butter, grape jelly, three cans of Tab. Only the cheese had been bought with my money.

"What do you think Tommy's doing right now?"

My shoulders tightened and I forced them back loose. I said what a friend must always say: "You're too good for him." I must have sounded convincing, because she gave me a wistful smile.

"You always know what to say." She made a quick air-kiss for me.

Damn it. I absolutely hated tonight. I grabbed the peanut butter and closed the refrigerator and looked down, carefully unscrewing the jar's metal lid and placing it on the counter as if that action required attention. But I had to look at her. Again: "You're too good for him," I mumbled.

"Can't help who you love," she said. Her eyebrows lifted in a question. It could be she was thinking about Tommy, or, I suppose, it could be she was thinking about me.

"Actually, I think you can," I said. I extracted a spoon from the dish rack, teeteringly full, because why bother putting away dishes that would be used again? I scooped up an overflowing glob of peanut butter that I slid through my mouth, spinning the spoon upside down, finagling with my tongue to suck off every gluey bit, half gagging and half wishing I would gag more, harder. I wanted to think only of this hunger for peanut butter, my desire, this need. If I thought about anything more, I would tell her. I would tell her. I would confess my mortal sins.

Somewhere deep inside, I understood the day would come when she would find out about me and Tommy and what we were doing. When I would have to admit the truth, to her, to myself; I would have to *say the words*. It could be any day, really; she'd found out about Tommy cheating with his old girlfriend out of the blue, when we were on campus for some professional society meeting she said she should go to because she was secretary. This was right before school started, and we were in the Harris Hall first-floor bathroom, the one with the pretty mahogany stall doors from the early 1900s, when we overheard some girls talking about him and his ex-girl-friend Sydney Moore and how cute they were reunited at the Theta picnic, keeping on with their gossip even when they saw us at the mirrors, knowing what they were doing, knowing exactly who Jess was. After the girls swished through the door, and I got that we wouldn't be going to the meeting, I looked at Jess's eyes in the mirror and said, "You have to do something, don't you?" and in that long minute afterward, I almost felt wrong for saying it like that, but then she nodded, and a few days later it was done. The engagement was off. No one planned for that but it happened. Maybe you could say I helped make it happen. I liked to believe that I wanted what was best for Jess.

I wondered what I would do if she found out about me and Tommy, where I would live, who would buy peanut butter for me—Jif, the good brand, not the cheap, oily Dominick's crap. Any day could be that day when she found out. Any day. Ask the Tylenol victims. I was a bad person, a sinner. Guilty. That's what the Catholics and the rest of them were counting on, that deep in our core each of us knew we were bad.

I jabbed the spoon deep into the peanut butter again. We did this all the time, drank from milk cartons, dug up jelly and ice cream with our fingers. Why dirty a dish? Germs didn't scare us. They didn't feel real. People dead from popping Tylenol weren't real, and neither was God and neither were the secret things I did with Tommy in a certain library bathroom.

"So come to church tomorrow," I said through a mouth of peanut butter. "Take communion. I promise you'll be disappointed. You don't even eat doughnuts, which is the real reason to go." I tried to picture her standing next to me in the back in a crumpled T-shirt and tennis shoes; my mind couldn't even get to that part, Jess sloppy.

She shook her head. "I—" and the phone burst out, louder than usual, the way the refrigerator light seemed brighter than usual, the peanut butter stickier. Everything tonight felt pushed too far. My heart beat like a bongo drum, knowing Tommy was on the other end, though there was no real reason for him to call either of us—only to confess. It had been a couple of weeks since Jess broke off the engagement. The spiral of begging and apologizing and explaining should be over. Too many people knew he was cheating with Sydney Moore, so Jess had no choice. He pushed and pushed and pushed, and the relief was that he'd been caught with Sydney, not me. We'd gotten away with it—we were both getting away with it—and that should be enough to keep us quiet. But I didn't stop. And neither did he. Like he wanted to be caught, which was why that ringing phone terrified me. *Slut.* I shoved more peanut butter into my mouth. I was going to eat this whole jar if I wasn't careful.

Jess on the phone: "You sound insane, Mother!"

I had missed something. How had her mother found out? Tommy had called her mother?

A moment later, she slammed down the phone and snatched her hand back, as if the receiver were toxic. She whirled continuously, facing me, away from me, facing me again. Her eyes were wild, like animal eyes; her mouth contorted and silent, without language for this moment. The spoon dropped from my hand and clattered onto the counter, and I grabbed hold, the laminate under my fingertips a hard, cool comfort. The words would come, the hellfire of each consonant and vowel, her hate burning into me, and I braced, ready, so ready for that hiss—*Slut!*—though my mind warned it didn't make good sense that Jess's mother would deliver this news or that Tommy would confess to Jess's mom.

Jess said, "My dad's on his way over and she says don't let him in."

"What?"

"I could barely get that with all her crying and screaming," Jess said. "And swearing. Yeah, my mother, swearing. Like a sailor! I couldn't listen to it, what she was saying."

"Oh, Jess," I said. Relief made it easy to hit the perfect sympathetic note.

"Goddamn it. She's insane." Jess folded her arms around her chest. The stripes on her sweater sleeves jumped into weird alignment. "How's she know those words? I don't want to hear my mother screaming that my dad's a goddamn fucking cocksucker. Oh my god." Her body folded and collapsed gently onto the floor. She leaned her back against the cupboard where we kept the pots. I slid down next to her.

"Probably just some crazy fight," I said. "It'll blow over. It has to." I spoke breezily, as if talking would create a wind that could blow a fight over.

"They never fight!" Blurted out like a true fact, like proclaiming the Earth round.

I chewed my lip. *Isn't it pretty to think so?* I wanted to say, but this wasn't the right time, and she wouldn't get it, how that line clobbered all assumptions; Hemingway wasn't on the Southern Women Writers syllabus.

The phone rang again, and we scrambled up. "Want me to—?" and I reached for the phone, but she slapped my hand, a big smack that stung; she hit hard, trying to hurt me, and then she shoved one shoulder against me as she went to the phone, rough enough to make me lose balance. On purpose. She snatched up the receiver and shouted, "I mean it, Mother, you're being totally insane and don't call again until you calm down and tell me what the deal is."

From upstairs, the landlord thumped on the floor with a broom handle.

There went the doorbell, *ring, ring, ring,* six or seven times without pause.

Jess stood with the phone a foot away from her ear, screaming, "Stop it! Stop it!" maybe directed to the phone or to me or to all the world. Red blotches sprawled across her cheeks.

Maybe she would hit me again for trying to help, but the doorbell kept going, along with the bang-the-door-down knocking, and one more time with the broom handle upstairs, so I ran to the door and flung it open, ignoring every scrap of training about peepholes and late-night strangers—because something had to stop this chaos—and there was Jess's father, an open trench coat slung crooked over his suit as if he were coming from the office at this hour, and next to him was a girl, and part of me thought, *Linda?* But no, because that was impossible. This girl was fourteen or so, holding a small, old-fashioned red plaid cloth suitcase. She clutched a feather pillow under one arm, and a worn baseball mitt dangled off her hand. A fringy leather purse hung at her hip, strapped diagonally across her chest, and at her feet was a larger suitcase in matching plaid. I snapped on the porch light so we all could see better, and what I saw immediately was that the girl looked like a younger version of Jess. Like Jess's father. Hawkish nose, wide-set eyes, long forehead. Her hair was wavy, and her eyes gleamed differently from Jess's without her fake contact lenses, more gray than blue, very pale. A lot about her felt pale, like a worksheet that had been copied too many times. Her head cocked like a robin's.

"Jess?" she asked.

"No, no," I said. "I'll go get her," but Jess's father grabbed hold of the top part of my arm, hard, meaning business—the way Jess had meant business when she slapped me off the phone—and he pinched deep into that spongy gap between muscle and bone. I forced myself not to flinch, to let the pain dig, to take it. That heavy, ugly pinkie ring he wore pressed in.

"You stay here with Penny," he said. "I'm talking to Jess alone," and he squeezed harder; I felt the tiniest edge of a fingernail. I hated too-long fingernails on men. I would bruise. The mark would last several days, and a flash through my mind showed my little sister with bruises, my mother getting her dressed for church, tugging a long-sleeved turtleneck over her head, the heavy silence of that moment, but the sharp flare in my arm right now dragged me back to here, to Jess's father, to his bulk. I nodded, moving aside—he would have trampled his way through—and as he stepped over the suitcase, I edged out sideways onto the porch, thinking I should keep the girl outside as long as possible. If I were outside, she wouldn't notice she wasn't inside, right? My reasoning felt sound yet surreal. I pulled shut the wooden door, then let the squeaky screen door close with a bang.

Outside had a crisp chill, that sort of autumn nip that got your hair smelling good, hinting of the sweet side of winter: snowmen, hot chocolate, mittens. Though actually I liked winter best, how guilt-free it was. Outside was cold, so you stayed in and read books. That was all there was to do in the winter. No picnics or gardening or walks in the fresh air or vacations or rounding up friends for swimming pool dates like the other seasons. Make a snowman if you felt like it, but no one cared if you did or didn't. Once you hauled yourself over the nightmare hump of Christmas, winter was ollie ollie oxen free.

Sometimes I truly admired how my own mind wandered inside itself, getting lost, going other places than where it was supposed to be. But Penny was staring at me, chewing the inside of one cheek, probably a bad habit, something she imagined no one could detect, but that side of her face looked caved in, unsettling me further. I babbled: "I'm Jess's roommate. Jess is inside. She was on the phone, but probably she's off now. She—"

"My mom ate one of those poisoned pills," Penny said.

I assumed I hadn't heard her correctly. I said, "Jess is..." but Penny's eyes teared and glossed, so I had heard. "Oh," I said. And, "Oh," again as Penny blinked and watched me and blinked harder. "Oh. I'm so sorry," I said. "So... she... ?"

Penny yanked the baseball mitt off her hand, dropping it onto the suitcase so she could swipe roughly at the tears her blinking hadn't caught. The pillow slipped to the ground, and she half kicked it. "So now I'm here."

I sort of reached an arm out to hug her, thinking she might expect that, but her body visibly stiffened, so instead I patted the sleeve of her jean jacket, kind of the way you pat a dog's head when you don't like dogs, which I didn't. Penny reminded me of that dog you find shivering on your porch on a rainy night that you wish had ended up on someone else's porch, the kind of dog your dad calls the pound on.

"She had a headache," Penny said. "She was cooking dinner and had a real bad headache from work and she said, 'Go get me a couple Tylenols, lovey,' and I did. Right off the bathroom counter, still in a bag. She swallowed them without water, and like five minutes later she thumped down flat on the kitchen floor."

"Oh, wow," I said. And I also thought, *Oh, wow, "lovey."* The word that belonged to Jess's family. *Lovey, pay the check so we can leave. How was your day, lovey?* The show-offy, "we're a perfect family with this perfect word" word that I hadn't realized I hated until I heard it in Penny's voice.

"I didn't know what to do," she said. "So I called up my dad, though I'm not supposed to, not even if it's important. But I didn't know what to do." There were more tears than she could stop; they rolled down her cheeks one after the other, the wet trail of them glittering in the porch light. Her shoulders hunched, collapsed, and her arms twisted tightly around her ribs. I stumbled back a step or two, tripping on the pillow. Here was the worst bad luck. There was not one bit of this that Jess was going to like. We heard Jess shriek, "Oh my god! No! *No, no, no, no!*" through the closed door, the closed windows. I wondered if her father would pinch her arm into a bruise. *He didn't mean it to be that hard,* I reminded myself, *he's under a lot of pressure obviously, or why else would he have brought this girl here?* Jess's half sister. Jess might slap him the way she slapped my hand. I thought about Jess's frantic, furious mother alone at home, dialing our number while we were at the dumb movie, calling, calling; thought about this girl waiting under that porch light at Jess's house, clutching her pillow, trying to ignore that screaming fight inside; about Jess's mother hurling words no one knew she knew. Cocksucker. This girl, not much older than my own sister, alone on the porch. Why didn't she have an aunt, for God's sake, some real family? Wasn't there anyone else? A wave of fury walloped me, deep tribal fury, as if this were all her fault—getting the Tylenol, winding up on my porch—as if it were her doing and she should have known better. But I closed my eyes, took a deep breath, opened them again. Forced out a smile, kept it there for a moment to make sure it would stick.

"What grade are you in?" I asked.

"Eighth," she said.

"My favorite grade," I said, though it wasn't. "One funny thing is I had to take shop class. We were the first girls who had to take shop—you know, for equality—and the teacher kept warning we'd all chop off our fingers with a saw because we were dumb girls. He had us make cutting boards, not lamps like the boys, because girls belonged in the kitchen and home ec."

"You liked that?" Penny asked.

"I liked when he was the one who shaved off the tip of his own finger with the jigsaw when he was yelling at a girl who hadn't sanded the edges of her cutting board enough." Okay, Penny had stopped with the tears and seemed to be listening. It was me the shop teacher was yelling at, but probably Penny didn't need to know that. I continued: "There were buckets of blood everywhere, and a bunch of the cutting boards were wrecked"—though ironically not mine—"and the girl, who wanted to be a doctor, wrapped a tourniquet around his arm, and he yelled at her that she was doing it wrong, but she got a special award in the end-of-the-year honors assembly. Then we had a sub for the rest of woodshop who smoked so much dope he didn't even notice we were girls."

Penny said, "I don't know what's going to happen to me."

I barreled on, pretending not to hear her: "Also in eighth grade I had the biology teacher who promised to swallow a live goldfish in front of every class on the last day of school. I don't know what that would prove, really, or teach us, or why parents didn't complain."

Penny didn't even barely smile, but as long as I was talking, she wasn't.

From inside, Jess shrieked, "I already have a sister and she's dead!"

"Linda," Penny said.

"You know about Linda?" I asked.

"I know about all of them." Penny looked down, scuffed one foot roughly against the wooden floorboards of the porch, following the line of the plank with her toe. She wore Frye boots, real ones, which looked too expensive to match the cruddy plaid suitcases and the lumpy pillow, and I realized that Jess's father had bought these boots. I imagined her ripping paper off the box two days past her birthday, or the week before Christmas, never a gift from him on the holiday itself.

"The cops were going to take me," she said. "I thought I was being arrested for killing my mom. But then my dad got all involved, and I don't know what's supposed to happen next."

"Do you have... a grandmother?" I asked.

She shook her head, yawned, kept watching her feet. "Me and my mom. Some aunt I met once is married to a preacher saving souls in Africa who's psycho, says my mom."

"Where do you live?" I asked.

"Near Wrigley Field," she said, a glimmer of a smile brightening her face as quick as a flashbulb snapping. She grabbed her mitt up off the ground and crushed it onto her left hand, smacked her right into it with a pop that was clearly satisfying, because she smacked it again several more times as she spoke. "Last summer I'd go hang out with the guys trying to get home run balls on Waveland Avenue, outside the park. My friends called me weird, but the guys were all crazy Cubs fans, kinda like me. They'd bring coolers and lawn chairs and everyone with a glove, and someone always had a radio to follow the game, and when they cheered inside, we all jumped up, knowing if the wind was blowing out there was a chance a ball might sail over, though they hardly ever did. Didn't matter. Harry Caray on the radio would go, 'It might be, it could be...' and we'd jump around, all happy because maybe the Cubs would win, and they'd toss me an Old Style. I never got a ball, but guys did, especially at batting practice. Getting a ball would be magical, like once in a lifetime. Sometimes my mom gave me money for bleacher tickets, and once my dad got us seats behind home plate and bought us programs, and we kept score like he did when he was a kid and he promised to give me his old scorecards. Back then he snuck into games with his friends, he said, no big deal. We went for batting practice, but I still didn't get a ball, so he bought me one off the souvenir stand, and I acted all happy, but that's not like catching your own ball yourself."

There was more—wow, she really was into the Cubs—but I couldn't listen, because it was impossible to imagine how this could work out, with Jess, with Jess's mom, even with Jess's dad. Impossible. I imagined Jess's father living all these years split right down the middle into two separate halves, the halves each wrapped up separately in tissue paper and placed into two separate boxes, the boxes going into two different rooms, into two different closets on two different floors of the same house... and then I imagined that house burning all the way down to the ground with the only thing left in the rubble those two halves of one life, right out there for everyone to see. I would like to think that I couldn't imagine such a thing, but I imagined it perfectly: how fantastic it felt, how exciting, keeping that secret solid and heavy in your chest, holding two halves of you so separate they weren't even really you anymore, knowing anyone less daring, anyone less smart couldn't do what you were doing, couldn't get away with it. No one saw they had only half of you, which was amusing and powerful: half of you was enough for them, more than enough; half of you was better than a whole of anybody else. So you told yourself. So you believed. Until that house burned down around you one autumn night. *Don't play with fire* popped into my head.

I realized Penny had stopped talking. Her silence made me nervous, so I said, "I don't know anything much about baseball. Three outs. Home run. Nothing intricate. I guess there's a lot of strategy?"

"Totally," she said. "I could explain some, not that I'm any expert, but maybe when we watch the World Series—if, I mean. I think it's going to be the Brewers for sure. I'm drawing up scorecards on graph paper so I can keep score, even—"

A dish or two crashing. A door slamming. A howl: "I hate you, thanks for ruining my whole life forever. You make me sick!"

Penny's face seemed paler, or maybe my eyes had adjusted to the yellow bug light. I should grab her hand and dash down the porch steps, lead her somewhere that wasn't stuffing her like a sack of groceries right back into Jess's dad's Audi parked on the street.

I smiled at her yet again. My smile felt weak, like watery tea made from twice-used tea bags. "This will all blow over," I said for the second time this night. Stupid phrase.

"I'm sure." Her voice was polite, as if she agreed that we'd reached the part of the conversation where meaningless bullshit was expected. She picked up her pillow, maybe anticipating that she'd be heading out shortly, shifted it into a tight wedge under her arm.

A car zoomed too fast down Ridge Road, then screeched to a stop as the traffic light up the block switched red. "That happens all the time," I said. "The light's blocked by tree branches. Someone should do something." I'd heard people complaining to the cashier at the little neighborhood market. I didn't care that much. I didn't even have a car.

"Linda killed herself driving," Penny said. "A suicide. That's what my mother said."

"I think it was just a regular car accident," I said. "Bad luck."

Penny gave me that same polite smile.

Another pause. I yawned, and Penny copycatted my yawn. She looked like a little girl yawning. Maybe if Jess could just see her.

I turned and put one hand on the doorknob.

"No," Penny said abruptly, grabbing at my wrist, letting the pillow tumble to the ground again. Her fingers felt cold and numb, almost dead—how lips feel after the dentist shoots in Novocaine. When I pulled my hand off the knob, she let go and picked up the sad pillow, pressing it against her chest, as if posing as a fake Santa.

"You should come in," I said.

"The story of my life," she said. "No one wants me." Calm, no self-pity.

I matched her tone: "She doesn't know you yet. Give her a chance."

"All I ever wanted was a real family like everyone else," she said. "That's the only thing I would ever pray for in stupid old church. And I guess maybe a home run ball, but that's selfish."

Jess's father swung through the door. His face was red and sweaty and he looked startled, as if he'd forgotten I would still be here. "She won't listen," he said, to me or to Penny or to no one, to the crisp autumn air. He paced off his excess energy for a moment, then settled about five feet away from Penny, leaning up against the slatted wooden railing, where the light was dim, and he angled his leg backward against the boards, once, twice, more, kicking hard and harder, until the wood crackled and splintered.

"I'm sorry," Penny whispered. She gathered in a deep breath before smushing her face deep into her pillow. I imagined the smell, the feel, like mine back home: slightly musty, prickly with feathers from ancient dead birds, the striped ticking soft with age.

"I'll try," I said, slipping through the door, into the living room, on to the kitchen. No Jess. The back door slammed. "Jess," I called, "wait up," but only half-heartedly, only to say I tried. Her car was parked in the back alley. I guessed she was going to drive; she'd been doing that since she and Tommy broke up. They used to like to drive Sheridan Road down to Lake Shore Drive really fast, after midnight, his black Porsche slicing ribbons through the dark. She wanted windows down no matter the weather, and I imagined the rough wind like sandpaper over her hair and face. "He doesn't go fast enough," she would complain to me when they first started dating and she was dragging in at four A.M. and there I was, wrestling with a paper or a poem or insomnia when my mind wouldn't shut up. "That car does one-fifty easy, but he won't kick it to the top. Fraidy-cat." "It's dangerous," I would say, playing the lecturing scold she wanted me to, and she'd say, "Now you're my mom? What, are you afraid, too? Or jealous? Come with us sometime." No, I wasn't her mom, and it wasn't that I was jealous that she was the one in Tommy's fancy car, watching the glittery Chicago skyline blur at a hundred miles an hour; that she was the one who got the ring; that she had those things and I never would. Honestly not that, or mostly not. But I knew she was lying: it wasn't Tommy afraid to kick it up, it was her. She was the one driving. Jess was afraid of fear, confusing it with weakness, and her solution was to bully herself into doing things that terrified her. I was the opposite, so used to fear I felt nothing.

I called again, just in case: "Jess?" A tire squealed, and she was gone. Probably she was driving home to be with her mother. Either way she wouldn't be back here for a while.

I took a deep breath, assessed the kitchen. I screwed the lid back on the peanut butter jar and returned it to the fridge. Set my dirty spoon in the sink for next time someone did dishes. This was as good as it was going to get. *Maybe there isn't an exact moment when one makes important realizations. Maybe this nothingness is what doing the right thing feels like,* I thought, as I forged a slow path back to the front door, uprighting the tipped kitchen table chair, tugging a crooked couch cushion straight, stamping flat an upturned corner of the rug, clicking shut the door to Jess's bedroom.

I hurried to the front door and yanked it open. Jess's father and Penny were halfway down the front walk; he was actually almost at the car, which was parked under the burned-out streetlight, walking faster than Penny, I suppose, in spite of carrying both suitcases, and I shouted, "Hey!" and the footsteps stopped and he turned around. I couldn't see his face in the dark. The upstairs landlord's lamp flicked on, sending a square of light out onto yard. A window squeaked open. "Hey," I said more quietly. "She can stay a couple of days."

"Really?" he said. He sounded annoyed, as if he had expected to be the exclusive architect of any plan. "Jess changed her mind?"

"Jess changed her mind," I agreed, delighted to be given an acceptable lie. "It's okay."

There was a pause, where I sensed him wrestling with Jess's alleged magical transformation, the whole top to bottom of it, but to question it would mean a longer, harder conversation. I figured he wanted to believe me so he would choose to, and I was right.

"Hear that?" he said to Penny. "It's okay. You'll stay here tonight, maybe a few days, and we'll figure out the rest. You'll see."

They spoke slowly, lots of pauses. It was only their voices coming out of the dark. I couldn't see their faces. Like listening to a radio, that detachment. What would happen, I wondered, before remembering it was happening to me?

"What about school?"

"You'll miss a few days," he said.

"I'll get behind," she said.

"That's too bad," he said, "that's just one of ten thousand things that's just too damn bad right now." The words were tight but not unkind.

He emerged from the shadows with the suitcases, which he plunked up on the porch; Penny slowly followed. Her Frye boots thumped the wood planks. "She doesn't want to see you right now, though," I hurried to say to him. "Still kind of mad. You know." Again, that flicker of a sigh: he knew not to believe me, but he wanted to.

"Right." He nodded, wouldn't meet my eyes, then rested one hand on Penny's shoulder, his fingers jerking in slight tapping motions.

You ass, I thought, *hug your daughter, hug her, hug her.*

He stammered the sentences: "I—I'll come by tomorrow, and we'll grab lunch, maybe buy you some new clothes at the mall. We'll get Jess to come along. God knows she's never said no to shopping. She'll pick you out some things, whatever you want." To me, he said, "I'll be at the Palmer House. Tell Jess to call me."

"Got it," I said. "The Palmer House." That wouldn't be cheap.

Quickly he bent over and wrapped half a hug around Penny; it was pretty awkward and uncomfortable looking—the pillow stuffed between them got in the way—but it may have been the best hug he was capable of with me standing there watching. Penny squeezed the pillow, squeezed deeper into this sad little hug, and her shoulders started heaving.

"Don't cry," he said. "Don't cry, lovey."

I gasped. For him to say it. This girl belonged to him. This girl was real.

"I miss her," Penny sobbed.

"I miss her, too," he murmured, glancing over Penny's shoulder to finally meet my eyes. I tried to keep my face impassive. I tried not to think anything. I tried to think about where we might have extra sheets and blankets, and then I realized Penny would have to sleep in my bed and I would have to sleep on the couch, in case Jess came back. I realized that Penny would be sleeping in the same room as the boxes of rocks Jess's mother had given me. I imagined her sleeping with her baseball mitt tucked up near her face. Seeing that would break open anyone's heart, even Jess's.

"I'm sorry, I'm sorry," he said, murmuring into her hair. "I miss her so much, too."

She clutched at him harder. "Don't leave me," she said.

He stepped back, keeping his eyes locked on to mine. "I'll be at the Palmer House," he repeated, like I should be impressed or something.

"Got it." I imagined that he had met up with Penny's mother there early on, when he first started cheating. That hotel was right in the Loop, near his office. He would be a man who valued convenience.

And yet. He was more than that kind of easy villain. I didn't think I was going to cry, but something prickled behind my eyes.

I said, "It's a really terrible thing that happened. I'm sorry. I know you"—the words had to be so, so careful—"lost someone, too." Then there was a picture in my mind of him kissing Penny's mother in a corner room at the Palmer House, pulling her shirt up over her head, years of him pulling her shirt up over her head with his big hands, his gaudy ring, his too-long fingernails. Maybe Penny's mother liked the ring, the fingernails. Or maybe Penny's mother liked that he bought real Frye boots for her daughter.

His eyes were larger than I remembered. They kept me transfixed, the way the refrigerator light had earlier, and I thought he should say something—like, maybe, "thank you"—but he simply stared at me. All action, all movement, seemed drained from his body.

"I've lost how many people tonight," he said. "I've lost myself."

So I stepped forward. Again, that same emptiness when I would have wanted to feel something, to feel "now I'm an adult." I snaked my arms around Penny, feeling the points of her shoulder blades, gently shifting the deadweight of her body off him and onto me. She slumped heavily against me, into me, hard enough that I stepped back for support from the splintered rail; she sobbed into her pillow, onto my shoulder, recklessly, as if she didn't care where she cried or for how long, as if nothing could stop her.

Once Jess's dad was free, he hurried down the stairs, down the sidewalk, his fancy shoes clacking on the pavement. He didn't look back, and I didn't blame him. I wouldn't have either. I dragged Penny inside before we had to hear the sound of his car engine, and I sat her on the couch and went back for her two suitcases, which I pulled into the entryway. I grabbed a box of tissues from the bathroom that I plunked onto the coffee table, next to Jess's mother's coasters. The sobbing had trailed down to sniffles.

"Such a long day, you probably want to go to bed," I suggested in the way that left no room for disagreement, and then I yawned to cement the idea.

She yawned back, reached for a Kleenex, and blew her nose. Her eyes were red-rimmed and swollen, and they traced the contours of the room, examining it as if she were an anthropologist studying an ancient culture; I imagined her taking mental notes to tell her mother... then remembering her mother was dead, so I jumped in: "You can have my bed, and I'll sleep on the couch. I'll set the alarm so there's enough time to get ready for... him, when he comes to get you for lunch tomorrow. Towels are in the bottom cupboard in the bathroom, and you can use my Crest. Did you bring a toothbrush? I don't care if you use mine, which is the red one, but I know that's kind of gross, so for sure we'll get a new one for you tomorrow. Um, what else? Want a glass of water? I'll be right out here the whole night if you need something. Or if you're hungry, there's peanut butter and jelly, or some cheese."

She said, "Where's Jess? Shouldn't I at least say hi to her?"

I was standing propped up against the recliner that came with the "furnished" part of the rental, an oversized brown-and-orange tweed behemoth that Jess and I despised because it smelled like cigarette smoke up close. Also, there were cigarette burns in the arm upholstery, which made me think of someone old and sad sitting in the chair smoking at four in the morning, almost falling asleep and burning down the house. Mostly it was just ugly. But I slid down into it. It was actually comfortable if you could get past its immense ugliness.

"Well..." I said.

She watched me, unblinking. The room felt suddenly quiet. I felt she was listening to me breathe. I held my breath until I couldn't anymore.

I'd forgotten how kids that age don't know the rules the way adults do. How kids won't hear "well" and immediately get the nuance of the situation, what isn't spoken but is as clear as an elephant crowded into a phone booth. And how hopeful kids are. The worst thing about kids, I thought, was all that hopefulness, especially when you were the one going to squelch it.

"So, nothing to eat?"

She shook her head.

"Where's your mitt?" I asked.

She pulled it out of her fringy leather hippie bag and set it next to her on the couch. I wondered if the purse was a hand-me-down from her mother or if she bought it at a yard sale or what. I thought about asking her, but finally I said, "Jess isn't here."

"Where is she?"

"She'll be back later."

"When?"

"Later."

"But she knows I'm staying, right?" Steady words, like water glasses balanced on a tray.

I said, "No. Not yet."

After a moment, she said, "He knew that, didn't he?"

I shook my head and nodded and shrugged virtually all at once, the actions of a marionette. But not like I could say, *Yep, your dad's the creep who left you here with me.* So I said, "You look tired." I was tired for real, thinking ahead to a long night on the lumpy couch, the gaps between cushions hitting the wrong places of my back; how it would be me shaking Penny awake in my bedroom tomorrow morning, dragging her into the day, wondering if Jess's father would show to pick her up and what he'd spend on lunch and shopping. And Jess returning tonight or tomorrow or eventually. And Penny's dead mother. It was so simple to take a Tylenol, the simplest thing in the world. "You must be tired," I pleaded.

"It's unfair." Penny looked me straight on and said, "This is what I prayed for all that time? This?" She waved one arm in a vague semicircle. Her voice burned with anger. "This... family?"

"Exactly," I said, standing up. Not nearly as poetic as "isn't it pretty to think so." But she was a smart girl. I liked that about her, though I knew being too smart made everything that much worse.

Part II:
The Beginning

Strategies for Survival #5: Practicality

(spring, freshman year)

Jess and I planned to be roommates sophomore year, going in together for the housing lottery. You hoped for a low number, so you could pick exactly the dorm you wanted. North campus or south. The difference was immense: no more trudging Sheridan Road to class, fifteen minutes there and fifteen back, icy winds daggering and slush trashing your boots. Frat parties were on north campus. Dorms with views of Lake Michigan were north. The library was smack in the middle. Communications and English classrooms were south. My work-study job in the admissions office was south. My other job answering phones at the divey take-out pizza place was south. I walked everywhere, and Jess had her car.

Jess wanted to live north, by the parties.

The numbers arrived in our mailboxes on a Saturday in March, sealed in a white envelope stamped DO NOT DISCARD. I was up early, needing a whole day in the library to read the articles on reserve that I'd put off until the test. My number was 37. It was the luckiest I'd been in my whole life. A number like that could mean the top floor of Shedd Hall with the shimmering lake framed by the window, a perfect view of the hugely full moon, glowing white as it rose out of the water. Or a corner suite in the new dorm on the edge of south campus, filled with fresh furniture un-sat on by a million asses, carpets without the ground-in crud of two million feet. Thirty-seven meant that whatever I wanted I could have. Nothing had ever meant that before. This knowledge was so overwhelming that I ran all the way to the library.

Jess's number was 3201.

"This is stupid," she said, crumpling the envelope. "Rigged."

Why anyone in the housing office would care enough to rig dorm rooms wasn't a concern of hers, or why she in particular would be conspired against.

"What's yours?" she asked. As potential roommates, we'd use whichever was lowest. We were partners.

I sneezed. Her Kleenex was softer than the brand my roommate bought and definitely was like silk compared with the cheap toilet paper in the hall bathroom. "Higher than yours," I said. I don't know why I said that. I guess I liked knowing something she didn't.

She groaned, then ranted harder. Her father could fix it for us, she said, he could fix anything. She said she'd die if they trapped her on south campus another year. She'd rather go live at home, she said. She'd heard there were dorks and burnouts who sold their numbers. She said, "I'd pay anything for a good number. Like something under a hundred. Like double digits."

"Wow," I said, "sell a housing number? Totally scummy." My used tissue looked pale on her roommate's desk.

"Right." Jess shook her head. "Still. Sure wish I knew who those people were right now."

What ended up happening was that she met Tommy at a frat party that night. He lived in his fraternity house, up on north campus. Jess decided that she absolutely would have to move to north campus no matter what, or she'd lose out on Tommy. She told me her dad called some people, and so by the time we reported to the housing office, she had a good number for us.

What also happened was that I knew a guy who knew someone who handed over a bundle of fives and tens in exchange for my 37: $135, bargained up from $120, when what I got from the pizza restaurant was $20 out of the cash drawer for a five-hour weekend shift of jangling phones, never sitting down, and endless complaints from rich college kids about their order taking forever.

The number Jess got for us, the number that snagged a corner room with a lake view on the fourth floor of Shedd Hall, was 37. A hundred and thirty-five dollars was so much money for me. But I should have realized there was always more.

Anyway, during our sophomore year, because Jess declared herself in love with Tommy, she spent most nights with him, over there at his single in the frat house, which she said reeked of beer and bong water and Polo cologne. Now and then, as I was changing into my good sweater or slicking on lipstick before meeting whichever guy promised he was into me, I caught a giant moon out the window. Everyone was right: on certain nights, the white moon hung suspended, tremendously huge and low, ascending from the waters of Lake Michigan. It might have seemed magical if I hadn't taken astronomy, where we learned that the simple fact was the moon is always the same size. This "moon illusion" was in our heads. Simply bend over and look upside down through your legs, the professor explained, and the moon would appear normal. "Not on the test," the professor had said, "just something interesting to ponder."

BAD GIRL

(spring, sophomore year)

Then this happened in April, near the end of our sophomore year, on a very warm, very sunny Thursday, one of those astonishing days when the sky over Lake Michigan widens ten times bigger, throbs a thousand times bluer. Dramas eddy all around—couples split up or accidentally create babies no one wants or shriek regretful words or whisper them under their breath. The thing is you don't know this. You remember only your own drama, though you won't recognize it as such until later.

He wore a blue shirt—nothing special, something vaguely denim with white buttons that were more lustrous than regular white buttons. Faded, milky blue, soft to the touch. Well, I didn't know it was soft because I couldn't touch it, not even the sleeve, not even that way girls might laugh too long at a dumb joke, that laugh the excuse to seize the guy's arm. Flirting 101.

But I wasn't allowed to do that with him, with my best friend's boyfriend.

Off-limits.

We were skipping our one o'clocks, the three of us, heading to the strip of south campus beach along Lake Michigan. He juggled two ratty lawn chairs; I carried the blanket. I would end up on the blanket—he and Jess would take the chairs. That's how it would be. I should have gone to class. There was a quiz—I'd already missed two or three quizzes or four. I would have to absolutely ace the final. I shouldn't have liked that pressure, but it was interesting, that tinge of excitement.

We complimented the day as if we had planned the weather ourselves: spring in Chicago had never been so warm, the sky never this blue. We talked as we set up the chairs, the blanket, the bottle of once-icy vodka lemonade, sweaty now in its paper bag. We talked as if no one in the history of the world had ever had such a conversation, such thoughts; as if we weren't surrounded by dozens of students cutting one o'clocks, pulling out icy vodka bottles.

"Take the chair," Tommy said.

"I'm fine down here," I said, sprawling across the blanket, automatically stroking the frayed corner that had been at my cheek when this blanket covered my childhood bed in Iowa.

"Don't be ridiculous," he said. "The chair is better." He plopped down next to me.

"Yes." From above, Jess's voice bumped in. "The chair is better. Don't be ridiculous."

He sat close. The shadow of one blue sleeve skimmed my bare arm. Neither of us moved, not even to breathe. The water seemed far away, though a quick run and you'd plunge in. The lake would be frigid this time of year. No swimming.

I had to breathe, so I turned toward Jess, who adjusted her sunglasses against the glare. She wore a black bikini bottom. Her legs weren't well shaved, so a band of goose bumps rose along each shin. There was a bikini top, but over it she wore a lavender tee with cut sleeves and a torn neckline; her shirt also looked impossibly soft. And expensive. If I owned that shirt, I wouldn't have had the heart to slash it up. I had watched her go at it with a big pair of cheap scissors. "What if you don't like it when you're done?" I had asked. "I'll buy another," she'd said, "and give this one to you." But she liked it fine. The color was good on her. She knew it. She cinched the waist in a side knot, unknotted it, knotted it again.

"Loose," I recommended from the blanket.

"You're right," she agreed, letting the shirt hang free. She looked like a picture in a magazine, an ad that makes you want to be there, makes you believe the product totally would be the thing to transform your life. That was how she always looked.

I had on elastic-banded gym shorts and a discolored high school mascot T-shirt that had shrunk. The thing I did was not wear a bra. My breasts were small enough that I could do that easily and comfortably, almost casually, but also the thing was that this tiny T-shirt was pale blue, virtually faded white. It was how to get attention.

But he was staring straight out at the water, not at me, not at Jess. His mirrored sunglasses reflected the unruffled lake and the empty sky. Near us: a noisy frat-boy Frisbee game with profuse arguments. Gaggles of sorority girls lay flat on their backs, absorbing sunlight, impervious to the proximity of the uncaught Frisbee, the tornadoes of kicked-up sand, the sky, the day, aware only of the glow of their serene radiance. A couple plunked next to bikes tangled in the sand, alternating bites of a sandwich, first him, then her, distracting me with the inefficiency of their eating. People were all around, the sun was all around. A guy with a beard flopped on the bare sand reading a thick paperback, but I couldn't see the title. I was thinking that if I could, I might feel less alone, though also maybe more.

I usually felt alone. Maybe he did, too, that guy rhythmically shaking sand from the pages of his book, and this ache might be something we shared. I couldn't tell.

After Jess and I met way back on that first day, she told me I was the only girl in the dorm she could stand for more than a couple of hours, the only person who understood her. She wasn't that hard to understand, I didn't think, but I understood not to tell her that. She wanted to be understood. Not me. This is how we knew we could be friends.

Jess said, "Someone sit in this chair, please." She laughed, but she was dead serious, so I stood up, then sat in the lawn chair next to hers. Both were the kind with frayed nylon webbing scratching your thighs. The flimsy aluminum legs shifted, then balanced for one unsteady, precarious second, and then I broke through, the whole thing collapsing me awkwardly onto the messy sand. A wide scrape gashed my elbow, stinging sharply.

"Oh my god!" I exclaimed, struggling to disentangle from the aluminum bars. My face seethed red-hot. It was the kind of thing that happened only to me, never to her, sitting all high and mighty on her perch. She had to have known—though rationally that wasn't possible, and she was working not to laugh at my wretched embarrassment. Grains of sand clung to the pulp of the scrape, and I rubbed to brush myself clean, grinding sand deeper into my skin. *Tetanus,* I thought, pushing my hand harder, like scrubbing a dirty pot, *infection, lockjaw, rabies, leprosy, Black Death, the plague.*

"You knew!" I accused, but she shook her head: "I swear no."

Tommy half rolled across the blanket and extended one hand so I could grab it and break free of the wreckage. I wanted his skin pressing mine, but not like this, in pity, so the sensation of his firm grasp was nothing. "You're okay," he said, telling, not asking.

"Back to the blanket for me," I said. "I know my place." Patches of sand clung to my bare limbs, and I felt itchy and filthy and doltish, punished for skipping my quiz, for wanting Tommy's skin on mine. But I didn't sit; I kept standing, reluctant to scatter sand on the blanket. Now I was the one towering over the two of them. I had become conscious of body language from a book assigned in my women studies class. I refused to step aside on the sidewalk when a guy headed straight at me. Often he didn't move so we collided, reeling onto the grass. I relished that my stubbornness messed us both up. The guys never bothered with "sorry," so me neither.

"Where'd you get these crappy chairs from?" Jess asked Tommy.

He shrugged. "The garage." He rented garage space for his car off-campus because he didn't want to park a Porsche outside. He was a senior, and the car had been a gift from his dad the quarter he got all A's. Jess told me he paid a grad student to write two papers and a take-home final for him, that was how the A's showed up. She also said he said that his father wouldn't care, that his dad just wanted to brag his kid got a 4.0, that his kid earned a Porsche 924 Turbo. And that his father would have bought the car anyway, but he decided to prove he could get the grades. It was definitely twisted, but also admirable, the vastness of the charade. The car was no good for Chicago winters, but it was the only Porsche 924 Turbo on campus, so that was the important thing. We'd driven to the beach in Jess's car, because there were three of us, plus the chairs. She didn't stress about parking on the street. You had to be at least a junior or a commuter to get a sticker for the school lots, so she racked up parking tickets that she sent to her father, who sent them to his friend, who sent them to his friend the alderman. Or something like that, where in the end the tickets disappeared.

Jess said, "Well, let's just enjoy the day anyway."

"I am," Tommy said, resuming his stare.

"What do you keep looking at?" Jess asked. "I hate when I can't see what you're thinking. Those power-trip, hide-your-eyes sunglasses."

That seemed like my cue, either to distract them from the day's hundredth silly squabble or to let them go at it in privacy, so I chose the latter and ambled down to the water's edge, rubbing at the sand stuck to my skin as I walked. It was only a lake, not an ocean, but I'd never seen the ocean, so this was fine. I was wearing flip-flops, but with water that freezing, I didn't want to get close, so I stopped at the wet sand line. Right then I was the only one standing near the water, and I tried to imagine that I appeared interesting or possibly even mysterious as I posed; I imagined that someone might pause to wonder who I was and what weighty, consequential thoughts I was considering, and that the person wondering—this man—might be older, a professor between classes, or a whippety jogger on the sidewalk beyond, distracted from the sweaty torture of running at catching sight of me at the water's edge as if I had risen from the sea. It was all silly, but no one needed to know my thoughts unless I told them, which I never did.

There was a slight fishiness to the air: dead alewives, which I had learned were shiny silver fish, thin but as long as a ruler, that washed up dead along the lakeshore every spring. I knew this because my poetry workshop was overrun by student poems lamenting the cruel cycle of life and the ephemeral nature of nature as symbolized by alewives. The professor rolled his eyes when the word was uttered, surely signaling a folder of insufferable alewife poems tucked into a cabinet, the typed pages chortled over during tweedy faculty meetings. I refused to offer commentary on alewife poems, hoping my silence made me seem dignified and impossible to please, like our professor. I'd probably flunk this class because I hadn't turned in my own poems for discussion, sensing they were juvenile and loathing their lack of sophistication, loathing myself for being unable to write anything better. But the professor liked me and had scribbled a note offering to review my poems privately, during office hours, and I pondered what that invitation might mean or imply, understanding it might mean or imply little. He was black, the first black teacher I ever had, which made him more interesting though it shouldn't have.

Bam, or *wham*, or *zoom*, or *whoosh*: the point being that I was roughly scooped from behind with persistent hands groping my waist and bare legs, fingers pressing and sliding inside my shirt, onto my naked skin, edging to my breast but stopping shy, then swooping for a feel, a squeeze, another, hands pawing, fingernails scratching; my flesh prickled and tense, abruptly alert in a way I hadn't known possible; whoops and cries like boys playing Indian warriors; beery breath panting across my face, along my neck; the slippery slick of someone's sweat; and I was being carried—or hauled or pulled or yanked or really all of those things: dragged, towed, heaved—into the lake by the pack of bare-chested boys who moments ago had been playing Frisbee, who had evidently grown bored and had seen me not as mysterious or alluring but simply as vulnerable prey, and I was plunged into Lake Michigan, getting "laked." Jess shrieked my name, and ice water hit, ramrodding through me, up my nose, over my eyes; my breath knocked senseless into bubbles and burbles; sand gritty on my knees and the heels of both hands. The world tumbled and twisted, was dark and wrong. I lifted my anchor of a head, forcing it backward, startled this scrap of instinct took hold, if that's what it was, and I surfaced to splashes and hoots and a curtain of water falling away. Hair flailing, and icy, icy, icy cold inhabiting me, coating me like new skin; the tiny, rhythmic clicks of my teeth absurdly loud in my head; my shirt clinging to my breasts, my nipples hard and tight and aware; water streaming down my body, which shook from cold, from fear; the sand squishy and murky and unknown under my toes, one flip-flop floating out of reach, the other simply lost—all of this under the pretty April sunshine, in front of everyone, like school recess, the boys high-fiving, shaking themselves like puppies, whooping off the water's chill and whacking shoulders and chests. One or two cautiously glanced back without eye contact, assuring themselves I hadn't drowned.

Is this what it's like to be chosen? I remember thinking, the cold confusing my brain. *To be Cinderella, stunned as the shoe slides on?* Jess shrieked my name over and over; she was up out of the chair, clutching Tommy's arm, waving at me, and I was shaking as I hurried up the beach to where she stood, running now, grateful for her, for the childhood blanket I had swiped over Christmas break, grateful that it waited for me with its frayed corner, tattered edges, and splotchy bloodstain from my first period, grateful to wrap myself in it and be invisible, and I reached Jess, and she said, "We're getting married!"

I stood for a moment, freezing, wet, bare and exposed, naked every way except physically—I might as well have ripped off the sopping T-shirt—and what Jess was saying seemed to make perfect sense, though it didn't, but everything with her made perfect sense because she made it make sense, and so I said, "Wow. Congratulations," thinking I should hug her but also that I shouldn't because I smelled like dead fish. I swallowed down a gritty bad taste, then kept talking— "That's so great. I can't believe it"—babbling conventionally; words looped out of me—what a great couple they were, how exciting this was—even as my mind thought this was a crazy plan, even as my eyes watched him watching my chest, my hard nipples an invitation, my body, maybe even my thoughts, as good as naked. His eyes widened and flickered, then drilled into my chest, and I saw the sunglasses half buried in the sand at Jess's feet. Another battle won, and this one, too: she would get the coveted flashy diamond, as enormous as a twenty-five-cent gumball machine ring, that gaudy, but real. I imagined what I would say to her about how pretty it was. I imagined those words in my voice, how pretty her ring was, her wedding dress, her condo on Lake Shore Drive, her matching Porsche; how pretty her life was turning out to be. She would be modest but unsurprised. Her life could have only this pretty outcome. Did I not know that? Of course I did. We both understood she wasn't me.

I arched my back, as if needing to stretch, but I didn't need to stretch. He slid his arm off Jess and bent down for the blanket, flapping it lightly, sending a cloud of sand fluttering free—"Careful," Jess fussed—and he handed the blanket to me so I could wrap up in it, cover myself. Our eyes locked, our fingertips brushed, and the cold coating my skin splintered, as if transformed into hard, glittering shards of ice.

He found me in the library that night, which wasn't exactly hard because I always studied in the carrels in the Asian collection. I couldn't read Chinese characters, so the books around me weren't distracting, and I liked the isolation of this underused section of the library and its long-settled silence.

I had suspected this was where it would be with Tommy—or with someone—the poetry professor, someone else, anyone. Even as I revered this quiet, I wanted it destroyed, which I couldn't explain. Also I knew about a single-use, staff-only bathroom with a snap lock inside tucked in a cranny off a short corridor. Jess had shown me last spring when she'd popped up to tempt me away from my books during midterms, demanding I join her for a Tab and M&M break, and she waved at the door with a careless motion and said, "That's where I gave Chris Roy a hand job that one time," and I nodded, trying to remember who Chris Roy was, thinking maybe he was from Hawaii, the one who Jess said always popped a Tic Tac before going down on her "not after, which I guess is a compliment?"

So I was in the middle of writing a generically pleasant critique of a dense poem about Saturn's rings for poetry workshop when I felt that tickle of someone watching, and I looked up at Tommy leaning against the wall across from my study carrel. He held a thick book with his finger marking the place and said, "Jess said you'd know what the fuck this poem means. She said you write poems."

"Let me see," I said.

He sidled over, positioned the book on the table between us, and spread the pages to Walt Whitman's "Song of Myself." A sharp, piney scent floated off his skin: Polo by Ralph Lauren. It smelled better on him than it did on everyone else. "It's so fucking long," he said. "What's it about?" He snapped his head back, thrusting a hank of hair out of his eyes. On the pages were underlines and checkmarks, cross-hatches and notations lining the margins in red ink, in curvy feminine handwriting.

"Are those your notes?" I asked.

"I buy used books," he said, "praying someone smart had them first." He didn't hesitate—as I would—to announce such a thing about himself.

Yes, I bought used books, too, but because they were cheaper. Most scribbled-in notations seemed dumb to me, with the wrong things highlighted. A Keynesian approach when my teacher favored Austrian economics. A die-hard feminist reading the novella my hundred-year-old white male teacher assigned.

"I can't explain this whole poem to you," I said.

"Jess said you could. She told me to come find you."

His face was too beautiful, with Irish skin, crisp blue eyes, long lashes, a tiny checkmark of a scar nestled under the perfect bend of one cheekbone, Kennedy teeth. That dark hair, tousled like he'd done it in a mirror before coming up here. Not that he had. But I guessed that he enjoyed the effect, the ripples he created. Later, I learned to recognize his style of arrogance immediately; later, I sniffed it out like a southern hunting dog, but here, now, it was something I couldn't yet identify, something alluring and mysterious, something that seemed the exact thing I thought I wanted. Then, there in the library—or at a party, or during office hours, or traipsing across campus—I believed it was the sex I wanted, wanting the man, any man, *a* man to collapse onto my naked body and say my name, to speak it sweetly, or whisper it all gravelly and rough, or at least, maybe, to think it. That.

But really what I wanted, what I wanted really, was this exact arrogance Tommy had lucked into. Only I didn't know then that I could acquire it for myself. All my life I had seen it exclusively in men. And in Jess, of course. Being in proximity, then, seemed all I could expect.

"Jess told you to come find me?" I said.

He repeated, "Jess told me to come find you."

My breath fell out of me, hearing that a second time, understanding it, and my head went feathery. Someone a carrel over shushed us, and we dropped into whispers.

"She told me where you study, that it's easy to find you alone up here with the chink books."

"Asian books," I softly corrected.

"Asian books," he repeated. "I know. I pick up bad habits from my dad. Can't help it." A sly smile, as if he wished I would call him a "naughty boy" and promise to spank him. He possessed that kind of simple mind. But a killer car. And that innate, from-the-crib, careless, easy, arrogant confidence he had been born into. I would never have that, pieces effortlessly locking into place, like loaded dice never coming up seven unless what you wanted was seven. I couldn't fathom. It was the way Jess had asked me on the way home from the beach, "Why aren't you angry at what happened? At those guys?" and from deep inside my blanket I had shrugged. Anger seemed to me inefficient, a churn of emotion with no movement. Being angry wouldn't make me un-wet or un-cold. "I would be furious," Jess had continued, "I would want to kill someone." I asked, "Who? Which one of them would you want to kill?" and she laughed, though I hadn't intended to be funny, and said, "All of them, of course." After it happened, one of the boys had sauntered over and popped the top off a bottle of Michelob, which he held out and said, "You're okay?" and when I nodded, he said, "I wanted to stop them." Jess said, "Get out of here, you fucking pig," and she grabbed the bottle, tilting it so a cascade of beer hissed into the sand at her feet. There was a lot of foam, which seemed dramatic. Tommy was off hauling the trashed lawn chair to the garbage can, which was probably why the frat boy thought it was safe to approach. He seemed shaken by Jess's fury but recovered, spiraling two fingers at his temples and announcing, "You're crazy," before slinking back to his herd, all of them chattering like monkeys, kicking sand over cigarette butts and bottle caps, taking turns spinning the Frisbee on one finger, shirts on, packing up. Jess said, "You have to be more angry," and she seemed angry saying it. I couldn't fathom any of the right things: I would have drunk the beer, I would have told the guy I was fine, as long as the scrape on my elbow didn't get infected from lake water. I would have laughed, so he'd get I was joking. I would've told him my name if he asked.

Now, I said to Tommy, "Did you read the poem?"

"Doesn't matter," he said. "I don't get poems. My mind won't work that way."

"Then why are you taking a lit class?"

He gave his head one sharp shake. "Guess I could switch to pass-fail. I'm a sinking ship. In over my head on this, on all of it." His face pinched, the sly smile switching to a disconcerting, tender grimace that I didn't like: "My dad wants me to be a lawyer. I'm joining his firm. I mean, after I get into law school. Wait list at three, and rejections from nine. It's a drag."

"It's too late for pass-fail," I said. "The deadline was last week." I knew because I had marked it on my desk calendar. I watched the day close in, then pass by, like a roar fading out behind me. "I missed it, too. So I'm just as screwed."

"Nah," he said. "You're smart. You know how to get by."

It made me uncomfortable when anyone talked about what I was like, when how could they possibly know? So I said, "Do you want to be a lawyer?"

"Of course not," he said. "But there's nothing else I can do." He fidgeted and windmilled his arms, suddenly nervous. He looked like a bug skewered on a pin, dying with a needle through its thorax, a colorful butterfly, sure, but one of a thousand, not a rare species, not anything exotic at all. I looked away, down at the words written in my spiral notebook. My handwriting needed more loops. I wondered if Jess knew he didn't want to be a lawyer.

"What are you doing when you get sprung out of here?" he asked.

I wasn't admitting to him I couldn't do anything either, that getting here was hard enough and I'd forgotten there'd be more, then more. It was his slick assurance I wanted, not his conversation. I said, "Chances are the poem is about sex or death. That's what they're always about, that's what professors say. So say that and you'll be fine."

He laughed. Another "shush." It was a super-academic school; people cared about their grades more than anything else, even getting drunk or stoned.

"Maybe we should go where we can talk for real," he said. Of course he knew how to make it sound natural, like hey, why not?

"I know a place." I stood up and got walking. He would follow. I should've walked without looking back, the way Jess would, but after a moment, I looked. He was a few steps behind, trailing his fingertips loosely along the spines of books on the shelves. He looked like a stranger, he was a stranger. I wondered if he was thinking about all those law schools that didn't want him, or about his dad; I wondered if he wondered what I was thinking and knew he wasn't. *Good,* I thought, *good.* This was why Jess knew to "never look back": the blank randomness of his face made me pity him.

I let him catch up to me, and when he did, I glanced away and pointed to the scuffed white door: "In there." I wanted my voice to sound confident. It did. He nodded, turned, and ducked slightly.

Afterward, he told me that Jess said blow jobs were totally disgusting. *You're the one marrying her,* I thought, but I corrected myself inside my head: *engaged,* because I knew it wouldn't work between them, and not because of this.

Later, I made my way out as the main library closed, when everyone with still more homework funneled down to the twenty-four-hour reserve room or pushed out onto the dark campus, into the dark night, the waves of Lake Michigan a distant growl, all of us pressing home to our dorms, walking with our brains raging like infernos, lit by all we had learned.

Finally, finally, I had learned who I was angry with. Finally, I knew how to punish that bad girl.

THROUGH THE DOOR

(spring, after college)

Time can slide itself forward, not only backward.

Sometimes late at night or at random, odd moments of random, odd days, I imagined Penny's grown-up life. I imagined her married. I imagined her divorced. I imagined her gay. With four kids, two, none; Penny referring to a fluffy black cat as her "fur-baby."

Each time I imagined Penny—loading a cart with organic produce or pumping the cheapest gas; barefoot and sprawled across a blanket at an outdoor classical concert; slouching in a subway seat, head propped against a grimy window; ordering a cappuccino—I reminded myself that she was without her mother, always, always, always. That on any morning, like Penny, we might wake up as one person but fall asleep that night as someone totally different.

That was a reason I took her in that night when we stood together on the porch, time suspended, both of us waiting to see what might happen. Let's call it the main reason.

Another reason was something she said the next morning, a stray comment I'm surprised to remember with the fury I do; something I'm guessing Penny remembers, though she may not recall telling me. That boy. Maybe she said a name, maybe not. The boy who told everyone he went to second base with her when he didn't. (Second base! That sounds almost sweet now, almost Mayberry.) That boy who thought he could do that to a girl, that boy who was *rewarded* for doing that to a girl. I hated that boy, and I had to believe Penny did, too, even as she later confessed her tremendous crush on him.

That boy—whose name I can't remember, whose name I maybe once knew—was all the boys and all the men who made me heap the blame upon myself. How was it punishment to that boy to take Penny in? I didn't know then, and I don't know now: only that it was. I was punishing that boy by pulling Penny in off that porch. Maybe that was the main reason.

Greg Tomlinson. And all at once, there's his name. That fucker.

This happened after that night and literally was impossible in affecting any decision as the two of us stood on that porch, precarious and alone. Yet now I believe it did. There are ways to escape logic when thinking about the past.

And there was another night, after I took her in, and we were eating a batch of experimental pizza bagels I brought home after working at the carryout. The new manager was testing them, thinking he might add them to the menu. I volunteered as guinea pig. He used terrible-tasting frozen bagels because they were cheap and, actually, about all there was back in that time and place. The pizza toppings helped.

Penny and I were at the kitchen counter, standing to eat out of the box. Penny said, "My mother was always late. Like picking me up. Was yours?"

"Not really," I said. Some of the green peppers were raw and some had been roasted; I was supposed to report back with opinions. Sausage crumbles or marble-sized dabs? What about the thick layer of sausage across the whole bagel top, with a hole matched to the bagel hole—was that fun or too much sausage?

She said, "Once when I was ten I sat in the grass of my friend's yard for three hours after a birthday party because my mom was so late."

"Why didn't you ask to wait inside?" I said, tilting grease out of a concave pepperoni slice.

She shook her head. "No way."

Too embarrassing. I knew. Too needy. I knew that, too. Too proud.

"They probably saw you from the window," I said.

Again, the head shake. "That's how come she was my friend. Because she understood to let me stay there."

"That's sort of screwed up," I said.

"Totally," she said. "But everyone needs that kind of friend, that person who gets who you are even when who you are is sort of screwed up."

"Needs," I thought, *not "wants." "Needs."*

Penny pushed aside the bagel topped with wedges of Vienna Beef hot dogs and rolled her eyes in disapproval. She said, "I was ten then. Now I'd go in, ask the mom to call up my mom or something."

"Sure," I said.

I was thinking about how Jess would declare a pizza bagel "idiotic" but who was practically never late, and how that was a tiny, tiny thing, but weren't friendships made of tiny, tiny things? So many tiny things you couldn't sift through them all.

"I miss her," I said, without meaning to, and Penny merely said, "I know," with the saddest smile I had ever seen, and that was why I let Penny through the door that night: that same sadness I saw on Jess's face sometimes, like when I told her not to worry on my birthday if no one from Iowa called me. Long distance was expensive, I chattered on, assuring her they'd all sent cards, the kind I secretly liked, with glitter layered an inch thick and something popping up when you opened the card, the exact type of card Jess had given to me minutes before, the card I displayed on my desk until enough time slipped by that I pretty much forgot about that desolate birthday, until now.

GIFT EXCHANGE

(winter, sophomore year)

Jess and Christmas confused me. Back in high school in Iowa, I'd steal my friend Janey a lip gloss from Drug Fair for Christmas and she'd steal me nail polish, and the lip gloss would be my favorite flavor and she'd really love the hot-hot pink of the nail polish, and we'd swap right then, both of us relieved. But Jess wasn't like that. For one thing, starting in November she'd dumped a swirl of hints that what she picked for me was totally amazing, totally awesome, totally, totally. Snooping around our dorm room didn't net any clues. The gift could be hidden over at Tommy's, where she spent all her free time, or in her car, or at her parents' house.

All my ideas were dumb. No college sweatshirt, because Jess wasn't rah-rah and she'd never wear school colors because "purple plus my skin tone equals sallow." I couldn't afford her favorite make-up brands, which were all from department store counters and hard to lift. She didn't read except for assignments. She was the first to call her musical taste unpredictable and suddenly now it was jazz, which I'd barely heard of as being something people our age might be into. Miles. Coltrane. Bird. Chet Baker. Why did he get two names and everyone else only one?

Freshman year Christmas had been a miracle. I took charge of a shopping bag someone left on the counter when picking up his to-go pizza at the takeout where I worked and answered the phone when he called. "Sorry," I said, "it's not here. Hope you track it down." Inside was a Marshall Field's box holding a glossy pair of scarlet leather gloves lined with cashmere. For a long minute, I wanted them for myself. But no, they had to go to Jess. She adored them enough to wear them around all winter. Not like a Marshall Field's bag was going to pop up again this year.

She gave me Lauren perfume that first Christmas. The woodsy-rosy sweetness was intoxicating, as was the size of that bottle, a ruby-red glass cube bigger than a grapefruit. I couldn't imagine this for myself, and she filled in when I couldn't stammer out my gratitude, lost in the shit feeling of having not picked out those gloves special: "I knew you'd love this," she said. "I knew it would be the most perfect thing for you."

This year, sophomore year, she buzzed endlessly about what Tommy might be giving her, so possibly a token from me would work if it was thoughtful. "Jewelry," she guessed, talking about Tommy, "which better be real gold, not bogus silver crud. At least fourteen karat, but I like eighteen karat better, don't you?" Me too, I assured her, also assuring her it had to be jewelry, mostly because Tommy seemed to me unimaginative, with the standard checklist in his head: roses were always red; gifts for girlfriends were earrings, bracelets, or necklaces; sex was with him on top. I didn't like him, or maybe I did; I barely knew him because Jess hogged him up for herself, and she was insane over him. It was impossible to sort out my exact feelings so I didn't bother. Her parents hadn't even met him, which at least I had. There was that.

Because of her insanity over Tommy, I didn't see Jess a whole lot and that was why the promise of the big present, I guessed. Guilt for abandoning me the whole fall. To hear her talk, it was a new car or a trip around the world. Last July, Jess's parents took her and Linda to Europe for a month for a big family vacation. Jess sent me a postcard of Big Ben: "Pretty big, haha," she wrote. "Fancy," my mother said as she sorted the bills and past dues from the junk mail. She slid the card to me across the kitchen table. I acted like it was no big deal and read the back. Then I passed it to Grace, who right away taped it to her bedroom wall. That was too pathetic to tell Jess, but I liked Big Ben up there, knowing that whenever she wanted, Grace could see somewhere that wasn't where she was.

It was the night before my last final and I'd be on a Greyhound after the test was over and still no present. What I had for Jess was a Chet Baker album. I just grabbed one from the record store, happy to spot his name on a plastic divider amid the rows of records. It wasn't even American. "Imports cost extra," the record guy said, but for once I didn't care. I was waiting for Jess to go first but also hoping she'd forgotten. She slouched in a chair at her uncluttered desk, a spiral notebook open as if to memorize lecture notes, but she was doodling stick men. The stress of this gift or not-gift was killing me. The stress of her around nonstop after weeks of not was also killing me. I had missed her, but sort of I hadn't. I'd been floating through classes and guys and random cliques of girls. She yanked me out of that, yanked me back. I'd started wondering what if I hadn't met her.

Suddenly she said, "Do you think Tommy loves me?"

"Did he say he did?"

"Of course," she said. "But only after sex."

There was a pause. I looked down at my notebook. In tiny letters, I had written in the margin, "Boring as death."

I said, "Then if he says he loves you, he loves you."

She said, "But only after sex."

I said, "Do you love him? Do you tell him?"

"All the time," she said, repeating herself for emphasis. "*All* the time."

"Guys are different," I said. "They don't like feelings."

"I don't like feelings either," she said. "No one does. And I can still tell someone I love them."

I said, "What about me?"

She laughed, a horsy sound, and tossed her pen into the air. It fell onto the desk with a small clatter, and she jabbed at it with one finger, rolling it from the desk onto the floor. "We're talking about my boyfriend," she said. "Tommy, who only loves me after sex."

I stretched my leg, nabbing the pen under one foot, pulling it toward me. I bent over and picked it up, then lobbed it back onto Jess's desk.

"Do you love me?" I asked again.

"You're like a sister," she said. "But a thousand times better than the idiot related to me."

"And?" I maintained my voice as a flat line of steadiness.

Finally: "You know I do," she said. "Don't be so stupid."

"You don't go around telling me," I said. I held the silence for a moment of dramatic effect, before announcing: "Tommy's like that. Just because he doesn't go around telling you he loves you, that doesn't mean he doesn't." I felt like the world's smartest lawyer, whisking all that out of my sleeve, presenting the ironclad case I had constructed. *Voilà!* I wanted to shout, but I wasn't exactly sure how to say the word correctly.

"Let's see when we exchange gifts tomorrow night," she said. She had bought him—actually bought for real—a pair of black driving gloves, handmade in Italy, and a leather portfolio with his initials embossed on the front for when he went off to law school. "Which reminds me..." Jess jumped up and reached into her backpack and held out a gift-wrapped box. "Merry Christmas. I can't believe I almost forgot!"

It was the exact width and length and thickness of the box for Tommy's gloves, and was it irrational to imagine I was trapped in a loop where the only gifts were gloves? I gave it a tiny shake, but nothing inside moved. "Is it a pony?" I asked, making Jess laugh. Sweat coated my palms as I tugged the shiny red store-bought bow, eased my fingers under the Scotch tape.

"Hurry up," she said, standing over me. "This is excruciating."

I got the wrapping paper off in a whole sheet, practically undamaged, and I doubled it over, doubled it again, creased it flat. There was a Marshall Field's logo centered on the box lid, but before I could get attached to a gift from Field's, she said, "That's just a dumb old box." Probably from last year's red gloves, not that she would remember.

I lifted the lid. Folded back slippery layers of white tissue paper. My heart thudded hard and heavy, like a stone dropped again and again. I was afraid. Inside was a ticket. Another swoop of irrationality, as I immediately assumed it was one of her many parking tickets, but she shrieked, "We're going to London next summer! You and me!"

Automatically, I dropped the box on the desk, pushed the lid back on top. "No," I said. "That's too much."

"I knew you'd say that," she said. "It's nonrefundable. Like it or not, you're flying to London with me in July."

"Oh my god," I said.

There was a moment to imagine this might be true, that I might go to London with Jess, that the postcards taped to Grace's wall would come from me.

"Told you it was big," she said. "Told you it was good."

Big Ben. Tea. Shakespeare. Whatever else there was in London. Everything there was in London.

Jess romped around the room, half skipping, half dancing. "We're going to London," she singsonged, and the words hammered my brain, "we're going to London." Abruptly, she halted and grabbed my shoulders and twisted to look at me, her turquoise eyes stabbing mine: "Well, so, let's hear it. Do you love me?" she demanded.

I was dizzy. The tiny dorm room was too dark and too bright, too empty and too full. I couldn't breathe. Sharpness pressed into my chest. My fingertips were icy.

"Do you?" she said. She dropped her hands off my shoulders, took a step back.

"Yes," I said, but maybe not loud enough because she said, "Do you?" as she cupped one hand around her ear.

"Yes!" I shouted. "Yes!" I shouted again and again. She heard, but she let me shout six or seven more times before dropping her hand away from her ear and hugging me. It was funny. Or we were laughing as if it were.

I thought I was going to leave the Chet Baker album in the room for her the next morning after my test, but I didn't bother. By then I knew I wasn't going to London. For one thing, no one had mentioned hotels or food or how my summer had to be devoted to working at least one job and probably two, or how I could possibly leave these jobs in July to traipse around London. So I didn't give Jess anything for Christmas that year. Tommy presented her with a robin's-egg-blue box from Tiffany that contained earrings in the shape of an X—"Like a kiss," Jess told me, "get it?"—designed by Paloma Picasso, whom Jess knew all about. Eighteen-karat gold. Jess loved them.

Eventually, the nonrefundable ticket was switched to Linda's name, which was Jess's mother's idea, who said it would do the two of them a world of good to spend some time, just the two of them, together, and what was better than travel to a foreign land?

SHADOW DAUGHTER

(spring, sophomore year)

Money was why I didn't smoke, drink, or do coke. If I wanted to, I found boys.

"He's not good enough for you," Jess might suggest, her suggestions always commandments. "His face is tedious. And that dragony breath. What do you see in him?"

I spouted clichés about still waters running deep while remembering how the boy drove me to a blues bar on Howard Street, putting down a twenty for as many shots of Wild Turkey as I wanted while the music pulsed my skull. If I thought about that, I wouldn't think about later, kissing him in his car, where he panted dragon breath into my ear and across my eyelids. Or when, with the sun coming up, I trudged to my dorm and its fluorescent-bright group bathroom, where I jammed two fingers deep into my mouth, crushing hard against the back of my tongue to make myself puke, the way to avoid hangovers, to not feel rotten the morning after.

Strangely, Jess didn't catch me and Tommy. It was his ex-girlfriend, the one I warned Jess about from the beginning, certain he would go back to her. Jess was only a sophomore, the whirlwind rebound, and no diamond ring would change that. Sure he was a senior, sure he panic-proposed to Jess in early April, but come on, the ex was Sydney Moore, a junior. Number one on the women's tennis team. A *Seventeen* model in high school. Naturally she gravitated to Theta, where rumor was she was a neat freak, screaming about toothpaste dribbles in the sink. She should've been set for homecoming queen but was too bitchy to win any election; girls gossiped about her the second she walked away. But she looked damn good framed by the bucket seat of Tommy's Porsche 924 Turbo, waiting while he ran in somewhere—picking up a deep-dish—a tiny, haughty scowl completing her tanned face. She and Tommy were last year's celebrity couple, and Jess was the evil slut who came between them, and I was a secret.

"I hate her," Jess howled, each word enunciated, each word brimming fury. "I hate him. I hate them both." She was sobbing and wailing, pacing our dorm room, stabbing thumbtacks one after the other into the bulletin board as if into the contours and crevices of his skin, obliterating him with pinholes. Maybe he wanted to get caught. He was supposed to meet Jess at the movies for the seven o'clock show of *Victor/Victoria*. She hated missing previews, so she bought the tickets because he was late, and Sydney Moore stood by the movie posters, hand on a hip, wearing a Fiorucci miniskirt that Jess owned except in blue, and the two smiled coldly at each other, did that terse nod thing, but when Tommy walked up and saw them both, he spun and ran. Nothing had been proven, but Sydney Moore whipped around in the opposite direction, her stride stiff and fast, so Jess shoved the tickets free into someone's hand and headed straight back to find me. She knew.

The worst part is that on that same night—before I knew what had happened earlier at the movie theater—I had been studying in my usual carrel in the library, and Tommy came for me, strolling the bookshelves across the aisle until I looked up, which wasn't long; I'd drop mind-numbing *Ulysses* at the whiff of anyone passing. Probably people guessed what was up, anyone sitting near the staff bathroom, anyone catching the two clicks of the door opening and shutting, the snap of the lock, semi-muffled by his fist. We didn't talk. He liked leaning ass up against the sink for a fast, rough blow job; he liked seeing me on my knees on that dirty mint-green bathroom tile. Jeans down partway. Boxers, usually blue. He grabbed my hair and held on, like it was beautiful, like Rapunzel's hair, which made me feel sort of pretty.

What was I getting out of it? Good question, though I didn't ask it.

He would vanish right after, and I'd drench my hands with pink soap, scrubbing each finger individually under cold water (even hot was cold in that bathroom), examining my face in the mirror. I was exactly who I thought I was, a girl from Iowa at a fancy college doing a reckless, awful, evil thing. I wouldn't leave behind even a used paper towel marking my presence, so I wiped my wet hands on my jeans, telltale dark streaks slashing my thighs.

Jess stuck her left arm straight out, tilted her hand upward at the wrist. She got the big diamond ring last week when Tommy took her to C.D.Peacock on Michigan Avenue. His dad in Louisville told him which store and called in with a credit card number, and after some paperwork, out strolled Jess, wearing the ring. I assumed she expected all the rest of it would be that easy. "I love this ring," she said now, toning her voice into thoughtful consideration, as if a challenging question had been posed.

"And him," I added for her.

"Him I hate," she corrected.

Easy to see how this would end. It was why men blinded women with glittery diamonds. Why I planned never to marry. But I went along: "It's a gorgeous ring."

She said, "My parents have rough spots, which I know you don't believe. But I never told you about when I was fourteen and came home sick from school, and my mother was crying in the bathroom. I asked what was wrong—you know, because you're supposed to; I mean, really all I wanted was to climb into their bed and have her bring me cocoa with little marshmallows and fall asleep to TV game shows, but there she was, sobbing, so I had to help her. She went, 'I'll tell you exactly what's wrong,' and then she said my dad had a mistress all set up in an apartment and everything."

"Wow."

"So, according to her this one time, which believe me was the only time she ever mentioned any of it, she started a secret bank account and was siphoning money into it."

I repeated, "Wow," the best response for something that was surprising and not.

"She said she wasn't leaving him because of me and my sister, because keeping a family together was *everything*, but also no way would he get away with it. She said—exact words—'It's not that hard to learn to love someone you hate.'"

"True," I agreed, watching Jess stare at her ring. Two carats, she had told me, an Asscher cut diamond, the most expensive cut in the world. I had never heard of such a thing, but I pretended to know all about it last week when she waved her hand in my face after getting back from downtown. "He insisted it should be the best diamond in the store," she told me, "and virtually flawless—like me," and while she talked, I thought about the bathroom tile pressed cold on my knees, that secret thing I clung to, like how praying might be if I still prayed. She said she wanted to let me try on the ring but it was bad luck, and when I said, "That's okay," she slid it off, saying, "Screw bad luck."

The ring was loose on my ring finger and the diamond heavy enough that it spun upside down, dangled in my palm. I twisted the ring the right way, half expecting a genie to appear and grant me a wish. But no, so I tilted my hand to flash the diamond before yanking off the ring, saying, "Too quick for bad luck."

Now. What about now? That was always a thing when I was with Jess, her snapping her fingers in my face to bring me back to now, to her. She kept me from drifting away, like clutching a string tied to a balloon. We both liked that, thinking I would be lost without her. Now she was saying, "After my mother told me all that I threw up. Like I want to right now."

I said, "You haven't even talked to him about it yet."

"I'm the one who got the ring," she said. "I'm the one he asked to marry him that day by the lake. Not her."

I'm the one in the library bathroom, I thought, before saying, "Why does everyone think she's so pretty? Her nose is too big."

She curled both arms around her chest, tightened them as if hugging herself. The ring disappeared into the folds of her limbs. I stepped over and squashed my hug on top of hers. She was shaking. She said, "When I asked my mom the next day about what she'd said, she accused me of too much NyQuil, that it was a bad dream, basically that I was insane to think that could be true. I was afraid to bring it up again. But I don't know. Men really are scummy pigs."

I thought about her dad, the richest man I knew in person, though not rich the way Tommy's dad was rich. Jess's dad was sharp, his body all angles like a wire coat hanger, and he finished your sentence if you weren't getting to the point fast enough; actually, he preferred making the point for you. Except for Jess; she talked over him when he bulldozed in, until he laughed and shut up. He planned office parks and found people to build them, though Jess told me he started out running vending machines, which I didn't know was a thing to be run by someone, but he never talked about work out at dinner because Jess's mom said all that bored her. He was the only man I'd seen in real life with two rings: a wedding band and, on his right pinkie, a knuckled chunk of gold with initials carved on the smooth top. I asked Jess if her mother had given it to him, and she thought that was so hilarious: "No woman would pick that out. He bought it himself." I imagined him coming home with that ring in a velvet box, not letting anyone try it on because it was bad luck, later saying the same exact words to the mistress. I imagined the mistress at C.D.Peacock, quietly shaking her head no, no, no, then yes. Whatever there was, people—and not only men—wanted more. I did. I wouldn't say so then, but if there was a mistress in an apartment, I knew there might also be a child, a girl, Jess's sister, a shadow daughter—a girl growing up to be like Jess's dad. How funny later, when I realized I was right, to wonder if she'd been named for money: Penny.

I shook straight the rumpled comforter, patted the pillow invitingly. I let Jess crawl into bed in her jeans and polo shirt, but I tugged off her flats. She murmured, "You're always here to take care of me." I sat in the dark with her as she slept, listening to her breathe. The next day, when I asked if she ever thought about questioning her dad about the mistress, she daggered me a frozen look and said, "Give me a break. You know my father's not that way." She arced one arm in instant dismissal of me and my rudeness, and the Asscher cut diamond flung dazzling sparkles across the morning sunlight. *Who's the one keeping together the family now?* I wanted to say, but didn't dare.

Jess hadn't told her parents about her sudden engagement. They hadn't even met Tommy, which she explained away, saying her parents refused to like anyone who asked her out. Her father didn't trust boys, and her mother didn't trust men. "They want me to be a nun," Jess said, "even though my mother doesn't trust Catholics." I reminded her that I was Catholic, sort of, raised to be Catholic anyway. "That doesn't count," Jess said, "because they love you, how genuine you are. They're always telling me how polite and quiet you are, and well-mannered. That's their favorite word for you, that I should be more 'well-mannered' like you." We snorted at that idea. But now there was this Asscher cut ring, making Tommy real. So when it was time to tell them over dinner—two days after the movie theater and Sydney Moore, after Jess decided that things looked better in the morning, and after Tommy had a mountain of flowers delivered and swore he ran only because he was freaked to see Sydney—Jess insisted that I be there to ease the way. "You're like an adult compared to me," she said, "and you know how to handle parents. Like you're gifted." I made a few dismissive clucks, but she barreled on: "I want you there so they really get I'm engaged for real, so they're ready to meet him. One surprise at a time." And the kicker: "Anyway, they like taking us out." *And I like getting free dinner,* I thought, right as Jess, knowing what I was thinking, nudged my ribs.

Getting ready, I picked my nice skirt, the one that closed up the side with a line of shiny black buttons, one or two of which you were supposed to leave open at the bottom, or possibly three. I went with four. Pumps with too-high heels. The periwinkle cotton sweater from Marshall Field's that I convinced the saleslady was from the half-off table. A new tube of Cover Girl mascara, the brand Jess recommended for me, and she also recommended I switch to black mascara and eyeliner, both more dramatic than boring brown. She had lots of opinions about makeup and loved that I took all her advice, unlike her sister, "always whining that foundation oppresses women. Puh-lease!"

Jess wore a slinky wrap dress with a deep V-neck. We were date-dressing for this dinner with parents. We thought we looked like adults. She decided on no jewelry except for the giant diamond ring.

"Your mom will see it right away," I said. "You flashing that thing around."

She said, "Let's hope. Maybe that will make everything easier."

"Won't she be happy for you?" I asked.

"Not about being engaged," Jess said. "But the ring. At least he has money."

"He's cute. And better manners than me," I said. *Please,* he liked to moan, *please.* Though not thank you.

"No one is as well-mannered as you," she said. "You're the queen of manners. They love you."

"Because I'm quiet."

"Exactly." She laughed in that way that made sure we both understood that she would never be quiet like me, or like me in any way, and we got in her car and drove to the Keg, Evanston's only fancy restaurant, and ended up sitting in the lobby, waiting for her parents, who were always late. Even when we knew they would be late, we rushed to be on time, which didn't make sense until I realized that Jess wanted to complain about how long she had to wait. They usually claimed parking problems, but the Keg had its own lot, so it wouldn't be that. It was her father pouring down one last drink before heading out, was what it was. Jess's mother had announced that one night when she and I sat in side-by-side stalls in the ladies' room, like I'd asked a question. I pretended not to hear. And I didn't tell Jess, though maybe I was expected to.

Now, as we waited in the paneled lobby in our date clothes with our black-lined eyes, Jess said, "What I need is a ton of luck."

"I don't think that's how luck is measured," I said. "We've gone metric."

She didn't crack a smile. Too nervous to listen. Too bad. It was the kind of joke she liked.

The hostess behind the stand—tall, thin, what the bad poets in my writing workshop would describe as "raven-haired" with "alabaster" skin—glared at the space above our heads. She was a hundred times prettier than me, even prettier than Jess, and definitely as pretty as Sydney Moore, but clearly she hated us anyway. We went to the school by the lake and she didn't. The equation in that town was simple.

I'm not them, I thought, trying to vibe the information. *I'm a fraud. I'm more like you than you think.*

But she kept up the scowl. And why not: here I was perched on a bench in the lobby, planning to order the fried shrimp, the third most expensive item on the menu she was handing us with a forced, hateful smile because Jess had requested one.

Jess said, "They do this on purpose."

"Do what?" For a moment, I thought we were talking about the hostess, but I remembered we'd never been talking about her.

"Make me wait," she said. "Like they know what I'm going to tell them. Like they fucking already know and don't want to hear it." She barely said "fricking" back then or "what the f," so "fucking" was a very big deal. I watched her pick at her cuticle until a skin shred ripped off, which she flicked on the floor toward the hostess.

I checked my watch. Twenty minutes. Maybe her father had needed a second or third drink. Maybe her mother wouldn't leave the bedroom, because that was another thing she told me once in secret, that lots of days barely seemed worth getting out of bed for.

The hostess said, "I'm only supposed to hold the reservation fifteen minutes." A mean little simper accompanied her statement. I kind of admired it. She was unimpressed with Jess, that's for sure. Not that Jess would care what a restaurant hostess thought of her.

"Then seat us," Jess said.

"Not until your entire party is here," the hostess said, and Jess's parents swooped in, flurrying apologies, and we jumped up for hugs and Jess pounced—"You're twenty minutes late"—and the hostess took in the fuss with a smirk, lasering her smoldering stare at me, which felt unfair because all I was doing was standing quietly in the background. I mean, it wasn't like my parents would come to campus—from Iowa or even if they lived two minutes away—to buy me and my friend fancy food. Also, I wasn't stupid like she thought; I understood exactly the cost of a free dinner. I wouldn't make eye contact with the hostess, though I felt her now wanting to.

Jess's father immediately got drinks going, pretty much before we sat down, asking what we wanted, though Jess and I were both underage, and I said, "Tab is fine," and Jess's mother shrilled, "Raymond!"

and arched an eyebrow, and Jess said, "I'll have a martini, shaken, not stirred, very dry, up, with a twist, and seriously—very, very dry, don't even think the word 'vermouth,' because I mean dry like a desert," and her father laughed and asked how many martinis she'd drunk in her life, and she laughed right back and said, "Enough to know how I like them," and her mother complained, "Raymond!" and he laughed again and said, "I'll have what she's having," pointing to Jess. Her mother ordered a half carafe of Chablis, and when the waitress looked at me, I wilted and said, "I'll have Chablis, too," so her mother changed to a full carafe, which is what she probably wanted all along, because she patted my hand gratefully.

Then we went through the menu, Jess's father reading off the specials that were typed up on a small card clipped to the center of the trifold menu, though that same card was clipped to our menus, too, and we listened attentively, then Jess said she wanted a small house salad because she felt fat and her mother said, "You have to eat something, lovey," and Jess tilted her head my way so I could put to use my alleged gift handling adults, and I remarked, "We had a really huge lunch," though Jess hadn't eaten any lunch that I remembered or breakfast. She was very take it or leave it about food.

The drinks came, and Jess's dad made the same toast he always did, which was a word or two in another language, probably Polish, since his grandmother was from Poland, and we all mumbled our imitation, clinking glasses, and the wine tasted like vinegar from a refrigerator, like sour medicine, sludge to slog through before reaching another, more desirable outcome, and Jess started coughing and choking because, of course, she'd never had a martini before, but once she could breathe, she announced, "I love it," and her father said, "That's my girl," and his swig was long and hard, so clearly he really, truly did love it, and watching him made me want to drink martinis someday, but to order them his way, not how Jess did.

"I like when there's an olive," her mother said. "And the gin soaks in."

Jess said, "Olives are fattening," and her mother sighed and sipped wine, but she didn't seem to love it the way Jess's dad loved that martini.

The waitress returned—she was older, tired looking, conditioned to people like Jess and her family, irritated only at the time lost going through the motions to get her 15 percent tip. "We have some specials tonight," she said.

"We're ready to order." Jess's father pointed at Jess's mother, who ordered the baked halibut, after twenty questions about how fishy it would be, and no side dish even though one came free, and no dressing on the salad, just lemon. Jess ordered a house salad with oil and vinegar and opened her mouth to say something else, but her father was pointing at me, and I ordered fried shrimp with French fries as my side and Italian as my dressing, because fried shrimp was my favorite food, which in Iowa I got only on my birthday, and only after enduring my mother announcing to the waitress, "This one with her champagne taste better marry rich, because she won't get it here." Jess's father ordered prime rib with a baked potato and "a mountain of sour cream" and, for his salad, blue cheese dressing, which the menu said was fifty cents extra, and then Jess's mother said, "I want a baked potato, too," and then changed altogether to the prime rib and blue cheese, and the waitress wrote it all down, and then Jess's dad looked at Jess and pointed and said, "She'll also have the prime rib and blue cheese," and Jess rolled her eyes and mumbled, "Dad," but when she saw the waitress's pen poised, unsure, she nodded and said, "Okay, prime rib. But no sour cream—a mountain of butter," and I was about to chime in that I changed to prime rib, but the waitress gathered the menus and walked away: clearly I wasn't one of them.

Jess's parents settled in their chairs, drinks cupped comfortably in their hands, and I thought it would be how it always was, them shooting questions at Jess about her classes or unwinding dull stories about people I didn't know, and her father interrupting to rail on the mayor or the economy, but Jess thumped both hands flat on the tablecloth so it was impossible not to notice that showy diamond and said, "You guys aren't very observant," and Jess's mother screeched and practically spit out wine as she grabbed Jess's hand.

"What the hell?" Her father's whole body clenched into itself. I was glad he had that martini, and probably so was he, because he gulped at it. It looked like he wished he had one in his other hand also.

The questions surged: *Who? What? Where? When? Why, why, why?*

The salads came and sat there until finally I started on mine. Lots of croutons. Crunching echoed in my ears.

"And why isn't he here tonight?" Jess's dad asked for the tenth or hundredth time. He reached for his salad, sliding it roughly across the white tablecloth to center the plate, chopping down with his fork the way bulldozers hacked into ground, probably not tasting a single thing; it might as well be dirt.

"Because I knew you'd be like this," Jess said. "You're supposed to be happy for me."

"We're happy," her mother said. "This is so sudden. You're not even legal for drinking."

Jess grabbed her martini protectively. "I can vote," she said. "And I'm the exact age you were when you got married."

It was a pause where everyone stared somewhere that wasn't at each other. And then Jess looked straight at me, like announcing, *Showtime!* and said, "You like Tommy, right?"

Their faces swung my way as if I were judge, jury, and God Almighty in one body. I badly wanted the waitress to show up with my fried shrimp, because chances were good that Jess was going to storm out in some sort of protest, and if the shrimp were here now, I'd at least get to snag one or two. Also, I wished I had one of those martinis. I imagined them tasting brutal and strong and true, like wiping a chalkboard clear of writing. I imagined erasing my own mind with crisp briskness. I sipped my wine, nodded to buy time, said, "He's really in love with Jess." The wine tasted worse than before. But I kept going, with the wine, with the words: "They're a perfect match. A very perfect couple. They're perfect together."

Jess's mother dumped a lot more wine from the carafe into her glass and a little bit more into mine. "Okay, lovey," she said, and her voice was thin. "So. I guess we want to meet him. This perfect man. I didn't realize you two were serious. When did he propose? There's nothing wrong with a long engagement, you know."

"For God's sake," Jess's dad said. "Don't encourage this nonsense."

Jess tossed back her hair. I think she was getting drunk, because her smile seemed sloppy and her black eyeliner and mascara were fuzzy. Or maybe I was drunk. But I'd had more at any frat party, garbage can punch made from Everclear and store-brand Hi-C. I was one of those people who didn't get drunk, or if I did, I hadn't yet found the amount needed to get me there.

"He's very romantic," Jess said. "He sent roses the other day. And once he wrote me a poem."

A limerick. "Jess" rhymed with "chest." Probably copied off a bathroom wall.

"Christ," Jess's dad said, waving at the waitress and pointing to his empty martini glass. He wolfed lettuce as if he had to have something to do or he'd keep spouting words, the wrong ones, like he'd decided to relinquish all control over the situation to his wife, knowing she'd botch it, looking forward to blaming her later for the mess.

Jess said, "I really love him. Maybe you guys forget what it's like to want to be with someone every minute of every day, but that's how we are." She made a fake pouty face at her father. "I want another martini, too."

"Christ," he said again, less forcefully, jabbing a finger at Jess's glass. "Olives this time," he called to the waitress, tipping the lemon rind onto his empty salad plate. Neither Jess nor her mother had touched her salad. The blue cheese dressing lay thick and viscous, like what pus probably looked like. Who could choke that down? Yet I knew I would order it next time.

Jess folded her arms across her chest. The ring was on the outside, impossible not to see.

Abruptly, her father laughed. "Arranged marriages. Those were the days. Call up your friends and they send over their sons."

"Who did that?" Jess said. "No one gets married that way now."

"Line up all the boys to look them straight in the eye," her father said, his voice expansive, louder. "Smart as you are, Jess, lovey, I know a hell of a lot more about judging character than any college girl. I know—" and he swooped his arm in a semicircle, knocking over the bread basket. "Hell." He pointed to the hostess, leading an older couple to a table in the back. "I could marry her and what would be different? Love is the least of it. 'I reeeeaaaally love him,'" he mocked.

"What do you mean saying 'her' like that? Because she works in a restaurant?" Jess said. "Anyway—"

"Raymond," shushed Jess's mother. "You're embarrassing."

Now his eyes dug into me. "You know I'm right," he said, finally lowering his voice, "tell me I'm right," and he jerked the gold ring over his knuckle and halfway up his finger, then started twisting it aggressively. "Let's hear what your old man would say if you came home tomorrow engaged."

Jess slapped both palms flat on the table, prelude to jumping up, though she stayed seated. "Honestly," she said. "You're embarrassing me and everyone else."

Her dad's eyes glittered, and I imagined their glint across a conference table while you signed the loops of your name, suddenly getting that you'd been screwed, or their dangerous flash rising out of a cluttered alley behind a bar after last call. How had I not seen his eyes this way before? I waited for Jess to leap up and drag me in her wake: our protest that would leave her childishly triumphant and me hungry, with no shrimp and too late for dorm food. I waited for her mother to hiss or screech or warn, "Raymond," but she sipped wine robotically, as if she had left the table, leaving behind this husk of a body. I waited, but there was only silence. The hostess glided past with a miniature, disengaged smile, as if she hadn't heard, though surely she had. Everyone had.

I said, "She's so pretty, isn't she?" and I don't know why I did. No one agreed or disagreed. I felt my face burning a horrible red, and my fingertips seemed dipped in ice. Because I knew exactly what my father would say as if I heard the words echo in the room: *With that huge-ass ring, you can buy your love somewhere else.* Actually, no, my father could not be that clever. He would say, *Quite a ring you got there. Hang on to whoever gave you that. As easy to love rich as poor.* But even that was too polite. He would say—my father would say—he really, truly would look at that ring and I knew he would say...

They kept staring at me, this awkward, unhappy, confusing family I could never understand, and I blurted it out: "He'd take one look at the ring and say, 'Bet there's more where that came from.'"

And the three of them laughed. They laughed hysterically in gulps and cackles, clutching the table edge and one another's hands and forearms. They didn't see that I wasn't laughing. The new martinis came and Jess's dad fished out the plastic sword spearing his olives and handed it to Jess's mother, who slid the olives into her mouth. The waitress took the two empty salad plates, mine and Jess's father's.

"You'll stay in school," he said to Jess.

"Of course," she said, giving the lie he expected.

No toast this round, just Jess's dad laying into his drink. I knew, watching that thirst, his vehemence, that I would bull down martinis and blue cheese, choking myself until I learned to love both, and when blue-cheese-stuffed olives for martinis hit Chicago bars in the nineties, I would feel vindicated.

Then her father said, "We love you, Jess. Whatever makes you happy makes us happy." The words seemed to suffocate him, and he tugged the rim of his shirt collar.

Jess's mom said, "We're eager to meet Tommy and welcome him into the family. I'd love for you to think about an engagement party this summer at the club to introduce him around. People ask about you; they'll want to know." There was lots more chatter, mostly between Jess and her mother. Her father cradled that martini. He seemed suddenly calm. I imagined him having another whole separate family with his mistress, another daughter making him proud but who was also disappointing, who wanted the house salad but got prime rib when he pointed his finger. Another daughter who would attend this fancy college, or who maybe would be the hostess at this restaurant. Or maybe he didn't know this other daughter existed. Maybe she was a secret, floating unnoticed like a ghost, never drawing attention, passing along edges, watching, observing, learning the way to be.

A little later, before the desserts and coffee came, Jess's mother stood up and announced that she was going to the little girls' room. "She likes to pee in a herd," Jess had warned me when I first met her parents, so now she smiled at Jess, who rolled her eyes and looked my way for a rescue, so I got up, but Jess's father pointed at me: "Hang on there," he said, so I sat down and Jess stood. The two of them walked toward the back of the room as sudden sweat dampened my armpits. I struggled to think when I had been alone with Jess's father. His eyes were half closed as he leaned back in his chair, regarding me as if I were at a job interview and failing it. I sat straighter. I picked up a spoon. Before I could tap it or turn it over, his brow furrowed, so I loosened my grip and flattened my hands on the table, palms down. I had to breathe, so I did that quietly.

Finally he said, "You're a good friend to Jess."

"Thank you."

He reached over and rested his hand on top of mine, patted my fingers absently. "I lost control earlier," he said. "I'm sorry you had to see that."

I shrugged. It was an uncomfortable silence. I suppose it was touching that he thought he owed me an apology, if that's what this was, if that's why he wanted to speak to me alone. I wanted to tell him that was why never, never lose control.

"I love my daughter," he said. "I would do anything for her, anything to help her, and I'm not on board with this engagement. That big ring is nothing compared to her happiness." His eyes were shiny for a moment, as if he might cry, but then they weren't anymore.

"I love Jess, too."

I truly did. I loved her in a fierce and confused way, like a sister. I loved Jess for saving me from who I was. What her father said made sudden and absolute sense of why I was doing what I did with Tommy: I was trying to save Jess back, because I wasn't on board with her engagement either, and her father, his hand now gripping my hand, pressing his heavy gold ring against my knuckles, understood all this.

I said, "Between us, I'm sure they won't get married in the end."

"Would you bet money on that?" he asked. Joke words. But his face was 100 percent serious, looking me straight in the eye, the way he had when he asked about my father.

"I never bet real money," I said. "But yes."

"Well, then," he said. "I think you know something." His hand pressed heavier now, and I couldn't slip mine away. The restaurant dipped into seamless silence, and he slanted his head in, close. Tiny black whiskers lined his jawbone. I smelled gin. I leaned forward. He said, "I think you know a lot of things."

"Maybe," I said. My heart beat extra loud.

He whispered, "You're prettier than that restaurant hostess any day." As if he read my mind.

The silence was tense, and I wanted to pretend I hadn't heard, but surely he could see that what he said had punched my breath out. I figured I'd remember this moment for the rest of my life, and then it was over because he sat straight, nodding to the far corner, to Jess and her mother returning, snatching his hand off mine so fast it was as if my skin had burned his with flames. He grabbed his water glass, cocked his head sideways as if puzzling the answer to a tough question. When Jess and her mom reached the table, he said loudly, "There's my two girls," in a voice that wouldn't fool anyone but did and half standing as they bustled out chairs and re-draped napkins across their laps. But they were in the midst of a conversation about how many bridesmaids and barely seemed to notice they were at the table.

Whereas I understood exactly where I was: in a restaurant I could not afford, with a family that wasn't mine, with a man whose hand grabbed my hand for too long. I didn't want to be evil, but I was. I was, even when I didn't want to be. As if what my father had done to me had left a physical mark on me that any man could read, that no amount of money would erase.

I smiled and stood up and politely said, "Excuse me." I walked across the restaurant quickly, my open skirt swishing, showing off my legs to anyone paying attention. It seemed like a long time ago that I had gotten dressed, and I wasn't sure how I had ended up in this outfit or why I had worked so hard to get this sweater for myself from Marshall Field's. My head buzzed and hummed with wine, and the tall shoes made my footsteps as clattery as hooves.

I could stay in control. It was only walking to the ladies' room. I wanted to stare at my face in the mirror, to see what they all saw. And I wanted to know for sure he wasn't going to follow me. Could I have at least that?

HOW WE LEAVE HOME

(summer, before college)

I.

Here could be the beginning, that summer in Iowa when we longed for adventure. We sprawled on towels on the glittering concrete of the pool deck at Mercer Park and sighed, arching our necks, flexing our toes, bemoaning how boring Iowa was, how bored, bored, bored we were—how we needed—no, deserved—adventure. We glopped handfuls of baby oil over each other's shoulders, desperate for any zinc-nosed lifeguard to swivel his head our way.

The adventure on my horizon was that I would leave for college in Chicago in three weeks. I hadn't told my friends. They saw me on the path we all followed: maybe the state school in our town or community college, living at home in my childhood bedroom, working a mall job. The only thing different would be nothing. Same people at the same parties at the Reservoir in their same run-down cars, same brand of beer bought from the same place that sold to minors, Dirty John's on Market Street.

I felt sorry for my friends, the dull blur of them. They sensed my pity—maybe read it as disdain—and all summer they'd been avoiding me, or cutting me with the slightest of slights, like not acknowledging my new haircut. It was okay. I floated a stratosphere or two above them. I was leaving. I was out. I was so out, and the poor things didn't even know.

At the same time, I missed them already, their clattering gossip about people we'd known since third grade. I was the one insisting on this afternoon at the pool. I wanted to bawl. I loved them so much. I wanted to tell them that adventure was stupid and all wrong.

My stomach curled and flip-flopped, so I pushed my salted nut roll to the edge of my towel. It seemed accusatory. Usually it was my favorite choice from the pool vending machine. I could smell the peanuts over the chlorine lacing the air, so I concentrated on the lifeguard scanning the blue pool, the screeching kids, the chubby moms clustered in the semi-shady corner.

"Well, I'm going in," Janey said, as she rose, all six feet one inch of her. She wore a glittery pink headband, too narrow for her crazy wad of dark hair—"That girl needs to learn control," my mother said about Janey—and Janey tugged off the band, letting it drop to the concrete as she shook free her hair. Her coppery skin glistened with baby oil; she tanned the best and showed off with white tank tops deep into autumn. Though she and I had been friends since seventh grade, it was an uneasy friendship, each of us certain we were better than the other without evidence backing us up.

She was too tall for our school, with too much hair, and just always too much something. After my new haircut, with five inches chopped off and bangs, she stared at my face with intensity and said, "God, your chin shouldn't be pointy like that."

Now, she glanced down at me sitting cross-legged on my towel and demanded, "Come with me." I scrambled up, startled to be noticed, grateful, nervous—so nervous that my bare foot crunched the discarded hairband as I followed her; I heard it snap. We moved fast over the stovetop heat of the cement, and the pain scorching my feet felt distant.

We sat on the lip of the pool, dangled our legs in the water. "I wish the water was blue," I babbled, "not clear."

"There's islands in the world where it is," she said hazily.

The lifeguard whistled at some boys dunking each other. "No roughhousing," he yelled. Whistle Nazi, we called that one, even as we flipped our hair when his gaze skimmed us.

"What if it's our last summer together?" More babbling. I should shut up already.

"Look," Janey interrupted. "I know you're pregnant. I already know that."

That hot sun was frying me. I half jumped, half fell into the cool, colorless water that should have been the cheerful turquoise of the painted walls and floor—I disappeared into the cold, scraping my hands back and forth against the rough cement to make them bleed.

What my mother said: *That girl needs to learn control.*

I could drown myself, never emerge, but I wasn't good even at holding my breath, and when my head bobbed up to the surface, there was Janey, sitting very still, staring over the water with the same abstract gaze as the Whistle Nazi. She said, "What are we going to do?"

"How do you know?" I asked.

"You're too quiet," she said. "That candy bar's been there all afternoon. And honestly, you know you're an unlucky person, always jinxed. You barely did it with Brad, like once or twice?"

That was fine—let her think it was Brad. That was better.

"I can't tell anyone," I said. "Not anyone. Not even one person."

We glanced at the clutch of girls, at my former friends, sun glare flashing off their oiled shoulders. One of them rolled over, and then another and another. I felt suddenly invisible.

"I won't," she said.

I had to trust her. So I asked, "How much money do you have?" She waitressed the late shift at Country Kitchen, when drunks and frat boys stumbled in for scrambled eggs and fried potatoes, and either they gave her excessive drunk-guy tips or else she got stiffed, no in-between.

She hugged her knees to her chest. "Aren't you afraid?" she asked.

"No," I lied.

"Were you going to tell me?" she asked.

So easy to lie. "When it was the right time."

She shook her head, hair flailing. I thought about the white puff of a dandelion gone to seed, blowing at it with one huge breath to make a wish. How little girls ran around backyards all summer blowing the tops off dandelions. I taught Grace to do that. This little girl could, too. Like me, she'd catch fireflies, and crook her eyes in her elbow at the parts of movies where animals might get hurt, and write her name across the dark with a lit sparkler, and eat her hot dogs burned black. All the things little girls did, things I did, that I taught my sister. But I shoved this little girl out of my head. I pushed her away, like pushing a swing on a playground and watching the body on it sail off into a pure blue sky. I would never think about her again. All I needed was Janey's tip money.

"What about him?" Janey asked.

"What about him?"

"You have to tell him," she said. "Don't you?"

"I don't *have* to do anything," I said.

"Wow," she said.

The moment fell heavily between us, separating us irrevocably but neatly, like a guillotine severing the head from the body. Every single person in the pool was screaming, yet I couldn't distinguish a word. Janey wouldn't meet my eyes, so I looked down at my wavy, water-distorted legs.

"Okay. I'll drive you," Janey said. "I can get the car." She and her older brother shared a crappy Pinto, the kind that might blow up if it got rear-ended. Her brother was a pothead and definitely mellow. There was nothing he cared about except pot and pizza. Janey and I talked about whether that might be a good life, pot and pizza, and sometimes we agreed it would be, and other times one of us argued it would be boring.

"I can take the bus," I said. "I figured out the transfer and the route."

She shook her head. "You can't take the bus."

Exactly why I didn't want to tell Janey, because I didn't need her being nice. I only needed her money. But I didn't know how to say that. So she would drive me there and call up afterward and watch me with shiny, sad eyes and hug me for no reason, hanging on until I squirmed away. I had to hate her, I had to. And she would tell: *I handed over every dime of my summer tip money to my best friend for her abortion and then she left town for college without saying good-bye. When I would have done anything for her.* I wondered how I would tell the story, until I remembered that I would never tell the story. That was the only bright spot: that all this could happen and no one would know.

"I hear it's not a big deal," Janey said.

"That's what I hear, too," I said.

She got up into a crouch and reached out her hand to me, wanting to help me out of the pool, but what I did when I took her hand was yank really hard and dodge aside, wrenching her headfirst into the water. She shrieked, and the Whistle Nazi about broke his whistle on us, and I watched Janey's big body lash and twist underwater, her limbs reorganize into standing, until her head emerged, her hair tamped and streaming rivulets, water beading her oily shoulders. She tugged both suit straps straight, then fixed me with her eyes. As the lifeguard yammered about roughhousing, I waited for Janey to call me a slut, to tell me to take the bus and pay for it myself besides. But she smiled at me, a too-wide, circus-clown, sad, sad, sad smile. Now she would always see me like this: pitiful.

II.

Maybe this story starts before that day at the pool. Maybe it starts when we were fifteen, sixteen, too old for the slumber parties we still organized, any excuse to flee our houses, dart free of our mothers' watchful eyes. Too young for dating, we tried anyway, none of us landing with the cute crush boys of our giggles and chatter, each of us compromising, so it was homecoming dance with whoever asked, always yes-thank-you, playing at gratitude to pimply-faced boys. We didn't talk about that boy passing us in the hall after school, that boy, the one raking his long hair back with both hands before slouching over the drinking fountain, that boy whose sudden presence in any doorway set loose a smolder of longing we knew to keep secret. Each of us kissed Janey's pothead brother, who was surprisingly tender, bestowing secret nicknames we pressed close to our hearts. We whispered them in our dark bedrooms during icy winters and sweaty summers. I was Desi, after confessing that I wanted Desiree for my French class name, hating the teacher who assigned me Claudette and called me arrogant. But he didn't count; he was just Janey's brother, just a pothead drifting through the fringes of the back parking lot, smoking dope in tricked-out vans. Though he was an excellent kisser; though he never pushed for more, recognizing his exact but limited role of First Big Kiss; though Janey didn't mind and we suspected he kissed her, too; and though we would never break tradition and *not* kiss him when our turn came, it was understood that kissing Janey's pothead brother was not enough. Understood that there had to be more, and some of us needed whatever that more was, or told ourselves we did.

"Desiree," "desired," "desire"... the clutch of the words, their pinch. Bearing down like a marble rolling through my brain, the echo of each syllable merging with the thump of my heart, aligning to the push and pull of my breath, melding with the drumbeat of my being, until I couldn't speak what the word itself meant to me: it was a throb I was never without, that was all.

My mother's baby brother was being divorced, which didn't happen much to people in Iowa back then, especially not twice. He landed on the battered couch in the unfinished basement, T-shirts and denim spilling from a Hefty bag after his wife kicked him out of their cheap apartment, because, he said, now she was a hot-shit secretary on the university payroll. Before, she spooned up lunches at South East Junior High, a hairnet lady no better than the others. Now, every morning she looped a paisley polyester scarf from Younkers around her neck and wore pantyhose. She kept the dog, which pissed him the most, he said, because she fed it table scraps so's it would get fat and lazy. "I only just grabbed up my guitars," he said, "before she was fixed to hurl them up the alley."

My uncle was a musician who slept all day and woke up about when my parents got home from their jobs. He'd trudge barefoot up the basement stairs, eyes watery and red-rimmed, his hair stiff with leftover sleep, a crunchy sheen to his skin, then saunter over for a mug-to-the-brim of black coffee from the fresh pot my mother put on for him right after she walked through the door. According to him, she loved him best of her brothers, even with him being the black sheep of the family till kingdom come, no matter what he did or how he proved himself, no matter if he got a gold record or if the Man in Black, Mr. Johnny Cash himself, recorded one of his songs. "People need someone to blame for how their stinking life turned out," he said, "and for a shitload of them, I'm it." That's how he explained it to me, when I sat up late at night, reading at the kitchen table, and he dragged in, the tang of cigarette smoke and butts coiled round him, shadows of rough brown liquor on his breath and smelling of something more, something leathery and sweaty that made me think of the secret pleasure of working a hunk of gristle: this essence later what I sought in every man.

He'd drop into the chair opposite me, ask what I was reading and half listen, his eyes scattered beyond me, beyond this kitchen where the stripes on the wallpaper mismatched by a quarter inch; my mother complained but wouldn't rip it down to put it up right. I'd go on about my book—as long as I wanted, because he didn't stop me—so I theorized about who the murderer might be in whichever Agatha Christie I was dug into. When I was done talking, he'd take a turn, telling me about the band and the bar, who hit it good, who was trash, who played stoned or drunk or strung out, something he scorned as "disrespecting the groove." He played guitar with a bunch of bands, his name bannering posters tacked up all around downtown; he was locally famous for his guitar playing, he told me, and I was oddly proud, as if scraps of that glory might blow my way if people at school connected him with me. When I asked why he wouldn't stick with one band, his own band maybe named after him, he said that was going to be forever the million-dollar question, and if he had the answer he'd know why he couldn't stick with one woman or one anything. We'd talk for an hour, maybe longer, and he'd suck down a mug of cold, leftover coffee and a juice glass of Wild Turkey, and sing lines from songs noodling in his head—"that's where the shit is, writing songs"—and once I was brave enough to ask him to write a song about me. "You betcha," he said, and did I want happy or sad, and "sad" was the right answer, and he said, "Good girl, it's in the works," and tapped his forehead with two fingers, but I never heard any lines.

He wasn't allowed to drink or smoke in the house because my mom was trying to quit both, but he did anyway on these nights. Mornings after, I'd catch my mother dumping the ashtray and rinsing the brown circle of bourbon ringing the juice glass, hurrying before my father was awake.

I watched his head tilt when he drank, my eyes tracking the path of the bourbon rolling from the glass on down through his throat, tiny, delicate muscles rippling along his neck as brown liquid tumbled its way down. He didn't mind when I snuck sips, and I felt—or I imagined I felt—his eyes watching the delicate muscles shift along my throat, too.

Some nights he didn't come home. I'd wait as long as I could stand, my face swallowed up in yawns, then tiptoe upstairs to my bedroom, intending to lie awake until the back door rasped open, instead dropping into immediate, dreamless sleep.

Then there were three nights in a row when he didn't come home and the ashtray stayed clean. I craved the ache and burn of his Wild Turkey, so maybe now I was an alcoholic, which is what my father called my uncle when he was out of the house, spitting the word at my mother because he thought no one else was listening.

Janey's pothead brother called me, wanting to go to a movie, but I said no-thank-you. When I hung up the phone, my mother didn't set aside *Family Circle*, but she said, "Not like you're collecting phone calls from boys every day, you know. Wouldn't want you to think you're too good for everyone. Be more like your sister, why don't you?" My sister was at the table drawing on the back of used worksheets, picking colors from a coffee can of old, dull crayons, sitting in the chair where I would wait for my uncle. The rims of her ears flushed seashell pink. She was only five or six, and terribly quiet, the kind of little girl who sat where she was told to sit, making it easy to forget about her. Somewhere in my heart I understood I was responsible for her, but I had to not think about that. She was so quiet that I could convince myself things would work out okay for her. I wanted her to say something, to talk or cry or shriek or pound fists on the table or fling crayons to the floor. To stop drawing happy-family figures. The last thing on earth that could be true was that I thought I was too good for everyone—though possibly I thought I was too good for Janey's pot-head brother, and yet it was possible that maybe, actually, probably I wasn't. But I had to tell myself that, yes, I was. No-thank-you, I had said, I had said that.

I marched upstairs to my bedroom and tried on shorts in front of the dresser mirror until I figured out the shortest pair, the Levi's cut-offs I made at the last slumber party. Then I yanked off my T-shirt and bra and slid on the bright red tube top no one but me had seen. In the mirror, my boobs looked like tomatoes, which wasn't a good thing, but this was the sexiest shirt I owned. Maybe not buy red next time. Later, with everyone in bed, I crept downstairs and sat at the table in my outfit, barely able to focus on *The Murder of Roger Ackroyd*. I knew who had done it because I'd peeked at the last page. I could have been reading harder, better books, but I liked Agatha Christie because the problem always got solved. Plus, with so many books, nearly a hundred, I could never read them all, or if I did, it might be a thrilling accomplishment. I longed for the tickle of bourbon skimming my tongue, the abrupt burn and razor slice of it, neck muscles tightening and loosening. I wanted the bourbon. I was an alcoholic. He had to come tonight. My thoughts mishmashed on top of themselves.

I must have set my head down and fallen asleep on top of my paperback, because I was startled to see my uncle in the doorway, a smile screwed sideways across his face. "Look at you," he said, ambiguously. He tossed his jean jacket onto the back of a chair with a soft *thump*, an even drape, like of course it would land that way.

Gravity had shifted my tube top, and I wanted to tug it higher, to my chin, wanted to run upstairs for a real shirt, for jeans that weren't chopped apart, but I kept my hands still.

"Look at you," I said straight back. He stretched his black V-neck T-shirt to sniff the armpits, one then the other. "I'll get glasses," I said. I stood tall in front of him, sweeping in a swift, giant breath that lifted my boobs, a trick we learned at slumber parties. My shorts bit tight at my crotch, and some of the cutoff fringe felt feathery against my leg. I idly scratched a slow, teeny spiral with one thumb.

"Glass," he said. "Singular. I'm not taking the heat for my niece turning up drunk." He looked away, stared at the misaligned wallpaper, and rested one hand up against a seam as if noticing it for the first time.

I got two anyway—jelly glasses with Scooby-Doo characters, because the real juice glasses were dirty in the dishwasher—making sure to reach up to the very top shelf of the cupboard, to the way back, balancing precariously on my tippy-toes. I plunked the glasses on the table and said, "I promise I won't get drunk." I trailed a finger in a lazy cross-my-heart that intersected the edge of my tube top, my finger flaring off the slope of my breast, as if launched from my nipple. I let it point directly at him. His hand on the wallpaper crunched into a fist that he dropped at his side.

"Probably should get myself some sleep," he said, sinking into his usual chair. I understood: certain words must be spoken and dispensed with. Like lines in a play, people were assigned specific roles for right now. "One drink," he said, reaching for his jean jacket, for the bottle tucked into the inside pocket. "Only one."

"One drink," I mirrored. "Only one."

He poured a half inch into my Scooby glass, an inch into Shaggy, and said, "Bottoms up." He lifted the glass to his lips, locked my gaze on to his as he watched me over the rim. A flick sent the brown liquid cascading down his throat, through those undulating muscles. His eyes pinned mine, and the rush of liquor tightened his face, almost imperceptibly, like something suddenly coated with frost, and finally a quick buzz of good sense made me afraid.

"The narrator did it," I said, grabbing *The Murder of Roger Ackroyd*. "The guy telling the story. He's lying the whole time." With both hands, I pressed the book to my chest, against the crack between my two boobs. Cleavage, it was called, though I had never dared call it that. The book was slightly sticky, or it was that patch of naked skin that was sticky. My heart hammered into the layers of paper.

"Shoot," he said. "Most about anyone leaves shit out when they're telling stories and lies their ass off. That's what a story is, a long, fearless lie unwinding." He extended a hand for the book, which I reluctantly gave him. He glanced at the front cover, then flipped to the back, his eyes skipping the words. With one thumb he riffled the pages. Then he let the book drop upside down onto the table. It looked stupid sitting there, just as I looked stupid sitting there in my tomato-red tube top and my cutoffs, with my ragged-edged fingernails, bitten and torn, that wouldn't hold polish more than a day without chipping. "You don't have to drink it," he said, nodding at my glass. Automatically, I curled my fingers, covering Scooby with my palm.

I'd been thinking about this bourbon for three days. I'd been thinking about Janey's pothead brother, and Janey and the rest of them whispering in the dark at slumber parties, and my mall job scooping warm Karmelkorn into cardboard boxes and plastic tubs. I wanted more than this forgettable college town in Iowa, more than what I had. I didn't know what I wanted, only that: more. How to get it, how to get it, how to get it.

I drank. Wild Turkey plunged into the pit of my body, into that hollow emptiness that I didn't like to think about, filling it with an explosion of blistering flame. It was bourbon I wanted, another inch.

Talk about Roger Ackroyd. Talk about the gig, a good one with a cranking crowd and a decent take. Two glasses of bourbon for me, bigger, taller. Five for him. We found the bottom of the bottle. When he grabbed my shoulders and jammed his lips onto mine, when his tongue scooped through my mouth, when he moaned my name—my real name, no childish nickname—and muttered, "Oh shit-shit-shit-shit," when his hand snaked down through my tube top and I straddled him right where he sat in my father's chair, when these things happened and then more things happened, more, I kept my eyes open. I saw everything. It was my own life arriving—finally—and there I was, watching it all spool loose.

The next day, my uncle told my mother from then on he was crashing in a friend's basement, on a friend's battered couch. But also he scribbled that address across a scrap of paper that he slipped to me, and the address after that, and the address after that, so I would always know exactly where to find him. Which I did.

III.

Maybe the story starts on another day, the day my uncle said, "You're a smart one," and meant it, said, "No, really," and then, "Really," and I said, "Smart enough to get out of here?" and he blew cigarette smoke into some circles and said, "Smart enough to want out." The word "how" throbbed in my brain, and I imagined driving away somewhere with him, my books and jeans in a garbage bag, a banged-up guitar case always slicing between us in the front seat, and "not that" pushed through the "how," and when he said, "Smart enough to find your own ticket," I thought, *Yes.* I thought, *I can't hate the man who thinks this.*

A college in another city would take me, if: if I convinced them my dream was to be a girl doctor or scientist, and I doled out heartbreak in an essay, and I filled out and signed financial papers myself; if I found a teacher—who was a man, who drank bourbon when he wasn't at school or when he was—one teacher who had gone to any college in any city, who could send someone important a letter recommending me. Problem solved. Maybe that's the day the story starts, when that silver gleam of light winked from the other side.

Or maybe the story starts at night, on the night I listened to my father's gentle shuffle on the hall's shag carpet, my little sister's bedroom door yielding to his hand, his murmur—heard or imagined—that she should stay quiet. The bed's squeak. The squeak. That squeak. Maybe the story starts that night, or the nights I sat up late in the kitchen, flipping through English murder mysteries, pretending I cared whodunit, the overhead light blaring at its brightest, listening. Maybe this story starts on the night my grandfather's footsteps traveled a different hall, to my father's little-boy bedroom, my father the one told to stay quiet, and no one sitting silent guard in the kitchen. Maybe there is nowhere for this story to start.

IV.

I didn't want to travel back home for Thanksgiving, so I expected Jess to invite me to her parents' house with her. Her parents told her I was "polite" and "well-mannered." They liked me. But she didn't ask. Every freshman on campus was chattering about Thanksgiving break, dying to get home. Maybe Jess thought I was like them. If I mentioned Thanksgiving, Jess jumped in with "That will be great for you to be back, won't that be great?"

There were reasons to go home: Dorm cafeteria closed, starting Wednesday. Library closed, starting Wednesday. If I stayed, I'd be eating pork-flavored ramen noodles out of my roommate's hotpot for five days because they were seventeen cents a package. My roommate hated my using her hotpot, claiming the water she boiled for tea tasted like meat. She hid it in a shoebox in the back of her closet. We loathed each other. If I stayed, people would feel sorry for me, even my roommate, whose parents booked her on a plane home to Fort Lauderdale.

For my Greyhound fare, I borrowed money from my roommate's purse and skulked around the laundry room pocketing stacks of people's dryer quarters, and I snagged the tip jar at the campus Cone Zone when the person scooping ice cream turned her back. Someday I would repay all of this, everything. That refrain circled in my brain like a bird trapped in a room.

My bus left Chicago at four A.M. Thursday, the cheapest fare, meaning I would pull into Iowa City around nine A.M., about when my mother started the stuffing. She loved stuffing, and Thanksgiving was the only time she allowed herself to eat it, so she would be in her best mood, listening to the Frank Sinatra records she took from the farm after my grandfather died. There was one he taught her to dance to. That one she played the most. With no one else awake, she'd keep the stereo low and she'd possibly be singing. I imagined pushing open the back door—a surprise, since I hadn't told anyone I was coming, because that's how expensive long distance was—my mother's startled smile (I hoped), a tight hug (I hoped). She'd hand me an apron,

151

and I'd start chopping onions right alongside her. We wouldn't talk; we were better off with a task, when we had something to think about that wasn't conversation, so we'd dice onions and celery, and there'd be the sizzle of real butter in the frying pan, and she'd sing "I've Got the World on a String." She knew each word exactly how Frank sang it.

Grace would be next awake, and she'd wrap her arms around my waist and squeeze. She wouldn't talk either, but she'd be happy. Maybe she'd sit at the table and read. Or she might draw. She loved to draw animals and families. Her lips moved when she read, but maybe she finally broke that habit while I was away. She'd tuck her bare feet up on the chair rung to get them off the cold floor. She'd draw a picture of me.

That's what I imagined. That's as far as I got.

The reality was I had to get to the house from the bus station. Usually I would expect to wait for a city bus, but none ran on Thanksgiving. If I called for a ride, the surprise would be wrecked. There would be talking. I couldn't stop at hello.

I stood at the pay phone, nickels scraping together in my fist. The huddle of people exiting the bus with me had dispersed immediately: collapsed into noisy, sloppy hugs, everyone exclaiming how great it was to see everyone, how great everyone looked, then dashing outside to waiting cars with running engines billowing white clouds that lingered like mist after the parking lot emptied. A single hovering taxi got snapped up, not that I had cash for a taxi, and not that that would work, Chicago me pulling up like a queen. "You come from Chicago in that thing?" my mother would say. "Well la-di-da to you."

The rain nailing the window looked vicious and cold, ready to jump the line over to sleet. I only had a backpack to carry, but our house was across town, two long miles, almost three.

Still, I didn't call. I couldn't. I imagined onions and celery sputtering in that pool of real butter, my thumb and two fingers crackling leaves of sage into powdery bits: the bottomless scent of sage and thyme and butter and my mother's Wind Song perfume, her only everyday indulgence. The turkey resting on the counter, a heap of pale flab pocked with goose pimples, but we would knead handfuls of soft butter onto it, up and underneath each fold of skin, then rain a shower of salt and pepper and paprika: our day together a fervent vigil of basting and peeking and worrying, aromas rolling in waves, our stomachs pleasantly anxious with hunger. Throughout, Frank Sinatra crooning and the slight clickety of the record reaching its end, my sister hopping up to drop the needle back at the beginning, sending Frank's orchestra on another round. The warm kitchen. The plates with the yellow roses from my mother's dead mother who I never knew, the dishes we weren't allowed to use unless it was a holiday because one might chip or break. Ironing the tablecloth, stiffening it with starch and chunky squirts of steam. The quiet morning. The morning like everyone else's morning: the people who had gotten off the bus, Jess with her parents in Oak Lawn, my roommate in Fort Lauderdale. A TV commercial morning. "What are you thankful for?" people asked on TV Thanksgivings, and right now, until I dialed, it was possible someone would speak those words today at my house.

The nickels were warm in my hand, and solid.

It would be my father who would drive to get me. My father would be there. Of course.

Finally I picked up the phone and pressed the coins into the slot, listening to their jangle and then the dial tone. I went through the seven numbers. I expected the bark of my father's sleep-rage—"Wha—?"—or my mother, a rough sigh, impatient as she eyed pans simmering on the stove. But the phone simply rang. And rang. Ten times, fifteen, twenty. I stopped counting. What a lonely sound, an embarrassing sound: a phone echoing across an empty house because no one was home. Not even a dog or cat listening. ("Pets eat," my mother said, "who can afford that?" She said something like that about everything.) I hung up, my money spitting back out at me.

You told us you were leaving. I could hear my mother's words as if she stood next to me, whispering them. *You left. You left us. You left* us. Only she wouldn't be bold enough to say "us," though I understood the "us" was there and, now, always would be.

The bus station wasn't a place where anyone would want to wait: two short lines of bolted-to-the-ground bucket seats in blue leatherette made it impossible to lie down, and the vending machine was stripped, except for one slot of flamboyantly orange peanut butter crackers. The drinking fountain dribbled water and out-buzzed the fluorescent lights overhead. I smelled little-kid vomit when I turned my head left.

The redheaded man at the ticket counter perched on a stool, looking my way, though it was possible he was merely staring into space, which is what I hoped. His eyes looked ironed flat, like his IQ might be in the double digits, like sitting here might be the only job he would have in his life. I hoped he wasn't watching me, worrying I might cry, wondering what to say. He wouldn't have missed the empty clang of the coins rattling down the chute. I suspected he saw countless sad stories unfold in the bus station, and I suddenly understood that mine wasn't even the saddest. Thinking that made me more pitiful, more embarrassed, and then he dipped his head and flipped over a page of comics in his newspaper with a soft rustle.

I didn't blame him. I looked like a loser. I had abandoned them, all of them—my sister, my mother, Janey, Janey's pothead brother who smashed up the Pinto two days before I went to Chicago, the teachers who wanted to help me, my uncle, even this dumb ticket man staring blankly at his paper—and how dare I think that after leaving them as I had that I could return any time I wanted. There was no one to call. There was no one here.

The ticket man said, "Next bus heading to Chicago pulls in at twelve-oh-seven roundabouts." He spoke loudly, as if making a scheduled announcement to the room, eyes directed upward, at the wall clock.

I nodded, appreciative of this sliver of kindness, and slumped deep into a bucket seat, backpack on the floor, straps tangled in my feet. I wanted to kick it hard across the room. Maybe I misdialed, or maybe they were in the bathroom or down in the basement where there was no extension. Maybe the phone company had an outage for a minute. I thought about trying again. Because where would they be? We always had Thanksgiving at home; there were out-of-town aunts and uncles and cousins who came, but they came to us, not the other way. I jumped up, hurried back to the phone, the man's eyes tracking me.

The coins were poised at the slot, and I let them go. *Chink, clink,* and that catch of the dial tone. I punched each number deliberately, pausing after the confirming beep, the random pattern of these numbers carved into my memory. I closed my eyes and listened to the ring.

There were two phones in that house, one mounted on the kitchen wall, crossing over the seam where the stripes didn't match. That phone was dull yellow, with a short cord, so you had to sit at the close chair of the kitchen table. Anyone heard what you said when you talked on this phone. The other phone was upstairs in my parents' bedroom; it was no-nonsense black and heavy and sat in the middle of my father's nightstand. A coil of thin cord attached it to the wall, and when you were feeling brave, you could grab that phone and let the cord snake behind as you walked into the bathroom, where you could balance on the edge of the tub for a halfway-private conversation, until he or my mother hollered to hang up already, or someone needed the bathroom, or you imagined you heard the slow creep of footsteps edging the door. That phone gave the illusion of privacy, but it wasn't private. That was the phone my father called my uncle on, threatening to sic his old high school buddy the cop if he ever came around again. "Or maybe I'll kill you myself," he said with slow, practiced calm, "depending on the mood you catch me in." That was the phone my mother used to call my uncle and arrange to meet at First National Bank downtown, so she could withdraw money from Grace's savings account so he could make rent. The day before I ran off to Chicago, I called my uncle on that phone, needing to tell him I was fine, that I was fine, that they said everything worked out fine, though he had no idea why I wouldn't be fine, but some girl named Sandy said my uncle had hitched to New York or New Orleans or somewhere last week and skipped out on rent again and could I... ?

I opened my eyes. Hung up the phone. I took my coins, dug out the last few from my backpack, and plunked them down the vending machine and ate six packages of peanut butter crackers for Thanksgiving dinner, and waited for the bus to Chicago. The man at the ticket counter dozed over his newspaper, chin bobbing above his chest, a light snore now and again. The sleet storm clawed at the large windows overlooking the empty bus bay. I thought about telling this to Jess: my mother's stuffing recipe, Frank Sinatra, the four of us linking hands around the table covered with the embroidered cloth my great-grandmother brought from Luxembourg, each of us listing three things we were thankful for, the buttery crackle of turkey skin, letting Grace win the wishbone battle, my mother dropping one of the yellow rose saucers on the floor but it miraculously not breaking, seconds and thirds on pumpkin pie, and sprawling on the living room carpet rubbing our bellies, all of us laughing at the same nothing.

I thought about my story all morning, waiting for the storm-delayed bus to drag in, and later, slumped in an aisle seat at the back next to a tattered man sniffle-shooting the snot back up his nose every two seconds, and on the el from the bus station while watching a mother half-heartedly joggle an ugly, cow-eyed baby against her shoulder as it squalled, and trudging from the el to the dorm under burned-out streetlights, kicking a dented RC can along the sidewalk; I thought about my story so hard that it became real, and I couldn't wait to tell Jess, who loved best that we were all laughing on the floor even though no one knew what was so funny.

Then Jess told me her story. It sounded about as good as mine, with her mother buying goofy matching turkey aprons for everyone, including her dad, and her sister reading a poem she wrote in school instead of saying boring grace, and Jess rolling out the pie crusts perfectly without any help. A great Thanksgiving, we agreed, great.

V.

Here could be the ending of our story. Which is that place where every story truly begins.

Part III:
The End

THE BEDROOM

(fall, junior year)

Early morning after the night Penny arrived. My neck was kinked, knotted as old-fashioned bakery bread, and my mind half caught in sleep, meandering through flutters of dreams—sitting at a picnic table with knights, chatter about swapping horses so I'd have a white one—and it came to me that I was on the couch. I dragged the pillow over my face, then remembered Penny, and I flung the pillow to the ground and sat up to stiletto jabs in my lower back. Apparently I had become an old lady overnight, and I gently twisted my torso one way, then the other, until the pain eased. The objects in the room were early-morning fuzzy, scribbled into place instead of cleanly drawn; the flurried, pale light in the window was still gray. I stood, thinking I'd pee and then read a chapter of my boring art history textbook until I fell back asleep, but walking out of the bathroom, I paused in the hallway. Jess's perfume. She alternated between Lauren, which I liked, which is what I smelled now, and Bill Blass, which was overly sweet, like cotton candy dissolving into the heavy air of a humid day. When I'd spritzed the tiniest squirt of Lauren onto my wrist from the bottle she gave me for Christmas freshman year, she'd lectured me not to be stingy, to spray two full seconds behind my knees and along the inside of one thigh. *Why only one?* I wondered, but I did as she said whenever I was going out, which made me feel reckless and decadent. I hadn't heard her come in, though I was right there on the couch, and she was a flouncer, not a tiptoer. I stood for a moment, sensing a forced quality to the stillness, as if something was about to make noise but was trying not to.

I stepped to her room and whispered, "Jess?" as I slipped through the door, partway open. It was like plunging underwater through way too much Lauren, and I hacked out a cough. There was Penny, hunched in Jess's desk chair, the tiny seashell lamp switched on to the lowest setting. She jumped up, dropping a cassette case onto the desk, mumbling a fast "sorry" at the clatter. Jess's makeup—silvery cases of Clinique, the pale green "bonus gift with purchase" samples she was addicted to getting for "free" from Marshall Field's—was heaped on the desk, with a tattle-tale smear of Raspberry Glacé ringing Penny's mouth, Jess's favorite color. The tube was rolled open, revealing the groove worn by Jess's lips, and I felt as though something very intimate was exposed. This moment should have been like catching a naughty three-year-old at play, something simple. It wasn't. Nothing about Penny felt playful, and I had the sense that she knew exactly what she was doing.

I waited for her to explain, but she remained silent, rubbing Kleenex across her mouth, smudging the lipstick into a pink shadow. She balled up the used tissue in her fist. "Over there," and I pointed to Jess's wicker basket for trash that she was forever emptying, irritated by any accumulation of garbage. Her makeup in a jumble would drive her crazy.

"I'm fine," Penny said.

One of Jess's composition books of lists was spine-up on the bed, opened flat, next to a handful of loose papers. I guessed Penny had been reading it. "You shouldn't be in here," I said. I tried to balance my voice exactly into the kind sternness of an elementary school teacher. *Her mother just died horrifically,* I reminded myself, *and her father dumped her here because there was nowhere for her to go. It's a world with a random murderer.*

"This is Jess's room," she said.

I nodded, pushed the door all the way open. Anyone else would have skulked out, embarrassed to be caught. Penny remained standing, one hand on the chairback, her leg bent so her foot was propped up against the inside of her knee like a stork, an uncomfortable pose to hold, but she seemed unbothered. She wore an oversized R2-D2 T-shirt with holes at both shoulder seams and white tube socks with red stripes bunched around her ankles. Her hair was lumpy, and I wanted to smooth it for her, to wipe off the rest of that lipstick with a damp washcloth and Vaseline.

She pointed at one of the framed photographs on the desk, Jess and her mother posing with cheeks pressed together at the top floor of the Hancock building, a view of tiny Chicago buildings behind their shoulders. I had taken that picture; her mother had invited us to Water Tower Place for lunch and shopping. Jess had bought red flats at Marshall Field's after trying on a dozen different shoes; on the way back, she said she planned to return them right off the el at the Evanston Field's, that she bought them only to make her mother happy, that the only thing that made her mother happy was shopping and spending her father's money as fast as he could make it, which I didn't know how to respond to. Penny asked, "That's her mom?"

I nodded.

"She's pretty," but the way she said it, I knew she didn't think so. I guessed her mother was prettier, younger, bolder, less nervous, more independent—all those qualities men want in their girlfriends but that get siphoned out after girlfriends become wives. Then I realized I knew who her mother was because her photograph was on the news last night before we left for the movie; she was the pretty secretary. Bright eyes, high cheekbones, wild blond Stevie Nicks hair, kind of like Penny's. Thinking back, her left side had been sliced off in the picture, as if someone—Jess's father?—had been cropped out. This whole other life he had, now crashing into this one. "And who's he?" Penny asked, pointing to another photograph: Jess and Tommy lying entangled on a blanket at the lakefront, Jess in linen shorts that needed to be ironed before every wearing, cute white tennis shoes, and perky socks. Jess thought her legs looked good in that picture and said that was the reason she kept it on her dresser. I pretended to believe her.

I facedowned the photograph. "We don't like him anymore," I said.

"He looks like one of those guys you think you like but who ends up being a big huge jerk," she said.

"Something like that," I said.

Penny said, "I liked a super-awful guy last year who told everyone he got to second base with me when he hardly didn't even barely get to first. Stupid Greg Tomlinson."

I said, "My advice is stay away from boys until you're like twenty-five. Even then, they're always trouble."

"Is that what you do?" she asked. "Do you have a boyfriend?"

"Not exactly," I said. "You should go back to bed." I yawned widely, first fake, hoping she would follow, then for real.

Penny pointed to the composition book. "In her diary she says she wants to marry a rich guy. Is that guy rich?"

"Put that back where you found it," I said. "You know you shouldn't read other people's private things."

"It's the only way to find out anything worthwhile when you're just a kid," she said. "Right?"

Of course she was right, but I kept my lips pressed in a tight line. I went over and snapped shut the composition book. "Where does this go?" I asked, though I knew: between the mattress and the box spring. My hands shook a tiny bit, I don't know why, so I folded my arms across my chest, very schoolmarmish.

"Guess what she wrote about you," Penny said.

"Stop it." Our eyes met in a staring match that I knew I would win, and I did, and she pointed to the bed: "Under the mattress," and I slid the notebook between the mattress and the box spring, up near the pillow. I straightened the comforter, pulled tight the sheets. I would know if Jess had written about me, and she hadn't. At least, not last time I looked.

"She's worried about you," Penny said.

"I'm the one letting you stay here," I said. "Maybe remember that."

"I just want to know her," she said. "She's my sister."

The iciness of that word, spoken with crystal enunciation. Maybe that was the moment I stopped trusting her, though of course what she said was true. *Sister*.

She grabbed the cassette off the desk, flipped open the case, which was empty. "We both like Blondie and the Police and U2—*Boy*. And that ticket stub from the Stones on her bulletin board for the Tattoo

You tour? How awesome is that? I was dying to go, but my mom said I was too young even though like all my friends were there."

"Blondie is mine," I said. "She borrowed it." Not really, but I didn't want Penny thinking she knew it all just because here she was snooping around Jess's room, reading Jess's book of lists and slapping on her lipstick.

Penny said, "Every time I fall asleep, I dream about my mom and she's telling me to go get her the Tylenol. In the dream I say no." She dropped the stork pose, thunking her foot back on the floor, then tugged at her socks, pulling them as high as they would go. She looked dorky-sweet, like a foreign exchange student on the first day of school. It was hard to know what to think of her, the snoopy sneak and just a little girl all wrapped up together, and I had to remind myself I had decided not to trust her. As if she knew what I was thinking, Penny quickly said, "Did you see the Stones with Jess?" She smiled, suddenly conversational, interested, as if we were cousins passing gravy down the table at family Thanksgiving.

"I don't remember," I said.

"Don't remember!" She shook her head like I had to be insane. "The Rolling Stones! Come on."

Of course I remembered that I didn't go. Tommy got great tickets from a scalper, and he asked Jess if she'd mind if he went with a friend instead of her since she didn't even like the Stones. Then he asked me if I wanted to go. *Who would ever know?* he said; it was Rosemont Horizon, the place was huge, and... the Stones! My favorite, which I didn't know he knew. I could tell Jess that I was going with one of the dopes from my poetry workshop, some guy who was trying to impress me with a big-deal date. It was a stupid and dangerous plan—I couldn't even imagine Tommy in public, me in public alone with Tommy; what we would talk about, whether we would hold hands—but I said yes because that's how much I wanted to see the Stones, and when I told Jess I was going, in the next breath she told me that probably she should go with Tommy after all. "I'm not leaving room for Sydney Moore to squeeze her fat ass back in," she said, and I told her she was paranoid and possessive and hyper-jealous and all that—dumping on her so much that she smirked and said, "Why are you so worried?" and I shut up. So I had to dress like I was going to a concert, leave to meet my imaginary guy, who wasn't picking me up, which was a whole huge lie of an explanation that made Jess lift her eyebrow in scorn. I named him Jake from reading *The Sun Also Rises* for the first time, and then I rode the way-out-there lines of the el for hours, because I couldn't think where else to go where absolutely no one I knew would see me. The next day I relived the concert with her, how great it was and how Mick was hot for an old guy and which songs were best, listing them out in her notebook, screwing up when I said "Wild Horses," which she couldn't remember them playing, and I said, "I meant, I just like that song." I remembered all that, and the flares of confused excitement when Tommy first told me he got the tickets for us, my mind flashing first on what to wear and then on his Porsche, but not on Jess. I told myself not to feel those edges of happiness ever again about anything he said to me, because that wasn't what we were about. It was like the time some guy Magic Markered on my dorm room message board, outside my door, "You make a dead man come," signing, "Cheerio, Mick Jagger," in a flourish, and I was proud, pretending to forget to erase it, though I knew I was supposed to be offended.

Penny was walking around the room now, rubbing her feet into the black shag throw rug as if she wanted to collect Jess's static electricity into her body. She fingered the Marimekko bedspread with the primary red flowers, brushing her palm along the needlepoint throw pillows of rabbits and goldfish and irises that Jess's mother had stitched during a phase when she was heavy into needlepoint. Even I got my own pillow of leaves vining around acorns because there were so many pillows stuffed into closets at Jess's house; she would have given me a dozen more, but Jess told her to stop, that it was embarrassing. I should have corralled Penny out, herded her back into my room where she could touch all my stuff, which would take about two minutes. And yet I understood. Sometimes I went into Jess's room when she was gone, just looking at her things, maybe trying to understand why she was who she was and why I was who I was. As if having a Marimekko bedspread—which is what I learned was also on my freshman roommate's bed—was an explanation. For a while, I was saving money, planning to buy one for myself, but when I thought it through, I understood that even if I had the comforter, I wouldn't have the Lanz of Salzburg flannel nightgown for frigid nights, and if I had the nightgown I wouldn't have the Top-Siders, and if I had the Top-Siders (which, actually, I did have—three dollars at a thrift store), then I would need the Fair Isle sweater in blue, and if I had it in blue, I would need it in pink and cream and heather... that there was no end to wanting and needing and imagining that just one more thing would be *the* thing, one more sweater, one more kiss, one more boy, one more anything. That endless yearning, that empty hunger, even when I knew it wasn't sweaters I wanted (though also, actually it was). It was to not care how many sweaters I had; it wasn't a number, but a word: "enough." And that word was impossible, it seemed to me.

Even so: the ritual of looking at Jess's room was like studying a place of completion, standing in the doorway to stare through a day-dreamy haze, not necessarily registering each item specifically, but admiring the tableau, like the picture of a jigsaw puzzle on a card table: not one piece missing. So pleasant, the way it was pleasant to be alone in a room in a museum, surrounded by walls of important paintings, each more perfect than the last, and then another room, and another. And then, here, the same topsy-turvy moment when it turned oppressive, and I was overwhelmed by this airless perfection, and I'd jam my eyes shut to break the spell, and once I was free, I'd tiptoe in and rearrange some small thing: slide a folder from the top of the stack to the bottom or dog-ear a random page in a book. I don't know why this was satisfying. Jess never noticed. But now and then, I thought something felt askew in my own room, and I wondered if she did the same thing when I was out, though I knew she didn't; it was just me hoping she had.

It occurred to me that Penny and I were not very different. Except that she was Jess's sister, and I was Jess's friend. But we were both in a precarious spot.

Penny was studying a framed poster of *Houses of Parliament* that had also hung on Jess's wall freshman year and last year. She touched the glass, circling her thumb around the image, then pushing down hard, purposely leaving an "I was here" print. She shot me a defiant look, as if she expected me to stop her.

"That's a print from a painting by Claude Monet," I said. "The original is downtown, in the Art Institute."

"That building with the lions outside," she said. "We went in school. The teachers kept screaming, 'Don't touch.' I wanted to, though. You know when someone tells you not to, how that makes you want to do it even more?"

"It's just a print," I said. "No one cares if you touch it." I stepped up to the poster and I don't know why, but I pressed my hand flat on the glass, overlaying Penny's thumbprint. Also leaving a definite mark. The glass was cool under my touch. She set her hand next to mine. "Anyone can buy this at the museum gift shop," I said. "Probably like ten bucks or so, without the frame." *Even I could buy this,* I thought, *or something better*; everyone loved Monet so much that I considered him a cliché. All the girls in the dorm taped Claude Monet posters onto their cinder block walls; I had noticed that even before I knew who Claude Monet was.

"I thought art was so special," she said.

"It is," I said. "This is a copy they make for normal people to hang in their house. The real one would cost millions of dollars."

"I thought anything framed was real art," she said. She didn't seem embarrassed to say so the way I would have been. Jess had laughed at me for saying *Mo-nette* instead of *Mo-nay*, for asking if the Houses of Parliament were in New York. After that, I was more careful.

"I touched a painting," I said. "In the museum. I put my hand right on it, right in front of everyone. People around me gasped. Then I got kicked out. But I had to see what it felt like." I felt shy admitting this, I don't know why, and I didn't even know why I was telling her. I knew the no touching rule, but there were so many paintings, and they were so... I couldn't say what they were. Only that there were so many. That had been the first time I went to an art museum, the first time I saw art that was real.

Penny plopped onto the bed, bounced a little, brought her wrist up to her nose and inhaled her scent—rather, Jess's scent. Then she stared up at the ceiling, moved her lips as if counting.

There was an uncomfortable silence. So I sat in Jess's desk chair and sorted the makeup, returning it to the drawer with the plastic divider tray, eye shadows here, lipsticks there. A soothing little task. When I got to the Raspberry Glacé, still open, I sniffed its waxiness, glanced in the mirror at Penny behind me, who tilted her head to watch. So I rolled and capped it and dropped it in the drawer—the last piece of the mess on the desk.

"I should go back to that museum sometime," Penny said. "It's probably better without teachers yelling. Maybe Jess will take me. I want her to like me so bad."

Our eyes met and locked in the mirror. Only a kid would dare express such naked want. She was a kid. Why did I need to keep reminding myself? I was supposed to say something comforting like "She will," but instead I asked, "Did he—did your father talk about her a lot?"

"I only found out this summer," Penny said, "when I heard him telling my mom about Linda being dead in the car crash. My mom was so mad, yelling that he was never supposed to say that name in her apartment, and so right then he got all mad and started screaming, 'Linda, Linda,' just like that, and my mom kicked him out and cried the whole weekend and barfed from drinking the whole bottle of my dad's special Scotch. It was all super horrible, and then I went to the library and found Linda's picture from the newspaper article and it mentioned Jess and Jess's mother and this whole other family besides me and my mom. I thought Linda was just some kid from being married before. I got all sick to my stomach like I was going to barf in the library, so I snuck the newspaper into the bathroom and ripped out the article and brought it home to show my mom. She was like, 'Get that away from me, I never want to see that picture again,' and I couldn't believe she never told me about any of them—because she knew already, she knew everything—and I said, 'My sister who no one ever told me I had is dead,' and she said, 'Those people aren't your sisters and never will be,' and she said it just like that, '*those people*.'" Penny flung herself backward on the bed, staring up at the ceiling.

"Wow," I said.

"I begged to go to Linda's funeral, but she said no and so did he," she said. "He was mad that I found out, and my mom was mad at him and me. I was grounded for a week, with no TV. Everyone was mad at everyone. I was that way of being mad where you don't think you can stand another minute, you know? I kept dreaming about Linda, like she was in the room with me, like a ghost, but she never said anything. She just stared at me from her bloody face."

She twisted her fingers nervously. I sat perfectly still. I knew there was more. I knew she wanted to tell me. I even knew what she was going to say.

Penny continued: "I was so mad at my mom, the maddest I've ever been in my whole entire life, for never telling me any of that. Not even one word. I think I was still kind of mad when she died." She gave a little cough, sort of a choking sound, as if trying not to cry. "I was the one who gave her the pills. Me."

"It was an accident," I said. "A crazy, random, horrible thing."

"Is it?" she said. "Even if maybe . . . maybe I was so mad that I secretly wanted her to die?"

"No, you didn't," I said. "No one's really that mad for real. Even if they think they are."

"I don't know," she said. After a moment, she added, "Have you ever been that mad?"

Me walking into the living room and there'd be my father, snoring in front of a baseball game on TV, and part of my brain would turn automatic: *Get a pillow from your bed, hold it down, you could do that, five or ten minutes,*" and then I'd walk upstairs and close the door and lean up against it until my heart slowed to normal.

"No," I said. "Never."

Another pause.

I said, "You had no idea about your dad?"

She swung her head wildly, her hair flailing no.

I said, "Well, that's how Jess is right now. She had no idea. This won't be easy."

"But I'm her sister," she said.

"Half sister," I corrected.

"Isn't that still family? Doesn't that count?" She sighed.

"Your dad will be here soon," I said. "You really should try to get some more sleep. And talk to him about all this."

"Think he'll actually show up?" she asked. "Half the time he doesn't, or he's late."

"He said he would."

She sat up, tugged again on her socks, first up, then down, unable to settle. "After they didn't let me go to Linda's funeral, I cracked his car windshield with the hammer out of our junk drawer. He doesn't know it was me."

"You shouldn't have done that," I said, giving the expected response because I was supposed to be an adult. Secretly, I thought it was the sort of thing I would want to do and, actually, probably was what Jess would do, not that I was going to say so. I moved over and sat on the bed next to her. "Or if you really can't sleep, I think there's cereal. Special K."

"That stuff's gross."

"I know," I said. "But it's the only cereal Jess eats."

"All I want is for her to like me," Penny said. I imagined that sentence circling her brain for these past months, round and round, gathering speed, ready to explode and shatter glass.

"I know," I said, and accidentally added, "Me too," which apparently Penny interpreted as me saying that I also wanted Jess to like *her*, because she leaned in and gave me sort of a hug, and a sort of murmur that might have been thanks. Which I suppose I did also mean, sort of, maybe. But mostly, I meant what I always meant when I thought about Jess: that I wanted Jess to like *me*. Which—maybe surprisingly—I never viewed as being in opposition to what I was doing with Tommy in the library. I suppose I imagined I was saving her from him, giving him the outlet and helping her; she thought blow jobs were disgusting, he had told me, and yet he wanted them, so I provided them. It made sense. That's what I told myself.

Or I suppose I imagined that the splinters of my life could remain separate because they always had. Seeing what happened to Jess's father had shaken me, but I knew that if I were him, confronted with the abrupt reality of Penny, I would have found a way, something all his money could handle or maybe another person to take her in, or, really, I would have taken care of it from the very, very beginning and that pregnancy test coming up positive. I knew, now, that he wasn't as tough as I was. Probably no one was as tough as I was. What I had done, been willing to do: that was how much I wanted to be here, had to be here. There I was, sitting on Jess's bed, reveling in my tiny bit of superiority, knowing I would never let myself get caught.

Penny was talking: ". . . going to get a print and have it framed. And then I'm going to—" and there was the click of a key in the back door and I said, "Crap," and jumped from the bed and grabbed Penny's wrist and said, "Shh..." and Penny snatched something off the pile of papers on the bed as I scooped them up, and Penny whispered, "Top desk drawer." I jammed the handful in there, hoping the back door was its usual sticky, stubborn self, and I half dragged, half pushed Penny into my bedroom and saw that thing still in her hand and plucked it away from her, thinking it was the used tissue, but it was a white envelope, folded in half, and I knew exactly what that was; I had been there when Jess had pulled off the ring and dropped it into the envelope, and I wanted to shake Penny so her teeth rattled like maracas, but all I said was "Jesus Christ, what are you doing with this?" and shoved the envelope into my underwear, at my hip, until I could sneak it back into Jess's room, and I closed my bedroom door just as the back door opened and there was Jess, startled to see me.

"What are you doing up?" she asked. Black mascara striped the skin under her eyes, which was puffy and pink.

"Couldn't sleep," I said.

"Join the club," she said. "My shitty father. I don't want to talk about it. Ever. He's a shit. All men are shits."

My blanket and pillow were on the couch, and if she saw, she'd ask why I was sleeping out there. I stood in the hallway and leaned, hoping to block the easy view through the cutout between the two rooms.

"I came for my stuff," she said. "I'm staying with my mom for a few days. She's a mess."

"Okay," I said. "I'm sorry. Is there anything... ?"

"If my dad calls..." She looked around suddenly, as if she were a dog catching an interesting scent. The room reeked of Lauren. I couldn't remember if we had put away the cassettes. The flipped-over photo of Tommy. Handprints on the glass.

"If your dad calls?"

"Tell him to go to hell," she said. "Tell him to find somewhere else for that girl to stay. Tell him that girl can go to hell, too."

"Her mother died," I said. "Don't you maybe think—"

"Yeah, and I hope her mother's in hell right now, too." Jess spoke loudly, as if aware that someone else might be listening, needing to make her message heard. She stood with her arms folded, dissatisfied, but after a moment, she swirled into her bedroom, and I tiptoed into the living room and tucked the sheet up under the blanket so at least she might believe a story about me falling asleep watching TV or something under a blanket. Then I sat at the kitchen table, too nervous to do anything else, but it felt awkward and weird to just sit, so I poured out Special K into a bowl and started eating it with my fingers—I preferred it that way; back in Iowa we ate tons of dry cereal since lots of times there wasn't milk—and listened to the bangs and scrapes of Jess pulling open drawers and sliding hangers in her closet. I willed Penny to shut up, not trusting at all that she would.

The envelope was tickling my skin, so I took it out of my underwear and opened it. There was the ring, the big, beautiful, expensive ring. I slid it on my ring finger. What if I showed up at the library wearing this ring? What would Tommy say, it glinting as I unzipped his jeans, the feel of the metal as I took his cock in my hand? The diamond felt heavy. Hard to imagine how much money it had cost. Jess hadn't told me, and I had known not to ask directly. To some ways of thinking, it could just as easily be mine.

Suddenly Jess shrieked, "Who was in here? Where's the ring? Where's the goddamn ring?" and my stomach knotted and a bad taste rose up along my tongue. The silence that followed was so heavy that I couldn't know if what I heard was real or not when Penny shouted, "I was only looking." Jess's scream was like nothing I had heard before, like something being slaughtered. And just like that, Penny was real.

Jess accused me of betraying her. There was more. That I should mind my own fucking business, and maybe I looked shocked because she shouted, "That's right, I'll say 'fucking' any fucking time I want." There was more. And more. And more. It all happened in maybe ten minutes, maybe less. I told myself not to remember the words, that words weren't actually important. Maybe I said, "I'm just trying to help a little girl whose mother died." Maybe she said, "Help your own sister, why don't you?" Maybe I remember it all.

I know that I closed my eyes, and I saw that painting I had touched in the museum: *The Bedroom* by Vincent van Gogh, a picture of a bed with a red spread and two chairs and pictures hanging on the blue walls, the bright paint thick like frosting, streaks and rows dancing across the canvas, so much paint, colors I had never experienced before. There was a semi-open window in this bedroom, which is where my eyes had jumped immediately, and looking long enough, as I did, it was clear the air outside the window smelled like something indescribable and beautiful, and there was a bird chirping madly, and that someone could lie for hours across that red bedspread and time would slow, then stop, then disappear. However crazy it was—and it *was* crazy, because it was only a painting, the exact same painting a dozen people behind me were staring at right then—I thought that if I could be there, inside that cozy little room for even just a minute, everything in my life would be perfect. I guess that was why I touched it, and also that was why buying a postcard or a cheap poster afterward couldn't possibly ever be enough.

GIVE THE LADY WHAT SHE WANTS

(winter, sophomore year)

In an ideal world, Jess's mom said she would see Jess at *least* once a week. In an ideal world, Jess said she would see her mom at *most* once a month. They didn't say these things to each other, but to me, separately. I didn't ask, they volunteered, each using the words "in an ideal world." This happened on the same day, when Jess's mom met us at the big Marshall Field's department store downtown for shopping and lunch. It was early February, and Jess hadn't told her parents about dating Tommy, so she warned me to keep quiet. But she wanted a new dress for Valentine's Day that would knock his socks off. "Or better yet, his pants," she said.

I was invited last minute, because Linda dropped out, claiming shopping was bourgeois, an opiate for the masses like TV and sports. "She's stopped washing her hair," Jess's mom reported, "and now it's baking soda instead of Crest like a normal person. She says she's not going to college, she's moving to Vermont to make yogurt out of goat milk, or maybe it was spin yarn out of goat hair. Who can keep up?"

We were at lunch in the Walnut Room on the seventh floor, where we'd gone straight off because Jess's mother said she needed coffee, but she ordered a glass of white wine. Jess and I had Tab. Jess ordered a chef's salad with oil and vinegar dressing, and her mother started out talking about salad but switched to chicken pot pie. They told me I had to try the Marshall Field's special sandwich so I did. I was hoping toothpicks with those frilly cellophane tips came jabbed into it, which wasn't very sophisticated, but they reminded me of Grace.

She loved them, and maybe I was thinking about her, her face through the window twisting into sadness as I boarded the Greyhound after Christmas break, and how on purpose I plunked into an aisle seat.

"Who cares?" Jess said, about her sister. "Let her hang out with stinky goat lovers. Probably be good for her to move away."

"No one's moving to Vermont," Jess's mother said. "That's too far."

We were seated at a round table for four, smack in the middle of the room, which reminded me of a historic mansion, with stately ribbed pillars and a dizzyingly high ceiling. Jess said there was a forty-five-foot Christmas tree every year where the marble fountain was, which I hadn't believed until now that I was scrunched here, feeling tiny. The walls were heavy oak paneling, and the tablecloths were crisply white, with cloth napkins, and soaking up any clatter was thick red carpet with twining flowery shapes. We sat in plush-bottomed chairs with wooden arms where the varnish was still shiny and unchipped. Everything felt like it cost a lot of money. I sat opposite the empty chair, imagining Linda there instead of the pile of coats, our eyes latching, both of us thinking, *Bourgeois,* at the same time; or imagining Linda here instead of me, Linda glaring quietly as Jess picked at her salad and Jess's mom peeled off and ate the top crust of her chicken pot pie, leaving the rest, Linda hissing that there were starving kids in some African country no one had ever heard of. Linda watching Jess's mom order a second glass of white wine, explaining the first one tasted off (though she drank it anyway); Linda *not* nodding yes when the waitress asked if she liked the special sandwich and its ladles of Thousand Island dressing, *not* shaking her head no to dessert because Jess did. And then lunch was over, and it was time to shop, and a knot twisted my stomach.

Jess's mother spent a lot of her time shopping, which I didn't understand could be a thing people spent time doing in real life. I thought it was something women did in TV shows and movies because showing what women did in real life would be boring. I had been shopping with her two or three times with Jess. She liked getting a couple of salesgals (that's what she called them) to roam the racks, scooping up dresses in different sizes and colors, parading them to the dressing room, where she tried on everything in a bustling rush, swishing behind curtains, then marching out to pose on the platform in front of the three-way mirror. That was what she loved most about shopping, it seemed, stepping onto that platform and staring into the mirror, examining every angle, every side, twisting her torso to admire and castigate. As much as she loved that, she loved even more when Jess was up there. "Turn around, lovey," she'd say, "those pants look loose; how many fingers can you squeeze in the waistband?" She was always jumping up to tug some part of the garment lower or higher or to the side, demanding that Jess bend forward to see if the V-neck "gave the world a free show" and telling Jess to raise her arms or hunch her shoulders forward. "Your butt looks too big," she would say, or "Your boobs are too small for that sweater," or "Your neck isn't long enough." She knew the Marshall Field's tailors by name and snuck them an envelope of tip money; "Every gal's best friend is her tailor," she'd announce to anyone listening, "you want that perfect fit." She didn't rummage the sale racks like I did and wouldn't buy anything just because it was marked down 80 percent; "It's no bargain at any price if it doesn't fit." She'd say that about a hundred times, tacking on, "Good fit is everything." And her favorite was: "To feel good, you've got to look good." The shopping trip ended at the make-up counter, where she'd finagle free makeovers that weren't free, because afterward she'd buy a bagful of creams and eye shadows and powders.

The thing was this was all annoying. Annoying to watch. Annoying to think about. All this fussiness and bossiness and so much money spent. Good fit *wasn't* everything. My guess was that Linda didn't like it either, not if in her ideal world, she was making goat milk yogurt. But Jess didn't seem to mind. It was the only time she wanted to see her mother, when shopping was involved. Sometimes she'd get off the phone and groan, "My mother wants to go to a movie with me on Sunday afternoon... can you imagine? The horror, the horror."

"It's so horrible to sit next to her in a dark theater?" I asked once. "Or is eating popcorn the horrible part?"

"Haha. The movie part's fine, but it's the 'let's talk about the movie,' the 'let's grab a bite.'" Jess made fluttering, chatty mouths with both hands. "Blah, blah, blah. All that work, finding the right things to say to her. At least with shopping, I end up with new clothes."

Today we were looking for a dress for Jess's mom to wear to someone's daughter's wedding at the country club, someone Jess's mom called "new" in a pinched voice, which I interpreted to mean the dress had to be show-offy. At lunch she announced that Jess and Linda were invited to the wedding, and Jess said, "No way, that's during finals," and her mom rolled her eyes and said, "Fine. Help me pick out something for Linda then," and she eyed me and said, "You're her size, aren't you?" and I said, "I guess so," because she had decided I was.

So we followed a trail of escalators to the floor with the fancy dresses, and Jess's mom got us one of the dressing areas in its own alcove and corralled a herd of salesgals, sending them on their mission of finding a tasteful cocktail dress for her—"maybe Calvin Klein or Calvin Klein–like, or Halston or Halston-like; think simple, clean lines with a little pizzazz," and a thousand more adjectives—and something for me playing the role of Linda, maybe in lavender or light blue; "She won't wear pink," Jess warned, so her mom added, "No pink. Nothing little girly, but not too grown-up either... she's still my darling little baby!"

Bobbie—the primary saleswoman working with us, a bouncy blond lady with lots of mascara who jerked her head in one hard nod to punctuate everyone else's sentences—said, "Periwinkle is great for you," and I said, "It doesn't matter because the dress is actually for her daughter who can't be here today. I'm just filling in since we're the same size," and Bobbie did her series of nods as if this all made sense, and Jess's mom said to me, "Maybe you need a nice dress for yourself? For a fraternity formal?" and Jess said, "Stop it, Mom. She can buy a dress or not," and Bobbie flashed an exaggerated wink and said, "We'll pick some things, just to see. Who doesn't want to admire herself in a pretty dress?" and Jess explained that what she needed was the slinkiest floor-length black dress they had, "one that shows off boob and leg, so high slits and a low, super-plungey neck," and her mom sighed and she and Bobbie exchanged looks under waggling eyebrows, with Jess's mom signaling an embarrassed apology, and Bobbie sending back sympathy about girls today and the complexities of daughters. "We have some great new looks for spring, so let's start there," Bobbie said, her voice as bright as a flashlight beam, and she hustled off, waving one hand at a couple of younger girls, roping them in.

"What's Dad doing today?" Jess asked.

"Something about taking in his car," Jess's mom said. "I don't know. That car's in the shop more than it isn't. He's getting to be quite the regular down there. He sends his love."

"No, he doesn't," Jess said.

"He most certainly does!"

"I just mean that, yeah, he loves me," Jess said. "But he didn't specifically say to you, 'Send Jess my love.' He never says things like that, so why do you pretend he does?"

"He says things like that all the time," Jess's mom insisted. "Honestly, Jessica."

"Okay, sure," Jess said. "Then you tell him I send my love right back." She flashed me a mocking imitation of Bobbie's exaggerated wink right as Bobbie walked back with three black dresses. Her face flushed, but otherwise she pretended not to notice, of course, and smiled hugely as she passed the hangers to Jess. "Hop right in that dressing room, dear," she said, and Jess ducked into a little room cordoned off with heavy, Walnut Room–ish drapery. Jess's mom and I sat side by side on a tufted bench near the big three-panel mirror. I felt like a member of an audience.

"I want to see those dresses on," Jess's mom called. "I don't want you looking trashy."

"Oh my god," Jess said.

I smiled at Jess's mom because I didn't know what to say. Jess never looked trashy, but also she wouldn't want to ever look like anyone's darling little baby either. Jess's mom checked her watch, which was slim and gold with tiny diamonds at twelve, three, six, and nine. Linda was right; shopping was bourgeois, though I had never heard anyone say that who had enough money to get clerks running around. I wondered what Linda was doing instead. That seemed safe to ask, but when I did, Jess's mom said, "Probably rolling out of bed. I swear, she'd sleep all day if we let her. Maybe she should, since she's a growing girl, but her father is always at her to set an alarm clock and show some responsibility. Early bird gets the worm and all that."

"Who wants a worm anyway?" Jess called out. There was the sound of rustling, a zipper.

"Birds do," Jess's mom said.

"Is she still flunking English class?" Jess called.

"Shhh!" Her mom looked around; we were in our own alcove, sure, but around us were other dressing rooms and mirrors and mothers and daughters sitting on tufted velvety benches. "Keep your voice down, Jessica, if you don't mind. We're not in a barnyard."

"Well, is she?" Jess stage-whispered.

"The teacher says she needs at least a B-plus on next week's test on *Hamlet*, though I don't think she's even read it," Jess's mom said, slightly leaning away from me. "It's going to be summer school, what with the math and all those absences in biology. And gym class. She just doesn't go. All she has to do to pass is show up, and she won't."

"'If I only had a brain,'" Jess sang out.

If I only had a heart, popped into my head, but I didn't dare say it in front of Jess's mom, though I was sure Jess would laugh.

"Your sister is plenty smart," Jess's mom said. "She just needs..."

"Let's see if any colleges think so next year." Jess sighed dramatically. "It's so very, very hard being the good daughter, loved by all, including English teachers. 'To be, or not to be... that is the question.'"

Jess's mom's face turned bright red. "Let me see that dress," she said. "I'm not paying for anything I don't see." She glanced over at me and mouthed a word that looked like "sorry," though I wasn't sure what she was apologizing for when Jess was the obnoxious one. Bobbie had busied herself sorting a rack of dresses, waiting to be returned to the sales floor. I suppose good salespeople knew how to pretend they weren't listening.

"Don't like it," Jess said. "Neckline for a nun."

Her mother sighed as two of Bobbie's girls returned, arms loaded with dresses for the three of us, and there was all that to sort out, Bobbie nodding after every opinion Jess's mom offered, and I was sent to a dressing room with a Linda-might-like-this stack and a you-might-like-this stack. I didn't have to lift a price tag to know that I wasn't wasting time with that second stack. Jess's mom slipped into her own curtained room, and a certain relaxed silence settled as we shed garments, flung clothes we didn't have to hang up properly, tugged carelessly at zippers and buttons, wanting to see only how good we looked and that the fit was perfect.

Bobbie chattered away squirrelishly—did we need other sizes? did we need heels? her friend at the costume jewelry counter could set us up, and on and on. It was like Jess's mom had wound her up and she'd keep running until we bought dresses and left, and I felt that pressure building, the question of who would outlast the other, Jess's mom, who had to try on everything in the store, or Bobbie, who had to compliment something every two seconds.

The plan was that if we liked something, we'd gather at the big mirror to consult. But I had no idea what Linda might want to wear: Puffy sleeves? Who liked puffy sleeves except five-year-olds? A high waistline? Or too much like the girl on my *Pride and Prejudice* paperback? I liked asymmetrical hems... would Linda? Jess's mom complained at lunch that all Linda ate anymore was peanut butter sandwiches cut diagonally, so I decided to assume yes on the asymmetrical hem and said, "This might work," and left my curtained room to step onto the platform. Naturally Bobbie over-gushed that I looked stunning, and she handed me sample black pumps, simultaneously frowning at my brown knee socks and keeping up the nervous-tic nodding. The dress was simple, so maybe a leftist high schooler flunking English and skipping gym wouldn't mind it: crooked hem, severely straight neckline, dropped waist, royal blue. Not a boob dress or a leg dress, but if I saw someone wearing this dress, I wouldn't mind meeting her.

Jess's mother emerged from the cocoon of her dressing room, wearing a raw silk suit with a simple, straight cut. "That looks great," I said, as Bobbie nodded, hands clasped rhapsodically against her chest.

"It's all wrong," she said. "But let's look at you."

I stood on the platform, wobbly in the wrong-sized pumps, and she prodded and poked and pulled as if I were a Barbie doll. She and Bobbie debated the cut of the hemline, which Bobbie called "fresh." She told me to lean forward to make sure the neck didn't gape, which it didn't, and she rubbed the fabric between her finger and thumb and scrunched it in her fist to see how badly it would wrinkle. Then she hiked up the skirt, digging for the care tag, which made her brow furrow. She never once flipped over the price tag. Then Jess came out in her regular clothes. "I hated them all," she said, and Bobbie shooed the minions back out to the floor for another round (the third? the fourth?) of black dresses. "Actually," Jess said. "I don't know about Linda, but this dress looks good on *you*. Minus the knee socks."

"Huh," Jess's mother said, stepping back to assess. Her eyes narrowed, making it hard to know what she was thinking. I stood very still as I pretended to look at myself in the mirror.

"It's a great dress," I said. "I'd love if my mom came home with this for me." Fat chance of that ever happening, which I didn't mention.

"Linda doesn't love much of anything these days," Jess's mother murmured.

Jess said, "Good luck even getting her to that wedding." And she sighed, her lips screwed up in a tiny grimace in the mirror that her mother acknowledged with a slight nod.

Bobbie stood by silently, her eyes roving to other dressing rooms, to other women, to less problematic places.

"Probably I should just take you to the wedding," Jess's mom said to my reflection, with a gloomy little laugh.

I looked at the three mes in the mirror, front, side, other side. I lifted my arms above my head, then lowered them, as Jess's mom directed, imagining myself at the country-club wedding, sipping champagne from a crystal flute, gossiping as we stood side by side in the ladies' room slicking on lipstick, complaining how banquet fillet was always overcooked, which was something Jess's mom had said at lunch, that she "just knew" the menu would be surf and turf because it was most expensive, though "everyone" agreed the club did a much better job with the prime rib. "Hahaha," I would go in my new bubbly laugh when something was meant to be funny, and I'd exclaim, "No, really?" in a pert voice at the end of the story. I'd know which fork when. Everyone would think I was the one supposed to be there all along. Someone would call my smile dazzling.

"It's a nice dress," Jess said, sidling in close to her mother. "Any-one would like it, even dopey Linda. And what you've got on, Mom, is fantastic. Look at your own gorgeous self in the mirror. You look totally thin."

I stepped down, and Jess's mom stepped up in her own heels and hose; she wasn't dumb enough to wear knee socks. The gold watch with diamonds glinted along her wrist—"Never leave your good jewelry in the dressing room," she reminded us at lunch, as if I had good jewelry to worry about—and her hair wasn't at all mussed from dresses going on and off. She rubbed her lips together and examined her reflections. I didn't know what she was seeing, because she quick-ly frowned and stepped away, saying, "This ivory washes me out. No. Absolutely not."

Several more black dresses arrived for Jess, and she returned to her dressing room with them, and Jess's mom told me to set aside the dress I was wearing, that I was being extraordinarily helpful. Then the three of us tried on a hundred more dresses, or what felt like a hundred more dresses, always with something wrong: too young, too old, too short, too long, too chalky, too blah, pouf in the wrong place, not enough of a waist, cuffs on the sleeves when there shouldn't be or no cuffs when there should be, too bright, too drab, gold buttons not silver, buttons not a zipper, a zipper that looked cheap, too scratchy along the neck, too tight, too loose, too wrinkly, too poochy, "no one can carry off pleats," and every other reason why this wasn't the dress—but that maybe the next one would be. It felt like every single dress Marshall Field's sold passed through Jess's or her mom's hands. Bobbie smiled and nodded and tossed out compliments like handfuls of confetti. The man who had started the store was famous for saying, "Give the lady what she wants," and Bobbie was following those di-rections to a T.

"It's so hard to find the perfect fit," Jess's mom said, and Bobbie agreed, telling Jess's mom that she had a very sophisticated eye.

Finally, there was a black dress Jess liked that her mom agreed wasn't trashy, and there was a long conversation about control-top hose, and Bobbie had suggestions about which brands she preferred and so did Jess's mom and so did Jess. I pretended to be sad when I told Bobbie that none of the dresses in the pile for me had worked, unfortunately, and when I handed them to her, she had to know I hadn't even tried them on; they weren't rumpled like Jess's discards. Bobbie smiled brightly and perked out, "That's a darn shame," and Jess's mom called, "Better to go home with nothing than something not perfect," and I expected Bobbie to nod her usual staccato of agreement, but she let out a tiny, accidental sigh instead, because of course my going home empty-handed wasn't at all better for Bobbie, who probably worked on commission, whose time was ticking away with us.

Jess plopped next to me on the tufted bench. "Sorry she's so crazy," she said. "I'd be dying if you weren't here. And Linda totally would freak, which would make my mother panic, and then there'd be all that to deal with." She slumped hard against the wall and did a very dramatic fake-dead-person face with her tongue lolling out. "Literally. I would die. You're saving my life with her, like usual. Keep it up, and you'll replace Linda as precious, beloved daughter numero uno."

I shrugged. "She sure likes shopping, doesn't she?"

"I'm pretty into shopping, but my mom *really likes* shopping lately, like *really* likes it. This is totally bad." Her voice dropped to a whisper. "Bet she doesn't even buy anything today."

There was a short silence. I understood suddenly that Jess's mom was a very unhappy person. The realization startled me, and I looked at Jess guiltily. This seemed like something she should know. When her eyes slid away from meeting mine, I understood that she *did* know already, of course, but that we were pretending she didn't.

Another armload of dresses came for Jess's mom, but none of them worked. Then she told me to try on the dress set aside for Linda one last time, for the final decision. I returned to my dressing room, and as I was changing I heard Jess's mom tell Bobbie to look for one more in the same size. "It fits her perfectly," Jess's mom said, "like it's made for her. Should I offer to buy it? One for Linda, one for her?"

Yes, I thought, but in the abrupt silence that followed, I flipped to no, imagining Jess rolling her eyes, shaking her head, her face tightening as she begrudged me this single dress, this nice thing that could be mine, that her mother could buy as easily as breathing. I didn't even need it. I didn't need it, I reminded myself. I could do without.

I stood exactly still so they wouldn't remember how close I was. Jess's mom said, "Your father can certainly afford a dress for your friend. And he owes me. He owes me whatever I want to buy."

"No," Jess said sharply. "She can buy her own dress if she wants to. Stop it."

"Stop what?" Her mother's voice shook. "Stop trying to be nice?"

Jess mumbled something I couldn't quite hear. Actually, I didn't want to hear. It sounded like "Mom, she's not your kid." Said nicely, not meanly, as if it mattered. Another mumble, then: "Anyway, buying more stuff won't"—something—"you don't"—something. My heart thudded in my ears.

"But this I can fix," her mother said, too loud. "Giving something nice to a girl who dresses like she's been through someone's attic." Rustling, maybe rooting through a purse.

"It's not that simple," Jess said. Or her mom? Suddenly I couldn't tell them apart.

"This one thing is. Just this one thing." And that was Jess's mom. "She has such simple little problems that I can fix if you let me."

Tearful sniffling. The rustling had been for Kleenex. No way could I go out there; plus, did they really think I couldn't hear them? Of course no way could I stay in here either. I imagined the store lights dimming, Bobbie's manicured fingers stabbing through the curtain; "Dear?" she would prod in an understanding, patient voice. I stared at myself in the narrow mirror centered on the wall. The dress washed me out, or it was the lighting, or it was that I felt pale or that I'd caught Jess's mom's infectious unhappiness. Seemed like a hundred years ago I was thinking about frilly toothpicks. I'd never thought of myself as simple, but of course I was.

There was no answer to this problem, letting her buy me the dress or not letting her buy me the dress. No one could be happy now, and anger sparked up: Jess couldn't keep her stupid mouth shut for once. I hadn't even wanted the dress, had I, until I thought it might be mine, until it fit. It was for Linda, Linda's dress, though it felt doomed now, and I lost confidence that Linda would like it or even wear it. Instead the dress would droop limply at the back of a closet, eventually getting jammed into a box for the church rummage sale or the Goodwill, and end up finally mine for five dollars a couple of years from now, out of style and smelling of damp cedar, something old and unwanted trickling down to me.

Bobbie's brisk footsteps came at the same time as her announcement: "That's the only one here in size six. But I've got a girl calling the Field's in Water Tower and Old Orchard, so don't you worry. We'll track down another."

"How kind of you," Jess's mom said. I imagined the fake smile, the glitter of tears framing her eyelashes; Jess's face averted, fumbling in her purse for more tissues, attention lasered on extending that task as long as possible; Bobbie talking down into the carpet, desperate not to lose the sale. I stared into the mirror, at the blurred edges of my figure sharpening into hard, taut focus.

I watched myself slowly reach for the zipper, snaking one arm along my side at my hip, but instead of edging the tab up with a tidy ratchet, I clenched two hands at the bottom of the zipper and pulled the two sides wide, hard, harder, yanking, stretching, and wrenching apart the fabric, splitting the dress along the seam. The relief of it, the simple relief. The dress was ruined. I had ruined the dress. And I had solved the problem, not that I expected to be thanked. "Uh-oh," I called out to the waiting women, making sure to sound appropriately sorrowful.

What happened in the end was that Jess got her slinky black dress and also a couple of polo shirts in spring colors, a red ribbed silk sweater, and a pair of plaid shorts that matched the red sweater. We all got makeovers at the Estée Lauder counter, and Jess's mom bought a gift set of White Linen perfume and powder for herself and a jar of facial scrub for Linda. Jess's mom decided she would drive to Skokie to the Old Orchard Shopping Center next week to pick up Linda's size six on hold, and also see what Lord & Taylor had, and maybe the Field's out there had different stock, so she might as well check there for her own dress. Jess got three pairs of control-top hose to go with the slinky dress and also regular hose, because she complained she was always running hers, but really she didn't like to hand-wash in the disgusting dorm sinks, so she threw away hose when they were dirty but still good. Jess's mom picked up a box of Frango mints for a hostess gift for a card party on Sunday afternoon. We checked the wedding registry and looked at the china pattern the country-club bride had chosen (Westchester by Lenox), which Jess's mom deemed "ostentatious," noting gold edging was overdone and utterly unnecessary, especially inch-wide, pretentious rims like that, and Jess and I said we absolutely agreed. While we were in that section of the store, Jess's mom decided to buy a "darling" tiny oval crystal picture frame, though she laughed that she didn't need it. We trudged into the men's department for dress socks and handkerchiefs, because Jess's dad always could use more of those, and she also bought a navy-blue V-neck sweater that Jess said he'd never wear. On a whim, she led us through the bed and bath shop, picking up a set of green towels on sale. All the things Jess's mom bought got rung up on her Marshall Field's charge card, the bill for which Jess's dad would get in the mail on the fifteenth and for which he would scribble out a check, simply paying the total, without asking if the day had been fun, without asking what all had been bought, without even knowing anything at all about this shopping trip.

After Linda died, I tried not to think about this afternoon and how Linda's absence that day now yawned into a greater, longer, vaster absence. Linda had been the favorite, according to Jess. Now she was gone. Only Jess was left, and a gaping hole, and a family smashed into pieces.

I tried not to think of Jess's mom rolling a silky hem between her finger and thumb, raising a faded T-shirt to her nose to inhale her missing daughter's inimitable scent. I tried not to think about Linda at all, though of course I did, and the clothes left hanging in the closet, the sweaters in the drawer, all of them my size, all of them with the potential to fit me perfectly.

Strategies for Survival #3: Silence

(fall, junior year)

It was cool on campus to talk about the Tylenol killer. Even at the frat parties I still went to, though I was a junior and should have outgrown them. I liked being there, especially alone, standing near the keg or the garbage can of punch, eavesdropping. The things I heard. "That pathetic dork," a girl would say to another, "telling me about his parents' honeymoon in Maui. How dare he think I care about Maui?" Or the girl going a mile a minute to her friend, "My boyfriend, you know, like totally is pissed because I like said Ronald Reagan was cute, you know, like for an old guy. I mean, I know I like said 'for an old guy,' you know." Or the guy who lifted his beer cup and toasted, "Here's to you and me and all the children in Africa!"

Now it was all about the killer on the loose, the murderer among us. Psych majors buzzed importantly with terms like "antisocial personality disorder" and "*DSM-III*." A freshman girl explained that no way was she using Johnson & Johnson baby powder until the killer was caught because nothing was stopping him from contaminating that, too, and her friend said, "You don't eat baby powder," and she said, "We don't know half the ways poison infiltrates." A group of drunk premeds argued about why the capsules contained ten thousand milligrams of cyanide when half a gram would do it: Simple sloppiness or purposeful misdirection away from a scientific suspect? Student government and poli-sci types round-robinned blame on Reagan, the CIA, Cuba, Brezhnev and the goddamn Politburo, the Trilateral Commission, and anarchists. "The Mafia, obviously," a voice behind me murmured, but when I spun around no one was there. Journalism students were certain the cops were protecting someone, but who? The religious studies students pondered the existence of evil.

As for me, I did what I always did at these parties: stand at the keg. Listen to words drift through the idiotic swirl, out from the loop-the-loop of people hammering at what they thought was important. Disappear.

Wait.

At a frat party, it was possible that no one noticed a girl alone for a long time, the single girl—you, me—standing quietly near the keg, until, finally, someone did. Someone would be slightly intrigued—slightly curious about this girl, me, wondering how and why she was standing alone. Someone would observe that this silent girl looked utterly comfortable within the quiet space of herself—of myself. This someone would not be so at ease himself, but he secretly would want to be; perhaps he longed to escape chaos for this coveted silence. The calm of the quiet girl would be noted and envied.

This someone comes early or maybe he comes late, but he always comes, like bills in the mail (my father might say), and as soon as he speaks, you realize the sham of your silence: you aren't comfortable at all. You aren't comfortable in this quiet place—what you are is trapped. And here's the person to rescue you, you think, to rescue me, to rescue the girl standing alone.

He says, "Who do you think did it?"

What about poor, sad Penny, you think, wanting her mother? This wasn't a game. You say, "I bet we never know. Bet he gets away with it. It will end up being the perfect crime."

"No," he says. "No, no. There's no such thing as a perfect crime."

You smile at him. Sweet boy. Sweet, sweet boy. Then you fuck him anyway. I mean, I did. I fucked them anyway.

Strategies for Survival #2: Denial

(fall, junior year)

There was also this. This shard of my life I thought could be kept separate.

I had seen Tommy on the night Penny got dumped off. When he found me at the library, it was the usual. He had seemed morose, almost sulky, taking his sweet time to come, making me work for it, as if seeing my effort was the truest pleasure for him, and afterward he shoved one hand through his hair and suddenly asked how Jess was. Her name was a bomb exploding, and I said, "Fine," a slice of a word, jagged as broken glass, but he said anyway, "Sometimes I feel bad about how it ended with her. I don't want her going through life hating me," and I said, "Don't be obtuse," assuming he wouldn't be 100 percent sure what the word meant, and he laughed, sort of, and said, "You calling me fat?" which was unamusing because it sounded like a question, not a joke, and I despised how easy it was to be right about the things I assumed about him. Then he said, "Seriously. How bad does she hate me? Thinking about her makes me feel goddamn shitty." He slowly tugged his jeans zipper, focusing his eyes on his crotch. The pathetic narcissist. He said, "I could do it all better if we could just start over, you know, a clean slate. I wasn't ready to be engaged, but maybe I am now." I let a pause build, curious, truly and sincerely curious, about what his autopilot brain might decide I'd enjoy hearing next, which was: "And why the fuck isn't she giving me back that goddamn ring? My dad is really on my case about it, so tell her I need it the fuck back."

I said, "That's what you feel shitty about? Jess? A stupid ring? That's all? Not anything else? Not one thing else?"

His body jerked straighter, no more slouching against the sink. It was almost as if light hit his face the exact right way, making him look clever. "She never told you why." A statement, not a question. A pretentious way to speak. Like he was my professor.

"About you at the Theta picnic?" I said. "She tells me everything." Jess and I had overheard two girls in the bathroom at Harris Hall talking about Tommy and Sydney together at some stupid sorority picnic in September. I thought people did that kind of stuff only in 1950s TV shows, but apparently not. She finally dumped him. "Going cold turkey," she announced, "off men forever."

"You really think I'd be caught dead at a Theta picnic?"

"Well, yeah," I said.

"Christ. And you always so smart." He arched his neck backward as if to loosen a kink. There was a small pop. I suddenly felt nervous for no reason. He said, "What it was, what it really was, was I didn't go to her sister's funeral."

My heart clattered. "Me neither," I said. "I didn't even know about it." I dropped into a near-whisper, and so did he: "She told me not to. She told me to stay the fuck in Louisville. That's what she said, exactly that: 'Stay the fuck in Louisville.'"

"Someone sent newspaper clippings," I said. "That's how I found out."

"That's fucked," he said, no more whisper. "Someone tells you to stay the fuck in Louisville, that's what you do, right?"

My reflection in the mirror grimaced. I would have gone, would've hopped on a Greyhound. I would have been there. I imagined myself wearing an old-fashioned but elegant black hat from a thrift store, a wisp of dark netting obscuring my face. Drawing Kleenex out of a velvety black purse and pressing it into the palms of people sitting beside me. The rippling notes of "Amazing Grace," wreaths ribboned with DEEPEST SYMPATHIES, murmurs about God.

I said, "You screwed up. Did you say so to her?"

"Yeah, well, you're so perfect," he said.

Except she didn't even tell me. He turned abruptly, our eyes meeting in the mirror. So unfair how good-looking he was, his easy life. His father had made some phone calls, wrote some checks—like I figured all along—and got Tommy into DePaul law school, a dozen el stops south. Provisional, but in.

She knew I wouldn't have had the money for a bus ticket. She knew me. She was saving me. A kindness. I had to think that. It wasn't true because I never said things like that to her, all direct like, "I don't have the money." But it could be true. I said, "You think that's worse than this?" I waved one arm in a grand semicircle, as if "this" meant nothing more than the hideousness of this poorly decorated bathroom. "It's all bad," I said. "All of it. And you were too at that fucking picnic. People were talking about it. Sydney was talking about it."

"At least Jess told me," he said. "She wanted me there. What kind of friend are you? Speaking of 'all of it.'" He circled his arm, mocking me, indicting me.

I backed away, bumping against the hand dryer that roared on. "Liar," I said, and he said, "You're a slut," as if the thought just occurred to him, and I said, "Then what does that make you?" hoping for enough time to escape, that the door would click shut before he would figure out that there was no equation for him, that me being a slut (and, yes, I was) was irrelevant to who he was. "You're a stupid liar," I shrieked at the door. The childish words echoed across the quiet library, and I was late meeting Jess for the movie and she hated missing the previews, so I leapt into a full-out run, footsteps thumping the carpet, pounding down the stairs, fast. Maybe I ran the whole way.

RECKLESS

(spring, freshman year)

Jess liked to talk about skiing. That's what her family did for vacations, ski down mountains in Colorado. Breckenridge, Vail, Aspen... the names were poetry written in a language foreign to me. I was from Iowa. There was skiing near Davenport, down a largish hill. Someone manufactured the snow. I didn't know what "powder" was, but I knew it didn't get dumped on a hill in Iowa.

"What do you like about skiing?" I asked her in March, when we met for the traditional nine o'clock study break by the vending machines in the library. There were no heating vents in the room, as if someone had decided that keeping us cold meant we wouldn't linger, which meant we'd get back to the books faster. It was a real possibility at this school. We made all kinds of paranoid assumptions. This would be the first year Jess's family wasn't taking a ski trip because Linda's spring break was a different week than ours, which Jess had been complaining about: "Like anyone notices if Linda misses a week of school. Because of her, no skiing for me." When I thought about skiing, I thought about going fast, about being reckless and icy air whipping your cheeks red, and that's what I expected Jess to say, that she liked hurtling down a mountain, flying. She racked up speeding tickets her father yelled about then paid. She walked fast. She talked fast. She was impatient and clawed through ideas fast.

But she didn't mention speed. She looked around like someone might be listening—which no one was, because a thousand different conversations clattered at nine o'clock break, a thousand shrieks of affected laughter—then lowered her voice so I could barely hear and said, "I like that my sister hates skiing. She's afraid, and I'm not. I like being braver than her and people seeing it. "

It felt like she wanted to say more, and I waited because I had never thought about someone purposely going out of their way to feel brave, but she stayed silent. So I asked, "Afraid of breaking her leg or something?"

Jess swirled her arm in a grand yet dismissive gesture. "The big baby. If only it was that because that makes sense, sort of, though no one's breaking their leg on the bunny hill. But no, she's afraid of my father. He does all the hard trails, the black diamonds, double blacks, even the backcountry, and she's always freaking that he's going to die out there, that the ski patrol will have to dig him out. So my mom goes overboard to make Linda feel better, yelling for my dad to slow down, which is crazy. He's really a great skier, everyone says a total natural, especially for someone who didn't grow up in the Alps or whatever. He's not going to die. Linda's just..." She clamped her mouth shut.

I stared at the vending machines, at the line of candy I couldn't buy because I didn't have any money. Right then I was that poor because I had given my roommate everything I had for my half of the phone bill, which still wasn't enough. Jess would have given me quarters— or anything I asked for—but I was sick of asking, pretending to her that I left my money back in the room. I imagined a whole life ahead of me asking, asking, asking.

I waved away the open bag of peanut M&M'S when she wiggled it under my face, offering to share. I smelled chocolate on her breath, peanut under the chocolate. She had accidentally dropped a green M&M on the floor that rolled under the chair opposite her, and now I stared at it when I got angry from staring at the brightly lit vending machine. Dinner had been the pits, *el ranchero*, which I couldn't choke down; it was processed gristle coated with a slick of bland, soupy tomato sauce and a dab of liquid orange cheese. Anyone with sense— and money—would order pizza or go out. I was starving.

"She's also afraid of horses," Jess said.

"Horses are big animals," I said. "And skiing's dangerous. Maybe it's okay to be afraid of those things?"

"It's lonely not having a normal sister." Jess held a red M&M between her finger and thumb, examining it as if it were a jewel. My stomach growled and I coughed as cover-up. But she didn't notice. "Anyway, I'm not afraid of anything," she said. "And neither are you."

"Spiders?" I asked. There had been an incident two nights ago involving a large spider in her dorm room. She woke me up and dragged me over so I could whack it dead with my shoe. I scooped up the carcass with a tissue, which I walked to the bathroom to flush because she didn't want it in her room.

Jess popped the M&M in her mouth, crunched down. That made a loud sound. Even though we were surrounded by people, it felt like we were alone. The overhead fluorescent light flickered oddly and quickly, like a surge. Then she laughed. "I was letting you be brave," she said. "I was letting you earn your keep." Her eyes met mine. Daring me.

There was a moment that felt long to me but maybe not to her. I decided to laugh. "I promise to kill all the spiders for you," I said, though big spiders creeped me out, and I hated smashing something dead only because it wandered up the wall of a dorm room instead of staying put outside.

She shook the last M&M into her mouth. She crumpled the bag and tossed it at the garbage can but missed, so I picked it up and dropped it in the trash. I didn't mind, I told myself.

Strategies for Survival #6: Thinking

(fall, junior year)

When headaches seized me now, I ate baby aspirin. I liked its chalky orange flavor and how my teeth ground the pills into dust. I popped four at a time, or six, or eight or more. They didn't fix my headaches like Tylenol did, but I chewed them up anyway.

The killer was out there running around. That's what everyone said. But it was equally possible that the killer had been mowed down by a city bus or died in his sleep, the sweet stories filling his obituary printed in the same paper calling him a cold-blooded killer in shrieking headlines. He might be the guy on the 11:40 jet to Oslo or the guy who delivered mail. He might be someone's dad, mowing the lawn. Everyone talked about when he would be caught. Talked about "he" and "him." As if women and girls never once might think about murder.

As if women and girls never once might be angry. Or desperate.

As if women and girls never once might scheme out an airtight plan, every detail considered, even, say, a detail like shredding written checklists into a handful of tiny pieces and stuffing some in the neighbor's trash and some at the bottom of a garbage can in the park and flushing the rest down a toilet in a McDonald's on an interstate highway crossing a long, lonely state. As if women and girls never thought this way, never lived a secret life or wondered about revenge.

As if women and girls never stood alone late at night, fingers gripping the edge of a porcelain sink, as they stared down their reflections in the bathroom mirror, letting silent questions accumulate: *Who am I? How did I get here? Now what?*

As if women and girls might never face only one hard choice after another; as if women and girls might never simply get so very, very, very, very, very, very tired of doing nothing, nothing but thinking, thinking round and round in vast loop-the-loops that never ended in a tidy circle—tired of not being allowed to do anything but think and think and think. As if women and girls might never *ACT*.

PRETTY

(fall, junior year)

Did Penny's mom want to be buried or cremated? Buried where? Ashes sprinkled where? A church? A priest? No one knew, Jess's dad told me on the phone. Jess was still down in Oak Lawn with her mother, but she was making at least some classes, because one afternoon I watched her from the bathroom window at my work-study job as she meandered across the plaza. She wore a burnt-orange coat that I hadn't seen before, but that was her walk: kind of jaunty, like a sailor in a movie musical. Two hours after Jess had left on Sunday, a locksmith came to install a deadbolt on the outside of Jess's bedroom door, which would ding our security deposit.

Penny had taken over my bedroom, leaving me on the lumpy couch. We had a routine where we'd wake up around nine and eat peanut butter on toast while *Andy Griffith* reruns played on the TV Jess's dad had bought for Penny that day he took her shopping at Old Orchard. During commercials, she and I chitchatted carefully about Mayberry and its citizens. Penny thought Andy should marry Helen Crump already. Penny wanted Juanita to barge into the courthouse one of these days and demand Barney buy her lunch. Penny said it was really sad that poor Opie was growing up without a mother. "Like me," she said, twisting strands of hair around her index finger. I agreed. I agreed with whatever Penny said during these mornings. We didn't switch on TV news because it was all Tylenol: the task force, the FBI, Mayor Byrne, gray-suited men from Johnson & Johnson and their calm voices.

After I left for my campus job, class, the library, or wherever I had to be, I think Penny watched game shows until Jess's dad showed up, which sometimes he did and sometimes he didn't. He'd drive her to a shrink's office, and there were lawyers and cops and government do-gooders and paperwork and sometimes meetings that involved her that she had to be at and, every so often, a packet of schoolwork that she never cracked open. But in the apartment, it was only TV— *Andy Griffith*, game shows, and, at night, baseball, the kitchen table littered with scribbled scorecards she had drawn on graph paper. Mostly she talked about *Andy Griffith*. She liked that the show was black and white, which surprised me. When I mentioned that eventually it changed to color, she said, "Gross. So Mayberry looked like every other stupid TV town."

Jess's dad said to call him every day at his office. His secretary always patched me through to where he was, even if I was parked on hold for ten minutes. I knew I didn't really have to call just because he told me to, but I was afraid not to. I guess I wondered what he had to say. And I had questions I was too chicken to ask.

First he'd want to know how Jess was, and I'd say she was fine. Then a pause where I would silently hope he wouldn't ask more about Jess and he wouldn't. We'd talk about Penny: Was she eating? Was she sad? Did I think she should get back to school? Had the "goddamn pack of jackals," the reporters, found her? What did she need? He'd given her twenty bucks to give to me for groceries—did she? ("Yes," I lied, so that was a mental note: *Ask her.*) He banged out questions like a hammer. I was surprised how sorry for him I was. Even sorry for him, though, I was still afraid of him.

He never asked anything about me. I wouldn't expect him to.

After the questions would come another, longer, deeper pause I didn't dare interrupt. He would sigh. I imagined him closing a door where he was, or swiveling his chair to face a wall, to tuck his voice deep into a corner. I imagined a priest in a confessional booth feeling as I did, uneasy about what might spill out of this disembodied voice. That's when he would talk about Penny's mom, whose name was Carla, but who was stuck in my head as "Penny's mom." How they met in a bar he went to sometimes in his old neighborhood, where a few people still remembered his Polish grandmother. How Carla drank coffee black and teased him for dumping in a heaping spoon of sugar. She was the nicest woman he ever met; she was an "angel" and a "real sweetheart." The stories should have been better, more interesting and less paint by number (she liked red roses and "pretty moonlight"), but I listened anyway, his voice crackling over the phone, sliding into a hoarse whisper. I was the only one who knew these things about him, about her, about them. It felt powerful to know. Frightening. Important. I felt chosen.

The stories ended when he said, "I'm sorry, goddamn sorry, because I didn't want any of it happening this way," and I would say, "I know. It's okay."

So Wednesday, when I was on a pay phone at the library, instead of hanging up after I promised it was okay, he blurted out, "They released the body," and even though we'd been talking for fifteen minutes and, before that, however many days about Penny's mom, I never thought of her as having a body, ever, but of course she did, and now something had to be done with it.

I jabbed my finger in the coin return, though I'd done that first thing before lifting the receiver. Rarely was money left behind, but just enough times there was, making me imagine living out my whole life checking, just in case.

"Should I bury her?" he was saying. "Or cremate her?"

Another pause.

"What should I do?" he asked.

I understood that wasn't a question he asked, often or ever.

"What should you do?" I repeated. "What do you think she would want?"

"To be alive," he said. "Goddamn it."

A guy wearing a Ghost in the Machine tour T-shirt sidled up to the phone next to mine. His coins jangled down the slot and he punched in a number that he read off folded-up notebook paper. He whistled aimlessly as he waited for someone on the other end to pick up. They didn't, and he hung up, raked a finger through the coin return for his money, and walked away, still whistling. He could have been the killer. It was that unknowable.

I said, "What does Penny want?"

"Ask her," he said.

We both knew I wasn't going to do that, because immediately he said, "Christ. I can't believe this. Why me? Of all the—"

"Bury her," I interrupted. "You can change your mind from that later. But not if she's cremated." Also, which I didn't say, explain *that* to Penny, tossing her mother's dead body into a raging fire.

"There's actual good sense there." He sounded startled. Maybe he'd forgotten I was on the line. Or hadn't expected me ever to say anything useful. I heard a rough knock on the door, and the phone clicked quietly without him saying good-bye or thank you. Jess had told me plenty of times that he hated saying good-bye, that he wouldn't if he didn't have to. He usually just hung up on her, and she said, "It's just how he is, which sucks."

So there was going to be a very small, very private funeral on Saturday morning. I agreed to go because I didn't have an excuse not to, since it was Saturday so no classes and no job. Plus—and the for-real reason—Jess's dad promised me fifty bucks to help with Penny, "babysitting," he called it. I certainly babysat back in Iowa, but that was for like a dollar an hour. "I would go anyway," I told him, which maybe was true, and he said, "She trusts you, she likes you," which also only maybe was true. Penny insisted on no one from school there, no one from her neighborhood. They hadn't heard from the aunt, even after telegrams and phone calls to the embassy of wherever in Africa she was. "They hated each other," Penny told me. "I met her like one time in my life, at my grandfather's funeral. She hugged me, then said it was really a shame my mother was going to burn in hell, because I seemed like a sweet girl."

"There is no hell," I said.

Penny shrugged. "You don't *know* that. No one does."

I was helping her get ready for the funeral, but I didn't know what that meant. Pick out something to wear, sure, and grab some Kleenex, but it seemed like there should be more, that this would end up being one of those memories weaseled deep into the darkest regions of her brain, planted there for the rest of her life, so everything had to be right. I didn't want her obsessing until she was ninety, thinking, *If only I...* or *Why didn't I... ?* about her mother's funeral, yammering to a parade of shrinks. She announced she hated all her clothes, including everything new Jess's dad had bought her, the bags and bags of things, most still with price tags. All she liked was a pair of Doc Martens, which turned her feet Frankenstein-huge and which didn't seem right to wear to a funeral or to anywhere. I was used to the preppy look, which I considered worthy of aspiring to, but she said oxford shirts and pullover sweaters were stupid, and plaid was her least favorite color. I was trying to get her to think about what Opie wore to his mother's funeral, making her see that Andy Taylor never would let his son traipse through a funeral in clunky black boots, and I was making some headway as we laughed, imagining Helen Crump in Doc Martens and a nose ring. We were in the living room, and clothes and shopping bags blanketed every piece of furniture, as if a suitcase had exploded.

"I like what *you're* wearing." Her voice lilted into a suggestion.

A slim black skirt slit up the back; a silky (but not real silk) black blouse with white pinstripes and a white Peter Pan collar; a wide black leatherish belt with an oversized crescent-moon-shaped silver buckle; black hose and pumps that were—like usual—too high to be comfortable. The pumps were Jess castoffs I dredged out of her trash last year—in front of her, so nothing secret, but I felt weird anyway, and if they didn't make my legs look a thousand luscious miles long, I wouldn't have kept them. Jess said they looked better on me than they ever did on her, though the soles were barely worn. Maybe it wasn't the exact outfit for a funeral, but it was black. *Why would I own funeral clothes? I've never been to a funeral,* was what I was thinking, that and how now I'd associate funerals with Doc Martens. I never bought a pair, even when they went mainstream, because of Penny, because it was so sad to imagine growing up and realizing your awful mistake of wearing clunky, rebellious boots to your mother's funeral, after she died because you had the very bad luck of happening to hand her a poisoned Tylenol capsule.

"Fine," I said, and I unbuckled the belt, dangling it off one hand like a snake. "Then you wear it."

"For real?"

"If you want." I gently kicked off the amazing shoes, one after the other, skittering them to Penny. She bent to tilt the shoes right side up and slid her bare foot into one, rearing up onto the heel. She balanced for a moment before sliding into the other shoe, abruptly taller than me, as if she'd done a year's worth of growing in two seconds. "Can you even walk in those?" I asked.

She rolled her eyes and nodded, then reached for the belt, which she looped around her waist. Fingering the indentation from where the buckle bit into the (fake) leather, she said, "You're so skinny," which seemed like a point scored for me.

I unbuttoned my blouse, something I had done countless times, but it felt awkward doing so in front of this girl, and I wanted to turn away. Since that would draw more attention, I forced myself to keep going, button by button, as she watched. I had on a bra, so she wouldn't see me bare-naked, and what would it matter if she did? I was being silly, and finally I fumbled through the last button and slid myself free of the blouse. A sudden chill prickled, lifting the hairs on my arms, and I pretended it didn't, as I stood there in my skirt and black hose and bra and handed the blouse to her. I really didn't have another outfit as funeral-esque as this one; I'd have to wear the navy Shetland sweater that was too tight around my armpits and sprinkled with wool pills I hadn't picked off. A dark gray skirt from a garage sale in Iowa that was a little too long, a little too big, with the zipper constantly twisting from my back to my side.

Penny said, "You look like those awful models in the Sears catalog, faking like it's natural standing around in bras and skirts." She exaggerated a pose, thrusting her chest forward like a Barbie doll.

I ignored her and unzipped my skirt, the ratchet louder than it should have been. The zipper stuck, which is probably why the skirt ended up at the Goodwill, because someone got tired of tinkering with it, impatient that it always needed the magic touch. I was pretty good with it. I had a feeling that Penny wouldn't be, that with her the zipper would finally give. I shimmied the skirt down my hips and high-kicked it her way. She snagged it one-handed.

Penny laughed. "Straight to the hosiery pages. Don't you feel sorry for those ladies in those pictures? They've got to know how stupid they look. They better get tons of money from Sears for looking so dorky."

"They do," I said, though I had no idea.

"Like how much?" she asked.

"Put on the outfit," I said. "Your dad will be here any minute." Even he wouldn't be late for a funeral. Of course the doorbell ding-donged right then, and Penny, still in the shoes, awkwardly thumped off to my bedroom and slammed the door, leaving me standing there half naked, looking and feeling as dorky as she had suggested. "Just a sec," I shouted, hoping he would hear, "hang on," and I was scrambling through the closest pile of clothes for a big sweatshirt or anything to cover up with, while also shoving the blanket and pillow on the couch into a more attractive wad, and the door creaked open, and then hard, heavy, fast footsteps, and I shrieked, *"No!"* and yanked up the pillow in front of me as Tommy strode into the living room. Something tiny in me bristled, half angry that it was him, not Jess's dad, catching me without clothes.

"You said come in," he said.

"What are you doing here?" As I hugged the pillow to my chest, it burped out a tiny feather that drifted through a patch of sunlight and landed on the rug. I dipped down to pluck it up off the carpet, even though there was plenty of dust and crumbs down there to keep it company, and rolled the feather between my finger and thumb into a tiny ball of white crud that I shoved up under my thumbnail.

"My dad is really on me about that ring," he said. "I've got to talk to her."

"She's not here," I said.

He looked around the room, eyebrows and forehead turning frowny, like he was thinking too hard. "Hey, is this a slumber party?"

"You wish," I said. "I'm not some dumb teenage girl having slumber parties. There's just someone staying with us, so I'm on the couch. If you have to know. And like I said, Jess isn't here and won't be back for a while. So you should go."

He crossed his arms. He was wearing a perfectly faded jean jacket over a white T-shirt. He kept his hands tucked under the tops of his arms, which was just as well because his hands were totally sexy. I liked thinking about them clutching my head, buried in my hair, those times in the library bathroom, or how they snaked along my waist when he slid himself up against and into and along my body, pressing close and rubbing deep. I liked to imagine them stroking my hair, cupping my breast, trickling down my ribs, finding the curve of my ass. I liked to imagine them knuckle-tight around the steering wheel of his Porsche.

"We can be friends," he said.

"We were never friends," I said.

"We're something," he said.

"Not friends."

"I'm sorry I called you a slut that night," he said. "You're not." He even sounded slightly sorry, or at least less smirky.

That night was a thousand years ago. It was almost confusing to talk about it. So I said, "Look. You really have to leave. She's not here, and I'm going to a funeral."

"Like that?"

"Haha. I'm getting ready."

"Who's here?" he asked.

"No one you know," I said.

"Whose funeral?"

"No one you know," I repeated.

He took a deliberate step closer to me, unfolded his arms off his chest, then used one hand to push back his tousled hair and tucked the other into a back jeans pocket. He slouched a bit, but the bad posture looked great on him. His modeling shot was *not* Sears catalog. It would be impossible to marry a guy this much better looking; every minute would feel this way. Only someone like Sydney Moore could withstand that pressure. I sucked in my stomach, not trusting the pillow to hide the fat.

"What're you thinking about?" he asked, moving one more step closer. I inhaled his piney cologne. He stood three feet away from me, the only thing between us this dumb pillow off my bed in Iowa;

it was too flat, too feathery. Feathers leaked. I doubt it had ever been washed, ever. I should wash it, except it would probably disintegrate like wet tissue.

"You really have to leave," I whispered.

"I will," he whispered back. One step more, one more, and then he was *this close*, his hand right up in front of me, gently grasping the tip of a feather, tugging it loose and holding it to his puckered lips, blowing, sending it flying beyond my shoulder, his breath raking my bare skin.

"I mean it," I said, still whispering. My cheeks felt pink, flushed. My spine tingled.

He dug his fingers into one corner of the pillow, pulled lightly, and I resisted, bracing my arms and squeezing, clutching deep into the fluffy mass. But it was only a pillow. I felt the elastic band of the pantyhose cut into my waist unattractively. If I only at least had the shoes on. Those shoes were magic. I felt short and fat, like a dwarf, a troll, a mushroom.

"Why are we whispering?" he whispered.

I shook my head.

"She's here, isn't she?" he asked in his normal voice. "You little liar." And with one hard slash, he wrestled the pillow out of my grasp, letting it drop to the floor. As he examined my awkward, half-naked body, my entire face burned, and I yanked my mind out of the moment and cocked my head and stared right back, unwavering, as if this moment was all about my eyes piercing his dark soul and finding it wanting, finding it amusing and small. I took a deep breath, feeling that superior look settle onto my face, that careful, untouchable composition the only weapon I had, the only weapon I ever had, that mask of utter boredom and vast superiority, and even though seeing it ratcheted my father's fury ten or more notches, it was so worth it to dig at him, to know my lofty silence infuriated him. My escape, even if only in my head; my way to show he didn't have all of me and never would, locking myself anywhere that wasn't here, any point in time that wasn't now, that was never now, never here, not this: all I had.

But this was only Tommy in front of me, dumb Tommy (they were all dumb, I reminded myself), and I released all that breath and said,

"Like I said, she's really not here, and I'm really getting ready for a funeral."

His eyes skimmed my chest, and I had to be pleased I was wearing my good bra, and that it was black lace, and that it was tight and stretchy. Even with all the other things I was thinking, I still thought that. I inhaled deeply, knowing my breasts would rise, knowing the lace was skimpy. Was this what I wanted, really, him looking at me that way?

"That ring is worth a fortune," he said. "More than my fucking car."

More than my parents' two cars put together, I thought, *more than their house, more than...* and I stopped. "Shouldn't have given it to her," I said. "Don't give anyone anything you can't afford to lose." My preachy voice grated condescension.

"I don't give a shit if you like me or not," he said. "A girl like you."

I shrugged, but my heart thudded loudly. I recognized that anger, I knew where he'd go next, and yes, he leaned in to scoop up my face between both hands, those sexy hands, and bent my head backward, forcing a slippery, slobbery kiss onto me, into me, his tongue wet and heavy like a sandbag slung through my mouth, and I couldn't break free if I wanted to, and I was supposed to want to. There was a stupid question in my head, and I was afraid I would ask it, so I bit down on his tongue—not hard, only just hard enough to notice—and he shoved me aside and howled, "Jesus H. Christ!" *The big baby,* I thought, *he should feel it when I mean it. Could have been his cock.*

"For the nine hundredth time," I said. "She isn't here." I thought about grabbing up the pillow again, but how weak would that be, like the question circling my brain, so I crossed my arms instead, like being at a frat party, watching guys be idiots. Sucked in my stomach. Tightened and adjusted my folded arms to jostle up my boobs and pop my cleavage.

"Tell her she's got to call me," he said, then paused. Eye contact seemed a struggle, and his gaze seared, sliding down and over and along my body, its scorch almost something physical on me. I watched him survey me, watched his eyes finally return to my face, his jaw tightening. "I'm getting that ring back. And you..." Another pause, truly considering me. Almost flattering. But I barely remembered why

I cared about him in the first place, until I remembered that I didn't care. His final judgment: "You're just fucking crazy."

But am I pretty? I thought. And I accidentally said it. Maybe if it had come out like a joke... But it didn't: it came out needy. Like I needed to know. Like I cared. "But am I pretty?" The words dangled. The question out of my head and into real life.

"Not really," he said.

I couldn't stop: I gasped.

If he had smiled, even a not-funny-joke smile or a malicious grin of revenge... but nothing. Only dismissal, his mind clicking somewhere else already. He turned to the door, one arm sweeping across the top of the bookcase, crashing through my alarm clock, a vanilla-scented candle, poetry books. The door slammed and the walls shook, and I crushed my eyes shut.

I knew all this. I knew it all, had known since forever, since I could first know anything. It was the answer I expected, even the answer I wanted to hear. But I didn't think he could actually *say* it. To me. To any girl. I didn't think it mattered.

I stood there for what felt like forever but wasn't. I wouldn't think about anything. I thought about the blankness in my head.

Penny coughed, and I opened my eyes and whirled around. She looked trampy in my skirt and those heels, rosy lipstick shellacked on and my black eyeliner circling her eyes, smudged like bruises. She clutched the doorjamb to balance in the shoes. It was disorienting; was this how people saw me?

Penny said, "That was Jess's fiancé."

"Ex-fiancé," I said.

"I heard everything," she said.

I shook my head. "Not much to hear."

"Even when you were whispering. 'Why are we whispering?' he said. 'But am I pretty?' you said." After a moment she added, "He's cute."

I never wanted to touch that pillow again, so I shook free the heavy blanket and draped it around my shoulders, pulling so the wool scratched my bare skin. Jess's L.L.Bean blanket with the big stripes. It was like I owned nothing of my absolute own. Jess's dad would be here any minute and I would be going to my first-ever funeral, where at least I could cry with no one asking why. "No," I said. "You don't understand."

"I think you still have that ring," she said. "You could give it back to him."

I shook my head again, the only gesture I felt I could control. "I gave the ring to Jess. She has it. It's locked up in her room." As I spoke, I gained strength, believing my own story, so I barged forward, blanket trailing like a wedding dress train, and said, "I have to get ready. Can't go to a funeral dressed like this, can I? Clara and Aunt Bea would really work the phones."

She laughed—forced and awkward—but pressed back out of my way as I passed, and I glanced sideways at her face, that combination of Jess and her own self, and reminded myself that she had no mother, had no one really, not me, and not even Jess's dad, and so I stopped in front of her and said, "You look really pretty," and she blushed and pushed at her hair with the palm of one hand, and I reached out and smoothed back some loose strands.

"Thank you," she said.

I smiled at her. I put everything into that smile.

"You know I won't say anything to anyone," she half whispered, as she loosened her grip on the doorframe and tottered toward the table.

"I know." And finally I was safely in my own room, leaning up against the closed door, listening to my heart explode.

It turned out that Jess's dad *could* be late for a funeral and was, also that he could reek of alcohol on a Saturday morning, that just-swigged smell lurking under the whiff of mint gum, and the hovering, foggy stench of last night's booze misting out of every pore, despite the elegant dark gray suit, despite no skin exposed beyond his face, neck, and hands, which gripped the steering wheel too hard. He wore aviator sunglasses. I had on a pair of Ray-Ban Wayfarers that I'd found by the vending machines in the library. Penny was the only one in the car with exposed eyes. I was sorry about that. It was a super-sunny day, hyper-blue. Lots of zippy bike riders, those people I imagined bouncing out of bed and staying busy all day, people who'd rather die than waste a pretty Saturday, racing from bikes to pancakes to leaf raking to grilling on their deck with friends to sitting up late telling funny stories, everyone tipsy on wine. I'd never be those people. We didn't talk much on the drive. I let Penny have the front seat. If Jess's dad thought her outfit was ridiculous, he didn't say so. He hugged her for exactly one second and said, "Let's bull through this," which sounded like something he barked to the men who worked for him. Maybe he didn't know another way. But also maybe Penny didn't realize that. Her mouth stayed a tight line, like a horizon you gaze at and never understand. I was glad not to be her.

There was no church service and nothing at the funeral home; we were going straight to the cemetery, which I didn't know was a thing people could do, until I remembered that Jess's dad could about do anything he wanted. What if it rained? I had worried when he explained the plans, until I realized that if it did, someone would be paid to set up a tent and find umbrellas and unroll carpet over soggy grass and shove the clouds over to Indiana. That kind of power, where things got taken care of.

The cemetery was a maze of gravel roads winding through jutting gravestones, marble mausoleums, and towering obelisks. Pale angels and cherubs and lambs. Crosses. Greek columns. There were heft and age here, and an overlay of remembrance, attractive to ghosts, I imagined, if I believed in them. It was about as melancholy as the cemetery I had viewed from car windows at the line where Evanston slid into Chicago, before Sheridan Road became Lake Shore Drive with its promised silvery gleam of skyline. That cemetery was centered inside one very tight, angular curve of the road, so that driving into Chicago, hurtling too fast, too late at night, you might think ironic thoughts about the convenience of being found dead in a car wreck at the cemetery. The lake pressed close on the other side, the road a thin ribbon between two perils, and it seemed that there should be a poem about this juxtaposition. I missed my old poetry class and that poetry professor. At our final meeting, when he read my last set of poems, he told me he was giving me a B, which surprised me, and suggested I work on the undergrad literary journal, that he could get me an assistant-something slot on the staff if I wanted, and I said maybe, because I didn't want him changing his mind about the B. He never said much of anything good about my poems, but possibly that was his way of teaching poetry, because he never did about anyone else's either. But I didn't want to work on the literary journal, judging people's poems. Most we wrote for class were so bad, and none would end up in the Norton anthology, so why bother? Our bad poetry didn't much matter.

Jess's dad whipped his car along the cemetery's gravel roads. It seemed he was lost but didn't want to admit it. The radio played a staticky newsy drone of AM interrupted by commercials for furniture sales and an upcoming monster truck show. I couldn't see much of Penny from where I sat in the backseat, just her one arm overhanging the side of the bucket seat. Even with the ripples of the blouse that arm looked tense, like taut wire.

I thought about my sister in Iowa, her skinny toothpick arms. I would catch sight of them during this past summer, when she was wearing a tank top or a bathing suit, and want to snap her arm in two, or bend it like a pipe cleaner, just to see if she would cry out. Not really. But sort of. Then her arm got broken for real and she had to wear a cast. But I didn't want to think about her.

Some of the gravestones looked very old: weathered, rough deep gray stone, the writing half erased and hard to make out from the car. Some names were easy to read, bannered across an archway or along the steps of a columned facade: HOYT, PINKERTON, CUMMINGS, PALMER. I didn't believe in ghosts. I didn't believe in being haunted. I wanted to believe that when you were gone you were gone, and that was it. I would definitely choose cremation, just to be sure.

I wondered if this was the same cemetery where Linda was buried.

Jess's father spun a U-turn in the narrow road, slashing tire marks into the grass, gravel pinging noisily against the car. "Goddamn it," he said. The outburst was startling, and I'd forgotten that he, too, would wrestle emotions today. I was the only person here who didn't care, the only person coming because I'd been promised fifty bucks. A few more fast turns landed us in a section we hadn't already seen, with fewer columns and simpler, smaller stones, more modern. I wondered if other Tylenol victims were in here, if their stones said TYLENOL VIC-TIM. Up ahead were a dull blue canopy and a few rows of folding chairs. Also cop cars and cops and FBI guys in rumpled suits and vans from TV stations and a dozen cars lining the road. Jess's father guided his car to the end of that line and killed the engine. The car felt lonely with no radio voice. He kept both hands on the wheel for a moment, maybe thinking about Penny's mom or that last drink he'd had, the jigsaw pieces of his secret life. Penny sighed. He leaned toward the glove box but straightened right back up as a cop in a pressed uniform approached. Beyond the cop stood a band of reporters and men with cameras with those long, top-heavy lenses that got close-ups from far away. I imagined Penny's raccoon eyes on the front page of the *Sun-Times* and the *Trib* tomorrow morning. I imagined her cutting out the pictures with scissors, saving copies of the newspaper, because that's what people did when they made the paper.

Suddenly Penny said, "I don't want to do this."

"No one wants to," said Jess's dad.

"Who are those people?" she asked.

"I got it." Jess's dad jumped out of the car to go talk to the cop, the door clicking shut behind him. His keys dangled in the ignition, and I worried he might forget and lock them in the car, so I stretched into the front and yanked them out. The engine key was warm. There was a key on the ring for a hotel room, which seemed sad and permanent.

Penny said, "I wish it was Jess's mother who was dead right now."

She twisted in her seat, her smudgy eyes glowering. She had bitten off most of her lipstick, so faded magenta rimmed her lips and stained the edges of her teeth. She moved with such ease that I realized she hadn't buckled her seat belt this whole time. Someone should have thought to make her. Me, I should have. She rolled her shoulder, shaking off my hand. "Stop acting like you care. You're only being nice because he's paying you to babysit me until he figures out how to ship me off to my nutty aunt. That's what he does, pays for things."

"I'm not getting any money," I said. The car had turned stuffy; sun pressed at my back, layered sweat under my sweater, on my forehead. *He cares about you,* is what I should have said. *He* loves *you. You, his daughter.*

"Because I take it," she said. "Every time I see him, he hands over cash I'm supposed to give you, but I keep it for myself."

He cares about you, I thought. *He loves you.* But what I said was "Let me guess. Your big plan is to run away." Why couldn't I say what I was supposed to? Because it wasn't true? Because it was? *He loves you.* Like a church bell endlessly ringing. *Daughter.*

"You can't stop me," she said.

"Don't be stupid," I said, and I hadn't planned to say any of this or even known I had thought about it, though of course I had, because I knew there were lawyers and meetings and interested parties, and I knew how the world worked: there would be money, lots of it, at the end of all this. Johnson & Johnson, the company that made Tylenol, was crashing in the stock market right now, but they were worth bajillions, and they'd dump a fortune on Penny and every family member affected—and even if they didn't want to, fancy lawyers would force them. A fortune. A *fortune.* This didn't even count the money sent by the people who read sad stories in the newspaper and mailed checks; there was a fund, Jess's dad had told me, that Penny would get a percentage of for her education, something people felt good about paying for. Doling out money helped shove away guilt, either guilt because the poison was crammed inside capsules from your factory, or guilt you felt over being happy someone else got the poison pill, not you, not your family—or maybe even guilt that you'd been living a secret life for like a thousand years. Penny had no clue how rich she would be, and yes, of course, her life was damaged—yes, yes, I got that, yeah, totally—but plenty of people—*plenty* of people—had damaged lives—just as damaged, just as terrible lives—and got nothing. Absolutely nothing. Only the wreckage of their life to haul around forever.

"You can't stop me," she repeated, less defiant, no oomph in the words.

"Do you have any idea how much money you'll get someday?" I asked, my voice rising and furious. "From the company who makes Tylenol? They'll hand over a bucket of money to you and the other families, or they'll be sued. I bet lawyers are working phones and dictating documents right now, even on a Saturday."

"What?" she said. Her face went slack, mouth drooping open.

"God, yes," I said. "You lost your mother. That's worth a fortune."

In the silence, I thought about how I should have shut up. How her mother was gone forever. "No one thinks about money the way you do" was the phrase buzzing inside. Everything I had done today was exactly wrong: saying this to Penny, letting her wear my slutty outfit, standing in front of Tommy half naked, aching to be in the library with him even after what he said. And more: Jess's dad telling me those personal things and me listening. I didn't even make Penny put on her seat belt, for God's sake. All of it, my whole life, was wrong, including whatever I might do next. Whatever I was going to do next was already wrong.

Penny opened the car door and scrambled out. I thought she'd run, but not in those shoes, and she hobbled her way to Jess's dad standing with the cop. The ground was soft from yesterday's downpour, so the spiky heels sank in, making her gait lurch, surely coating the shoe with mud I'd have to scrub off. The photographers lifted cameras, pinning her to this moment.

It seemed I was jealous of her, a girl whose mother was dead; jealous of a girl who accidentally killed her own mother. What kind of terrible person was I? The keys were still in my fist, and I let them drop onto the front seat where Jess's dad would see them. I couldn't stay in the car. I would have to get out, too. Fifty bucks, fifty bucks.

I watched Jess's dad drape his arm around Penny's shoulders as he and the cop talked. The cop gestured to the reporters; apparently there was some boundary they couldn't cross, a designated place to stand. Probably I should join them, the pack of jackals, peddling papers off everyone's misery, like Jess's dad said. He was in the paper now or on the news, labeled "speaking for the Mitchell family," offering statements like "The family is grateful for your prayers and good wishes. We hope the perpetrator of this horrific crime is apprehended, and we urge anyone with information about this crime to come forward and share what they know with the authorities or call the anonymous tip line. No further comment." I imagined Jess and her mother switching channels in a huff or crumpling the paper into the trash. I imagined Jess's mom secretly thinking, *Those bags under his eyes... he's not sleeping well.*

I got out of the car, careful not to accidentally press the door lock button. The cop had backed away, growling something at the cameraman from channel 9, and Jess's dad caught my eye and waved me over. "Can't keep the reporters away," he called. "Goddamn it." I glanced at them, and immediately cameras lifted, so I positioned my back to them the way he had. "We'll pass by with Penny between us," he said, "so they won't get a clear shot of her. They've been warned because she's a minor, but nothing shames those mercenary beasts."

"I don't care," Penny said.

"Yes, you do," Jess's dad said. "And even if you don't, I care on your behalf." He hooked his sunglasses over Penny's ears, balancing them on her nose. They were too big for her and crooked—I wanted to straighten them for her but didn't dare get in the way as he roughly shuffled Penny at me. One of her feet twisted, and she clutched my arm so she wouldn't fall, but he didn't notice, saying, "Let's go," and he rushed us toward the canopy and the folding chairs, which were positioned on a section of rolled-out Astroturf. Up front, resting on a white-sheeted table, was a dark wooden casket with brass handles topped with a spray of pink flowers overflowing down the sides and, next to that, gigantic wreaths, most of them creamy white flowers, but one made of all red roses, like maybe a hundred or more, shaped like a heart, which I knew was his, not ordered by his secretary. MOTHER, said a ribbon on the biggest white wreath. There were at least two dozen leafy potted plants lined up on the grass in front of the casket. The foil wrapping the pots was dull silver. A murmur rose as black-clad people perched in the chairs turned and caught sight of Penny. Cameras clicked as we passed the reporters.

Penny clung to my arm, and it felt like dragging her, she could barely walk, and she accidentally stepped out of one shoe and would have fallen to the ground if I hadn't caught hold of her. "Christ," muttered Jess's dad, but he paused, stared straight ahead while Penny fumbled her foot back into the shoe, but when she buckled a second time, she raised one foot after the other, so the shoes dropped off sideways into the grass, and she continued on in her (my) black tights. It had to be the saddest thing to see in the world, this girl wearing too much makeup in this thinks-she's-so-sophisticated college-girl getup, stumbling stocking-footed across wet, muddy grass to a folding chair in the front row of her mother's funeral. She was only a little girl. Anyone could see. And see that Jess's dad and I were two strangers.

There were people who seemed to know her, trying to make eye contact as they sniffled into tissues, but she kept her eyes fixed at the ground, and mostly I did, too. I wondered if her feet were cold. Maybe she didn't notice. She'd probably run my tights, so I hoped this wasn't a good pair. And that mud. I would have to do hand-wash tonight. Jess always asked to throw in something with my hand-wash because I did it more often than she did since I had fewer bras and hose and tights to rotate through. It was kind of a joke between us. "The soap's in the sink anyway," she'd say. She never reminded me that she bought the Woolite, but also I never forgot.

Jess's dad guided us to the front row, to seats cordoned off with white ribbon, not that they needed to be since nobody was brave enough even to sit in the second row. We would be a solitary island up front. I went three chairs in, and Penny plopped next to me, but he stayed standing in front of us as if he had something to say. Without sunglasses, his eyes blinked and squinted. Either they hurt from the light or from being bloodshot and hungover. I thought I should grab hold of his hand, or that Penny should, but she and I sat perfectly still. Suddenly, silently, he turned, and I twisted to watch him stride back down the aisle, pausing for a few murmured words to a thin man with a trim red beard and earnest eyes, and then he was gone, cameras clicking along the line of reporters, their muffled questions like birdcall and then silence, and it was impossible to miss the slam of the car door. I braced for the engine to start, but when it didn't, I remembered the glove box, the bottle. He needed a drink. I thought of Linda and wondered if he sat with Jess and Jess's mom in an island of three or if he had hidden in the car. He wasn't coming back.

The man with the beard walked gently up the center aisle, as if on tiptoe. He wasn't a real priest but he was some sort of religion, and he stood up front and talked. I didn't find his words especially meaningful, just the something that had to be said, but behind me, I heard snuffling and choked tears. Penny stared at her feet, which she flexed and twisted in a kind of distracting way. Now and then she half smiled, and I didn't know why or what that meant. I couldn't tell if she was listening to the man or not. I wanted her to, because later she surely would want to know what he said, but even I couldn't pay close attention, and I was older and had learned in college how to note-take tedious ramblings that might show up on a final.

I was thinking about Jess. She should have called me at least maybe once. I wondered what was in her mind, what she was thinking about Penny, about her dad, about these crazy things happening all at once to her family. Maybe she was thinking that I should have called her. We'd never had a fight like this before, and I couldn't figure out what was normal.

I remembered exactly what she said that morning when she found Penny, after she accused me of betraying her, after grandstanding about fucking saying "fucking": "I always thought you cared about me, but I see I was totally wrong." That was fine; I expected her to be dramatic like that, extravagant with the "always" and "totally." What I didn't expect was: "Everyone warned me to watch out about you, but I didn't listen to them." *Everyone who?* I wondered. *Them who?* Before I could ask, she kept on: "You don't fool me. I know all about you." And I would have laughed, thinking she had to be joking with such ridiculously melodramatic statements, things my poetry professor would shame with a tidy red ink box on the page; she might as well have announced, *Aha! It was Colonel Mustard in the library with the rope,* but then she said, "Stop sponging off me. You're so cheap, I can't stand it. I'd be embarrassed to wear someone else's hand-me-downs. It's like you're poor."

She stood perfectly framed in her doorway, gripping both sides of the door with her hands. I stared at her chipped nail polish, which meant she was back to chewing her nails, a habit she'd really worked hard to break.

I couldn't let her know how that felt. The depth of what she'd said. But she already knew. That's why she said it. So I smiled. Hard. I thought my face would collapse. Finally: "I'm just trying to help a little girl whose mother died," I said. "Your sister, by the way."

"That's right," Jess said. "My sister. Not yours. Help your own, why don't you, if you're so keen on helping someone's sister."

"My sister is fine."

She smiled at me. I smiled right back, matching her. We smiled and smiled. This lasted forever until she surrendered. Luckily, the next thing she said was "That little bitch has my ring, doesn't she?"

"She'll hear you," I warned. Penny was in my bedroom, door closed. Surely she was pressed up against it, listening.

"You tell her to give that ring back," she said, "or I'm calling the cops, and don't think I won't. I don't give a shit what my dad says."

"It's not really yours anymore, is it?" I said.

That was exactly when she left, lugging an armload of duffel bags jammed with clothes, shoes, and makeup. Maybe I should have been relieved, but I was drained dry. *I can explain,* I thought, *come back, come back.*

Now, the guy was done talking. I hoped there might be someone hired to sing, but no, which seemed depressing. People held back from walking up to the casket, waiting for Penny to go first, but she stayed sitting, staring at her feet, so I sat with her, and eventually people ventured up to pat her shoulder or reach for her limp hand, people crying and sniffling into wadded Kleenex, murmuring about how terribly sorry they were and how her mom was a wonderful lady and promises about heaven and angels. Penny slouched through that onslaught as she had through the service, with the minimum amount of words, the minimum facial expressions. Someone brought over the shoes—which were wrecked, by the way—but she left them there on the ground, and the minister handed me a business card with an official, printed phone number and one he had scribbled on with pen for me to give to Penny later; "For when she wants to process this," he explained. A young-looking woman in a jean skirt who was the guidance counselor from Penny's school also gave me a business card, and the principal, with wheezy bad breath, handed me a large sealed envelope filled with letters from students at Penny's school. The stack of leftover prayer cards was at least an inch thick, and a lady told me I should take them; I guess there was a minimum order, but how sad to see them all. People pressed flowers into Penny's hand, folded-up bills. Someone asked if they could take a potted plant to a grandmother in a nursing home, and I said, "Why not?" so then a bunch of people grabbed pots. What did it matter? A few people wanted to know where the lunch was, and I said there wasn't one, which made them shake their heads. No one asked who I was. No one told me they were sorry for my loss, which was okay, because I didn't have a real loss, unless I was allowed to count Jess and maybe Tommy, not that they were anything like a dead mother. Jess's dad didn't come back, which, if he was drunk, maybe was a good thing, but also maybe a bad thing, because he was the one who should collect the business cards and envelopes, and maybe there was a lunch planned that he hadn't mentioned to me.

After a long time it was over.

Men gathered along the perimeter, needing us to go, wanting the folding chairs and white ribbons, waiting to roll up the Astroturf, ready to bury the body. Even the reporters and TV vans and cops had driven off in crunchy sprays of gravel. The only car left was Jess's dad's, and now parked across the road from it was—I was pretty sure—Jess's Volvo. But I said to Penny, "Are you done here? Do you want to pray or something?" She shook her head and trudged toward the cars, finally removing the sunglasses, folding them shut. I watched for a moment, certain she'd return, that it couldn't be so simple to leave behind her mother's body, but maybe it was the only possible way. Like tearing off a Band-Aid, though the comparison felt stupid even to think. Nothing to do but follow. Halfway to the car I realized I'd forgotten the shoes, which I decided to leave behind. I wouldn't want to wear them after today, no matter how great my legs looked.

I caught up and touched her shoulder, the pointy knob of one of her bones jabbing the thin fabric of the blouse, then I pulled back my hand. "Hold up," I said. "I'm thinking Jess might be talking to your dad. That's her car parked there anyway."

"I'm not afraid of her," she said. But she stood still, arms crossed. Lipstick smeared one cuff. Impossible to soak out that stain. "Think she still hates me?"

"She showed up," I said, which was as hopeful as I could be. "So maybe she's getting more used to the idea that she's got another sister now." Not that it mattered if she was used to the idea or not, since Penny *was* her sister, like it or not.

Penny said, "I guess I shouldn't care. He's my dad, too. Even if he's crappy."

"He's not crappy," I said. "Maybe he's confused."

"No," Penny said. "I'm pretty sure he's crappy. Don't pretend." She sighed, lifted one foot, extended her toes, gazed down at them for a moment. "Not like we're walking home, so let's get it over with."

"We could take the el," I said, having no idea how far an el stop was or why I said that. But why not grab Penny and whisk her safely out, away from Jess's fury? If there wasn't an el, there'd be a bus. I could get her home. I could rescue her, be the one "speaking for the Mitchell family."

"You're afraid," she said.

I shrugged. "No."

"I said I wouldn't tell," she said. "I mean, I know you didn't have to let me stay. So I owe you something, right?"

I looked back. The chairs were already being loaded onto a truck. Different sad people would be sitting on them tomorrow. That fast.

"What I said before—"

"Stop," she interrupted, and her eyes went glossy.

"I shouldn't have—"

"I mean it, stop." She hunched away from me, scraped roughly at her cheeks with two fingers, which she flicked against her thumb, as if the glittering tears would fly off and disappear into the grass. "I'm not going to cry. You wouldn't trade places with me for all the money in the world. No one would."

An uncomfortable silence built. My mind flashed to watching Grace color, the comfort of crayons gliding over paper. But I was here, and I pondered what might be the right thing to say. I hoped it was this: "Sounds like the cue for 'Opie learns a lesson' music," and I crooned my bad imitation: "Waa-wah-waaaaa. Sittin' with Paw on the porch, talkin' it all out." *Laugh,* I thought, *please.* "Waa-wah-waaaaa. Honesty is the best policy. Crime doesn't pay. Bullies hurt inside."

She laughed, sort of, more like a choked-back squawk, and wiped away another line of tears. *Money can't buy happiness,* I imagined Andy drawling on that porch, scuffling a loving hand over Opie's black-

and-white cowlick, Aunt Bea beaming behind the screen door with homemade cake for everyone. I squinted at the sun, until my own eyes teared and I looked away.

The car horn did a quick staccato, and Penny jerked as if she'd been shot. Delaying was making everything worse, and I marched us to the car and pulled open the backseat door and slid all the way across, and Penny came in next to me.

"Look who's here," Jess's dad said, unnecessarily, unwaveringly flat and neutral, as if this statement truly could be an observation.

Jess turned to peer at us from the passenger seat. She wore a wide-brimmed black hat, as if dressed for the extremely dramatic part of Grieving Woman, and I realized she had intended to sit at the funeral. Her father had asked her to come. And she had. Because she cared about him, because she loved him. No fifty-dollar bribe. Her head tilted as she examined Penny, light and shadow carving the same hollows in her cheekbones that were in Penny's cheekbones, and she twisted further in her seat, for a deeper, longer, harder stare, then sucked in a big breath and said, "So you're Penny." Not one quiver.

I smelled a tinge of alcohol, either on her breath or in the car in general. I imagined her and her father swigging down the same glove box bottle. I remembered what Jess's mother told her once: keeping a family together was *everything*.

Penny nodded, her body shrinking deeper into the leather. Jess's dad got all still. I didn't know what would happen next. Or what I wanted to happen next. I mean, I wanted them to get along. That was what I wanted.

"Hi... Jess," Penny finally said. Her voice was small. "I, um, always thought I would like a sister, a cool older sister."

Jess said, "First thing is get you a haircut," then she reached—*She doesn't always like being touched*, I almost said—to stroke the hair draping Penny's face, coiling a few strands around one finger, before letting them spring free so she could push back the hair from Penny's forehead. "No one thought to clip these bangs? We've got to show off this pretty face." Penny started to speak, but Jess rolled on: "I'm excellent at cutting bangs. I can do it when we get home."

No lie. She really was good, caring about being perfectly straight. She trimmed her mother's hair, and Linda's, and mine. But she didn't trust anyone with hers.

Jess's father laughed, though nothing sounded funny to me, and started the car. The monotonous AM radio voice prattled, but immediately Jess spun the dial to XRT for music, which came up with Muddy Waters's "Sweet Home Chicago." "I love this song," she said, "don't you? Doesn't everyone?" She didn't need an answer. She knew she was right.

I was the only one still not breathing as we wound our way out of the cemetery and merged into traffic. "What about Jess's car?" I asked at one point, and because no one answered, I glanced out the back window and there it was, trailing us, breaking away at the first light to go the opposite direction we did, Jess's mom driving it home to Oak Lawn. That's when Jess said, "You know, Penny, me too. Sisters are amazing. They just really are. I wish you knew Linda. She sure was a character, right, Dad? We all miss her like you wouldn't believe."

Strategies for Survival #7: Balance

(summer, after freshman year)

I hadn't paid Janey the money I owed her. I told myself it was a gift. No one said "loan" or "pay back," or if they did, I didn't remember. The first time I saw Janey in Iowa the summer after freshman year, we talked really fast about a hundred different things, tumbling words as if that could make us the same as who we were, as if that would catch us up. But I was playing a part. Being away had changed me, and she was still here, which was impossible to overlook. One thing she said was that she'd thought about visiting me in Evanston, almost did it; that she was desperate to blow out of town and I was the only person she knew who'd gone anywhere. I told her to visit any time and stay as long as she wanted. Then we ran out of things to say. I hadn't mentioned Jess's name, and I wasn't going to.

Instead I asked about her pothead brother, how he was.

"He only likes boys now," she said.

The word I knew for that was "fag," but I couldn't say it. It felt ugly on my tongue and would be uglier in my voice, not right for that fuzzy-haired boy with wistful brown eyes who had kissed each of us with sweet delicacy. *Desi,* he had crooned, the only one trusted with the silly secret of my imaginary French class name, Desiree. It would be boys now: boys relishing his kisses, whispers filling boys' ears. But if I didn't say that word, I didn't know what I could say. Something big had changed, or maybe it hadn't changed at all, because maybe he liked boys all along, even when he was kissing me.

"My dad kicked him out of the house," Janey said. "My mom cries all day. No one's talking to anyone. Our whole family's shredded to bits. I don't want to be there. Or anywhere. I don't know where I want to be. Just out." She sighed and looked up at the ceiling, then back at me like what she wanted wasn't up there. "No one else knows. And I'm not talking about it."

We were at Country Kitchen off Highway 6 where she waitressed. I came in to apply for a job, but they wanted experience and didn't count answering phones at a pizza takeout. The manager wouldn't even pick up my application form to file it somewhere when he trudged away. Janey was on break, slumped across from me at one of those narrow two-person booths. A colorful stand-up card was tented between us, my side advertising the Country Boy burger. She was drinking coffee, black. I'd never seen her with coffee before. She grimaced as she sipped, like coffee was one more chore. "Why did I tell you?" she said. "Damn it."

"I can keep a secret," I said.

"Still"—she pointed to my application, my neat printing, the blue ink—"you should've lied," she said, "told them you were a waitress anywhere. They never check."

"Guess so."

"Maybe you don't *really* want to work here," she said.

I shrugged, gave a glance around, but not one thing registered as memorable. "Seems okay enough." That was the lie. She knew it. Janey wasn't dumb. The air smelled like bleach and burger grease.

"Maybe you think you're too good now," she said.

"Come on." I forced a smile, forced it to look natural.

Her face went sour as she tilted her cup to get at the last of her coffee.

"Just remember," she said. She clutched the cup really hard, so hard it shook the tiniest bit. "I know who you are. I'll always know who you really are."

I wanted to jump up or at least stand. I even kind of wanted to hit her. But the tiny booth pressed me in and clambering out would turn me awkward as a giraffe. So I leaned in close enough that my breath puffed the table card forward half an inch as I said, "Like how you knew your own brother? You don't know anything."

"You owe me," she said. "And always will. Even if you give me all the money in the world. How's that?"

She slithered from the booth, then spun and clunked her coffee cup into a plastic bus tub perched on a folding stand. It hit with a clatter, shifting other dishes, but Janey kept walking.

I couldn't park there forever, and I wasn't about to pay for a Country Boy or even a Tab at a place I wasn't invited to work at, a place I was too good to work at, but I sat for a moment, waiting for Janey to get back to the kitchen so she couldn't watch me leave.

I thought about her brother, kissing me, kissing all of us, while secretly longing to kiss a boy. I knew what he gave us, but was it possible he got nothing back? I thought about his tongue gliding the contours of my mouth, how soft and gentle his every movement was, the trace of his fingertip skimming my cheekbone; how fragile this was, not because we might get caught, but because the moment would dissolve into the flatness of memory once we stepped aside. I thought of all the girls he had kissed back then, our names pattering in my head like summer rain.

I thought about Jess for some reason, and the time I was hanging out in her dorm room, watching her peer into her lighted magnifying mirror as she plucked hairs from her eyebrows with a pair of tweezers. "Shaping them into perfection," she said. Once she finished, we'd be off to a frat party I didn't care about. Pinpricks of pink welts rose at the root of each hair as she extracted, one by one, swiping the tweezers across a Kleenex after each go, entirely focused on this task. Left brow, the right, the left, the right. Like Ping-Pong. Perfection. The repetition and her solemn concentration turned me silly. "What if you accidentally end up plucking them all out trying to keep even?" I had asked, uncomfortable, unwilling to stroke my own bristly caterpillar brows, fearing the tedium and pain of tearing individual hairs out of my flesh even as I envied the task and its precision.

She wasn't silly back: "Guess I'd just draw them on with eyebrow pencil," she said, distracted as she aimed her tweezers and yanked. "Fix them that way. Act like that's what I wanted all along. Like it was my choice. Who'd notice the difference anyway?"

TWO GIRLS

(fall, junior year)

There were logistics to discuss. The plan was to drop me off in Evanston. They'd grab Penny's things, then turn around for Oak Lawn. Penny would stay down there. Jess would stay there. Maybe Jess's dad would stay there, maybe. I would stay in Evanston. I would get back my bedroom. Jess would return to Evanston and school on Monday. Maybe Penny would stay permanently in Oak Lawn. Maybe Jess's dad, too, maybe. This was Jess's mom's plan, that Penny should move into Linda's old room, while everyone else sorted things out and talked to lawyers and shrinks and marriage counselors.

The car ride was opposite of the earlier, silent one, as Jess played talk show host, barraging Penny with fifty million questions about school and classes and what music she listened to and her favorite TV shows. Penny answered each question cautiously, as if being interviewed for a job, as if a wrong answer would trap her at the bottom of some list. It wasn't *The Andy Griffith Show* for favorite TV, but *The Dukes of Hazzard*, which I knew she despised but the kids at school liked. Baseball was "okay." Her face seemed paler, and she tugged at the blouse sleeves, yanking them over her wrists, sliding them as far up as they'd go, unbuttoning cuffs, buttoning them right back. All that scrutiny beelined at her, Jess's high-beam spotlight of attention. If Jess noticed Penny's nervousness, she didn't ease up.

Jess's father was driving fast again, gunning through yellow lights, flying wide on curves. He was in a hurry. Maybe he was afraid of tipping our fragile balance. This was before anyone fussed about people driving drunk, not that he acted drunk, just quiet and anxious. He barely said a word, even when Jess would say something like "Dad, did you hear that?" It was like he needed talking around him but didn't care if it was the radio or Jess. It occurred to me that I could have been the one talking on the way down. I could have done that, played Jess.

We pulled up to our street without anyone mentioning lunch, though it was after two o'clock. On TV and in movies, people were always eating after funerals, and now I got why: first, I was starving, and second, and really, eating was something to do that wasn't feeling sad. Some people at the cemetery had asked about what would happen afterward, emphasizing that word, "afterward," and they were startled when I said nothing. For a while, I half thought they meant "afterward" like the afterlife, and I was flattered they wanted my opinion, but finally I pieced together that "afterward" meant people expected lunch, possibly with drinks, definitely with a table's worth of homey food like macaroni and cheese and ham and casseroles.

"I'll wait out here," Jess's dad said as he backed into a space on the street, "while you two girls run in."

The thing is there were three girls in the car, not two, and his saying "two" like that made me feel like everyone understood something I didn't, because really fast Jess said, "Got it. We'll be quick," and Penny nodded, also really fast, not looking at me. She had barely looked my way this whole time, even with me sitting next to her in the backseat, the two of us a foot apart on the black leather. Only one or two furtive glances, like secretly checking my reaction, and I wondered what Penny had decided my reaction was. I didn't think I had a reaction. Maybe I had. But they both knew they were the "two girls" and I was only the other girl.

I was on the traffic side of the car, and because the road was busy I couldn't right away open the door, and in that time, as Jess and Penny scrambled out and I waited, Jess's dad said to me, "Hang on," so I lifted my hand off the door handle. Then I didn't know what to do with my arm, which suddenly felt annoying plopped in my lap and annoying hanging at my side, so I wedged it behind my back, leaning onto it, which was totally uncomfortable, but which also made me feel better. It occurred to me that he told me to hang on because he had my fifty dollars. I looked out the window, at Jess and Penny getting to the porch steps, Jess fumbling around her clutch purse for the key. She didn't like key rings, so it was just a loose key that she was always losing. She was wearing a boxy, old-ladyish, nubby black suit that maybe was her mother's and that looked exactly appropriate for a funeral. Maybe Jess's mom wore it to Linda's funeral. And the dramatic black hat. That was pure Jess. I imagined Jess gazing at her reflection in the mirror—hat on, hat off, on, off—and finally her mother touching her shoulder and saying, "I like the hat, lovey." Jess and Penny stepped inside, and I couldn't see them, only think about the two of them alone together for the first time, ignoring my mess in the living room as they went searching for what Penny needed. I'd cleared a drawer for her and space in the closet, but mostly she flung her clothes everywhere. At least the new stuff was in shopping bags, easy to pack up. Then I'd get my bedroom. I hadn't missed it much, only that the bed was less lumpy than the couch. It wasn't a space that felt like mine. No space ever felt like mine. Penny's baseball mitt was out on the coffee table, for when she watched baseball playoffs. I wanted to tell her don't forget it, or her blank scorecards that I'd copied on the Xerox machine in the work-study office.

Penny would know that it was smarter not to mention Tommy. Anyone would know that. Penny owed me. I wondered which stories Jess would tell about Linda, if Jess's dad would take a picture of Penny and Jess to put in a frame and display on his desk.

Jess's dad had been talking and now was at the end: ". . . so, yeah, I'm chickenshit for not sitting up there. I couldn't do it." He watched me in the rearview mirror, sunglasses back on, but they looked wrong on him, borrowed, like they actually belonged to Penny. I wondered if he had cried while he hid in the car. I was feeling like I might cry right now, though I'd be so angry if I did. I crushed my shoulder into the seat to make my twisted-up arm throb. That sharp clarity.

I said, "This was the first funeral I went to." I thought he might turn to gaze at me full-face, but no. He stayed shrunk to the sliver of sunglasses in the mirror. I added, "It was so sad. Even not knowing her, I was sad."

"That bastard," he said. "Killing random people for kicks. What kind of sick mind... ?"

"Think they'll catch him?" I asked.

"Hell yeah," he said. "They have to."

"Or what?"

"Huh?"

"They have to, or what?" I said.

Two motorcycles ripped by, both with girls riding on back, their long hair whipping like flags. We watched them, and then for a moment after, we watched the space where they'd been.

He shook his head. "I just can't get over the sick mind that takes away a kid's mother for absolutely no reason and no logic. What kind of world are we living in? Nothing can be the same now, not with that kind of evil loose among us. Mark my words."

I imagined my poetry professor boxing up those sentences, scribbling "melodramatic" in the cramped angles of his handwriting. Any time the word "evil" showed up in our poems, he'd scorn us with "melodramatic." Mostly what that did was send people to the thesaurus: "wicked," "malevolent," "immoral." There was a bunch. But it seemed wrong not to be allowed to call something evil if it was. I said, "I know. They think it might be a disgruntled employee."

"Then have the balls to shoot your goddamn boss in the face," he said. "Or quit your goddamn job. Don't take down innocent people." Red flooded the section of the back of his neck that I could see. "What law says you're going to love every minute of this life?" He yanked off his sunglasses and tossed them on the passenger seat. Then he wiped both eyes with his thumb (crying?) and angled his gaze back at me in the mirror. I wished he would just turn around. "That's something important to learn," he said. "I tell Jess, but she doesn't want to listen."

"Actually, I think maybe I know that already," I said.

"Good," he said forcefully. "Better than what they'll teach you here. School of hard knocks gets you somewhere, is what I always say."

I nodded thoughtfully, fake-pondering his advice. Really, what I was wondering was if maybe he created the second life for himself because he got tired of not loving every minute of his first life, or if a shrink would explain that he needed love or power or danger. All those lies like confetti everywhere, and dashing between two houses, the double "How was your day?" Exhausting to keep up, if not impossible—I mean, impossible if you weren't Clark Kent—and I realized right then that Jess's mom knew all along. She had to know. What he did was too much to hide. How else could Penny be on her way, accepted, to Oak Lawn this soon? Because someone could know something and not like it and just pretend it wasn't there. Someone definitely could do that. They could make that choice, imagining it would be easy.

The silence didn't feel especially comfortable. I couldn't tell if I was supposed to leave now and wondered why he didn't just hand over my money. No cars were coming up the street, so I could push open the door if I wanted. I unfolded my arm, that creepy pins-and-needles sensation cascading down the cramp. "Well," I said.

"I thought Penny would lose it," he said, sort of abruptly, as if he'd been having a conversation in his head and this answered a question that had been asked. "Poor kid. She's some tough cookie. My mother died when I was nineteen and that about killed me. I'm not ashamed to admit I talk to Ma out loud every day. God, but I miss her. I was her baby, the youngest, spoiled rotten to the core, and everyone knew it. But I didn't cry, not one goddamn tear." He sounded proud of himself, proud of Penny, but I was ready to explode into a mess of sobs, even though it's not like I had something specific like a dead mother to cry about.

I squinched shut my eyes and counted backward from a hundred, an old trick I taught my sister that didn't work but always felt like it might. He was going on about his mother, a "perfect angel," but I didn't listen. Numbers marched through my head. My sister said when she counted each number glowed a different color, all the way from a hundred down. A hundred was always silver, she told me. I didn't know there were that many colors. I wondered what she was doing right now. Maybe she was at a birthday party, watching someone twist balloon animals. A cake with pink frosting roses and a choice of chocolate or vanilla ice cream. My sister would choose chocolate. She loved chocolate ice cream. She even wanted it when I treated her to Baskin-Robbins during the summer—out of thirty-one flavors, she wanted chocolate. That's how she was, very loyal.

I was crying, but silently—streaking tears that I couldn't rub away fast enough with my sweater sleeve, hoping Jess's dad wouldn't notice while he rambled about his mother. But he shut up and suddenly blew his nose with a startling honk, and maybe he wouldn't count that as real crying, to keep intact his record of "not one goddamn tear."

"What's taking so long?" he asked.

"Want me to go see?"

"Better leave them alone," he said. "Let them get used to the idea that they're sisters."

He switched off the car, and the silence was disorienting. My armpits were sticky sweaty, as if they'd been that way for a while but now was the first time I was noticing. And still the tears, so I lowered my head so he wouldn't see. I felt trapped in this car, in this day. I should be reading *The Portrait of a Lady* for class on Monday, worrying about Isabel Archer, not myself, worrying about the next paper I'd have to write. I liked the book so far because I liked any book where women were stressing about getting married. There was something so quaint about that being your biggest problem, though I knew the professor would explain that it was a serious problem and a serious book and not quaint at all. "Quaint" was one of my favorite words, and I barely found occasion to use it.

Quaint, quaint, quaint.

Jess and Penny were sisters, which I had known all along. I had known that. Like Linda and Jess. Me and Grace. It shouldn't be any kind of bombshell to think of them this way. It was biology.

I straightened up and flung back my hair. Gave a fake yawn. "You said you'd pay me fifty dollars for helping with Penny today."

"Right," he said, distracted. He slapped both hands along his suit jacket, the hokey way men do when it's time for money to show up and they pretend they don't have any. But this wasn't that old trick; he dredged his wallet from an inside pocket and flicked through the bills. He pulled out three and folded them in half and half again and then stretched his arm backward over the top of the seat without looking at me. "Sixty," he said. "A little bonus."

I reached for the money and left it folded, sensing that to examine it would be tacky. Sensing that taking it was tacky. Sensing that I was tacky. "Thank you," I said, trying to keep my voice low enough that he might not hear.

"Buy yourself something nice." His voice was normal enough, but I wondered what he meant: "Something nice" versus those too-high shoes? Versus my thrift store skirt? But I realized these were probably the casual words he threw out any time he doled out money to women—his wife, Jess, Penny's mom, Penny. *Buy yourself something nice.* It should have been nice that he said them to me, but it didn't feel nice, so I said, "Actually, I'll be buying groceries and paying my half of the electric bill."

He seemed startled but ultimately uninterested. "Okay then."

"I mean, this is a lot of money for me," I said. "That's why I asked you for it. I didn't want to, but I really need this money. I need it."

"Do you want more?" he asked.

Finally he turned around. He wasn't smiling, but he didn't look angry. He looked like he was waiting.

I didn't understand what he meant. I didn't want to ask him to explain, because I felt like I should know, I should know exactly. He should mean nothing. He should mean, *I have lots of money and it's no big deal to give you some of it.* But I wasn't sure if that's what it was. There was that dinner where he held my hand and told me I was pretty. I knew secrets about Penny's mom. This was the second time I was alone with him. *Hang on,* he had said then, that other time. Maybe he told everyone to "hang on," and I hadn't noticed. Maybe "hang on" meant something, too.

"Do you want more?" he repeated.

"Well," I said. "I mean, well. What did you have in mind? What would I have to do for it?" As soon as I spoke, I knew I had made a disastrous mistake.

"Good god," he said, his eyes drilling down into me. "What do you think I am? Jesus fucking Christ. Nothing. I have nothing in mind. You have to do nothing." He yanked more bills from his wallet and thrust them at me, fanning them out. "Take it."

"I—I'm sorry," I stammered. "I didn't mean..." but I didn't finish, because there were three fifties in that fan. Three fifties and a twenty and a five. That was books next quarter. That was a month at my work-study job. That was more than my half of the rent. "I don't want—"

"Take the money," he said, shaking the bills. "It's all I got on me."

He wouldn't miss it. This was a pair of shoes or a bracelet for Jess's birthday, or a couple of nights at the Palmer House after getting kicked out of home.

I took it, folding it in quarters like the other bills. He would have just stuffed it back into his wallet. No one had to know. I mumbled, "Thank you," which seemed like a safe thing to say. I squeezed the wad of cash in one hand because I was too embarrassed to grab for my purse on the floor. Also, because I liked gripping so much money at once, $235 combined. I got dizzy thinking of it, but also thinking how it wasn't that much, that $235 was what he walked around with all day as if it was no big deal.

He spoke in a professor's lecturing voice: "And just so the record's straight, this thing with Penny's mother wasn't about money. I loved her. And I love Penny. And maybe this is too complicated for someone like you to understand, but I love my wife and I love Jess, too. God-damn if some college know-it-all is going to judge me."

For him, I thought, *for him maybe it wasn't about money. But what about her? He shouldn't be so sure,* is what I thought. But I said, "I know you loved her. I'm sorry."

He barreled on, maybe not hearing me: "And you should be more goddamn careful. Not everyone..."

A sudden pause, maybe him thinking he should stop. I remembered the hard, glinty angles in his eyes and Jess telling me he always had to be right. He wasn't going to stop. I squeezed the thick wad of money in my hand. Mine. No matter what he said next.

He said, "Think before you go slapping prices on everything. It makes you look cheap. Don't be cheap."

I repeated, "I'm sorry."

He shook his head. "You're not someone I want associating with my daughters."

It was a struggle to speak. Finally this, a whisper that he heard perfectly: "You don't get to choose."

"My checkbook says I do," he said. "Ask."

Another pause. My stomach lurched. I should jump out of the car. I should tell Jess. I should call him a hypocrite. I should scream. I should scream rape. I should ask how much. I should not be cheap. I should shut up. I should shut up.

I felt shitty, just as he intended. He might as well be my father leaving the dark room, that final brush of his hand along the top of my head lingering on my skin. Pushing me underwater, leaving me to drown.

The front door slammed, and Jess and Penny emerged, each loaded with a row of shopping bags, and a big black Hefty slung over Jess's shoulder like a Santa pack. Penny pressed her raggedy pillow between her ribs and one arm. Her baseball mitt was looped off the tips of her fingers, and she waved it, as if explaining something to Jess. The Doc Martens clumped heavily on the wooden porch.

"Go," Jess's dad said to me, twisting the key to start up the car, and as I slid out of the car, Jess and Penny slid in, and he said in a voice that was barely his, "Here's a great idea. How about Walker Brothers for one of those great big apple pancakes?" and Jess said, "Oh, yes! You ever had one, Penny? They're aaaa-mazing," and I pushed the car door closed, not slamming because Jess's dad didn't like that, but not gently either, and partway up the walk, I turned around to watch them drive away.

I hadn't asked, so there was that. But I had wondered, and there was that, too.

Now they were gone—anyway—and I had nothing—anyway—only the bills I squeezed in my fist.

I crushed my eyes shut, started counting backward. *It was worth it, worth it, worth it,* sang the numbers in my head as they sailed through, on their way nowhere.

I was alone the whole rest of the day, with so many things to do to keep busy. I felt divided, split precisely in two, with half of me accomplishing to-do list drudgery, and the other half of me watching that girl work, wondering why she needed herself to be busy. I took back my bedroom, sliding shirts into drawers and skirts on to hangers. I wadded up the accumulation of empty, pleated Frango mint wrappers from the pound box Jess's dad had bought Penny, which explained why she barely ate. I yanked her blond hair snarls out of my comb. I couldn't find two of my oversized sweatshirts or my off-white ("oatmeal") polo shirt, and my lipsticks had been ransacked. She left only the pale shades, and since I never wore those, I pitched them, and then I went through all my makeup and threw away the eye shadows that were cheap drugstore brands because Jess had turned me snobby about Clinique. Penny left behind a clot of dirty T-shirts, three tube socks, and an unopened package of hair bands. I retrieved my fake pearl necklace from its hiding place in the toe of my winter boots and rolled up the three fifties and tucked them in there instead. The twenties, I buried with my underwear; yes, that was the first place anyone would look, but I always figured that they'd stop looking if they found something. I returned my books to the shelf, largest to smallest, and then I changed to alphabetical by author but that looked sloppy, so I went back to according to size. I threw away my nail polish because Penny had mixed up some of the brushes and colors and left caps loose; she'd also painted her initials in Evening Plum on a corner of the dresser. The boxes of rocks in the drawer looked untouched, but I lifted each and rattled it, making sure. It was a dry, scratchy sound, almost melancholy, like something I'd heard before but couldn't quite place.

I scrubbed the bathtub, though Jess was the one who took baths, not me. I sprayed Windex on the bathroom mirror and the mirror behind my door and wiped with an old piece of newspaper until there were no streaks. I liked the smell of Windex, so I sprayed it on a couple of kitchen windows, too, but ran out of newspaper. Rags and paper towels were no good, according to my mother, leaving lint and streaks.

I ate the rest of the peanut butter, all the limp celery, and I thought about ordering a pizza but I didn't, though I could afford to and could tip. That was the luxury, the *choice* and choosing no.

I wanted to sleep but I wasn't tired. The phone hadn't rung, though I hadn't been listening for it to. I could go to the library to study. I could go watch the on-campus movie, always some big blockbuster on a Saturday night. I could find a frat party. I could find a guy at a frat party. I could do all of those things, one after the other, if I planned the night right, starting at the right time, which was now, or in five minutes, or in twenty minutes, or at quarter past at the latest, or in an hour if I skipped the library or the movie, which usually had two showings anyway.

I sat at the table, I sat on the couch, I sat in the ugly tweed chair. There was no place I wanted to sit, no place that was comfortable. Standing was worse and felt aimless. I stared out various windows, but all I saw was my own dumb reflection because it was dark.

I tried to get back to reading *The Portrait of a Lady* but closed the cover almost immediately. It wasn't about marriage at all. It was about money. All the books I thought were about marriage were really about money. How had I never understood that?

I thought about the murderer, maybe bored with Saturday night, staring out his window, eating his cruddy celery, jotting notes on what to do next: 1) get more cyanide; 2) sneak it into Frango mints at Marshall Field's; 3) chuckle quietly as people died. That easy for anyone to stir a handful of poison into dorm spaghetti sauce or sprinkle it on top of the pizza I had almost ordered earlier. Utter power, like God. That was what he wanted, power—I felt sure of it and wanted to tell someone, but there was no one to tell. It was scary to understand that about him.

FROM IOWA

(fall, junior year)

"We're women of the world now," Jess said. "Aren't we?"

"Sort of," I agreed. It was our first night together in the new apartment, and her parents were finally gone, so like a party. All afternoon, her dad had hauled furniture as directed, this corner, that corner, this room, the other room. Jess told him how to rearrange my bedroom. She had a sharp eye, making him angle the bookcase in the corner, not push it flat and boring against the wall the way I would. Jess's mom left for an hour and returned with a car trunk full of shopping bags jammed with more stuff to squeeze into this two-bedroom, one-bath, on the first floor of a stacked duplex, with closets like phone booths and half as many electrical outlets as someone would need. We ordered pizza from a place in the new neighborhood. Jess's dad ate all the nibbled crust edges littering Jess's and her mom's plates. No one mentioned Tommy and how if he and Jess were still together that's who would have been pushing around the furniture and paying for the pizza.

Now, Jess slouched sideways across the arms of the ugly brown La-Z-Boy. She had threatened to haul it to the curb, but I said they'd charge us since it was listed in the lease. She snorted. "They should thank us. It's grotesque." She sprawled in it, crumpled like a Kleenex, and even with a ton of boxes to unpack in her bedroom, she found a composition notebook and wanted to write a list in honor of, as she said, "escaping my parents."

I'd been waiting for her to mention her sister now that we were alone, but she hadn't. Linda. Linda. An echo off the walls. No one had gone to London that summer. Beyond the sadness, Linda's absence shifted Jess's family like an earthquake upending a line of buildings. Her mother and father barely spoke, with Jess the only thing left to agree on. Jess talked more, desperate to plug the gaping hole in their hearts. The ache I imagined filling Jess, overflowing: the agony of her easy scorn and silly complaints about her sister, and the abrupt finality of what she'd done and hadn't done. I knew that ache. Who wouldn't want to escape?

I was lying on the couch, and because the couch also was written into the lease, it, too, was wretchedly ugly—mustard slipcovers with the texture of a soggy pile of half-decayed leaves—so I didn't feel bad plopping my shoes on the cushions. My mother had spent the whole summer nagging me to sit up straight and stop slouching and to get my feet off wherever I set them, table, chair, couch—anywhere that wasn't the floor, basically. It was the sound track of that summer, "Get your feet off..." My boss at Kentucky Fried Chicken warned I'd get varicose veins if I didn't prop up my feet and lifted her pants to show me a network of blue scarring her legs, but my mother said I was too young and why didn't I get something real to worry about?

I kneaded one of the throw pillows before sliding it under my head, trying to settle and get comfy. These were the pillows I remembered from our dorm room last year, and it was reassuring to see something familiar, round and blue with stripes, square and yellow with polka dots. Classes started in a week, though I'd been here alone since the first, waiting for Jess to escape her parents.

Jess and I were drinking Tab, though I'd dropped in a scoop of vanilla ice cream, which appalled her: one calorie versus a million. "It's competing interests," she lectured about the Tab float, and also about my other great food invention, potato chips dipped in cottage cheese. Pat Benatar played on Jess's stereo (which her dad had hooked up, stringing webs of wire to get the speakers precisely right), begging to be hit with our best shot. That song was my secret anthem, though so many people liked it that I pretended not to. The room had drifted down into that early darkness where someone stands up to turn on a light, and the mood shifts. Jess had just snapped on the floor lamp behind the ugly chair. Almost always, she was first to go for the lamp.

Now Jess said, "Here's the new list. Men Every Woman Should Kiss at Least Once."

"Always with the men," I said. "You really need a women's studies class."

"Like I need to study how to be a woman?" she said. "Seriously, this will be good. A list of a hundred essential kisses. Like every girl should kiss a musician. Remember that frat party with Eddy Clearwater playing, and me afterward totally making out with the drummer?"

Musician, check, I thought. "A boy with a motorcycle," I suggested. "A lifeguard. Someone on Valentine's Day. A stranger at midnight on New Year's."

"Slow down," she said, scribbling. "You've kissed all those guys?"

"And don't think I'm stupid," I said. "I know what you mean by 'kiss.'"

"Just kiss," she said. "Really. Like, just all sweet is all."

"A boy in the best fraternity," I said. "A boy in the worst fraternity. In the rain. Under a starry sky. A boy with a great car. A boy who can fix a car."

Still writing, she said, "I'd never kiss a boy in the worst fraternity. You know what they look like."

I said, "According to Benjamin Franklin, ugly women make the best mistresses because they're so grateful."

"Then you take that disgusting frat boy," she said. "Take Benjamin Franklin, too. My boy with a great car I guess was Tommy."

Hearing his name startled me, and I had to speak before she noticed my reddening face. I said, "Should I kiss him to knock that off my list?"

The pen froze straight up.

"Just kidding," I said.

"He was a good kisser," Jess said. "Maybe sometimes too wet, but better than too dry, like those pecks from my old-lady great-aunt."

"You want tongue from your great-aunt?" I asked.

She laughed. "Just please get your own guy with a great car." It wasn't a sharp tone, it was a joke; we were joking. Still, in my head: *Check.*

So I kept talking: "A guy who drives three hours to see you. A guy with an accent, preferably British."

"Remember that French guy we met on Rush Street who thought we were models?"

"He said that so you'd kiss him."

I thought she would laugh again, but she twisted herself to sit up properly and stretch out her legs straight in front of her. Because they were cramped, she would claim, and crunched sideways in the chair, and achy from loading and unloading boxes, but really she was secretly admiring them, how long and tan they were (which they were, maybe even better than Sydney Moore's legs). I knew her habits.

She said, "Me, my turn. A guy you meet on a plane. A train."

"The el," I said, which just came out. That was forever ago, that first fall, when I was someone else. I couldn't think of another guy. I couldn't think. I scrambled to smile or smirk, to look lighthearted. I slurped Tab through the straw, distracting with noise.

"You kissed a guy on the el?"

I shrugged one shoulder. "You ride enough, it's bound to happen. So add a guy on the Greyhound bus. Dry lips. You wouldn't like him."

She scowled, tapped the pen in quick patterns of three against the notebook. "I don't have el or Greyhound bus."

"I don't have plane or train."

"Because you don't take planes or trains," she said.

It was supposed to be silliness, not a contest, not a conversation. I rattled them off: "A guy you work with. Your boss. Your teacher. Your professor. Bartender. Waiter. Busboy. Black guy. Jewish guy. A guy who can whistle really loud through his lips. A professional athlete. A guy at a beach. A guy who's prettier than you. Any guy and then later that same guy's brother or cousin or best friend."

"Whoa," she said. "Too fast. I can't get all these down."

"A guy who can start a fire without matches," I said. "A guy who trained his dog from a puppy. A guy who can field dress a deer. A guy who cooks as good as a chef. A guy who—"

"You're saying you kissed all those guys?" she asked. "For real?"

I gave another ambiguous shrug and let her writing catch up while the list in my head tilted, darkened. Damn it. Guy who drives an eighteen-wheeler. Guy who's your friend's brother who's really a boy who likes boys, who's a fag. Guy who deals coke that you get free. Guy who buys dinner and a couple of drinks, guy who only buys the drinks, guy who brings a bottle of what he likes. A guy you meet for blow jobs in the library. A relative, a guy you're related to, a man, a man you're related to, a relative...

I barreled onward, though Jess was flexing her writing hand: "A guy you have a huge crush on who you didn't think knew you were alive. A guy who's going to inherit a boatload of money. Married guy. Married guy married to a friend, married to your best friend." *Shut up,* I thought, as Jess tossed the notebook and pen onto the carpet that had been unrolled, then rerolled and moved and unrolled again to center it properly.

"Enough," she said. She lifted her half-full glass off the (ugly) coffee table, spun it to rattle the ice cubes, then set down the glass without drinking from it. "I'm your best friend, so I should know everything about you. Have you kissed all those guys?"

"You said it was a list for what we *should* do," I said. "A hundred kisses before we die. A wish list."

"You want to do all those things?" she demanded. "Even if they're wrong? I mean, your friend's husband?"

"Don't you?" I asked. "Now that they're on a list? Don't you secretly sort of want to a little bit? You know, to be bad?"

There was a moment where she opened her mouth, about to say something. Maybe *I'm engaged,* before remembering she wasn't. Or maybe she didn't like me assuming she wanted to be bad. Anyway, I sensed the whole Tommy and engagement thing remained unsettled. I wasn't about to trash him unless she started. The one she thought she wanted to kiss was him.

I said, "What is this list for then? If it's not like a shopping list for you?"

She sighed. "I thought it might be fun."

"Is it?"

Another long sigh. My feet on the couch cushions looked huge. Size nine. Maybe that's why my mother didn't like seeing them. She wore five. Elvis loved dainty, delicate feet on women, she often pointed out. Not that it mattered now with Elvis dead, but my mother bragged that people said she was a ringer for Priscilla.

"It's just a silly list," I said. "Like Zittiest Boys in Astronomy."

"Don't you want to fall in love?" she asked. "Get married?" I watched flickers of complication cross her face, sadness but something trickier, and I paused before passing along my usual lie:

"Of course."

"Then you have to stop... this," she said. "Picking up boys on the el."

She chose that one. Yes. We knew each other that well. I jabbed my straw deep into my drink, through the ice cream and to the bottom. There were things I could admit. She called herself my best friend. What if I admitted them?

She waited.

"He was a man," I finally said, "not a boy. With amazing green eyes and a chin dimple. Worked in the pit at the Board of Trade, which is how we met; he was still wearing his jacket, and I asked about it. They stand out in the pack of men hustling down on the floor, he said, so everyone knows whose guy you are. Working down there is like shoving your way through a football game, waving your arms and screaming all day, then going out to get wasted. 'Nothing like it,' he kept saying, and he cracked up laughing when I said I wanted a job just like that, told me I wouldn't last five minutes and shoulder-slammed me, about knocking me off my feet. 'That's just what's going on in the can,' he said. So he was kind of drunk, I guess, and when he grabbed my hand and yanked me through the cars, I was like, *Why not?* We wedged into one of those unused conductor compartments, and there we were, you know, like from a movie."

I stopped. I had been talking too fast all of a sudden. I had to stop.

"And?" she asked. Her fake-casual tone prickled the bare skin of my forearms, lifted the hairs. I set my Tab on the floor, then rubbed my hands fast against my arms to warm them.

"Brr." I smiled pleasantly. "At Howard we transferred to different trains. End of story."

He said, *I know you want it,* and he wrenched back my arm and wrestled up my skirt, pinning my body where he wanted it, and a jagged hook scraped the middle of my back, dug into me, dug in, and he said again and again, *I know you want it,* like convincing himself, and I wondered if I did, if I really did, and if I did, how did he know? How did he know? It was over fast.

I added, "No idea what his name was."

She said, "You don't have to do that."

A little prim of her, and exactly why I was careful with the story, inventing the chin dimple for charm, stopping when I was supposed to—exactly like I'd been taught. I felt awkward, so I picked up the Tab again, sipped politely, silently.

Jess said, "I promise some guy will come along and love us the way we deserve to be loved."

"How do you know—" I started, then stopped, and she thought that was my whole question, because she launched into the fairy tale about the "right one" and the usual bullshit bull crap. I only half listened, because my question wasn't that. My question was: How do you know I deserve to be loved?

I thought about my mother growing up in Iowa, a young girl with exquisite, tiny feet, letting herself kiss strangers on buses or in bars. Maybe she was like Jess, expecting and waiting for "the one." And there was my father, maybe "the one" or maybe not, probably not, but she was tired of waiting. Marrying him meant no more men on the list—that she understood clearly. And—she thought, she was so sure!—marrying him would also mean no more wanting. But what I could tell that girl in Iowa is that nothing, *nothing*—not the marriage, not the list, not anything I knew—was ever the end of that constant ache, of wanting to be wanted.

I tuned in as Jess wound down, finally saying, "Anyway, I should get organized or something."

I said, "Me too," even though I'd unpacked when I moved in on the first, and I didn't have half as much stuff as she did, so it wasn't such a big deal. I took an hour, tops.

But neither of us moved. The room was shadowy, lit by the pale blue glow of the stereo receiver and the single floor lamp. I remembered a girl on our dorm floor freshman year who got kicked out after her roommate busted her for growing pot under a grow light. The roommate expected to be given all A's on her report card, like a reward, and of course she wasn't, and everyone hated her behind her back. I missed the pot-growing girl, who popped a lot of popcorn that she shared with anyone around, but I was happy that thin glowing line of purple seeping under the door was gone. The funny thing was that even with it not there, I still saw it every time I walked down the hallway late at night. Lots of things that were gone had a way of going nowhere. Maybe Linda, too.

I said, "Doesn't freshman year already seem like a long time ago? Or even last year?"

Jess said, "You know, I'm still thinking about that guy on the el."

"Forget him," I said. "If I don't even know his name he can't be 'the one,' right?"

"Like maybe there's something you're not telling me," Jess said.

"I tell you everything," I said. I shook my head for emphasis. Jess liked emphasis. She was very dramatic, dramatic enough to be a theater major.

"I just..." She trailed off, waiting for me to ask, *Just what?*

Instead I said, "Do you tell me everything?"

"Natch," she said, drawing it out, then adding, "Did you know that comes from 'naturally'? I always thought it was a separate word. I mean, look how it's spelled. It isn't even logical."

I laughed.

It could have ended there.

She said, "I just think you're that kind of person who holds a little back."

I set my Tab on the floor and stretched my arms wide open, as wide as they would go.

Now she laughed.

I imagined blurting out, *You're right, I do have a few things to tell you, some whopping big secrets, and one stupid man on the el isn't even where it begins or ends.* I imagined my secrets bubbling out, words spilling and gushing like water from a broken hydrant, words flowing so fast I couldn't stop if I wanted to, every last secret out where Jess could see it. Would she listen past Tommy? I wondered. Could she look me in the eye for any of it, see who I really was?

And after. I imagined Jess's face, and then her mother's face when Jess told her, and then her father's face when her mother told him, and all the faces after that. I imagined the rest of my life, knowing they knew my horrible monster-self. Once I let those words out, they couldn't go back in. They would turn real. What happened would be real. I imagined mumbling, *Just kidding,* afterward, but way too late. I imagined Jess telling it later, turning this moment into a dinner party story about her sad, crazy college roommate. I imagined being the sad, crazy college roommate for the rest of my life. *From Iowa,* someone might remember, half remember, *wasn't that the girl?*

Jess was uncharacteristically lost in thought, not noticing me and how I was observing her. Maybe she was also imagining. She tucked her legs up into an inverted V, propping her feet on the edge of the chair cushion and folding her arms tightly around her shins. She bowed her head and balanced one cheek against her kneecap, closed her eyes. She seemed to shrink into the tiniest scrap of space possible. Jess sat that way for a long moment while I watched her. I tried not to think of anything except how almost alike we felt right now. The moment would pass. It always did.

I had escaped Iowa. I had escaped.

Part IV:
Where Every Story
Truly Begins

THE SILVER GIRL

(summer, after sophomore year)

Nearing the end of summer. I smelled like fried chicken because I always smelled like fried chicken because the only place that picked me up after I got fired from selling popcorn at the movie theater was the Kentucky Fried Chicken on Muscatine Avenue. I had to swear I was sticking around Iowa City into fall, which wasn't any part of my plan. I was back here only for the summer, only to make money for school, only around for the cheap living. But I was a good liar.

People I knew bought fried chicken. Janey. Girls from City High who spent the day tanning at Mercer pool because they didn't need jobs. Guys who were or used to be big shots on the football team. Parents I'd babysat for. These people ordered snack packs and buckets but never said hi, because they didn't look at my face or see beyond the ridiculous candy-cane-striped smock and the poufed-up hat that made me look like I had an Afro. They just didn't see me. Which was fine.

People probably wouldn't like fried chicken so much if I told them what went on in the back. But I kept my mouth shut. I couldn't lose this job also. I needed the money. I needed the free chicken that I brought home to Grace so she got decent food during this stretch of however long it was and would be, with our mother moonlighting nights at the bakery while also answering phones for the radio station. If there wasn't chicken, Grace would be eating Frosted Flakes out of the box, because that was all our mom thought to pick up at the 7-Eleven in the twenty minutes she had for shopping between shifts. Cereal and bologna and Wonder bread for my dad's sandwiches, but that was his. My mom didn't eat. She'd taken up smoking again and said she wasn't hungry. She said cigarettes had zero calories, and same with black coffee. She would live on that for the summer, she said, and lose ten pounds. But she didn't look thinner to me, just tired. We barely saw her. She was a ghost passing through walls, either late to somewhere better than here or sleeping off a handful of pills.

Grace ate only drumsticks and biscuits. She wouldn't touch coleslaw or the mashed potatoes. I couldn't blame her. Coleslaw and mashed potatoes should be homemade, cooked with love or at least affection. This food was institutional, not nourishing. Just something going down our throats.

I took on every available shift, snapped up anyone's unwanted hours, and I was so tired that summer, so greasy and tired, but every night after work, however late it was, I sat at the kitchen table with Grace while she nibbled at a drumstick or two. She played she was a chipmunk sometimes, making lots of teeny-tiny bites, packing meat in her puffed-up cheeks until I told her to swallow it. She was that young, still pretending things. I wanted her to outgrow this habit and also I wanted her not to, not quite yet. My mother wasn't around to nag her to go to bed, so she waited up for me. She said she wasn't tired, which kind of made me mad, because I was tired all the time, all the time. I could have slept for six days straight, was how I felt.

"You tell a story and I'll draw the pictures," Grace said. "Like a book." Grace had eyes that never seemed to blink, often pinned right on me, like they were accusing me of something. I hated her eyes. I hated how tired I was always, and being this tired at twenty years old. Maybe I also hated my sister, though I wouldn't dare say so.

Those eyes. A blotchy smear of grease around her lips. Uncombed hair. Chewed-up fingernails. She never asked for anything, only a story she could draw. If I stopped bringing home chicken, she wouldn't ask why. She'd just go back to handfuls of dry cereal. She was used to not asking questions.

So I invented a story for her that we called "The Silver Girl." For Grace's birthday, I gave her new crayons, the sixty-four box with the special sharpener right inside, because the most she'd had before was forty-eight. The silver crayon was her favorite, so I gave her a story for it. She had sharpened it already half a dozen times, making it the shortest in the box. It would disappear by the end of summer. She liked silver the best, she said, because it was second best, not as good as gold, and she felt sorry for it.

Every story started with "Once upon a time." And each was separate. The Silver Girl didn't string along in never-ending, world-saving adventures; she was invented fresh each time I told a story, meaning I didn't have to remember what happened before. I could simply start with "Once upon a time." The Silver Girl had absolutely no history or past. We liked that about her.

"Once upon a time," I began, "there was a girl who lived in a cave."

"Make it the woods," Grace said. "I like drawing trees."

"A cave," I said. I always started with the Silver Girl in a cave. I liked to insist, and she liked me to insist.

"A cave, but a cave in a forest," Grace said, with a quick, shy smile. She didn't smile much because her front teeth came in crooked and some idiot in her class last year went around calling her "mule-mouth." Our father thought that was funny, so he called her that, too. Our mother didn't hear because she wasn't around, but she wouldn't have heard anyway.

"Hmm..."—fake dramatic pause—"okay, a cave in a forest." I always let Grace win, which she knew, and she started drawing. I said, "This girl who lived in a cave that was deep in the forest was called the Silver Girl, because everything about her was the color of silver: her hair was silver, her skin was silver, her eyes were silver. She was totally silver."

"Even her toenails?"

"Even her toenails," I said. "Everything was silver. If she tripped and skinned her knee and it bled, the blood was silver and then the scab that came later was silver, and if there was a scar, it was a skinny silver line streaking across her silver skin."

This was how every story began, talking about how precisely silver the Silver Girl was. Was her stomach inside her body silver? Yes. Was each tiny eyelash silver, each hair in both eyebrows? Yes. If she sneezed, was her snot silver? Yes. Did she have silver freckles? Everything about the Silver Girl was silver. If she got zits, they would be silver, and so would the goo that came out if she squeezed them. Often that was the whole story, how silver the Silver Girl was. I'd repeat "silver this, silver that," until "silver" sounded like a made-up, nonsense word, but that's what Grace liked, so I did it her way. I never got red-faced, slamming my hand on the table, yelling, *I said she's all goddamn silver, so she's silver, every goddamn inch of her!* Even after half an hour of body parts, even when we verged on disgusting, I was calm: "Yes, her poo is silver, and what she wipes onto the toilet paper is also silver."

I don't know why Grace liked this litany of questions so much, but she did. She wanted to ferret out a loophole but was relieved she couldn't.

Sometimes the story moved ahead. Grace would let me know when. "Were there animals in the forest?" she might ask.

Whatever she asked, I said yes. A theater major told me this was the theory of improv comedy, to always say yes. "Yes, there were animals in the forest where the cave was. Two elephants, a herd of ostriches, and a rhino named Sam." That was Grace's favorite name. All her Barbies were named Sam, all her stuffed animals. Now and then she slipped and accidentally called me Sam, making my heart break just a little because she apologized right away though I said she shouldn't.

We might veer off into other animals: "Were there fawns?" "Seventeen fawns, each with a different pattern of spots on their backs," which made for good coloring. Or we might scoot past the animals, with Grace asking if Sam and the Silver Girl played games together. "Yes," I would say, "she and Sam went swimming in the lake on sunny days, but when it rained, they sat on the floor in the cave and played board games." Did they play Parcheesi? Did they play Chutes & Ladders? Candy Land? Chinese checkers? Yes, I would say to each game, adding that Sam got the red markers in Parcheesi because red was his favorite color and the Silver Girl got to be the top hat when they played Monopoly. Or maybe the Silver Girl would be planning a birthday party, so what cakes should she bake—chocolate, angel food, spice, white, yellow? And what was she going to serve with her cake? Caramel corn and corn dogs and dog biscuits, because a dozen puppies were invited, and those biscuits from a tube you banged open on the counter... Yes to whatever Grace proposed.

They were stories of no drama. The end would come when I fell asleep while talking, my head propped in the upraised palm of my hand, my elbow balancing the weight just so. Not that hard to do. Droopy eyes, swallowed yawns, each word weighing a ton, and then I was asleep, blissfully free from the Silver Girl's ice-cream flavors. That's how tired I was all the time that summer. Only for a couple of minutes, and I'd startle awake, terrified I'd made a terrible mistake. But there was Grace coloring, crayons lined up, her bottom lip stuck between her teeth.

And there were the naked chicken bones on a napkin. My sister ate every scrap of chicken and shred of skin, down to the hard gray bones. Those bare bones looked too much like her skinny arms and the jut of her elbows as she colored. This was the moment when I lost my patience and snapped that it was time for bed, that it was way past midnight or one, and that she had to go to bed *now*—as harsh as a whisper got, because waking our father would be a disaster—and we'd tiptoe up to her room and she'd ask me to stay with her and I'd say I would and she'd say, "I mean all night this time," and I'd say again that I would, and she'd catch me with her unblinking eyes, and I'd repeat, "All night. I'll be right here next to you all night," and we'd squeeze into the skinny twin bed wedged between the wall and dresser and she'd say, "Promise," and I'd take in a deep breath, being patient again, and exhale all the air out into one word: "Promise," and I would mean it. I would really mean it, and she would cozy herself in, one arm slung over an old teddy bear with a missing eye that she'd had about since she was born.

But I left as soon as she was asleep, which I could tell because she'd twitch—arm or leg—and then I'd shimmy myself out of the bed, careful not to jostle her, and I'd go to my own room. I mean, how was I supposed to sleep, two of us crammed into a twin bed, with her rolling around and twitching, that crusty, smelly, drool-soaked teddy bear in my face? How was I supposed to sleep? I had to sleep. I was so tired.

She didn't know. She never said anything the next day.

On this night, there was a full moon that people would call pretty if they happened to notice it and were the kind of people to have the energy to think about those things. One of my coworkers dropped me off, but the whole drive he stammered about his friend's near-suicide last spring. "Lucky he took the razor across, not lengthwise," he said, and I involuntarily glanced at his own wrists, covered by long sleeves, as he stared straight ahead, maybe expecting questions.

I had found out about Jess's sister a week ago, and we had talked on the phone once, mostly about the apartment, a whole conversation where Jess didn't say her sister's name once. The folder of newspaper clippings was still in its envelope on my dresser. I had accidentally set a glass of water on it, leaving a crinkly circle across my address, blurring the ink. I never liked the girl who sent the clippings; her dorm room smelled like something burned. I didn't even like her handwriting. Jess might never have told me about Linda if I didn't get these clippings. I imagined showing up for school, maybe asking how Linda was, and Jess making up a story: "She got accepted to study abroad," she might have said, sending Linda off to Spain for her senior year of high school. It would have worked. It was possible that Linda might have died and I would never have known. I couldn't decide if that was sad and, if it was, how sad. Maybe that wouldn't have been sad at all. I didn't like imagining Linda in her Mazda with her friends, laughing one minute and bloody and mangled the next. All the girls in the car died. I didn't know why Jess would want this to be a secret. I didn't know if I should have pretended not to know instead of calling Jess up right away. I wondered if Tommy knew, wondered if he thought about my hair in his hands, wondered who gave him blow jobs when he was bumming around Europe those three weeks with his dad's credit card. I imagined myself at Linda's funeral, sitting next to Jess and her parents while an organ played sad hymns. She should have told me. But she didn't.

So those were the things I was thinking about when I walked inside that night, with a cardboard box of two drumsticks and four biscuits and a handful of honey packets. My mother thought open bottles of honey attracted ants. I didn't like honey that much, but it was free to take if no one was watching.

It wasn't Grace waiting for me in the kitchen but my father. Like ice knifing deep through my gut to see him slouched in his chair at the head of the table. He was supposed to be asleep.

I stopped in the doorway. Bright light hammered off the ceiling fixture, a globe shape with a too-bright bulb. "Where is she?" I asked.

He wore a light blue pajama shirt with a mat of curly dark chest hair overflowing the V. One button didn't match. Another hung off a loose thread and should be yanked and sewn before it got lost in the laundry. His elbows dug into the table as he shifted his weight. He squinted, surprised I was here.

"That chicken?" he asked.

I left the doorway and set the box of chicken on the edge of the table, nudging it toward him. It slid halfway there, but he didn't reach for the box.

"Don't want any," he said. "Just a question."

"Yes, it's chicken," I said. "From Kentucky Fried. Where I work fifty hours a week." *In case you didn't notice,* I filled in inside my head. But it was good when he didn't notice. I didn't like him noticing now, his eyes roving over my red T-shirt, my shapeless red-and-white-striped smock dotted with blobby grease stains that I had to wash out before my boss yelled at me. Lucky the dumb hat was crushed into my purse.

He should have been upstairs, asleep. He was on a new shift for summer and had to be up at 4:30, so he went to bed super early. We were supposed to tiptoe barefoot all the time and whisper. No TV after nine. If the phone rang, "goddamn it" came charging through the bedroom door. He hated the new goddamn shift and he hated his goddamn boss and the goddamn economy. That was really why I was so tired, because I could barely sleep until the door slammed at five, the car revved twice, and he was gone. None of us could.

I studied the sag of his face, how heavy the skin looked on his cheeks and jowls. Beard bristles glittered. They would be rough and scratchy now, shaved clean by morning.

He said, "Your mother took Grace to Mercy Hospital."

"What happened?" My heart skidded through five or six beats. "How come no one called me at work?"

"Just a broken arm," he said. "No big deal."

"*Just* a broken arm?"

"Kids break arms all the time," he said. His eyes met mine, locked me into place.

He opened his mouth to say more, then stopped. His tongue was bright pink, as if he had sucked on a Popsicle recently. One thumb swung down suddenly, crushing a gnat into the plastic place mat. There was the empty Popsicle box behind him on the counter. It had been half full this morning when I ate an orange one for breakfast.

Then he said, "You broke your arm. Remember?"

My words flashed out: "Is that the same way she broke her arm?"

His eyes narrowed, and tiny muscles in his face tightened. "She slipped in the bathtub."

I looked away, to the Formica counter beyond his bulk, to the empty box and its zingy colors. I spoke quietly, slowly, a mumble really, or possibly I contained the words inside my head: "Haha," I said. "I guess that is like me then."

"What's that?"

He had heard me fine. I said, "Nothing. I hope she's okay."

A flicker of something on his face, something that made him pause a half second before spitting out, "I'm not taking shit from you. That fancy school doesn't impress me." He didn't stand, but his figure sharpened into focus, looming itself into my mind. The room filled with the stench of chicken and grease and my own putrid sweat, like I was marinating in it. No escape. I hadn't wanted to come back here yet again for the summer, but it was the cheapest thing I could think of. I would never be back. This wasn't a home. There was a wad of cash in a paper bag under my mattress, as thick as my fist. Home had nothing to do with anything. I had to breathe, had to remember to breathe this time.

The slamming door made us both jump. He receded, blurred, and I sucked in air.

"We're home," my mother called. Her voice was cheerful, optimistic, a TV mom's voice, a pretty lady reading lines off a piece of paper. "We're fine. Grace is fine. She was very brave. It's all fine." Each "fine" scraped inside my skull, each cheery note.

She glided into the kitchen, holding Grace close by her good hand, the Sunday purse knocking up against Grace. Grace's hair was matted down on one side, and a sucker stick angled out her mouth. She was barefoot. There was a Band-Aid on her knee that wasn't the kind of Band-Aid we used. She wore a pink T-shirt with an applique of a double-dip ice-cream cone, one of my old shirts that was too big, hanging down practically into a dress. Her right forearm, her drawing arm, was encased in a clunky white cast, stretching from the edge of her knuckles to just below her elbow, hammocked into a cloth sling. Her zoned-out eyes seemed to be struggling to figure out the room. She looked thinner, which wasn't possible, because I had seen her this morning, when I promised I'd take her swimming on Saturday afternoon even though I was supposed to work all day Saturday.

"Does it hurt?" I asked.

She shook her head.

"Want some chicken?"

She shook her head again.

"Just a simple break," my mother said. "I saw the X-ray myself. Nothing complicated. Kids are always breaking something, the doctor said. He was very nice." She talked fast, while heaving her purse higher up her shoulder and tugging the empty stick out of Grace's mouth, which she tossed onto the counter, maybe aiming for the Popsicle box because she hit it. Then, finally, she looked over at where my father sat as if it was now his turn to speak.

"What else did the doctor say?" my father asked.

"That's all," she said, pausing before repeating, "Yep, that's all. Just the usual. Keep it dry, don't scratch if it's itchy, try to keep the arm elevated. Don't go poking around inside the cast or stick anything down there. Lucky." She bent down and smushed a kiss on top of Grace's head, rested both hands on her shoulders and gave her the gentlest shake. "You scared us, little lady." Grace's head bobbled, then she looked at the floor. I thought she'd tell them she was sorry, but actually she didn't, and it seemed like there was a moment when we were all waiting for her to apologize and my mother said again, like it was a cue: "You scared us, little lady."

"You bet," my father said. Jovial. His teeth were like a wolf's.

"She's not a little lady," I said. "She's a kid. She's ten. She's a little girl."

My father clenched his smile, narrowed his eyes at me.

"Surely you're familiar with figures of speech," my mother interrupted. "God, I need a cigarette." She fumbled in her purse for a crumpled pack, shook out a cigarette, but her twitchy fingers dropped it on the floor, which got her muttering as she picked it up, swiped it twice against her skirt.

Grace spoke suddenly: "Doing that doesn't kill germs. You should throw it away."

My father snorted, his version of laughing. "Gotcha."

"Christ," my mother muttered. "No one's dying from a dirty floor." She shoved the cigarette between her lips, dredged a Bic lighter out of her purse. The cigarette bobbed as she spoke: "I'm out fifty bucks. Might as well catch up on some sleep since I missed my shift. That'd be nice, wouldn't it?" She cocked her head, staring straight at me as if she expected an answer.

So I said, "Sure," but she kept watching me, and how was I the one to blame for the missing shift? I wasn't an adult; I couldn't take Grace to the hospital even if I had been here. Which I wasn't. I needed the hours, too.

My father moved in the chair, ratcheting the legs against the floor.

The air in the room turned heavy, unbreathable.

Not my fault, not. I crossed my arms, uncrossed them, let them hang stiffly.

"It's fine," my mother said. "Everything is fine. Grace is fine. Like I said, lucky."

My father slapped both hands flat onto the table and stood. Grace's shoulders jerked at the abrupt noise. "Bed," he said. "Good idea. Get some sleep. Goddamn morning comes too fast."

My mother snapped her lighter, lifting the flame to the cigarette. Her face loosened, released its tension, and she smiled. She was still looking straight at me, but that smile wasn't meant for me. Even relaxed, there were plenty of lines crisscrossing her face. Eventually these lines would dig through the same places on my face. Jess was terrified of wrinkles, so she slathered yellow Clinique lotion into her skin twice a day. My mother said Pond's cold cream was good enough for anyone.

And finally she turned, the flame out, the cigarette lit. "Gracie, let's get you to bed." She exhaled smoke and watched it dissipate.

"I'm not tired," Grace said. She drew her fingertips along the length of her cast. It was pure white except for one scribble toward the crook of her elbow, which I touched.

"Who's that?" I asked.

"The doctor," my mother said, "which was very nice of him. We'll all sign your cast tomorrow morning, Gracie. That will be special."

"It was prettier all perfect white," Grace said. "I don't want people messing it up." She gave a snippy sigh and scrunched her face.

"Somebody's had a long day," my mother said. "Somebody's very tired and doesn't even know it." A stream of smoke huffed out, like a dragon. She dropped another kiss onto Grace's head.

"But I'm not tired," Grace said. Her good hand plucked at the sling, fingers sliding up and down the cloth. My mother nudged her hand away.

"Stop messing with that cast," she said.

"Your mother told you it's time for goddamn bed." My father's face reddened to that splotchy color we all understood, and my mother sucked hard on her cigarette. Grace closed her eyes. I had painted pink nail polish on her toes last week and most of it had chipped off already. Then she painted my toes but didn't do a very good job. Not that anyone saw. I wasn't allowed to wear sandals to work. I knew Grace wanted a story. I knew she was afraid. She didn't know that right now she could think about something dumb like nail polish.

"Are you talking back?" my father demanded.

My mother's cigarette was stuck halfway to her mouth, smoke spiraling up. I thought about Grace trying to be so careful with the little brush but still slopping polish onto the skin of my toes, how that tickled. We giggled so much; maybe she had been messy on purpose.

All those lines on my mother's face. She must have been so depressed every time she looked in a mirror. I couldn't imagine her ever young.

I spoke cautiously, the way to approach a bristling dog: "I can put her to bed."

My mother's nod was the barest movement.

"I can take care of it," I said.

Grace chewed her bottom lip, sucked on it with tiny puckery sounds—the new tic after being forbidden to put her thumb in or anywhere near her mouth. She tried to keep this a secret but couldn't. My mother sighed but didn't flick her thumb and two fingers hard at Grace's jaw, which was what she usually did when she caught Grace.

"It will be fine," I said.

My father glared at me, a heavy look of lead. I stood straighter. Ash from my mother's cigarette drifted to the floor. She always let the ash get too long, like going for some record.

"Don't you go upsetting your sister," my father warned. "Or stirring up things that don't concern you."

My mother's cigarette finally made it up to her mouth and she drew in deeply. The red tip glowed. "She won't," my mother said. "Even if... Grace is still woozy."

Abruptly, Grace tugged her arm free of the sling and punched out her arm straight. "It's heavy," she said. "And hot. See?" The extra bulk of the cast turned her arm misshapen. "My arm is ruined," she whispered.

No one looked at my father. No one looked at Grace's arm. No one looked at anything or anywhere. It was just a moment to be gotten through, and eventually my mother told Grace her arm was fine, and my father told Grace that he'd take her out for a Baskin-Robbins double-dip tomorrow, and I told her that I had an amazing new story about the Silver Girl, and when we were all finished talking about all that, my father stood up and lumbered up the stairs, noisy as a bear, footsteps clomping hard and fast overhead, though we knew exactly how quietly he could walk that hallway when he wanted. My mother spun and followed, leaving a contrail of smoke. I snapped off the overhead light, which left only the hazy bulb over the stove. Noiselessly, I pulled out a chair for Grace and helped her settle in. Then I brought the crayons and paper from the rug in front of the TV, and I silently joined Grace, slipping into the shadows around the table.

I could ask her what happened. Though I knew. I already knew. And she wouldn't tell. Ask, and I'd just be forcing her to lie, to use my mother's easy word: *Fine. I'm fine.* Ask, and I'd have to admit that the lie was all I wanted to hear.

I unfolded the top of the chicken box, trying not to gag on the explosion of greasy air, the fried smell a slippery fog your hand reaches to swipe away, like fanning at my mother's cigarette smoke, though by now I'd given up on that, since waving it away got her going on how ridiculous I was, that a little smoke never hurt anyone, that maybe I'd lose some weight if I bought a pack of Virginia Slims now and then.

Grace fumbled for a drumstick with her left hand, tilting it awkwardly toward her mouth, maneuvering with her lips before biting down, no chipmunk nibbles, but laying in deep as if she hadn't eaten for a while. I thought I'd asked if she needed breakfast before I left for my ten o'clock shift, but maybe not. She wouldn't simply say, "I'm hungry," like anyone else's little sister. She finished in about two seconds and grabbed another.

"So I don't get to sign your cast?" I asked.

She shrugged. "It's messy."

"Really?"

She chewed, swallowed, then slid a thin bone out of her mouth, which she set onto a napkin. I thought about that chicken leg snapped in half, the force needed, the jagged splinters on either side of the break. *Kids break bones all the time. Doctors patch them up. Bones knit together, as good as new.* I heard the words in my mind, a doctor's soothing voice saying them.

"You're worried about your cast being messy?" I asked. "Or is it something else?" Maybe she would tell me. I thought I knew. She didn't want his name on there. He would go first, signing with a permanent ink marker, a big fanfare of a signature.

She grabbed a biscuit and teased it apart. But she struggled to tear open a packet of honey; the cast was awkward, her fingers slippery. I took the packet, bit down along one edge, then pulled until it popped open. Sharply sweet honey dribbled onto my tongue. I said, "I didn't know you like honey."

She zigzagged a drizzle along the split biscuit halves and nodded. "I like honey since always." Her eyes stayed down as she added, "It's better if no one signs. Not even you." All her concentration was on not looking at me, on keeping the honey-soaked biscuit level on its left-handed way to her mouth.

"Okay." Fake smile. Not that I cared about signing her cast. *Not even you.* I asked, "How long will the cast be on?"

Another biscuit, another packet of honey, which she handed to me, which I tore open with my teeth. Honey dripped onto the straw placemat, and I rubbed the sticky dot with my thumb, imagining a trail of ants scouting this spot, thinking, *Jackpot!*

It felt like a lot of silence piling up. Even her chewing was quiet. She seemed different tonight, and maybe my mother was right, that she was woozy. I said, "Time for a story? The Silver Girl?"

She said, "I can't color with this stupid thing." She lifted her forearm, then let it drop heavily on the table, a hollow thump.

"Color left-handed."

"It's not the same," she said. "I want to draw normal."

"Once upon a time," I said. "There was a girl who lived in..." I paused so she could interrupt with "the woods," but when she didn't, I continued: "Who lived in a cave."

Grace crumpled a dirty napkin and tossed it at the side of the chicken box. Then she slumped into her chair.

"Did you hear me?" I asked. "The girl lived in a cave."

Silence.

Like it mattered. Like it really truly mattered where this imaginary girl lived, or what happened in this silly, waste-of-time story. I poked at the bubble of a semi-healed grease burn on the underside of my wrist. The size of a quarter. I imagined a scar years from now, reminding me of this time and place. I drew in a breath and said, "Once upon a time there was a girl who lived alone in a cave in the woods," and Grace slid a piece of paper over and picked up a green crayon, as if powerless to resist the cue. I continued: "And what was remarkable about this girl, the Silver Girl, is that she was all silver. Her hair, her eyes, her lips—everything was a beautiful, shimmery silver, like sunlight dancing across a lake. Like the biggest moon you've ever seen. She was extraordinarily beautiful, of course, and—"

"Why is she alone?"

"Well, not alone-alone. There were lots of animals in the forest, and her best friend was a leopard named Sam." Grace liked to draw spots, so leopard was an inspired choice. Also, it seemed easy to draw spots left-handed, easier than stripes anyway.

"Does the Silver Girl like being alone?"

"She has Sam," I said. "So she's not really alone."

"Sam ran away last week. Does she *want* to be alone?"

"You are sooo talkative tonight, missy," I said, and I gave an awkward laugh. I felt trapped, every answer dead wrong. "Maybe," I said. "But mostly no. That's why she has Sam, right? Because no one likes being alone."

"You do," she said.

I invented quickly: "The Silver Girl is alone because she's in exile."

"What's that?"

"When a town sends you away for doing something really awful and wrong."

"What did she do wrong?"

I pointed to the paper. "You're not coloring."

She swiped wild green streaks across the paper, her eyes still on me. Usually she focused really hard on coloring; I imagined the world blocked out of her head as she drew trees and zebras and picnic baskets. If only she were really good at drawing. No one cared how much you liked drawing, only if a horse looked like a horse. Grace said, "What did she do wrong?"

The room darkened and tightened. I was just trying to tell a story. I wanted to talk about animals in the woods. I could have, I suppose. Pushed Sam harder. But the rule was to say yes to what Grace wanted. I said, "That was the weird thing. She didn't know what she did wrong."

"So they sent her off to exile anyway?" Now Grace grabbed a reddish crayon with her left hand, rolled it along the table. "The people in that town are mean."

The red crayon rolling back and forth, back and forth. I imagined the thoughts in her brain, back and forth. If I wanted to ask, I should do it now. Silence—like a pile of leaves, like snow, like something drifting up high while we sat and watched.

Grace said, "Then how did she know that what she did was wrong?" She watched her rolling crayon, and I reached out and rested my hand on hers to make her stop. Her skin felt sweaty. My burn bumped against the table, flared.

"Well."

"What if it wasn't really wrong?" Grace slid her hand out from under mine.

I had to invent again: "Everything she looked at turned silver. That's what she did." I stood and collected up her napkins and chicken bones and honey packets and stuffed them into the chicken box and then balanced the box on top of the overfull trash. I could take it out tomorrow. I had taken it out yesterday or the day before. Seemed like no one took it out but me. I imagined a river of garbage flowing through the kitchen two weeks after I left. I set the Popsicle box on top of the chicken box. Like pick-up sticks, that same care not to screw up with the wrong movement.

"You've got to get to bed," I said. My voice shouldn't have sounded so desperate.

"I'd like everything silver," she said. "Wouldn't that be pretty?"

"Okay," I agreed, relieved. "Yes. It was pretty. Silver squirrels eating silver acorns, silver leaves blowing off silver branches, silver birds with silver nests, a big silver lake with silver sand castles on the shore and silver-tipped waves crashing in, rolling up silver seashells. Whatever the Silver Girl looked at turned silver, if she looked long and hard enough. If she concentrated." I held one hand over my yawn; my hand smelled like chicken.

"I bet that was how she turned silver," Grace exclaimed suddenly. "She looked at herself in the mirror and concentrated really, really hard! And maybe that's what they didn't like, her changing, and her being all silver in their boring, old, ugly town, so she had to leave for exile and go somewhere silver to fit in."

"Hey, who's telling this story?"

"Chicago!" She bounced in her seat. "Chicago is silver, with a lake. Maybe the Silver Girl is there. All those big silver buildings. She was there, I know it."

"How do you know about the silver buildings?" I asked.

"You sent me a postcard that one time," Grace said. "Of silver buildings. I never get mail and it was so exciting that day I did, so I put the postcard under my mattress to save forever."

I'd forgotten sending the card my first fall, after I rode downtown on the el. I walked along Michigan Avenue, from Grant Park to Water Tower Place to the Oak Street Beach, and there was Lake Michigan sprawled out in front of me like it was all mine. I never felt freer in my life as I did that minute, like I'd finally reached the place I was supposed to be, and then that nag of guilt remembering Grace, so I bought a postcard of the skyline at Osco and mailed it. I should have sent other postcards, one every day, to show her how much more there was than the crud of here, than imaginary caves in imaginary forests; that the something more was real. I would this fall. So easy to buy some cheap postcards and lick a stamp. All I'd have to write was "Wish you were here." It was the thought.

Another mind-stopping yawn. She wasn't coloring anyway. I said, "Let's look at the card. We'll go to bed and look at Chicago, and I'll tell you the names of the buildings and we can pick which one the Silver Girl lives in."

Grace shook her head. "I don't have it anymore." She slid the stack of paper across the table, started shoving crayons willy-nilly into the box, some upside down, jamming them in when they crowded the rows, pounding on them with the flat of her hand. I tugged the box away from her. "Or the big clock."

"I thought you said you saved it. What happened?"

"Daddy threw them away."

There was a moment of stillness, then she shifted her cast, which caught on the placemat, knocking it to the floor. I stamped my foot down on it, pushing it farther under the table. "Why did he throw away your postcards?" I asked. I imagined the words leaving my mouth in a silvery whisper.

She stared down at the empty spot on the table in front of her. She wasn't going to cry; she didn't ever cry. It would have been easier if she

271

did. She shrugged, shook her head. Finally she had an answer. Finally she said, "Because I did something wrong."

"No," I said. "No, you didn't."

She reached for her crayons, but I slid them out of her reach. She went back to silence.

"No, you didn't," I said.

"No, you didn't," I said.

"No, you didn't," I said.

She didn't blink when she told me that her arm hurt and that she wanted to go to bed, and that the doctor who put the cast on smelled like onions, and that our mother stole a magazine from the hospital waiting room.

"I'll stay with you," I said, as we tiptoed upstairs. We fell quiet as we passed through the hallway, resuming our conversation only when we were inside her room, with the door shut.

"We're not going swimming Saturday, are we?" she asked, tapping her cast with one finger.

"We'll do something else," I said. "Dairy Queen. Maybe a movie." I should've told her I'd be working Saturday. But she knew I needed the hours, needed the money.

I helped her into bed—she decided to sleep in the shirt because the armhole of her favorite pink nightgown wasn't big enough for the cast to go through—and I lay down next to her and clicked off the lamp. Her cast bumped up against the wall as she thrashed through the sheets for the ratty teddy bear, which she clutched with her cast arm. I waited for her to ask me to stay with her all night, and finally I said, "I'll stay with you tonight." I meant it. I really would. I stroked her dandelion-fluff hair, brushing it off her sweaty forehead, finding a slow rhythm. *If only boys knew that this is what we wanted,* I thought, *everything could be so right and simple. If they knew. But we would never ask.*

She was already half asleep. She mumbled something, maybe calling me Sam; I really couldn't hear what she said. She was talking into the teddy bear's fur.

I thought about my own broken arm back when I was eleven and how scary the skin looked once they sawed off the horrible cast: pale and fishy, the texture of marshmallows. *Not even my own skin anymore,*

I thought, *nothing here belongs to me.* A strange thing to think at only eleven, but I remember thinking it. We didn't get Christmas presents that year because we had to pay the doctor, or that was what they said. Grace was too little to remember; "She doesn't even know what Christmas is," I remember my father saying. I hung up a stocking anyway, and one for Grace, and one for my mother, but in the morning they were empty.

"I said don't touch me." Grace swatted my hand away, crooked her arm up protectively over her forehead. I immediately tucked my hands under my armpits, pressed so the grease burn tingled. She didn't want to be touched. *Not even me,* I thought, and the three words ricocheted around my head until pretty soon they didn't.

I lay on my back, listening to Grace breathe. It was a steady sound. I watched the blank, dark ceiling. If I stared too long, it pressed in, closer to me, and I'd look away to the sliver of light along the closed door. I felt the burning white of Grace's cast. Something hot, an ember, something that would spark up. Something we were all afraid of, even him, at least a little bit.

There was one moment when she woke up. "Where were you?" she asked.

"I'm right here," I said.

"No. Then."

Nothing I could say. She knew. She knew everything. Maybe she wouldn't remember this in the morning. But in case she did, I forced myself to slowly say the truth: "I needed the hours. I wanted the money. I'm sorry." My words were tiny pinholes in the dark.

For hours, I couldn't sleep. Or maybe I was asleep. Maybe I dreamed all of this, everything.

Footsteps. The toilet. The shower. Footsteps. The door. The car. Gone. Safe. For now.

The light was shadowy as I tiptoed from Grace's room to my own. I had barely half an hour before my mother would be up, so I stuffed clothes into a duffel. I threw in the half dozen books that would break my heart to leave behind and lose forever. Makeup, notebooks, a handful of pictures of the Silver Girl, a pillow, some framed photos of Grace. I had left boxes of my winter things, my bedsheets, in Jess's garage, so I could travel lightly, and I liked how that sounded in my head, *traveling lightly,* and how hefting my single bag onto my shoulder felt. Remarkable to learn how little one might need. *Traveling lightly, traveling lightly.* The words fireworked through my head, exploding into joy and relief. That wad of bills under my mattress, all the money I had in the world, went inside the envelope of the clippings about Linda. It wasn't sad to realize I had so little. It was how to move fast.

I was pulling the door shut at the second snooze of my mother's alarm, and I walked through the dim streets to the bus stop. Because I was wearing a tank top, because I was walking a certain way, a guy pulled over and asked if I needed a ride and I said I did, to the Greyhound station or actually to Chicago, and he said he wouldn't mind dropping me off at the interstate if that was really what I wanted, and he had long black hippie hair, probably a PhD student at the university, and I told him that was what I really wanted. Heading home, I said, and he said he hoped I had a nice visit.

It wasn't so bad—the truck driver who picked me up did chew, which was messy and disgusting, but he told funny stories about growing up in Lubbock, Texas, that made my stomach hurt from laughing as he drove us straight east, into the rising sun, on into Chicago, and he dropped me at an el line, and from there I figured out a city bus the rest of the way and I got myself to Jess's parents' house, and they were shocked to see me on their front porch, but Jess's mom started crying when she hugged me, and I went into Jess's room and bounced on her bed to wake her up and she said, "Oh my god!" and I don't remember how I explained everything or if I did—my parents were getting a divorce, my parents had to go to Lubbock to take care of a sick relative—I had stories ready, but they didn't matter, because though it had been weeks, Jess's parents were so wrecked about Linda's death that they didn't talk to each other, and Jess was sleeping late every morning, staying up until three watching old movies, doing nothing to drag them over the humps to the end of each day, and so it was easy to see who I was and what I was there for: I played Jess. I talked. I told stories. I made them laugh or at least smile. I asked questions like what did they want for dinner and what brand detergent should I pick up at Dominick's, and I told people on the phone that

Jess's mother wasn't home when she was, and I weeded the garden and cut the grass, and I washed the cars and even did a pretty good wax, and I handwrote thank-you notes for flowers and casseroles and signed Jess's mother's name. Jess couldn't do those things. They needed me. Who was the favorite now? I thought, ashamed of the question, embarrassed by my longing.

Mostly, I was the person to talk to so you didn't have to talk to the person you didn't want to talk to. I was the person always around, meaning people had to stay polite. I hadn't planned this out, not any of it. But there was an empty space and I fit myself into it.

At Jess's house, I slept in one of her twin beds, the door to Linda's room always tightly shut even before her mother installed the deadbolt. No one spoke Linda's name. There wasn't a photograph displayed anywhere in the house that I saw, and maybe it had always been that way or maybe not. Some days her mother went back to bed after lunch, pulling the curtains, lying there in the shadows as the Cubs game played on the radio even though she hated baseball. Her father worked until midnight. Bottles clanked at the bottom of the trash bags I carried out to the cans. It was all familiar to me. It was how to make something fine when it wasn't.

For the first time in forever, I relaxed, just a little, for the ten days before the lease on the apartment started and I could move to Evanston and wait for Jess and wait for school and sit alone in the quiet, empty apartment, safe in my exile.

TERRIBLE BEAUTY

(fall, junior year)

People were calling reporters to announce they were the Tylenol murderer. Or driving to police stations and demanding to see the chief. Or sending letters to newspapers, Congress, and President Reagan. There was a ransom note, which everyone thought was more real than the attention-craving kooks. Apparently it was a thing, that certain people liked confessing to splashy crimes, wanting to grab glory and get their picture on the front page. An article in the *Trib* said almost two hundred people confessed to kidnapping the Lindbergh baby in the 1930s. In the 1940s, fifty people told cops they murdered the Black Dahlia, some movie actress I never heard of. "It wastes I don't know how many man-hours sorting through these false leads," said one of the detectives. "Lot of these folks are so sure they did it, they beg for the lie detector to prove they're right." There should have been a name for the syndrome, something a hundred letters long, Frankensteined together from German words, because there were more crazy people than anyone knew, or maybe more guilty people.

I read all this in the *Trib*, which still came each morning, though the bill was due back on the day of Penny's mom's funeral. Jess was the one who was supposed to write that check. She was required to read a newspaper for poli sci, with pop quizzes 10 percent of the final grade, so she signed us up for a subscription. With that bill unpaid, any morning would be the last, but the paper kept getting flipped up onto the porch. The uncertainty made me value it more, so I made sure to page through, reading the comics and the Tylenol murder articles. One day would be the last before the paper stopped. One day would be the last before Jess came back. I just didn't know which day. I didn't know when.

On the morning I read about the false confessions, I had an appointment with my poetry professor from last spring. It was getting where I had to declare a major, so I wanted to ask about creative writing even though he'd given me a B. I was also planning to ask him about alewife poems, if he saved a folder of bad poems that students had written. My thought was to amp our relationship into something sophisticated, like the two of us could talk for real, not only about class and school. I imagined drinking sherry with him, or whatever poets drank, and maybe he'd tell me about his trips to London and Ireland, about seeing Yeats's grave or Shakespeare's house. I imagined us cozied in front of a fireplace, holding tiny glasses of sherry, me listening to him recite a new poem, and he'd ask what the title should be, and, with a confident little smile, I'd suggest "Element," and that's what would be printed in *The New Yorker*. Maybe that was why I was reading the paper so carefully, so if current events came up, I wouldn't sound dumb. Last night I threw a half dozen combinations on the bed before picking the fuzzy lavender sweater to go with the black jeans that were almost too tight but only almost. I really wanted Jess's black boots that she always let me borrow, but her room was still deadbolted, so it was my own ratty pair. I guess I was anxious about the meeting but also eager. If Jess were here, there'd be a pep talk, her telling me I was a great writer and the sweater was amazing and to spray perfume on my thigh. Except for Jess not being here, everything was normal. It was all so normal.

The TV was on for noise, not the channel with *Andy Griffith*, but Donahue's yammering. I didn't want the people upstairs or anyone walking on the sidewalk outside thinking I was a girl all alone, though I was. Like the title of a painting: *Girl Alone*. Me, staring pensively. Me, alone.

Rent was due in two weeks. If I used the money from Jess's dad I could pay the whole month myself. But then I wouldn't have that money anymore. Really, I didn't know what was going to happen.

Because then there would be the month after that. And the lease was in her name anyway.

The *Trib* ran the murder tip line number every day, and it was announced on the TV news and even the radio. I had it memorized. When I couldn't sleep, which was every night, I recited the numbers in my head, forward and backward. I multiplied them together, one by one except for the zeroes, over and over, until I finally reached the exact same answer twice.

I imagined someone like me who knew those numbers by heart, punching them into a phone, saying, "I did it. I'm guilty. Drag me to prison." Hoarse whisper or gutted scream? It was a twenty-four-hour tip line, so would you call in the morning, first thing, before losing your nerve, or would it be three A.M., your call waking the cop on duty, one or both of you drinking or drunk? Would they trace your call? Would someone be pounding down your door before the words were the rest of the way out? The steely click of handcuffs, the blurry mumble as you got Mirandized, lights blaring red and blue through your drawn curtains, the whirling drama of *you, you, you,* your confused neighbors peering through slats at windows, noticing you for the first time. Would it feel exquisite, exquisitely painful, your arms cranked behind your back, wrists bound tight in those heavy cuffs, the cop roughly shoving your body forward? *I did it,* your mind spins, *yes, I did it, and it's my fault, me, I'm the one.*

I imagined it like leaning against a boulder, and leaning and leaning, until finally it's torn loose, barreling down a hill, and it's gone. The relief. And the ache. What there is now is emptiness, and they send you back home, because you *didn't* do it, because you're no one, you're nothing. The neighbors seeing that, too. But your secret heart still knows. Guilty.

I would have to leave soon for my professor's office, twenty minutes away, based on how fast we walked at this school. We walked fast because of the damn fucking cold, or because with only ten minutes between classes we had to book it between north and south campus, or because that was how to pretend it was okay being alone with everyone else strolling in cozy, laughing groups, or because we saw that hateful pig of a guy from the other night, or because your coat wasn't close to warm enough for Chicago but nada money for a better one. Lots of reasons to walk fast.

But I shouldn't skip breakfast again, not that I remembered much food in the fridge, just half an inch of skim milk and a piece of left-over mushroom pizza in tinfoil, which maybe would keep my stomach from growling during my meeting and maybe keep me from wasting money on ice cream for lunch at the Cone Zone. So I went to grab the pizza to wolf cold but found clustered on the second shelf a six-pack of Tab, two strawberry yogurts, an egg carton, a stick of butter, and a container of small-curd cottage cheese. Immediately, I wondered if I had possibly bought all this and forgotten. Was I truly so absentmind-ed? Was anyone in real life absentminded enough to walk to the corner store, drop items into a basket, dredge out a ten, match idle answers to the cashier's idle chitchat, lug home a brimming grocery bag, and arrange these items fortresslike in a corner of the refrigerator? And not remember?

I stared at the food as if it might evaporate. I hadn't bought those things. Jess was here. I flicked my eyes to her bedroom door. It looked locked, but of course it would: it was the kind of deadbolt where you needed a key both to lock and unlock it. She might be inside. She might have only stopped by. I had been in the shower. I had been asleep. She could have snuck in. She might still be here.

I would be late if I didn't leave now to meet my professor. I walked to the TV and snapped it off.

"Jess?" I said.

No scuffled sound of someone trying to keep quiet, no answer, sigh, or breath. I couldn't see her keeping quiet for long, without running to the bathroom to pee or to check herself in the mirror with the good lighting, to study her new eye shadow or look at her hair another way, or to ask me how to spell "discombobulate" (she was the world's worst speller, and until she met me she assumed commas were random), or to get water because she believed in eight glasses a day, or, really, just because she wanted to say hi to me. Just to say hi to me. That she wouldn't do that is what I couldn't imagine, even after everything.

With the TV off, the silence was piercing. I tiptoed to her door, pressed my ear against it. "Jess?" I whispered. "Are you in there?"

The furnace whooshed on, the refrigerator hummed. I heard a gurgle in an upstairs pipe, the leaky toilet tank burring to life, a car horn honking, the deep-chested bark of a dog on the sidewalk, the endless beat of my own heart, the imaginary sound of the ocean ringing through both ears as if I were holding a seashell. I could have looked for her car, but that was easy. I was afraid it was there, afraid it wasn't.

"Where are you?" I spoke in my normal voice, suddenly a thousand times too loud, startling me, and I refused to feel afraid so I shouted, "Where the fuck are you, Jess?" and I hammered both fists against her door, until the bones in the sides of my hands felt pulpy, and I rattled the locked door, raging at it, twisting the knob, wanting it to snap off in my hand. Finally I howled, clawing the wood, gouging streaks and scary grooves across the varnish, splintering fingernails and trashing my polish.

Her car wasn't anywhere.

I was ten minutes late to meet my professor, but he barely cared, waving one hand in a slow semicircle as I tapped the half-open door and slid inside. "Good to see you," he said, before starting one of those long pauses I guessed someone taught him to do, where the other person breaks and speaks first, absolutely frayed by the pressure of his silence. He pulled that in class all the time. I could wait him out most times, but right now I brimmed with nerves.

"I think I maybe want to be a writer," I said. "Would you take me in the writing program?" I was breathless, from walk-running all the way down Sheridan Road to University Hall on south campus. It was one of the oldest buildings on campus, always hot and crowded, students roaming and circling with thick down jackets draped over their arms, backpacks mashed and tangled. I was in such a rush that I hadn't taken off my coat, simply flinging myself into one of the wooden chairs, the one not teetering with double stacks of skinny-spined poetry books.

"There's paperwork," he said. "Everyone has to apply." He reached for a coffee cup but didn't sip, just held on to it as if his fingers were cold, which had to be impossible since it was about a thousand degrees in this fourth-floor office (one dinky elevator for the whole building; I'd stormed the stairs two at a time). He looked so, what, "poetic" sitting there in his V-neck like all the English department people wore, with his spidery, dark fingers curled around that pretentious mug, a picture of Shakespeare on the side or some other guy in a neck ruff, and I just knew the saying his fingers covered up was something like "What fools these mortals be!" or "The first thing we do, let's kill all the lawyers" and that it was a gift from a now ex-girlfriend who'd bought it at some Shakespeare festival. What was sherry anyway? He probably drank cheap beer like everyone else. He was pretty young for a teacher, maybe thirty. But already he had a book of poems that won a prize, all about his dead brother, all sad. I read them last spring in the library, months ago, but one line I couldn't forget: "But grief is like a dream, interesting only as our own." I mean, really, that I had tried hard to forget it, but I couldn't. It was too sad to forget. So even though his coffee mug was stupid, there was that unforgettable line, those poems, along with his dark skin and a rebellious tangle of braids spilling down his back. The creative writing major had fewer requirements than the English major, so mostly there was that. I could grab the paperwork and go without a meeting.

"I know," I said. "I'll apply and everything. But I want—no, I need to know if I even could. If I even could be a writer, I mean a real one." That wasn't at all what I had planned to say, not even close. I didn't know I was thinking this. I sounded weak and needy. I sounded sad like the line from the poem. I sounded all alone. I sounded lost. This would be how the fake confessors would talk, I realized, like lost, needy people who were all alone. "Do you keep copies of those really bad poems from class and make fun of them?" I added. "You and the other teachers? Like at a faculty meeting, do you all compare the bad ones? The ones about the dead alewives symbolizing the circle of life and stuff?" As I spoke, I struggled out of my coat, which was hard to do while sitting, and I got trapped by the sleeves, thrashing around like a flipped-over bug, like Gregor fucking Samsa.

Still circling the Shakespeare mug with both hands, he leaned back in his chair, which squeaked melodically, watching until I finally freed myself of my stupid coat. I almost knocked over the stacks of poetry books. Dozens of baby bookmarks jabbed out the top of each book, the markers made from ripping tiny slivers off a normal sheet of paper. His chair squeaked again as he resettled in it. There was one small window to my left, and a slant of sunlight angled in, so sharp it was like it had weight. This silence was going to kill me.

I said, "Did you put any of my poems in that folder?"

I said, "Like, I wasn't very happy with that one about the staircase and the footsteps, you know, from when we were talking about personification. Did you put that one in that folder of really bad, dumb poems? Did you let anyone else read it?"

I said, "Did you laugh at any of my poems?"

I said, "That really happened, what I wrote about. That was real. Those footsteps. Those."

I said, "That was my life."

I said, "That was me."

It sounded like these things I said were each separate and that it took a hundred years to spit them out. But probably it wasn't even a minute, and the whole time, he was watching my face. The whole time, he was listening to me, and finally he brought the mug to his lips and took a sip. Then he said, "Yes. I do think you could be a writer. I do. And yes, a real one."

"Oh." I hadn't expected that answer, or any answer. I jumped up and grabbed my coat, hugging it to my chest. "Okay, thanks."

He laughed, though nothing seemed funny to me. Sweat dribbled down my back. My face felt puffy and hot and pink. "Fill out these forms," and with one hand, he peeled a couple of pages off a giant stack. "The deadline is next week. And please type," he added. "I remember your deplorable handwriting."

Deplorable. I made a mental note to use that word more often. I took the papers, debating whether to hold them pristine in my sweaty hand or stuff them into a crinkle in my book bag. I held. "Have you seen Yeats's grave?" I asked. Finally I was able to grasp at one of my prepared questions, getting back on track for the sophisticated meeting I had planned.

He seemed startled but said, "I have. Have you?"

Have I? Me? He didn't know that I had never been on an airplane, let alone gone to Europe; that before coming to this school, I hadn't even understood Ireland was split up, or known who Yeats was or why we said Yeats one way and Keats another though the words looked like rhymes; that I'd never had a black teacher, let alone a black teacher who wrote poetry and who had seen Yeats's grave. I shook my head no but felt oddly buoyant.

When he spoke, I could tell it was a piece of poetry by that reverent lilt he got when quoting the real poets in class (he certainly did not read our piddly work with this voice):

Cast a cold Eye
On Life, on Death.
Horseman, pass by.

He said, "The epitaph on the stone." Another silence, but different, the kind of silence where everyone is thinking, and surprisingly he spoke first: "Noting that things carry on after we're gone. That life and death are..." He peered closely at me. "Well, you're smart. What do you think?"

I said, "That's nice," though of course the quote was much more than nice, and nice was about the stupidest stupid word I could have said about those lines, which were more words I couldn't forget even if I tried. To distract myself, I concentrated on the skinny line of sweat tickling my spine and how unbearably hot I was. *Pop the window and get some air,* I wanted to shriek. No wonder he was always hacking coughs in class with this petri dish of an office. It was the worst one in the building, hopefully because he was so young and hopefully not discrimination against the only black English professor.

"I'll fill this out as soon as possible," I said, rattling the papers in my hand to add authority. Then I crammed them awkwardly into my book bag.

"Very good," he said. "Welcome to the sweet torture of the writing life."

My smile felt embarrassed and confused, but maybe he saw beyond it, because he went on: "'A terrible beauty is born.'"

Later, I learned that line was also Yeats, from "Easter, 1916," the famous poem about the Irish rebellion, a breakthrough for Yeats and his political evolution. Later, I saw Yeats's grave in Ireland for myself, and a scruffy grad student took my picture beside the tombstone, my fingertips deep into the famous words etched into the stone. This professor and I crossed paths again, the first time at a poetry reading in an incandescent city I'd always considered more dream than destination. And crossed paths, and crossed and crisscrossed, until our lives were entwined. He gave me Baldwin and Portugal; I rescued his pages from the trash; we whispered by candlelight and murmured on balconies and argued long-distance, and when it was over, we stayed in love for a long time after.

Later again, I couldn't say when, I realized that what the professor said to me this day was what he would say to any hopeful cluttering his office. He was merely doing his job as director of the creative writing major, reeling in students to keep his department funded and placate the dean. I had not been tagged as a special person of genius. I was not some extraordinary talent waiting to be properly honed. He neither said nor implied that, not any of that, which is so clear in retrospect. But such is random luck—that we don't recognize it's luck as it happens, or that it's random—and those casual, tossed-off, empty sentences of his became an open door beckoning to me, a haven to step inside.

I plunged out of University Hall into the crisp blue of October, thinking about Yeats, half expecting to see a horseman. I felt slightly important, like this feeling might last forever. But there was Sydney Moore, posed in front of the Rock, staring as if it were some sort of oracle at Delphi instead of what it was, a semi-embarrassing school mascot—I guess, if an inanimate object could be a mascot—centered in the plaza, perpetually painted and repainted with a mélange of Greek letters. That was the thing to do with the Rock late at night, splash it with paint and your Very Important Message (PHI PSIS RULE!) and stand guard until morning to make sure it wasn't painted over by a competing group's Very Important Message (PHI DELTS RULE!). Rumor was the Rock was actually an old drinking fountain that had been coated with years of paint layers, turning it into a misshapen lump the size of a VW bug. Not that anyone believed this story, but it was more interesting than the truth of it just being a rock.

I stood still as purposeful students zigzagged busily, their brains buzzing about important meetings with professors and reserve reading in the library and band rehearsal, like a scene in a movie where everything else speeds up until it was only me and Sydney both motionless, linked in some significant way. So when Sydney turned and started walk-running, it felt right to leap into her wake, following. She sped along the asphalt path that wound behind University Hall, continuing over by Annie May Swift Hall and the library, the path eventually leading on to the student center and, beyond that, if she kept going, to the lake. She wore sweatpants with her sorority letters slapped across her butt and red high-tops, which I coveted immediately. On top, a purple sweatshirt baggy enough to look swiped from a boyfriend or an ex, perhaps Tommy.

There was no reason to follow her, just that everyone else was moving with such purpose. I had purpose, I reminded myself as I slid into my coat on the run, I had a goal, the most immediate being to type up my application for the creative writing major and, more immediate than that, to get myself to my Victorian Novels seminar that met in ten minutes, where my clear purpose was to make pertinent remarks about *The Portrait of a Lady* so I would get a good grade, the purpose of which was to get a high enough GPA to land me into business school or law school and to get good grades there and meet fancy friends who would help me get high-salary jobs in interesting cities, who would invite me to the kind of parties and weddings where I would be a bridesmaid and meet the man I would marry, who would also have a high-salary job in the same interesting city. There was a whole path of purpose ahead of me, ahead of all of us, but instead of putting my head down and following it, today I trailed Sydney Moore through campus.

Her dusty-blond hair was in a tight ponytail, bobbing in a perfect, hypnotic arc, never too far one way or the other. Maybe the ponytail was her choice, but in my experience ponytails meant unwashed hair. Also in my experience: unwashed hair meant unshaven legs and possibly unbrushed teeth—but this was impossible to imagine of Sydney, so must be she was late for something, and she simply tumbled out of bed in a crazed rush. One shoe was untied, but she didn't stop to fix it or notice when the lace dragged through a puddle. People hurrying in the opposite direction lifted hands and waved, mumbled "hey," but she kept her head low, rarely even a nod. She knew about everyone, or everyone knew her anyway—even when there wasn't a hello, there was a sign of startled recognition on the faces blurring by. She kicked through leaves, veering to knock through the biggest heaps, and even found a loose rock that she kept going for a while, knocking it fiercely forward.

I was getting farther from where my class met, but I matched her pace even as the sweat built up again. I realized I had never spoken to her, maybe never heard her voice. Tommy had loved her, presumably—though I couldn't imagine him murmuring "I love you" without chortling immediately after.

Something about the liquid blue of this particular sky sharpened everything I saw, making me expect meaning from these ordinary things: the crunch of leaves, the glinting windows of the three library towers, Sydney's vivid red shoes, William Butler Yeats. My mind filled with anticipation, unsure of what I was anticipating. Almost like when I was a kid, walking home after school, the house key loose in my coat pocket, my fingers running over its grooves and ridges, and a voice stuck in my head: *She's on Eastwood Drive now, and at the corner, she turns right. Here's where the tied-up black dog lunges and barks. Time to cross the street again, so she looks both ways. She's cutting across the yard. She's at the porch. She's at the door. She's opening the door. The door's open. She's inside.* My heart banging, my breath rattling, though no one was home, only me.

Sydney dashed onto a dogleg that led around the side of Baxter, the student center, and to a little-used back door, which she pushed through. Baxter was boxy and glassy and aggressively modern, seemingly built from spackle and cement, all open space, all cold floors and sharp angles and echoes, utterly lacking in nooks and the colors and shapes most people would identify as homey; you couldn't even think a word like "chintz" without feeling mortified. It was like, *Here's a new student center for you people, but don't get comfortable.* There was a grill—grease a specialty—and the Cone Zone for ice cream (both places I visited too often); a game room with pool (dominated by frat boys) and Ping-Pong (dominated by Chinese grad students); meeting rooms for clubs; the student newspaper headquarters; the place to cash checks with a student ID; various administrative bureaucrats scattered in offices; a "quiet room" filled with reasonably soft chairs, racks of magazines, and dozing students; a push-pin map for people hoping to hitch rides to various cities; and the campus bookstore, where we loaded up on textbooks and rah-rah, like the purple sweatshirt Sydney wore. This is where she ended up, swooshing through the glass doors, so me too, several steps behind and slowing my pace, curious to see what she was buying—spiral notebook? Tampax? Did Sydney Moore use Tampax? I was sliding my book bag into one of the lockers at the front of the store, ready to stalk Sydney through the aisles, but she was already at the open cash register. Not like she was much noticing the existence of other people, but I scooped up a copy of the student newspaper and flipped to the angsty personals in the classifieds, pretending I might be the "Kant-carrying brunette in the libes at 9:00 break." I could stare at the paper while spying on Sydney in line, sighing and shifting her weight; she was even less patient than Jess. I couldn't make out what she was buying; something small and purple was crumpled under one arm. Pom-pom hat for next week's football game? Puffy mittens for winter? Freshman year, right when I got here, I splurged on a purple football jersey with a number printed on the back that I thought was arbitrary but that I later found out was supposed to be your graduation year. I was off by one, so wearing the shirt made me feel like a fraud, like trying to pass myself off as older. Worse, I felt like an idiot, the girl too stupid to buy a school T-shirt. I barely wore it except in Iowa, where no one knew my screwup.

Sydney slouched up to the front of the line, her wad of purple piled on the counter. The clerk was a student, a tall girl snapping bright green gum, with hair dyed a brittle blond and broad stripes of an unflattering blush swiped across both cheeks. Theater major for sure, someone expecting to be the center of attention, and she spoke in a brassy voice: "Hey, Sydney."

Sydney pivoted her attention to the girl, straightened her spine and shoulders, and managed to look regal in her ponytail and sweats. "Oh, um, hi... um?"

"Kathleen."

There was a pause. Sydney didn't blink, and her famously pouty lips were pinched tightly together.

"From—"

Sydney sighed sharply. "Look, I'm in a rush and I just need to pay for this." With one finger, she nudged forward the purple thing. Her voice wasn't what I had expected, very flat, like a straight line, not fluttery at all.

"From Philosophy of Language and Communication," Kathleen said. "We were in the same discussion group." She clicked her fingernails on the keys of the cash register but only to make noise, not ringing up anything.

Finally Sydney focused on Kathleen and gave a curt nod. "I remember." Anyone could tell that was a lie. A cluster of giggling girls swooped from the aisle of beer mugs and shot glasses, and Sydney pawed the purple thing, covering it with one hand until the girls disappeared back into the merchandise.

"Yeah, remember?" Kathleen prodded. "That TA was a real dick."

Sydney crossed her arms over her chest and drilled Kathleen with a hard, narrow-eyed stare, like a magnifying glass lasering sun onto hapless ants roaming a sidewalk. "Do you mind?" she said, as she delicately hitched one edge of her sweatshirt to retrieve a folded bill from her waistband. "I just need to pay for this." She let the bill drop onto the counter in a colossal bitch move.

Kathleen popped her gum, then lifted the item with both hands and gave it a little shake. It was a toddler-sized hooded sweatshirt with a cartoonish Willie the Wildcat on front, exactly what the old people scooped up at homecoming for their grandchildren.

"Sure that's not too small for you?" Kathleen said, flashing a theatrical smile like she was still convinced they were great friends.

"It's not *for* me, you imbecile," Sydney snapped.

"Jesus, it's a joke," Kathleen said, smile collapsing into an audible huff. "You really need a sense of humor."

"You really need to do your job and ring this up," Sydney said, "and shut up already. Just shut up, please, just shut up. Shut the fuck up, you fat fucking bitch." The words were fast, nearing hysteria, and Kathleen stared at her, glassy-eyed and confused, until Sydney added, "Okay, Katharine, please. Just please ring it up and put it in a bag and just please let me get out of here." She forced a smile.

Kathleen looked about to say something, mouth open as if to speak, but then she cocked her head sideways and gave it a quick shake as she got the register dinging and the cash door swinging open. She counted out the change silently, and Sydney didn't recount or examine the bills, simply folded them in half and half again, crunching them in her fist as Kathleen shoved the tiny sweatshirt into a plastic bag. I mean, oh my god. What had I just seen?

"Thank you," Kathleen called sarcastically, "come again!" and she spun around, abruptly spotting me. Her face reddened, and I felt so sorry for her, but I wasn't sure if a smile would help or not so my face froze into a grimace, and Kathleen grabbed at her hair, dredging it up off her back in an affectedly casual way. "Jeez, and I let her copy my notes for that class, and plenty of times. She never would've passed without me." Her voice was shaky.

"I guess," I said.

"Pure bitch," Kathleen pronounced. She crossed her arms over her chest and sighed deeply. "You saw what she did, the kind of person she is. Why is someone like that? Why are you friends with her? What's wrong with you?" For a frozen moment, Kathleen waited for my answer, so I shrugged and grabbed my bag and hurried away, thinking I should get to class where I was already late; thinking, *I'm not her friend, obviously I'm not, anyone can see how different we are.*

And there was Sydney, in line at the grill, tiptoeing and leaning to shout her order at the half-deaf man in the white paper hat. Probably he should be fired for his perpetual crankiness and the way he pretended not to hear orders, but the greasy ooziness of his patty melt was sublime. Just one bite and a new zit or two leaped up, but so worth it—though I couldn't imagine Sydney craving patty melts. I mean, supposedly they deep-cleaned the grill only once a year, the day after graduation, and I'd heard stories about a rat nest in the exhaust fan, and once I was sitting one table over from a guy who found a bolt in his cheeseburger. But, really, I couldn't imagine anything about Sydney anymore. Why she would freak out at the student bookstore over a sweatshirt for a baby, why she'd call a chatty theater major a fat fucking bitch, why she was running around campus looking like she'd been scraped off the bottom of a trash barrel. I was suddenly conscious that she might be furious if she caught me following her, so I ducked over to the wilted salad bar, pretending to check the soups that never changed: chicken noodle or tomato. Both as salty as an ocean, but no one fussed if you swiped crackers, which I did, jamming them in my coat pocket for later.

The fry guy grabbed a plastic plate off the stack and dumped an entire basket of French fries onto it, which he handed over to Sydney, who walked to the cashier and paid with one of the bills in her hand. Double or triple order of fries, easy, with that just-out-of-the-fryer glisten. Crinkle cut. I hadn't eaten that leftover pizza in the fridge, and my stomach whined, but I had my crackers, I guess, so I trailed Sydney to a section of empty tables far, far away from the windows overlooking the lake where everyone normally sat. In case she looked up, I ducked over to a bank of pay phones, pretending to make a call. Sydney wolfed those fries, not pausing for ketchup, not once wiping her fingers on a napkin. The bag with the tiny sweatshirt was a lump on the table across from her. She kept staring at it, or maybe she was just staring as she pumped fries into her mouth, an assembly line of eating.

Then the plate was empty. Five minutes, tops. She circled the pad of one fingertip around the dish and licked that finger—for the salt?— then stared at her finger for a moment. She jumped up, leaving the plate on the table, ignoring the laminated signs posted every five feet telling us to bus dirty dishes to the bins. She scrunched the bag and strode across the room—eyes focused on the floor, but she was interrupted by scattered "heys" from various groups sitting at tables, so she stopped twice to chat, foot tapping, arms crossed, the plastic bag crushed under her elbow. She didn't smile. She seemed to stand too still, except for that single tapping foot.

Then she was at the Cone Zone, and the acne-scarred boy behind the counter gawked and twitched and blushed pink as she ordered and pointed; he scooped a double-dip of chocolate chip (my personal favorite) into a sugar cone and she set a couple of bills directly onto his outstretched hand, which made his face go pinker. He turned for change from the cash register, but she was already walking away. "Hey," he called after her. "You forgot your change," and then, "Sydney!" as if it were the magical word he'd never dared utter, but she was off, and so was I, trailing up the stairs, past the posters and notices taped to the walls, the concerts and bikes for sale and roommates wanted and typing services at super-low prices; she took the stairs fast and hard, thump by thump, up to the third floor, to the big chairs overlooking the grassy lakefill and the flat blue of the lake rolling along and over the edge of the horizon.

Sydney strode to the far glass wall and stared straight ahead, biting through the ice cream, her perfectly straight front teeth hacking off chunks. It was a cold, painful way to eat ice cream, chewing through it fast enough for a brain-freeze headache. There was no pleasure in these treats. Pleasure wasn't the point. Clearly.

Sunlight streamed in through the glass, and the blue beyond of the lake and the sky were dizzying. Her vivid red shoes, that lace still untied, still dragging. I was aware that I had skipped class for this. But what was this? I wasn't her friend and never would be. I couldn't possibly know Sydney Moore after trailing her around like a psycho for forty-five minutes. I wanted to say something to her, something like "I get it," even though I didn't get anything. I wanted to disappear. I wanted to have chosen earlier to go to class. That plastic bag, the mystery of that bag wedged between Sydney's ribs and her elbow.

She was down at the cone already, crunching slabs off it. Ravenous. The cone disappeared, and she licked her lips, then wiped them with her palm.

Right then Sydney whirled around, accusing and so fast that I couldn't react, because her legendary blue eyes, exactly the same sharp and dizzying blue of the sky outside, pierced mine, locked up mine. My mouth dried to dust and dropped open. My knees went to Jell-O. It might be the first time in my life I would faint for real. I didn't, I couldn't—not in front of her. I gulped in air, more, and steadied.

She was gazing right at me, but also through me, like the window, like I was glass, like I wasn't there, I was without substance. I thought, *We've sucked the same man's cock,* but luckily I didn't say it. I thought, *Someone thinks I could be a writer,* but I didn't say that either. I thought, *Two girls stare at each other, and one is pretty and the other isn't.* And finally I thought, *I know you.* And I said it: "I know you. Who you are. I know who you are." *But so what?* I thought. So did everyone else on campus, as I had witnessed.

She blinked quickly, reached both hands to wipe her eyes with her index fingers, and the bag fell with a plasticky whisper, landing just next to her foot.

I imagined Tommy whispering her name, remembered everyone we passed saying it.

I imagined how unhappy she might be. More unhappy than me maybe. More unhappy than anyone. I felt right to imagine this.

I bent down to pick up the bag, I don't know why. Because it was just there on the carpet, practically on top of her ankle, and she wasn't doing anything about it, so I knelt down and grabbed the bag—surprised it didn't feel like anything except what it was, a plastic bag, barely any weight to it—and I stood slowly, the bag in my outstretched hand so she could take it, so she would see I wasn't swiping it. There was a moment where we just stood there, me with the bag in my hand and her not taking it, and I thought I should say something, so I said, "You dropped this," which was a very obvious thing to say, but the words made her blink again, and it was like I was following her for exactly right now, to be the one waiting here to retrieve the bag.

Suddenly she whisked toward the hallway that led to the ladies' room. "You dropped this!" I called after her. A loop of words I couldn't escape, the cue she missed. My apparent purpose thwarted.

I waited for a minute. Was I supposed to follow her? Would she come right back? It occurred to me that if the receipt was in the bag, I could return the tiny sweatshirt for cash when Kathleen was on break. I waited another minute. It wasn't like she didn't know she'd dropped the bag. *You dropped this,* I had said. *I know you,* I had told her, when we didn't know her at all.

I tiptoed down the narrow hallway, halting at the bathroom door, the sound vivid and clear and horrible from where I stood, hacking and coughing, choking and heaving. My own gut clenched as I imagined her finger jamming down her tongue, pushing, prodding, digging deeper; I imagined the tile stony against her knees; I imagined the dark, bitter burn spreading up and into her throat, that familiar taste, the pleasure of that pain; I imagined warm bile spilling over her finger and hand, tumbling into the white maw of the toilet. I imagined her kneeling ass-up over the toilet, Greek letters in clear view, the red Converse high-tops a bright anomaly. Begging her body for more.

The plastic bag abandoned in my hand, the tiny purple sweatshirt not the simple gift, as I had assumed, for a sister, niece, godchild, neighbor. Or it was, but it wasn't. The wallop in my gut, the sickening thump of knowing: there had been a baby. There had been a baby and now there wasn't. Like me and that baby I didn't have. I ached for her, and for just one tiny second I ached for myself.

Some choices you can't think about ever again once they've been made. You have to tell yourself that. Isn't that what being tough was? That steady course forward, bulling through. Damn it.

I listened for another minute as Sydney Moore purged, a long minute that brought me no vindictive pleasure.

I didn't know what to say, how to save her. Not Sydney, not myself. Not Grace. Damn it. Damn it again. I stared up at the ceiling, down at the gray carpet, up again, down. Finally, I dropped the plastic bag on the floor and did what I'd learned to do: I left. I chose to leave. And I didn't look back.

Back when we were freshmen, Jess had been asked to a fall formal by a freshman guy she barely knew. He was in her soc class. They had whisper-chatted in the library, both of them cramming for midterms in the special room kept open all night for the desperate. Another time she gave him a pen in class because his ran out of ink. That was all.

"And then Thursday he was like, 'I need someone to go to this dance with me,'" she reported, "'on Saturday.' I mean, really. He's telling me this on Thursday."

She'd be doing him a huge favor, he explained, that as a pledge the guys would totally give him shit if he didn't show up with a decent date.

"That's exactly what he said, a decent date," Jess said. "That I looked like the kind of girl who'd already have a dress."

Which was true. Jess had tons of formal-ready dresses to choose from, and right now they were spread out across her dorm bed an hour before he was picking her up. ("I told him hell no was I taking the el and he better find a car somehow," she said.)

"You could have said you were busy," I said, knowing exactly why she didn't, wondering if she would cop to it.

She fingered the black sequined dress with the dropped waist that was the current favorite. "I felt sorry for him," she said.

"And?" I prodded. I don't know why I cared, why I needed her to confess the truth. I would have done the same—said yes—though anyone could glance at me for half a sec to see no way would I have a dress already, that I'd need time to scour thrift stores for something unique enough to pull the shift into "vintage" from "used." I pushed again: "Why'd you really say yes?"

She laughed. A lot of times when I dug into her like that, she laughed, as if she knew exactly what I was doing and found it amusing. She liked me catching her bullshit. "You win," Jess said. "I said yes because somehow that dork got into ATO. He must have a father, an uncle, and a hundred cousins who are ATOs. Legacy." She flung aside that black dress and pressed a different black dress against the curves of her body, staring at herself in the mirror. "Maybe I'll meet someone else there," she said. "Someone better. You'd do the same, right?"

Her eyes met mine in the mirror, locked them still, because we both knew about her boyfriend back home, Mitch. Also that Mitch had been her high school friend's boyfriend first and that the friend stopped speaking to her. We both knew these things, and I knew I should have been appalled and yet she knew I wasn't. Already we liked this about the other.

The five dresses were pretty, arrayed on the bed like a black-and-silver rainbow. The scent of lavender rose from the silvery-gray one when I reached for it. It was simple, like a slip, but glittery. Very short. I inhaled, imagining the occasion that had come before, Jess spritzing perfume behind her ears, in the crooks of her elbows, behind her knees, on one thigh. Until I met her, I sprayed perfume only on my neck.

She still watched me in the mirror. "Try it on," she commanded. Maybe it was the lavender or the slick fabric, but I yanked off my T-shirt with one hand as my other tugged the buttons of my Levi's. I wriggled the jeans down my unshaven legs, stepped out of them, and bent to roll off my knee socks. I twisted my arm to unhook my bra. Then I let the dress drape over the top of my head—the cool cloth like a tickle of water flowing down my body—and the shimmers flashed before settling against my skin. I sucked in my stomach and stood next to Jess, assessing myself in the mirror. I looked good wearing this dress, better than Jess had, and this style suited my stick-straight body, not her curves; this pale color was mine, not hers. I imagined sparkly earrings, high heels, perfume dabbed behind my knees.

Jess tossed the black dress on the bed behind us, where it landed on top of the others. She said, "You go."

"What?"

"He won't care. Anyway, I think I'm feeling sick." She coughed delicately. Our eyes locked in the mirror again. "Just..." and she pulled a sparkly bracelet off her wrist and slid it onto mine. "Just maybe meet someone with a friend for me."

I stared at myself in the mirror, inhaling lavender, watching the bracelet catch and fling tiny glints of light. I looked into my eyes in the mirror. This was what she wanted.

It was easy to believe Jess had never cared about Mitch. I think maybe she called him up that night and dumped him over the phone. Or it was the next day. Not long after anyway. "He was just baggage from home," she said. "Time to jettison that deadweight." Same with that former high school friend whose name I forgot, if I ever knew it.

The ATO dork was happy enough to have a girl, any live girl—the brothers had nicknamed him Pugsley after the Addams family kid because he was a dead ringer—and he spent the night rubbing his hard-on against me during slow dances and scoping my neckline, trying to trick me into bending too far forward. This was the first time I saw Tommy, who was in ATO (always on the verge of being kicked out for bad grades, always skimming by). He was at the formal with Sydney Moore, who came out of the stall of the ladies' room at the Drake Hotel while I was at the sink slicking on lipstick. She didn't wash her hands. Maybe there were times when I didn't either, but I always, always washed my hands if anyone else was in the bathroom. She didn't bother looking into the mirror because she didn't need to, I guess, because she already thought she was perfect. As the door swished shut, one of the girls pressed a lipstick O into a tissue and said to the other, "I heard she had an abortion when she was sixteen," and the other said, "No, it was her married sister who took the baby, when she was fourteen," and then they suddenly looked at me, and though I pretended I hadn't heard, they glared and one sighed sharply and the other tossed her balled-up tissue right past me at the garbage, so I left to let them talk as mean as they wanted.

Tommy sat with Sydney at a table up front, his chair tilted back on two legs, balancing, as he smoked a cigar. She whisked a hand through any smoke that drifted too close, and she didn't smile unless she was talking to a boy. If she got stuck having to deal with someone's date, she basically stared straight ahead, boredom shadowing her face.

When I got back to the dorm at three A.M. I tapped on Jess's door, and when she cracked it open, I told her that I saw the man she was going to marry, and she laughed and called me totally drunk, which I was, on Black Russians, which I'd never had before, which I wouldn't drink ever again because I was up all night puking.

I never told Jess the man she was supposed to marry was Tommy, even after they got together, and I never admitted I remembered him from that stupid dance or why I did. But there was a moment when Tommy was walking along the perimeter of the dance floor, a drink in each hand, and I was standing alone while Pugsley was "going wee-wee"—his excuse to escape and snort coke with his buddies in the "little boys' room." As Tommy passed, without skipping a step, he thrust one of his drinks into my hand, saying, "You need this more than I do," and kept going, but then turned, walking a few steps backward, calling, "You're too cute to give up on men because of one asshole," meaning Pugsley. Meaning, I guess, that he had noticed me. I hoped he might say more, but he was already back at his table with Sydney.

Chivas and soda, which I later found out was his drink because his father drank it. I still order Chivas thanks to Tommy's dad, a man I've never met and never will. Chivas isn't the cheap stuff, especially not back then.

He noticed me, but to feel sorry for me. So Jess could have him. Anyway, I didn't want to get married and she did, and she was someone who needed to get what she wanted and I wasn't. *Find someone,* she had told me, so I did.

After I left Sydney Moore puking in the Baxter Center bathroom, I wanted to be somewhere specific, and the most specific place I could think of was class. So I got to Harris Hall, smiled through the professor's sneer—"Lovely you decided to join us"—willing my face not to redden, and slunk into my usual chair around the seminar table, ready to soak up gallons of her wisdom about Henry James. The midway break came ten minutes later, and I was lined up at the drinking fountain when it snapped together that Jess could be at the apartment, changing the locks on me. I bolted back for my coat and book bag, then ran out of Harris, dodging through the herd race-walking up Sheridan, running for several blocks until I was too exhausted and had to slow. I didn't really believe this was possible, that Jess truly would lock me out, and yet, actually, I did. It was confusing to be in my mind, all stirred up and jostled. Nothing made sense, except the comfort of simply following the path I traveled every day, that straight shot up Sheridan, left on Noyes, five blocks to the el tracks, and then diagonal through the park to our back door. I suppose there was weather, cars, bicycles, autumn leaves and birds, the rattling el, but I didn't think to notice any of that.

The lock in the back usually stuck anyway, so I swooped to the front door, scanning for clues: the same locksmith van that had sealed up Jess's bedroom after Penny moved in. My clothes heaped on the front porch or spilling from the garbage cans that the upstairs neighbors had hauled out. Her car. But there was no evidence, not in view anyway, which didn't mean evidence didn't exist. For example, no one parked in the back spaces on garbage day because the guys were careless about heaving the lids around.

My key slid in, the lock sighing a soft *click*, and the door opened. Not that I relaxed any. My heart thudded harder in my ears.

I walked in, half breathless, immediately smelling Jess's Lauren perfume, which I inhaled in quick, deep gulps, until I practically felt calm, or calm enough to get to the next room, where I dropped my coat and crap on the ugly couch.

Jess was sitting at the table, sliding a glass of Tab around in the slickness of its water ring. I felt kind of frozen where I was, watching her through the cutout to the dining area. She wore a high, loose white turtleneck—the collar crawling so far up her neck it looked like she didn't have one—printed with an oversized grid of thin black lines, like a blowup of graph paper—three boxes across, three down. An orderly grid of nine. Her sleeves were pushed up to her elbows, and I noticed the heat was cranked hotter than usual. On her wrist, her watch with the pink leather band, loose and dangling the way she liked, so the watch face could twirl to the inside of her arm. Without looking at me she said, "How was class?"

It seemed like an invitation, or half of one anyway, so I edged closer, into the archway that led into the dining area, where I stood, framed and centered I imagined, and I rested one hand up against the wall. She was wearing high-waisted white wool pants, "winter white," she called them, her favorite color she told me a long time ago, and I had nodded, not knowing what made a white "winter," but accepting that apparently something very specific did. A skinny black belt with a spiky silver clasp on the side looped three or four times around her waist. The look, which felt chosen for this moment, could be on a magazine cover.

I knew she didn't care about my class, but we had to start somewhere.

"Good," I said. "Good enough, anyway." It was a safe, dull question, like one she would ask her parents, where no one listens to the answer because they just want words rolling around. Her parents always took forever to address even the most boring question, so I added, "Her voice is like a drill through cement. And on and on she goes. Just like the Victorians, I guess. Trollope wrote like fifty books."

I wanted to feel normal. But I couldn't chatter forever.

In the silence that followed, I realized that the pattern was that I waited for her to talk and then I answered back, that we talked about what she wanted to talk about. Or maybe I was wrong. Maybe it just seemed that way. But I had been alone so much lately that I was pretty sure I was right. That she talked first, and then I talked. It was unclear who picked that pattern, or if it was that our patterns fit from the beginning.

So I launched into a story I thought was funny about this professor, something she had said last week, and I was doing a pretty drop-dead imitation of her voice, but abruptly Jess lifted one hand, like a cop, like *stop*. The gesture prickled my skin, and I shut up mid-word. I had been about to slide into the chair across from her, but I stayed standing. I looked at my hand on the wall. My knuckles were ugly.

She said, "Penny told me something."

My heart banged back up into my ears. I stiffened, all inside and along my body. I couldn't stop that hammering heartbeat, but I could stop listening to it. I willed myself to not hear it. I didn't hear it. I studied my knuckles, which seemed even uglier than I thought. Too big, too lumpy, even for knuckles. "Knuckles" was an ugly word. My knees and elbows were also quite ugly, very bony, as my mother liked to inform me. This moment wasn't a surprise—what Jess said wasn't a surprise—but it felt like one now that I was pulled into it.

"How is Penny?" I asked, trying to be all casual, like saying, *What's for dinner?*

She abruptly tilted the glass of Tab, 90 degrees, 180. Brown liquid pooled and spread, waterfalling onto the chair, to the floor, ice cubes skittering along the tabletop. She set down the empty glass, quietly but definitively.

Now I *couldn't* sit down; the chair was drenched in Tab. The paper towels, if any were left, were in the kitchen, beyond where she sat. A can of Tab cost fifty cents in the library vending machine. I couldn't help knowing that. I would always know those things, also that I would never purposely spill Tab while wearing "winter white" and probably not even drink Tab while wearing "winter white" because I would worry about stains and dry cleaning bills.

"She saw you kiss Tommy."

I said, "Penny's a liar."

She said, "Penny's my sister," with the same casualness I had tried for, but pulling it off completely.

There was a mean pause, and I sort of caught my breath. It was the kind of silence where you couldn't breathe, where you instantly felt smothered or something. So I said, "She has your ring. She stole it."

"I know," Jess said. "She confessed."

I could not react. I could not react.

"Not her fault she lost it. You know how she is." Jess was pensive for a moment, nibbling a fingernail. My focus stayed steady, not reacting, until Jess said, "With Tommy. She *saw* you."

That thick silence again. Feeling it made me so angry. I swallowed.

Finally: "Once," I said. "Because he was mad at you. And anyway, *he* kissed me."

Her face scrunched, confused and startled, like maybe she hadn't actually entirely believed her *sister*. Like she had wanted to believe me, but now I wouldn't let her.

I smiled. It felt like an odd, inappropriate smile, the kind you regret later or right away. She glared at my smile, and it seemed like I really should stop smiling. She was so serious. This was so real. I shouldn't smile my way through something this real. I don't know why I smiled in the first place.

She said, "I hope he was worth it."

I said, "He isn't."

She said, "I know he isn't. I know that. He's a shit-turd. He's an absolute shit-turd."

"I guess I thought..."

After a moment, she asked in a sharp voice, "You thought what?"

"That you're too good for him," I said, too fast.

"Oh, ha," she said, eyes rolling. "But *you* weren't. How sweet of you. How fucking sweet. Thanks."

In the movies, these kinds of conversations took forever. There were a lot of dramatic pauses, lots of waiting. I could stand here for hours, I thought, and we would get through, and it would end like in the movies with a hug and things the same. My palm against the wall felt sweaty. Slippery. If I pushed too hard, there was sort of a suction cup sensation keeping my hand stuck. It was like a game to guess what Jess would say next. If it were a game, I would get a very good score, because she shook her head and said:

"I really loved you, you know. I thought I found the one person in the world who understood me."

I said, "I do understand you," because I totally did and because now Jess was crying, which cued me to start up my own crying, my tears keeping hers company, my agony matching hers, equal melodrama. Tears stained our faces; her mascara streaked down black. Probably mine, too, since we wore the same brand now. She didn't like waterproof. It was too stiff, she said. *Sister,* I thought, not wanting to, that word.

"I trusted you," Jess said. "You know all my secrets."

I said, "You know mine."

It seemed smart, ping-ponging right back to her, but she slapped her hands on the wet table, flinging droplets everywhere, and declared, very dramatically, "I don't even know who you are anymore." She slumped forward onto the table, letting her head drop onto her folded arms, her hair draping over and into the puddle of Tab, and as she cried, I watched her shoulders shake and quiver. Her shoulder blades were shaped like shark fins. I couldn't cry if she wasn't watching me. She spoke now in a muffled wail: "I don't even fucking know who you are or if I ever even knew." I understood I was supposed to feel bad and I was supposed to apologize. I watched her cry, but it was hard. She was right. She didn't know my secrets and certainly wouldn't want to.

"I'm sorry?" It came out a question, not a statement.

"You're not the person I knew," she sobbed. "Making me laugh, and taking care of me, and agreeing my parents are crazy, and keeping me sane. You know, just being my one true always-forever friend."

I should have apologized again for real, as sincerely as I possibly could, and fixed it between us. It was still fixable. But the person she was crying over didn't exist. I wasn't the girl Jess was brokenhearted about, not me with my ugly knuckles and scuffy thrift store boots, not me who secretly trailed Sydney Moore for forty-five minutes, then left her all alone, puking in a public restroom, abandoned.

I said, "Jess, really, I'm so sorry. About all of it. Letting Penny stay here and eating your groceries and everything with Tommy."

She sat up, the tips of her hair damp with Tab. "What's 'everything'?" she asked. Her eyes were so bright. I didn't like looking at them, but I kept my gaze steady.

"Nothing you don't know about," I said.

"That he kissed you," she said.

I nodded.

"Once?"

I nodded.

"Is that all?" Her voice was oddly kind.

I nodded.

"Because you could tell me," she said.

"Nothing more to tell," I said.

"Because I really want to know the truth," she said.

"That is the truth," I said.

"I need to hear you tell me the actual, real, honest-to-god truth for once," she said. "You owe me that. Don't you think?"

The ice cubes looked smaller already. I was surprised there was ice. I couldn't remember filling the trays. What did I owe her?

"The truth is," I said, "that he was mad at you and he kissed me that one time. And you weren't even technically still together when he did. That's the truth, and either you can believe me or not."

The phone rang, but neither of us moved to answer. It rang four, five, six times, seven, eight. I knew she was counting, too. After ten, it stopped. "Probably no one," I said.

She said, "It wasn't just Penny. I talked to him, you know. He told me everything."

I felt sorry for her, with her smeary mascara and cheeks splotched pink, and this silly tough talk, like she was some kind of private eye looking to bully out a confession. I couldn't imagine that conversation, not at all: Jess firing out questions or listening to him say "blow job," or him describing the library bathroom. I couldn't imagine Tommy admitting anything, him being more honest than me. I had to pee, I realized, desperate for that relief. I shifted my weight. Why stand here, I wondered, stuck in this dumb conversation, as forgettable as any sunny day, when the life waiting ahead was so far beyond worrying about a melodramatic rich girl in her pretentious white pants? As years passed, how many times would I think their names? "Cast a cold Eye," Yeats said, the writer said. These things would simply slide away, forgotten, Jess and Tommy and what I had done, all of right now, even the Tylenol killer, who would be nabbed by the cops and prosecuted and either clutter up a prison cell or sizzle in an electric chair. He would explain how he did it and why, and the reasons would be evil, but there would be reasons we could know and hold on to until we forgot them. All was nothing in the end.

"Come on," I said. "Stop it. It's fine. Everything is..." That damn word. *Fine.*

She said, "I know you'll feel better if you just tell the truth. If you confess. Like Penny. She told me everything, and now..." She held up both hands, fingers crossed. "She's the sister I always wanted." She knew, she knew, knew, knew, knew how to say that. Like a knife.

"Jess," I said. "Come on. Please stop."

She didn't: "Look at you, with that ratty hair and sweat pouring out and nothing in the fridge and the hem dropping out of your jeans. Rings around your eyes like a raccoon, your hand all jittery. Literally, I've never seen you such a mess. Are you sleeping at all?"

"Stop it," I repeated, very in control, totally in control, the control of control.

"And yeah, who are you, anyway, always wearing my clothes, kissing my boyfriend, eating my food, trying to steal my sister?" she said. "Do you even have a mind of your own?" She calmly enunciated each syllable, like explaining to a foreigner. "You're half a person, just totally copying me. All surface and nothing underneath."

The gut punch of that. The goddamn gut punch. But I would take it to the end, I would take it and take it and take it. Finally I spoke, coolly, all inquiring-minds-want-to-know: "What does that mean, nothing underneath?" The question ached like too much sugar.

She looked disappointed, as if I had latched on to the wrong thing. "Come on," she said. "I swear whatever the truth is, it's fine. I just have to know. I can handle it. Be honest. Just be honest. I can take it."

And here I laughed, which I shouldn't have, so much worse than smiling, to laugh when someone melodramatically swears they can take the truth, that they want to know, that you *owe* them the truth. Because fuck the fucking truth. What truth did I have *underneath* that Jess would want to hear? That my father—? That my uncle—?

Never.

Her complaining that she didn't know me was my ultimate victory, my intention. I didn't *want* her to know me. My only safe bet the whole rest of my life was never revealing the damaged, horrible person I was, the terribleness I was capable of. That truth? That's what she wanted, all that? Fine, give it to her. Give it to her, give it to her, I would give it to her. She would see, she would see and she would hate me, and what a relief that would be. What a relief.

I said, "You're right. I gave him blow jobs in the library whenever he wanted. He wanted a lot."

Jess howled and called me names. I stood there and let her. Those names were nothing new. I'd heard them all before. They were the names I called myself.

Then I said, "I can move out, though actually I'm paid up on rent for the month."

There were more names. More howls. Jess was dramatic and noisy, and she threw the glass, which shattered into a million crazy pieces I would sweep up later with the broom Jess had bought.

I said, "You knew what I was doing. You had to. I mean, you're not stupid. You told him where I studied in the library that one night last year. You told him to find me."

She called me the sickest person she had ever met. She told me to leave by the weekend. She told me my name wasn't on the lease. She told me not being on the lease was like not existing. She told me I was dead to her for the rest of her life. She waved her arms around and paced. She grabbed another glass off the dish rack and threw that, too, a clean one, which was a shame. *Why not a dirty one from the sink?* I thought. She told me that it was going to be like I had never even been here.

There was more. A lot more. I let her yell. It felt good. It felt as good as I had imagined. She told me I'd betrayed her. She called me Pontius Pilate, though I think she meant Judas, and she yelled when I corrected her.

The upstairs people banged on the floor to shut us up. That's when Jess left. She told me to get out before tomorrow at five, that she was changing all the locks. I asked her about the rent money and she said, "Fuck you and your rent money."

She left.

Jess was gone.

I cleaned up the mess. I mean, why not? I'd cleaned up lots of broken glass before. It wasn't any big thing to sweep up glass afterward. I felt nothing. I felt oddly calm, calm for real. This was all over. Everything was over, and that calm was everywhere, like fog, like vapor. I felt like the smooth, silvery surface of a mirror.

She said she had never known me. Well, she knew me now. *She knew me now,* I thought, letting water run over the last paper towel on the roll so I could dab up any splinters of glass the broom missed along the baseboard. Those tiny, glittery shards were dangerous.

She knew me now, I thought again and again, over and over, like song lyrics I couldn't shake or finish.

Because I'd gotten immune to those four words echoing in my head, it was a surprise, later, in the middle of the night, in the middle of not-sleeping, in the middle of crunching down a handful of baby aspirin, to realize the powerful truth of them, that yes, Jess for sure knew me now. In the middle of the night, not-asleep, I understood that now she saw me for who I was. Now she hated me, just like all the rest of them did. I wondered why that was what I wanted, and in that instant the calm shattered, a tremendous rock hitting the surface of my silent pond. The truth, I saw then in the dark, was that what I had lost was everything. And what the "everything" actually was, it was, well, everything. She had seen me with her own clear eyes, all along, and she had loved me. What she had seen was who I wanted to be, who I hoped I truly maybe possibly was or at least could be. Normal, like everyone else. Her friend. Not that other person, that monster.

Strategies for Survival #1: Numb

(winter, junior year)

The winters I remember in Chicago had a specific dark and endless quality, as if distilled to some deeper, purer essence than the winters in Iowa, though it was cold and snowy back there, too. In Chicago, the snow came and wouldn't leave, only accumulated, until the concept of "white" was a thing to loathe. The low gray of every day's same sky; slush ribboning the streets, piling up along the curbs, and the smacking sound of tires rolling through the mass of it; the scrape of shovels battering against cement; the piercing chafe of snot inhaled back up into a raw red nose; circling fingers full of Vaseline into salt-stained dress boots, massaging mink oil into shoes for waterproofing and stainproofing, the greasy rank scent, the fluttery questions, best ignored, about what mink oil really was, where it might come from; the flick of Kleenex popping when pulled out of a box one after the other; sniffles ricocheting across the library stacks, the distracting echo of that, rereading the same first paragraph over and over, highlighter pen clenched between fingers and thumb, uncomprehending; hat-mashed hair and chapped lips and hangnails catching inside gloves and dry skin, flaky skin, lifeless skin; sparks of static electricity snapping off doorknobs; the heavy, dull food of the cafeteria, brown meat, white potatoes, tinny-tasting green beans with the texture of mush, noodles and more noodles and more noodles; the radio DJs and newscasters and their damn positivity, the manic cry "Good morning!"; crunching across snow; seeing a girl in a red scarf slip and fall on ice across the street as people streamed around her, late for class. And the wind. The wind, the wind. That Chicago wind.

Possibly it was different for people living in the city itself; possibly winter amid glittering glass buildings felt different from our winter up in Evanston. Though Chicago was an easy el ride, we stayed locked in the library all winter, studying endlessly for the good grades that would sail us into grad school, med school, law school, business school.

I didn't want to go to any of those places, but I was accustomed to compliance, so I locked myself in the library like everyone else. Winter quarter was the only time I got all A's. Winter quarter was when we learned "existential crisis" in philosophy and "major depressive disorder" in psych; when we contemplated our doughy, abject bodies taking up space in the shower and found them inadequate; when whatever we most wanted to avoid—that guy, her, no job offer, *Moby-Dick*, whatever shit we hauled here from back home, the professor's red pen and mocking gaze, a missed period—ambushed each of us from within the shadowy dark.

To cope, we punished ourselves. This was when we took on the bears: tough classes, tedious requirements outside our interests, the eight o'clocks. The thinking was, nothing to do but study, so grind away. The thinking was, if your roommate committed suicide, they'd award you pity A's, and if you were the one committing suicide, at least you'd escape winter (we assumed; possibly we were already in hell). The thinking was, there had never been a year when spring didn't eventually show up, but just as we couldn't really believe that rumor about a roommate's suicide boosting our GPAs, we couldn't believe in spring either. It was something we remembered hearing about, once at a party, from a drunk guy with shit for brains. We didn't believe it. It was hard to believe in anything during those winters.

Lake Michigan was too vast to freeze like a pond, but the waves crashing on the sandy beach piled up and froze into thick, rugged layers of uneven ice, stretching out into the lake. One winter in particular I often stood at a certain window on the fifth floor of the library and stared at those frozen waves. I had moved back to the dorms, to a single in what we called Suicide Hall, though it was actually named after an alum who had donated money, as were all the buildings. Jess had a new roommate in the apartment, some theater major from Indiana called Molly.

Sundays were the worst: reading and papers due Monday, none started; lingering regrets from any parties scrounged up the night before; a hangover hammering across the afternoon; pulling on the last pair of clean underwear; the usual problem of no dorm food served Sundays. I was thinking about these things around three P.M., staring out this window at the frozen lake. I could order a small pizza or trudge into town to Burger King. I could shake out the pockets of my backpack to see if a five-dollar bill might magically appear. I could buy M&M'S from the vending machine and bull through, an expression I wanted to shake but couldn't.

Instead, I tugged on my boots; got into my coat, hat, scarf, mittens; left *History of England, 1066–1660* flipped open spine up so no one would steal my carrel space; and walked to the lake.

Footprints crisscrossed the snow on the beach, but no one else was out right then. The wind swooped in off the lake, so hard I imagined I could see the curve of it. The hawk wind, they called it. Like being grabbed, like talons. The name was right. Ten degrees? Less? Certainly not more. And wind chill. Even with my scarf pulled up unattractively to just under my eyes, my face went numb. My breath came out wet, and the scarf stiffened. My eyes watered. I shoved my hands in my pockets. I thought I would stand here, looking out for a minute or two, then go back before freezing to death. I couldn't see the open water from where I stood on the snow layering the ice layering the sand, all of it layering the beach. Forgotten words: "Beach." "Sun." "Jess." All there was was gray, and gray was all there was: frigid waves, sky, the lake beyond. Through my hat, listening to the muffled pull and roar of the gray waves, a gray sound.

Afternoon, technically, but the landscape was infused with the quality of twilight where nothing felt exact.

The ice looked thick enough to walk on. How could it not be? The frozen waves were more than six feet tall as I clambered up them, rising off the snow-covered beach. I told myself this was safe. If it weren't safe someone would have posted a warning sign. If it weren't safe, I wouldn't do this.

No one knew where I was.

It hurt to breathe. The wind knifed my silly winter coat and the sweater underneath. The surface of the frozen waves tilted and skewed, crunchy here and slippery there. I moved slowly. Swaths were streaked with sand and dirt dredged up from the bottom of the lake; areas were rough and areas were smooth. I thought of the texture of an unshaven face. Always the churn of more waves, flung up against the wall of ice, again and again.

I was walking on top of the lake. I was standing on waves.

The air thickened. Maybe I was shivering. My boots felt heavier to lift, my feet transformed like marble. I was desperately cold. Still, I trudged out, away from the beach, away from campus where people were clicking on desk lamps and reaching for the phone for delivery, something for dinner. The seagulls were somewhere else, the alewives gone. Under the sound of the fresh waves pushing forward, I felt an uncomfortable silence. I wondered if anyone was looking out a window, if anyone saw me right now.

There was an edge. There was an edge where I could stand and finally see the murky water below me, that edge where waves were neither water nor ice, and chunks of them slopped and sloshed into white foam. I stood there and watched, feeling the sky shift two more notches closer to darkness. As cold as the air was, the water would feel colder.

There was no one to warn that I might fall in, that the ice might not hold, that I might slip and break my leg, that I shouldn't be thinking what I was almost thinking.

Would Jess come to my funeral? I wondered.

I thought about Linda facing this same choice, maybe, and the sad, silent wreckage she left behind, and I wondered what we could have said to her. And Jess with a different choice, also a hard one: Choosing to love Penny. Choosing Penny. Choosing love.

And me.

People in books could escape, men in books could hit the road; escape for them was hopping on a raft, or jumping in the car and revving the engine and disappearing into the night. But girls, or girls like me anyway, we looked back.

I loved Jess for her generous, crazy self and because she chose me when I longed to feel chosen; but also, mostly, truthfully, I loved her because I thought she saw the person I ached to be, the girl free from a past. She saw the me I created. Maybe she could have seen more if I hadn't been afraid. Maybe all of this, each word, was true for the both of us.

I left my sister behind. Abandoned her. I didn't have a choice, I'd explained to myself over and over. I had imagined saving her plenty of times, the pillow over our father's stupid sleeping face, a crazy and grand gesture, like the last chapter of an Agatha Christie novel... voilà!

Say it again. I left my sister behind. She was the one who knew the real me and my dark confusion and fumbling, who suffered because of my failures, and what did she do when confronted with that? Grace loved me anyway. I left because I thought I had to save myself. I left because I couldn't save her. But looking down into that black water, I saw what was true: that my sister would be the one saving me.

I turned around. The wind was easier against my back, almost forgiving when I wasn't fighting it.

Back at the library, I knew I never would have jumped. Easy to think, back at the library.

When I got to my dorm room later that night, I heard the phone ringing through the door. It was a stupid expense to have my own phone when no one called me and I called no one, but also it seemed like something you just do, have a phone and a phone number. Maybe someone would call me someday, I had thought. Anyway, now someone was.

My fingers were stiff from being out in the cold, sort of half frozen, and I fumbled the key, racing to unlock the door, and my book bag crashed down my shoulder onto my elbow, sending my arm askew. The phone kept ringing, though each ring felt like the last. I wasn't used to this lock, which turned right instead of left, like where I lived with Jess. Ringing, ringing, and my mind clicked into place as the key did: it was Jess. I pushed the door open, flicked the light switch. No one else would call me. That's who the phone had been for all along. Understanding this was like suddenly being able to feel warm blood surge through my own body.

My single room had no decoration, which is exactly how I liked things now. About the only thing to see was books lined up. A desk lamp. Everything else went in a drawer or the closet. I dropped my book bag onto my empty desk, next to the phone.

The phone was black. A pretty color didn't cost extra, but a phone you didn't expect to use much should be black, I thought.

I watched it ring.

Did I want to talk to her? My bones, my insides, still felt hollowed out from the cold at the lake. I had another chapter to go over before my test in English history. I wanted to concentrate on planning the long, maybe winding trail of phone calls from this black phone that would begin tomorrow as I started doing what I had to for Grace.

I lifted the phone receiver to my ear; it felt oddly heavy. "Hello?" I said. I assumed she'd hang up. That had happened when I first got the phone, that someone would call and I'd pick it up and no one would be there. "Hello?" I said again. I heard breathing. Someone was there. I knew she was there. "Jess?" I said.

"Hi," she said.

"Hi," I said right back, that same old habit of mirroring her words. She said, "It's Linda's birthday today."

I remembered that phone call after I read the newspaper articles saying Linda died. I didn't know what I was supposed to say, and Jess said things I didn't expect, and there was no plan for the way to feel better.

"How old is she?" I asked.

"Seventeen," she said. "Jesus. I lost my virginity when I was seventeen. That feels like forever ago. Everything feels like forever ago."

I slid my key ring into the outer pocket of my book bag because that's where I always kept it now. "Yeah," I said. "I hate when things feel like forever ago, especially if it's really only a few years. How does that happen?"

She said, "I wish I liked her more. I was always so jealous of her."

"You did like her," I said. "Inside, you loved her. You know that." I sat on the bed and twisted the black phone cord, tightly entwining one finger into its rubbery spirals.

"She just seemed deeper than I was, more important. Like the way she looked at the world, the things she said. You'd never believe she was a kid, with what she was thinking. Like once she told my mother a house was a container for people."

A brief *whoosh* came from her end of the line, maybe from opening the refrigerator. I imagined that cold light washing over her face, the kitchen table in the shadows, dishes stacked in the drainer, and I had to stop.

Jess said, "I was jealous of you, too, you know."

This was like the key clicking in the door, something swinging wide open. That she could feel that. I said, "That's crazy."

"It's all crazy," she said. "Penny says hi."

"Really?"

"Well, she would if she knew I was on the phone," Jess said.

"Tell her I'm a Cubs fan now thanks to her."

"She's making all of us into Cubs fans," Jess said. "My dad's getting tickets for Opening Day this year, in the spring."

The spring, I thought, just as Jess said, "I wish it was spring right now."

The tip of my finger had turned purple red. "Spring will be here before we know it."

"I hate when people say that. So fake."

"Me too."

Just like those early days in the dorm room freshman year, sitting side by side on her bed, ideas and thoughts and words spilling out in torrents, each of us soaking it all up.

I said, "I don't think there's anything to say that will ever make you feel right about Linda. If there is, I don't know what it is."

"Try," Jess whispered. "Please just try." She sniffled. I wanted to cry, too. It was only luck that I hadn't lost my own sister. The purest kind of lucky luck that won't go on forever. Grace. Thinking her name calmed me the same way taking in a deep breath did.

I wanted to say something important, something that could be written in a book, in a poem. I pulled off my hat, dropped it on the neatly made bed. This room could be in a brochure, it so lacked personality. Not even any trash in the trash can because I emptied it every day. I didn't want anything unnecessary in here. I didn't want accumulation.

"Jess," I said.

"I've always liked the way you say my name," she said. "Like the S's are softer or something in your voice. Say it again."

"Jess," I said. I thought I might cry, but not yet.

She was. I imagined her wiping away tears that way she did, sliding both index fingers along the bottom rims of her eyes to sop up runny mascara.

Jess said, "I hate the winter here. It's so cold. It's a goddamn deep freeze."

I said, "Everyone hates the winter. Only idiots like winter."

"With the world filled with idiots," she said, "I guess there are plenty of people liking winter."

I knew what she was doing because I was doing it, too. She was making jokes because she felt so awful. Because talking about winter filled space and time. Because to lose a sister must be the worst thing in the world.

"Were you at the library?" she asked.

"There, and the lake," I said.

"The lake!" That dramatic shriek of hers. "Are you crazy now? Talk about freezing cold. And dangerous. What if you fell in?" Her voice cracked. We knew the answer: I would have died.

Yet I didn't.

"I thought about Linda while I was out there," I said.

"Maybe you knew it was her birthday," Jess said. "Maybe part of you knew even if you didn't know-know."

"I think so," I said. "Why else would I go to the lake right then, when I could go to the lake any day?" I scrunched the phone between my ear and shoulder, unlooping and tugging my scarf free with one hand. What if life worked that way, with secret currents carrying us in the direction we needed to go?

I said, "I don't think you can understand Linda or what happened or why, or at least not now, or I don't know. But I think you can find a way to live even knowing that you don't know. Like, maybe knowing you can't know is something. That that's what we all have to do, is find a way to live. But it's hard. It's like maybe the hardest thing there is."

Jess blew her nose. Then she said, "Don't you want to hear why I'm jealous of you?"

I could barely speak, but I did: "Okay."

"You know so much," Jess said. "Like you've been alive forever and learned all these things I'll never understand. Like, I always thought if you'd just tell me even half... And the way you move through the world, like the Devil's daughter, remember that? *Get out of my way. I belong here.* Like, you've wrestled your way in and here you are."

"Wow," I said. "I'm not that at all."

She said, "Like I got in through an open door, but you crawled through the window."

"The door's better," I said.

"Not really," she said. "So, what did you think about when you thought about Linda?"

I unzipped my coat, which was weird to do because I thought I already had. But I couldn't get it off unless I took my finger out of the phone cord, which I didn't want to do. Not until it was so purple I couldn't stand it. I left the coat on, gaping open. I said, "I thought about how sad she must have been. And how sad that she didn't see all the love around her."

Jess let out a choked sob. "Really? Did I love her? All I did was complain."

"My god, Jess," I said. "You loved her the most of anybody. Sisters always love each other the most of anybody. It's just how it is. Like how I love my sister."

I listened to her fight the crying, and then she said, "Grace. That name is perfect."

"I picked it," I said. "Before she was born, they asked what I thought the new baby's name should be, you know, a joke or something to make me feel involved. I was so in love with the Little House books that I said, 'Grace,' and they actually decided that's who she would be. I was really proud." I couldn't remember if I ever told that story to Grace. There were so many bad things from our past, but that was one good thing. I couldn't wait to tell her.

Jess said, "Linda was the name my mother picked, and Jessica was the name my dad picked. Isn't that weird, dividing it up? Maybe that's why I was jealous of her, that she got my mom's choice."

I said, "Your mom calls you 'lovey.'"

"I know," Jess said. "It's just that after someone is gone, maybe that's when you think of all the things you should have said to them."

"That's why it's so hard," I said. "Because we can't say those things when they're around, but also we can't say them when they're gone either."

Jess said, "I caught her calling Penny 'lovey.'"

"Oh my god," I said, and something ripped through me, like soft skin tearing. *There should be a scar,* I thought, *something thick and hard.* I looked at my finger: almost pure purple, almost.

Jess said, "I was surprised, but I liked it. It's nice. It's the right thing."

That's what I was jealous of, that—that acceptance. This casual love.

I hadn't cried yet. I decided I wasn't going to.

Then Jess said, "My parents didn't call me today. I thought they would, and I waited and waited, but they didn't." She sighed. "Maybe I knew they wouldn't. Maybe I just had to wait and wait to know for sure."

"I think they just don't know how to talk about Linda right now."

Jess said, "She's still my family even though she's gone and everyone's afraid to say her name, right?"

"Oh my god, yes!" I said. "Forever."

"That word again," Jess said.

"That word again," I repeated. "Sometimes it's the right one."

My finger was purple. I was just about to release it when Jess said, "All this doesn't mean back to us. I don't think I can ever do that."

"I know," I lied. Maybe I did know. I wasn't sure what was the lie.

"Maybe he didn't mean anything to you, but he did mean something to me," she said. "Maybe it was stupid that he did, but he did. I really loved him, even if it was stupid to."

"It wasn't stupid," I said. "Nothing about you is stupid."

"But you're the only one I could talk to today," she said. "There's that. What does that mean?"

"Something." I twirled the phone cord off my purple finger, that perfect condition of nothingness before all the feeling flooded back into it. Then I tried: "Jess—"

"No," she said, and abruptly she hung up.

I listened to the dial tone for a minute, but she wasn't coming back, so I hung up. I took off my coat. This call should have made everything worse, but somehow it didn't. It was like waking up, like when I stepped into the library after being out in that cold lake air. The things I had said were true and honest, and we agreed: even if someone is gone, they are always there. That was how sisters were. That was how I saw my sister, anyway.

I reached for my pillow and finally cried.

TODAY

(summer)

Grace and I are walking to the campus to look at the lakeshore. I've brought her to the school to show her how pretty it is. It's that kind of perfect June day that shouldn't exist in real life, but because we're incredibly lucky, it does and we're right here in it. We ride the rattling, jiggly el and hop off at my old stop, Noyes, then stroll east, toward the lake. She holds my hand because she likes to do that when she's in a new place. I don't tell her that we're near where I used to live with Jess. I don't tell her anything about the old life I had: typing papers at midnight and the Chinese books in the library, heating water in a hotpot and the heavy Chicago sky pressing down on the twilight, how soupy-warm Jess's dorm room was when we'd sit side by side barefoot on her bed and write our lists and talk about a million different topics and nothing at all while the light around us thickened. Grace doesn't need to know those things now. Those things are gone anyway. I don't miss them. They never felt like mine.

We pass the tennis courts where ponytailed girls whack balls back and forth in an even rhythm, and we watch for a minute. They rarely miss. They're good at tennis. Everyone should be good at one thing. I still don't quite know what that thing is for me, but I suppose I'll find it. Grace could be good at drawing. She drew a picture of me last week that we taped to the wall. I imagine I'll own that drawing forever. In it, I'm smiling.

When we're done watching the girls play tennis, we wait for the light, then cross Sheridan Road. When I lived here, I barely cared about the light. I might cross against it, betting that the zooming cars would slow for me, but now I consider things like *What if they don't?*

We skirt the clusters of brick fraternity houses. The Rolling Stones blare through a screen door. Some boys are playing Frisbee on the quad. They're shirtless, and they're good at Frisbee; the orange disk snaps and sails. They look carefree and happy, but I know it's possible that they aren't. That they may look one way and be another. There's a pause where their gaze latches upon us as we pass. I walk a little faster. I would meet their eyes and look them dead-on if I were alone, stare them down into motionless silence. But Grace is beside me, holding my hand.

We pass one of the north campus dorms. If I had been assigned to this dorm when I was a freshman, I never would have met Jess. I squeeze Grace's hand. A breeze picks up when we get behind the dorm, and we curve our way to the lakefill and the walking path along the water. It's what someone means when they say "summer breeze," the exact lightness, this precise refreshment. She's getting excited, bouncing as she walks, swinging both arms. "Look at the lake," she says. "It's gigantic. Are we swimming in it?" She sounds doubtful. She's still a shy girl. I don't think she wants to swim in a lake this big so I suspect she'll be relieved at my answer:

"The water's freezing now," I say. "Maybe later in the summer, at a beach. Today we're just going to walk, over where all those big rocks are." I point ahead. They're not really rocks, but jagged cement slabs piled up along the shoreline. This was how the lakefill was built back in the sixties, dumping into the lake masses of torn-up cement chunks and tons of landfill materials when the Port of Indiana was built for the steel mills. So, unwanted dirt and trash basically. You wouldn't know that if you looked around. This beautiful, grassy park was part of a plan, a way for the school to create land where none existed. It's almost impossible to imagine the school without the jutting peninsula of this park and its pathways, a place where bikers and walkers and daydreamers and students dreading their final exams can escape to. The catalogs and brochures all include a picture of the lake, usually right there on the cover. I bet lots of students were lured to this school because of those pictures of this lake, because of this exact scene we're walking into right now. I always like to remember that it's secretly garbage we walk on, that this park isn't really supposed to be here but is anyway.

I tell Grace that the kids at the school, like maybe those guys we saw playing Frisbee, paint their names on the cement blocks before they graduate. "Why?" she wonders, and I try to explain what tradition means and why some people might want to leave part of themselves behind before they leave a place, why they might like thinking that something of themselves is left there, wanting to feel they've made an impact, that a place—the place they love—is ever so slightly different, thanks to their presence. I ramble on, noting that people also like to take something of a place, maybe something to carry with them. My explanations and ramblings are half-hearted, because my idea of leaving has been to slip through, the way water slides through fingers. Maybe there will be a day when I want to care about tradition, but for now I like it best when things feel fresh and clean.

She says, "Maybe we could paint our names someday," and I tell her sure.

We're quiet for a while as we walk. It's a nice quiet.

We merge onto the asphalt path with the bicyclists and joggers. There's a woman walking six dogs at once, leashes a crazy tangle, and Grace and I laugh that one dog is a towering Great Dane and another is teeny-tiny and yappy, busy dancing between the Great Dane's legs. It's the kind of day where seeing this would make anyone laugh. "Think his name is Tiny?" I say, pointing to the Great Dane, and Grace is still a kid so to her I'm hilarious.

We round the bend by the observatory, a white dome jutting out of its own prong of land. I had signed up for an astronomy class because I thought we'd get to go inside the observatory and see the stars, but we didn't. My astronomy class was for nonscience majors, so we looked at pictures of stars in our textbook and on slides the professor projected onto a big screen in the barely dim auditorium. The stars were for the real science people.

Now we're walking south, right along the edge of the jumbles of concrete, the lake six feet below, lapping the bottom of those piles of cement. Ahead in the distance stretches the silvery Chicago sky-line, glittering like a line of jagged teeth. From this vantage point, the buildings look minuscule, like children's blocks, like one kick would knock them down. Yet if I were in the thick bustle of Michigan Avenue, I would be overwhelmed and dwarfed; I would be the one easily knocked over. I'm still holding Grace's hand.

It might seem a funny turn that now I work as hostess at the Keg, Evanston's fancy restaurant. I smile at everyone who sashays through the door, students and their credit card–wielding parents, prom couples, townie families celebrating anniversaries and birth-days, businesspeople in their buttoned-up suits, faculty groups host-ing visitors and job candidates. It's easy for me to be nice when I'm there, even to people who aren't especially nice to me. I just smile at them as long as it takes until they smile back. And I take summer classes at Chicago Circle. It's mostly a commuter school, so hardly anyone lives in the dorm, and most people have other jobs, usually more than one. The teachers are smart. My class is focused on Her-man Melville and Nathaniel Hawthorne. I started out nervous to read *Moby-Dick* because it's eight hundred pages, but I love it. Last night I read the first chapter out loud to Grace just for fun, and she liked it. "Call me Grace-mael," she goofed in a deep voice. "Call me Grace-mael," and she danced around the kitchenette being silly. I like watching her be silly. I hope she'll be silly more often, whenever she feels like it.

You can't always escape the past just because you want to, is what I might tell someone today, and maybe you shouldn't want to escape all of it, every scrap. I like to think Jess taught me that. Or maybe I taught her. Anyway, I like to think we'd agree on being alike like this.

Jess and her family haven't come into the Keg yet, but they will. I'll smile. It's possible they won't see me, even as I lead the four of them to their table and hand over the menus with the specials typed on index cards that I clipped there at the beginning of my shift. I rec-ommend the fried shrimp if anyone asks. Also the walleye, which I had never eaten before but which is delicious. I'll watch them from my hostess stand, watch how they'll talk and share bites of food and laugh at a funny joke and squabble over hurt feelings, how they'll be a family together. I'll watch, and I hope I'll be happy seeing them that way.

And. Well. Say it. There's some money in the bank. Not enough, but more than I would expect. Maybe it shouldn't be my money technically. But now it is, and anyway, I think of it as our money, mine and Grace's, and that makes what I did feel better during the times I worry about it. The round, burly man at the pawnshop didn't ask any questions. He said he had a daughter who looked like me, and he showed me a picture from his wallet, so it wasn't a lie, and when I left he said, "God bless," and meant it. I'll have to tell Grace someday. Not today. I tell myself those kinds of people have lots of insurance. Those kinds of people think they're protected against loss. I don't know why Penny claimed she lost the ring. Maybe she thought she owed me. Maybe she felt sorry for me. I don't know why Jess believed her. Maybe the same reasons.

There were authorities to call in Iowa and papers to sign and words I won't forget. Both my father's fists walloping their way through my mother's face as cops barreled up onto the front porch, my mother shrieking, "She did it, not me," the cops hearing that, the neighbors too, the echo: "She did it." Things happened that were ugly, so ugly. Grace was there for some of them. They will probably haunt us. Not today. Today is only for this, for now.

They haven't caught the Tylenol killer, and maybe they won't. I should be surprised but I'm not. People get away with things they shouldn't.

We're midway through our walk along the lake, and I decide here is the perfect place to climb down onto the rocks, to get ourselves closer to the water. Maneuvering isn't difficult or scary; each rock is at least the size of an armchair cushion but thicker, and many are stacked flat, almost creating a tier of stepping-stones. At the bottom shoreline, the slabs protectively slant and jag upward, making it hard to get all the way to the water. That's fair. They don't want anyone to drown. The rock piles appear random, chaotic, but surely this barrier at the bottom is planned. The water is freezing anyway, so you wouldn't jump in even if you could. But plenty of people clamber down the rocks, to find a flat one so they can sunbathe, or read, or stare into the soft waves or deep into the horizon.

Scads of names and messages decorate the rocks, their bright colors and diverse lettering a cacophony: BUGGO LOVED AHERN; JEANNIE JOHNSON, CLASS OF '81; LET US GO THEN, YOU AND I... ; the Greek letters of various fraternities and sororities; TECH RULES!; GO CATS!; BUDS 4-EVER; and lots of names and dates, some faint and faded, from five years ago, fifteen, longer. *I was here, I was here, I was here.* The words surge along these rocks like a tide. The air smells distantly like fish, delicately, just enough to remind us we're somewhere different now.

We scramble across the rocks and around the scattered people lounging on the rocks, me leading, holding Grace's hand and guiding her to the flat parts, helping her stretch her step over the dark crevices where snaky vegetation bobs in the water below or lies dank. I make sure she puts her feet only on safe spots, and we claim a flat, sunny rock all to ourselves and sit cross-legged facing the water.

"Down there is Indiana," I say, though there's nothing to see beyond the triangles of sailboats, beyond water and more water. "And directly across is Michigan," I say, gesturing at the narrow line of the horizon. "Up north are the fancy suburbs, Winnetka and Wilmette and Lake Forest, and someday we'll go visit that white lighthouse. Past all that is Wisconsin. And down there, of course, is Chicago." I point to these various places, visible and not, and her eyes follow my hand. I imagine her remembering this day until she dies, the day her big sister brought her to the lake for the first time. I hope she remembers this.

In my pocket is a handful of small stones, pebbles really. I bring some with me, a few at a time, whenever I know I'm coming out here. I'll do that until the boxes are empty. I scoop them from my pocket and divvy them up into two neat piles, putting the extra on the pile closest to her because there's an odd number.

"What are these?" she asks.

"For making wishes," I say. "We'll throw them into the lake one at a time, taking turns, and make wishes. Whoever's last gets their wish to come true." She'll be last; I rigged it that way. That's why I say that, so her wish will come true.

"Are they special?" she asks. "Are they different from regular rocks?"

"You're right," I say. "These are special. You start."

She selects one of the pebbles that Jess's mother left with me, ex-amines it by turning it around and around in her hand, thinking, as if there's one way to hold it that's luckier than other ways. She still believes these sorts of things. That's another thing she's good at.

Then she scrunches shut her eyes and tosses in the stone, throwing so hard it's like she wants to hit Michigan. It barely plinks, that tiny pebble hitting this whole huge lake, but when she opens her eyes, I see that she's almost quivering with the importance of this wish. "Your turn," she says. "You."

I pitch my pebble underhand so it arcs high across the blue sky and I lose it in the water's shimmer. On another day, I might throw it hard, wanting to hit Michigan myself, even knowing that's impossi-ble. That's okay. I already got my wish.

I guess if Jess wants to find me someday far off in the future, she will; she's like that. She might, might not. I know I'm not getting mar-ried and my name will stay the same. One day, my name will be print-ed on a book. If Jess wants to know who I was—who I am—she can read that. They all can.

For now, next time we come to the lake, I'll bring paint, and Grace and I can write our names together on these rocks, just for fun and to show we were here. Now, this is the beginning. This is home.

HISTORICAL NOTE ABOUT THE TYLENOL MURDERS

The basic facts are as described in the novel: In the fall of 1982, seven people in the greater Chicago area died after ingesting tainted Tylenol capsules that had been filled with cyanide and returned to drugstore shelves. As of this writing, no one has been convicted of the crime. However, while writing *Silver Girl*, I did take some fictional liberties, along the lines of creating a fictional murder victim and tweaking the timeline of events.

If you would like to read more about this crime, I recommend the online articles "A Bitter Pill" by Joy Bergmann, originally published in the *Chicago Reader*, and Bergmann's follow-up to that piece, "The Tylenol Mafia," also published in the *Chicago Reader*.

Additional source material included *Tymurs* by Scott Bartz.

ACKNOWLEDGMENTS

I have only one list to scribble in my composition notebook, People to Thank Effusively... though I cannot possibly prioritize and arrange and number. I'm grateful to each of you, more than I can say.

Kerry D'Agostino is the best agent in the world; she absolutely believed in this book from the beginning! And how lucky I am that *Silver Girl* landed with Olivia Taylor Smith at Unnamed Press! (Really, I long to use more exclamation points here because I am so grateful and so delighted to be working with these two women and with everyone at this fine press.)

Thanks to the editors of the following journals where various chapters of this book were published; I appreciate your early vote of confidence and your thoughtful edits: *Cincinnati Review, Hudson Review, Gettysburg Review, Midwestern Gothic, River Styx, WIP (Works [of Fiction] in Progress)*.

Completing this book was a long and complicated journey, so how delightful that I spent some of that journey writing and revising in these lovely places, each offering a writer what she craves most of all, time and space: the Writers' Colony at Dairy Hollow, Fairhope Center for the Writing Arts, Hambidge Center for the Creative Arts and Sciences, Hawthornden Castle International Retreat for Writers, Kimmel Harding Nelson Center for the Arts, and Virginia Center for the Creative Arts.

Many chapters in this book started as prompts composed in fifteen-minute bursts in my monthly prompt writing group. I'm honored to work alongside these writers on the second Wednesday of every month: Michelle Berberet, Nancy Carson, Mary Daly, Joanne Lozar Glenn, Lisa Leibow, Mark Morrow, Grace Morsberger, Lauri Ploch, Charlotte Safavi, and Nina Sichel. And thanks to Maribeth Fischer, whose example inspired me to form our group, after she told me that she wrote pages and pages of her own beautiful novels while writing to prompts.

The students and faculty at the Converse College low-residency MFA program in Spartanburg, South Carolina, are an avid and joyful audience, eager to hear from my works in progress, quick with compliments and challenging questions. I always emerge from the cocoon of our residencies feeling inspired. Special thanks to our MFA director, Rick Mulkey, for being an excellent administrator and a dear friend.

There are writers I turn to time and time again, who are always there to cheer, console, advise, and grab a drink (or two). Thanks for your continued friendship and your generous wisdom: Marlin Barton, Sandra Beasley, Michelle Brafman, Mary Cantrell, Susan Coll, Dan Elish, Rachel Hall, Anna Leahy, Carolyn Parkhurst, Amy Stolls, Susan Tekulve, Paula Whyman, Elly Williams, and Mary Kay Zuravleff. Also, I'm thankful that my tribe of Facebook writer-friends feels to me more like friends than simply "friends." I've learned so much from all of you.

After writing a book set in a college, surely I must thank all my writing teachers, especially these folks, some from way back when: Mary Kinzie, Arturo Vivante, Jeff Lipkis, Tim O'Brien, Mark Richard, and Richard Bausch.

Thanks to my parents, Donald and Catherine Pietrzyk, and my sister, Susan Pietrzyk, and her partner, Tanya Olson, who remain unfazed by and utterly supportive of this author in the family. I love the enthusiasm that exudes from Veronica Grogan, Cynthia Weldon, and Gerry Romano. And I honor the memory of Ann McLaughlin, who taught me much about shaping a novel.

Finally, last on this list, but always first in my heart, Steve Ello. At the end of one story, I am fortunate to find my new beginning with you.

BOOK CLUB DISCUSSION GUIDE

Note: *There are no right or wrong answers to these questions; they are intended to provoke lively conversation.*

1. Why is the narrator unnamed? How did you feel about that element of the book?

2. Why is this book not told in chronological order? What are the benefits and ramifications of this choice?

3. In what ways is this narrator unreliable and untrustworthy? In what ways is she also painfully truthful and honest?

4. How did your feelings about the narrator and the (sometimes harrowing) decisions she makes shift and evolve over the course of the book?

5. Have you had a complicated friendship with someone, perhaps reminiscent of the narrator's friendship with Jess? What kept you in that friendship? Or what eventually led to the end of that friendship? What keeps Jess and the narrator together?

6. The Tylenol murders took place in 1982, and product packaging and surveillance security have been transformed as a result. Does this crime feel like a relic from an earlier time? Or are there elements to these murders that feel relevant to today's culture?

7. These girls feel tremendous pressure to behave a certain way. Who applies this pressure? How do the characters find escape from these relentless expectations? How would you compare these expectations with your own experience coming of age?

8. How do the various characters in this novel treat and consider material goods? Their appearance? Are their concerns superficial? Why/why not?

9. In "Pretty," the narrator accuses herself: "No one thinks about money the way you do." How do you think about money? Have your views changed over time? How do you imagine other people think about money?

10. In "Two Girls," the narrator thinks, "*Utter power, like God. That was what [the Tylenol killer] wanted, power—I felt sure of it...It was scary to understand that about him.*" How would you describe the narrator's interpretations of power? Are there times and situations where she has power, or imagines she does? When is she powerless? Why does she think about power so frequently?

11. How does the physical landscape reflect and provoke the narrator's experience?

12. What is the role of stories within this book? How many different stories are told or are alluded to? Why does Grace like hearing about the Silver Girl?

13. How would you describe the narrator's view of personal relationships? How has she come by these feelings? Do her views change over the course of the novel?

14. In "The Bedroom," the narrator writes, "That endless yearning, that empty hunger, even when I knew it wasn't sweaters I wanted (though also, actually it was). It was to not care how many sweaters I had; it wasn't a number, but a word: 'enough.' And that word was impossible, it seemed to me." Do you think it's possible to have "enough"? Why/why not?

@unnamedpress

facebook.com/theunnamedpress

unnamedpress.tumblr.com

www.unnamedpress.com

@unnamedpress